305

DATE DUE			
SE 1 2 '00			
SEP 1 4 '00			
NOV 2 1 '00			
AR 1 9 03			
4-19-06			

7/00

JACKSON COUNTY
Library Services

HEADQUARTERS
413 West Main Street
Medford, Oregon 97501

THE CRITTER

And Other Dogs

**Also by Albert Payson Terhune
in Large Print:**

Lad: A Dog
Lad of Sunnybank
The Way of a Dog
Grudge Mountain

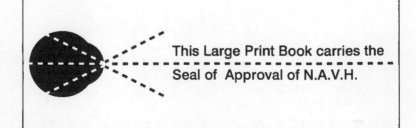

This Large Print Book carries the
Seal of Approval of N.A.V.H.

THE CRITTER
And Other Dogs

Albert Payson Terhune

G.K. Hall & Co. • Thorndike, Maine

Published in 2000 by arrangement with HarperCollins Publishers, Inc.

G.K. Hall Large Print Perennial Bestsellers Series.

The text of this Large Print edition is unabridged.
Other aspects of the book may vary from the original edition.

Set in 16 pt. Plantin by Minnie B. Raven.

Printed in the United States on permanent paper.

Library of Congress Cataloging-in-Publication Data

Terhune, Albert Payson, 1872–1942.
    The critter and other dogs / by Albert Payson Terhune.
      p. cm.
    ISBN 0-7838-8745-0 (lg. print : hc : alk. paper)
    1. Collie — Fiction.   2. Dogs — Fiction.   3. Large type books.
  I. Title.
PS3539.E65 C7 2000
  813´.52—dc21   99-089942

CONTENTS

I

WILD HEATHER

Champion Bruckwold Heather had brought home many a cup, many a medal, double-handfuls of blue ribbons and winners' rosettes, and several hundred dollars in cash prizes, from the big dog shows.

As a result she was tended and guarded and conditioned and pampered as though she were heiress to some super-imperial throne. Never in her two years of life had Heather caught so much as a mouse. Never had she known the disreputable joys of rummaging garbage-pails. Never had she had the miles of sweeping cross-country gallops which are a collie's immemorial heritage.

Her balanced rations were served to her on sanitary pewter dishes. Her daily exercise was a walk of precisely two miles on the end of a leash, supplemented by a carefully supervised half-hour of wandering around an enclosed half-acre lot.

The Bruckwold kennels were inordinately proud of her. Her owner dreamed of founding a glorious collie dynasty from her future puppies; a race of sublimated show-type collies which should make Simon Bruckwold's name immortal in dog-show annals.

From Scotland, at a cost of $2,700, Bruckwold imported a mate for her — the peerless British collie champion, Kirkcaldie Cragsmere. This Scottish paragon, alone of all dogdom, was deemed worthy by Bruckwold to sire Heather's wondrous progeny.

But the day before Kirkcaldie Cragsmere was due to arrive in America, one of the Bruckwold kennelmen got exceeding drunk. When he carried Heather's evening meal to her he fumbled awkwardly at the drop latch of her yard's door in closing it after him. The iron pin dropped, unheeded, to the ground, instead of fitting into the socket. The heavy yard gate swung slightly ajar.

There was an odd uneasiness in Heather's blood on that winter night; an urge to rove instead of settling down stolidly on her cedar-mat bed as usual. There was invitation in the half-open yard gate. Nature for once was out-calling mere lifelong environment.

Through the doorway trotted Heather, a little scared at her own temerity, and out into the deepening dusk.

Aimlessly she wandered about the grounds. Then she followed the driveway out into the main road. Here the going was smooth. Her sense of adventure quickened. For perhaps a mile she ambled along the road. A passing car halted abruptly a few rods beyond her. A man descended to the ground and came back toward Heather.

The collie made no resistance when he laid hold of her ruff. She had known nothing but kindness. Her temper was gentle. She was used to being handled by strange judges in the show ring. So she stood still, even waving her plumed tail gently.

The man's fingers were exploring her throat in search of a collar and license tag. He found neither. Apparently this was a mere stray dog, one hundred per cent eligible for the pound. The man was poundmaster at the village of Hampton, seven miles distant.

In this capacity he received from the township a dollar for every stray dog he could pick up, and an extra dollar for every unredeemed dog he put to death. Thus, ever, he was on the alert for such chances for revenue. That he was far from his own bailiwick, now, and returning from a trip to a dogskin dealer's at the county seat, did not deter him from picking up this friendly lost collie and lifting her into his car.

To the dog-show world, Bruckwold Heather represented something close to $2,000 in cash value. To the poundmaster she typified merely a much-needed dollar, and perhaps a second dollar if she should remain unclaimed for forty-eight hours.

Dollars were few, just now, in the Hampton poundmaster's line of industry. There was but one dog, at present, in the backyard pen he used as a pound. This was a savage male bull terrier his net had caught that morning when the

9

hungry stray was too busy looting a garbage dump to note the poundmaster's sly approach.

Into the pen, with this sulkingly ferocious brute, the man tossed Heather; as soon as he reached home.

Next morning, when he came out with a panful of moldy scraps for his prisoners' breakfast and swung wide the pen's narrow door to take the pan in, the bull terrier launched himself voicelessly at his captor; digging his teeth deep into the unprepared man's forearm and hanging on like grim death.

Back staggered the poundmaster under the impact. He smote with his free fist at the rage-wrinkled head whose jaws were grinding so agonizingly into his flesh.

Heather had shrunk back in terror at the din and turmoil of the attack. Now, unseen by her struggling jailer, she slipped out through the pen's doorway and made off at a gallop.

She was wretchedly homesick. Above all things, she craved to get back to her own peaceful kennel, to her human friends there and to her food. She was rumpled and dirty from her night in the filthy pen. Nervousness made her tongue hang out. A light foam dripped from her lips.

As she rushed down the village street some one set up a screech of, "Mad dog!"

This asinine cry lurks ever in the fear mists at the back of the human brain, ready to spring to noisy life at the faintest provocation. In an amazingly short time a group of men and boys were streaming along the short street in full pursuit of the harmless and friendly little collie.

Their yells terrified Heather. The thud of their chasing feet lent the speed of dread to her own fast pace. A stone whizzed past her head. Another grazed her hip, painfully. Heather proceeded to grow crazy from panic. Unseeing, guideless, she tore along the street at express-train speed, whimpering and gasping. Out beyond the village she ran, and into the open country.

The miles flowed past; but ever she seemed to hear that howling man-pack at her heels and to feel the whiz and the sting of the volley of flung stones. Unseeing, unthinking, scourged by that crazy yearning to outstrip her human tormentors, she fled.

At last her straining muscles refused to carry her further. Sheer exhaustion began to clear the panic-cloud from her bewildered brain. Her sweeping and scrambling gallop slowed to a trot. Presently she slid to a halt, then dropped heavily to the ground. There she lay, fighting to get her breath.

Bit by bit her breathing waxed less labored. Bit by bit the wiry young strength seeped back into her worn-out body. She got waveringly to her feet and looked about.

She was in the middle of a hillside wood. The nearest house in sight was fully two miles away. All around her were brown forest, broken here

11

and there by browner clearings. She had not the remotest idea whither her mad flight had carried her, nor that she was a full fifteen miles from the kennels of her birth.

To some dogs is given the mystic homing instinct which carries them unerringly over scores of miles of unknown territory, back to their owners. Many collies have this odd instinct. But many more have not. Most assuredly Champion Bruckwold Heather had not. Her pamperedly sheltered life had not been of a kind to waken such occult power.

She was lost. Irretrievably lost.

Ordinarily, in this predicament, she would have sought the nearest human, for food and for shelter and for companionship. But this morning's harrowing experience had broken to pieces her loving trust in mankind. It had taught her that strange humans chase dogs and stone them and try to kill them. It had implanted in her undeveloped mind a mortal fear of men.

Remember, please, that this had been the first painful or exciting or even interesting occurrence in her entire cut-to-order life. And such an experience was certain to burn indelibly deep into her sensitive organism.

From somewhere just ahead of Heather, in the woods, sounded the trickle of water. It reminded her that she was torturingly thirsty. She moved forward into a steep glen where ran a shallow brook newly loosened from its clogging burden of ice.

Never before had Heather drunk except from her sanitary and oft-scoured pewter water-dish. But never before had water tasted one-millionth as good as from this half-frozen brook. She lapped up pints of it, raising her head now and then for breath, then continuing to drink.

In front of her there was an outjut of rock under the shale-walled side of the glen. Beneath this roof a riffle of dead leaves had drifted. The nook was sheltered from the damp February wind, and it was dry. Heather curled herself deep in the leaves. She fell asleep almost at once.

When she awoke, night was falling. She drank deep again from the brook. Then she was aware of a compelling hunger. She was aware, too, for the first time in her cotton-wool-wrapped life, that getting food may sometimes be a problem. The knowledge increased her teasing hunger and it drove her forth from her shelter on a quest for supper.

Ever, up to now, humans had provided everything for her. They had solved all her simple difficulties. Hence, toward the abode of humans she bent her steps. True, humans had turned out to be murderous enemies, to be shunned and dreaded. But where there were humans there was food. Always that had been Heather's experience.

She raised her head and sniffed the still night air sharply; without the remotest idea why she sniffed or what she hoped to achieve thereby. Then, still not consciously aware why she was doing such a thing, she loped off through the woods, sniffing occasionally as she ran.

Soon she came in sight of a farmhouse's lights. She slackened her pace and slunk forward, stomach to earth, on a tour of inspection. Around the house she crept, her nose ever busy in its quest for food. At a dairy door she paused. Here on the dead grass had been set a bucket of sour milk for the pigs' next morning meal.

Heather plunged her dainty nose into the bucket with no daintiness at all. Long she lapped the acridly nourishing milk. At last the edge of her famine was dulled. She moved on to a second and larger pail, near by. The pail was full of table-scrapings, and the like, also designed for the pigs' breakfast. Heather nosed aside some wilted green stuff. She drew forth a lump of underdone bread — token of a failure in the day's baking.

This she gorged. She was helping herself to other edible bits amid the conglomeration of swill, when she heard the knob of the dairy door turn. Swift and noiseless as a shadow she disappeared into the night. Her hunger was appeased. Now she sought the lair she had found during the day.

For weeks Heather continued to creep through the darkness, every night, to feast on the pigs' breakfast. Her innate daintiness and her fear of being heard made her nose too delicately in the pail to scatter any of its contents. Thus her nightly visits went unsuspected by the occupants of the house.

14

Also, this late-awakened forage instinct taught her to chase such rabbits as she encountered in the woods. At first she did this with so little adroitness that the pursuit always ended in failure. But, without realizing her own improvement, she taught herself by instinct to stalk her prey and to anticipate by a fraction of a second a running rabbit's doublings. In like fashion she became a moderately good stalker of game birds and she learned to scent the underground haunts of field mice.

But never was she an inspired hunter. The farmhouse's pig-food was still a welcome addition to her fare.

This pig-provender became more and more useful to her as the weeks went on. For she found herself growing slower and lazier and heavier, day by day. The clumsiest rabbit or grouse could elude her now. But for the farmhouse folk's habit of setting out the sour milk and swill every evening for a hired man to carry to the pigpen early the next morning, she must have starved. Even the nightly two-mile trip, between the house and her lair became a burdensome effort.

On her return from one such foray, Heather sank limply on her side, among the leaves, muttering and whining. Then, feverishly, she began to scratch the leaves together in heaps, pawing them here and there, never satisfied with the results of her bedmaking.

At sunrise she was still lying there, weak, languid, but at peace. Nuzzling against her furry underbody were three squirmy puppies, about the size of rats. Sightless, vehemently hungry, they nursed with avid greediness; digging their almost hairless little claws deep into their mother's fur and chuckling to themselves.

An expert dogman, viewing the newborn trio, would have had scant trouble classifying two of them as baby bull terriers. At least they were much more like bull-terrier pups than like anything else. But the third had all the general aspect of a collie.

The same expert dogman, a few days later, would not have had to classify the two infants that resembled bull terriers. For both of them were dead. Like so many dogmothers, Heather ate the two, almost as soon as they died. This with the canine instinct to keep the nest clean, and through no taint of cannibalism.

But the baby that looked like a reasonably pure-breed collie lived on. Lived and throve. For his was the nourishment which otherwise would have gone into the feeding of all three pups.

And now Heather took up the burden of life afresh; working hard for her son's livelihood as well as for her own. Foraging was easier, every day. For April had come. The woods and fields were turning green in sheltered places. Birds and squirrels and rabbits grew daily more plentiful and fatter and less timid. And habit was teaching Heather to hunt better and more wilily, as time went on.

No longer did she bother to visit the farmhouse dairy yard. There was food and to spare, all around her; food which her increasing reversion to the wild rendered more and more palatable.

The puppy was pudgy and strong and inordinately fat. Now he did not resemble a rat, nor even a well-fed rabbit. He was growing at an incredible rate. His mother's new-waked instinct made her change his diet, when he was five weeks old, to such game as she brought home to the nook from her daily rambles. With an atavistic joy, the puppy learned to love his new fare; and to growl horrifically as he sank his needle-sharp milk-teeth into the breast of some fresh-killed pheasant or quail.

He did not need to be taught to hunt. Perhaps, from pre-natal influences, the stalking of game was wholly natural to him; even when he was still too young and unwieldy to put on the necessary spurts of speed. He followed his mother afield as soon as he could travel with any certainty on his thick legs. And he watched her in vibrant excitement as she stalked and killed.

By the time he was five months old he was joining her in these stalks and in heading off rabbits she drove toward him. Slowly and with much difficulty had Heather become a huntress. Never was she a gifted performer in the role. But the puppy was born to it, as much as is any young wolf.

Soon it was he, not she, that did the bulk of the killing. It was he, not she, for example, that learned the wolf-trick of cutting a fat fawn out of the wandering deer herd or from beside the doe, and of driving the bleating fugitive into a ravine pocket whence there was no outlet; there to pull it down at his leisure and to devour the feast with Heather.

When they were not hunting or sleeping, there was a spot to which Heather used to lead the way, almost daily, from the time the pup was strong enough to follow her so far. This was a tumble of rocks atop a knoll which overlooked a stretch of hillside pasture land. Amid the huddle of split boulders there was ample space for the two dogs to lie or sit unseen and to scan the fields just beneath them.

There, for hours at a time, they remained. There was a magic fascination, to Heather, in what she saw from the rock-tumble eyrie. She herself did not know why the spectacle stirred her so. But she seemed able to impart its keen interest to her young son.

To a human onlooker there would have been nothing dramatic or exciting in what the two dogs watched. Such a human would have seen only an extensive rock-pasture where grazed about a hundred sheep; and another and lower pasture with twenty cattle browsing its lush grass.

Yet Heather could not keep her eyes from the occupants of these two spacious fields. She had no such red impulse to chase or kill any of the silly sheep or their stiff-legged lambs as was hers when she and the puppy came upon a herd of deer. She felt no desire to harm these sheep. But she found their every motion of absorbing interest.

For ten centuries her collie ancestors in Scotland had won their right to a livelihood by herding and guarding sheep and cattle. Hereditary instinct was gripping mightily at Heather's heartstrings; and in only slightly lesser fashion at her son's. The cattle in the more distant pasture were also most attractive to the two. Some urge they could not at all understand awoke in the brains of mother and son; an urge that had no objective and that certainly was not for destruction.

And so, hour after hour, they would look down upon the grazing creatures, lying silent, tense, in their double vigil, their eyes straying from group to group.

Once in a while a human would go to one or another of the pastures, to inspect the flock or the herd. At such times the pup would glance sidewise at his mother, as if for explanation of the queer biped and of his presence. At such times, too, Heather's upper lip would curl in something like a reminiscent snarl; at sight and scent of the kind of creatures that had chased her out of civilization.

Once or twice, when the wind was right and the human who was inspecting the cattle and sheep passed within closer distance to the knoll, Heather could catch his scent and could identify it. She knew it for one of the several scents which had reached her from indoors; and by means of footprints on the dooryard ground, on the countless nights when she had pillaged the milk-bucket and swill-pail outside the farmhouse two miles away. The man must belong there, she knew.

Then came autumn and then the stripping of the trees by a gigantic invisible hand and the searing of the sweet meadow grass into brown-gray. The man whose scent Heather remembered came with two other men. They drove the sheep from their pasture and off to the farmhouse folds. The next day the three drove away the cattle, in like manner. And there was nothing left to entertain and excite the two dogs, from the rock eyrie on their chosen knoll.

Winter laid its strangling white grip on their world. Lean days followed. Game was scarcer and scarcer. The dogs sometimes had to range for many miles for a single square meal. They grew gaunt beneath their mighty winter coats. Yet they were as hard as nails. And by constant hunting they managed not only to keep alive, but to keep strong and vigorous.

The puppy went on growing. He was much larger now than was his pretty little mother. His chest was deepening — the chest he inherited from his bull-terrier sire, along with that sire's terrible fighting prowess. It was always the pup nowadays that led the hunt. Yet always he gave Heather the lion's share of the kill. His tender adoration for her was complete.

After months of lean dreariness the snow was gone and the earth began to array itself in green. On a May morning mother and son visited the rocky knoll for the first time in months. A nameless Something told them the two pastures no longer would be empty. And they were right.

Below them, in the farther field, some twenty cattle grazed. Up a rocky and twisting lane, from the direction of the farmhouse, the three men were driving the hundred sheep toward the nearer field.

The close-set bars of this pasture's fence were down, as they had been all winter. Toward the bars, along the steep lane, the men were trying to pilot the milling and jostling sheep. The task was anything but easy, sheep being perhaps the silliest and most erratic and annoying members of the animal kingdom. The men had their hands full, to keep the flock from bolting or scattering or trying to turn back. But after violent effort the drovers brought their foolish convoys to within perhaps ninety yards of the pasture bars.

It was then that an enormous red mongrel came charging up from the direction of the faroff highway — a dog owned by a shiftless laborer in the valley below; a dog that ranged the countryside at will and had proven himself a pest and a menace to livestock for miles around. A dozen farmers had long been seeking positive evidence to connect him with a series of henroost-slaughters and lamb killings.

The sight of so many moving sheep apparently went to the red brute's brain and deprived him of his wonted craftiness. For now he was coming straight for the flock, head down, jaws slavering. The men shouted. One of them ran at the advancing dog with stick raised, while the two other drovers tried in vain to keep the flock bunched and free from panic.

Eluding the man with the stick, the mongrel hurled himself into the welter of baaing and scattering sheep. Slashing murderously right and left as his prey fled in every direction, he caught one yearling, pinned it to the ground, and tore out its throat. In what was almost the same instant, he was up and after another victim.

The sheep dispersed to every point of the compass, running wild, crazy with fear. All over the hillside they scattered, for a full quarter-mile; so that no man or no ten men could hope to round them up within a day. Ever among them, quadrupling their runaway panic, dashed the giant red mongrel. As he ran he pulled down a second sheep, slew it, and was away again after more victims. Then —

From nowhere — from the sky itself, it seemed — appeared two collies, galloping like the wind, their mighty pale golden coats aflame.

The three men shouted aloud in sheer despair at the advent of these two presumptive allies of the great red killer. The situation was beyond their control. All they could do was to stand impotently and watch the trio of sheep murderers go on with their horrible work.

But in the next breath the farmer whose scent Heather had recognized caught the arm of one of his two hired men. He pointed unbelievingly toward the rabble rout of pursuer and pursued.

The two collies had been racing side by side toward the scene of slaughter. Now, as at a signal, they separated. The younger dog flew, head down, toward the red killer. Heather made a galloping detour of hundreds of yards, until she was beyond the farthermost of the scattered sheep. Then she wheeled.

Deftly she turned back the group of sheep she had just flashed past. She headed them toward the men. Then, racing in and out, she caught up with single strays, turning them in like manner and driving them into the bunch she first had halted.

Ever augmenting the numbers of the bunch by whirling side trips for more recruits, she kept her captives in close formation and she kept them moving steadily, if unwillingly, in the direction she had chosen for them. It was pretty herding. It was as neatly and as swiftly and as deftly achieved as if by a life-trained sheep-dog. The spirits of a million brilliant herd-collie ancestors were shouting their atavistic secrets to her.

Again and again, here and in Europe, has a novice collie shown this miraculous hereditary skill at rounding up sheep. But to the three onlooking men Heather's work savored of stark magic. From her to her son their bulging eyes kept shifting, and back again; after the fashion of folk who view a three-ring circus.

The younger collie did not swerve nor slacken his headlong pace as he bore down upon the huge red mongrel. The latter, by scent or by instinct, became aware of his approach.

Whirling around, as his teeth were about to close on the shoulder of a ewe he had just overhauled, the red dog was barely in time to brace himself for the collie's charge.

The two dogs came together with a shock that threw them both off their feet. On the instant they were up again, mad for battle. The red mongrel was a famous warrior. Dog after dog, throughout the valley, he had killed in fair or, preferably, unfair fight. He was eager to use his most deadly and foulest tactics on this pale-gold intruder that was interfering with his glorious sport of sheep-slaying. But the task of getting rid of the new foe seemed suddenly more difficult than the mongrel had expected.

Never before had the young collie fought. But in his veins ran not only the blood of a thousand redoubtable pit bulldogs — invincible fighters all — but also the collie strain which gives its possessor a speed and elusiveness in battle and a quality of being everywhere and nowhere at once. The combination of the two strains was teaching its ancestral secrets to the youngster; even as atavism was telling Heather how to round up and turn a horde of panicky sheep.

By sheer weight, the red dog sought to bear

down his smaller and lighter foe and to get the desired death grip on the jugular or at the base of the skull. But the collie dived under the plunging rufous bulk, slashing deeply the other's under-body, then writhing free and tearing into his shoulder.

With a roar, the red giant shook loose and hurled himself afresh at the collie. Four times in as many seconds, he sought to crush and pinion the lighter dog. Four times the collie was not there as he lunged. Four times, deep slashing furrows in the red dog's coat attested to the efficiency of the pup's countering.

Then, as the collie sprang nimbly aside from the fifth lunge, his hindfeet slipped on a wet rock and he crashed to the ground. Ragingly the red dog threw himself into the slaughter.

But a collie down is not a collie beaten. There was no scope for the pup to get to his feet or to roll aside, before the gigantic red bulk was upon him. Nor did he seek to. Instead, as the huge jaws snapped shut on a handful of mattress-like hair and on little else, the collie struck upward for the mongrel's briefly unguarded throat.

His collie swiftness and accuracy enabled him to secure the vital grip. But his bulldog strain's all-crushing jaws enabled him to make the most of it, in one quick and body-wrenching motion.

The red dog slumped to the ground, his throat as completely torn out as had been the throats of his sheep victims. The pup wriggled from under him and stood for an instant, panting and looking about him. Then he saw Heather and what she was doing. Immediately the pup was in rapid motion.

And now the dazed onlookers saw both collies at work among the scattered sheep; as perfect a team as though they had been trained to herding, all their lives. Steadily, rapidly, the scatter of sheep ceased to be a scatter. Firmly, compactly, the protesting beasts were herded and bunched, in spite of anything they could do, and they were headed toward the pasture bars. Every time one of them tried to break formation, it was pushed back into place as readily as if a solid wall of collies surrounded it.

The gray-white jostle of sheep moved toward the bars. Not one of them was hurt or so much as bruised. For, after the custom of the best type of herd-collie, the two dogs were as gentle as they were deft.

At the bars there was one more futile mass attempt to balk. Quickly it was frustrated. The flock was urged into a gallop. Into the broad pasture they cascaded, all of them, from first to last. The panting dogs stood in the gap, side by side, to frustrate any stray's possible attempt to double back and to escape.

Then only did Ellis Slater, master of the flock, find his voice and come out of his daze of wonder.

"I — I've read about such things," he blithered to his gaping men. "I've read about them in Dad's farm-books. But I never believed it. If it wasn't for those two collies we'd have lost forty sheep before the red devil was through with them. And it would have taken us maybe days to round up the rest. I'm going to find who owns the collies. If I have to advertise for him. And I'm going to offer him his own price for the pair of them, even if I have to put a mortgage on the land to do it."

As he talked he and his assistants were hurrying toward the bars where stood the golden dogs on guard. Heather and her son did not run away as the three men came forward, though memory made Heather shiver as if with a chill.

They waited until Slater and his hired men were too close at hand for the sheep to try to bolt past them. Then — once more as if at a signal — the dogs darted off.

Unheeding Slater's pleading calls to them and the blandishing whistles of the two other men, mother and son made for the sheet of underbrush which covered the upper half of the hill. Into this they melted from sight, like a brace of wolves.

Their work was done — cleverly, gloriously done — the work to which they had leaped by instinct at sight of the red mongrel's onslaught. Now they were free to take up again the forest life they loved; to turn their backs on their brief intercourse with humankind, and with no desire to renew it.

With eager joy, the Wild returned to the Wild.

II

DYNAMITE

He was not wanted. He was as unwanted as a wrinkle, or as a boost in the income tax. He was a collie pup — furry, pretty, eagerly friendly. His name was Kenneth.

He was given to Margaret Bryce by a man she detested. That was one reason why Kenneth was unwanted. Another reason was that Margaret was afraid of dogs and that neither of her parents had any experience or interest in them. Margaret was for sending Kenneth back at once — the moment the messenger boy deposited the small pup in the big basket at her feet on the veranda and handed her the note from Mallon.

But her parents would not have it so. They liked Mallon. They liked his gentleness with women, his outdoor ways, the tinge of the wild that seemed to cling to him. Besides, he had more money and more common sense about its use than has the average youth of twenty-seven. Wherefore they encouraged his visits to Mossmere, and they reproved Margaret for her unreasoning prejudice against him.

So now when, after one disgusted look into the

shiny wicker basket, the girl demanded that the messenger take it back to the donor, both her father and her mother vetoed the return. For a wonder they managed to do so with such vehemence that Margaret yielded. But she yielded about as graciously as might a sick wildcat.

The messenger departed. Mr. Bryce opened the basket. Out onto the veranda floor floundered a mass of dynamically energetic fluff. The puppy was soft and fuzzy and adorably awkward. His eyes alone gave special promise of his future, for they were dark and wise and deep set. Around his ridiculously shapeless little neck was an enormous cerise bow tied with the inept fingers of a man little used to such exploits as the manipulating of cerise satin.

"He looks like a tipsy Teddy bear," commented Margaret, eyeing poor little gamboling Kenneth without approval. "And this note is as absurd as the puppy. He says he is 'sending me a chum'; and that 'no gift in the world can be more precious to the right sort of girl than the right sort of collie.' Then he speaks of me and the wretched cur as 'thoroughbreds both.' Did you ever hear such silliness?"

"Mallon meant it all right," ventured Mr. Bryce.

"That's the whole trouble with him," complained Margaret. "He always means everything all right. Well, how about it, people? You said I mustn't send the little brute back. I'm most certainly not going to take care of him. Daughterly obedience stops, one station short of that. Here he is. But I'll be blest if I feed him or do anything for him! Ugh!"

This expletive was wrung from her by a violent onslaught from Kenneth himself. The puppy, freed of his basket, had explored with hesitant steps the expanses of the veranda. Then all at once remembering he was far from home and very, very lonely, he cantered gushingly up to the nearest human — for comfort and for petting.

This nearest human chanced to be Margaret. In active repulsion the girl shoved away the pudgily effusive youngster. The push sent him rolling over and over on his fat little back. As Kenneth gathered his feet under him, scared and amazed at such reception to his loving advances, the elderly gardener came plodding around the side of the house on his way to the orchard. Mr. Bryce hailed the interruption with relief.

"McLaren!" he called. "You're a Scot. So you must know something of collies. They're your national flower or something, aren't they?"

"Yes, sir," responded McLaren, solemnly; "cauliflower."

At his own egregious witticism, the Scot began to laugh gruntingly with infinite relish.

Bryce, after blinking dazedly at him for a moment, granted a vague chuckle to the awful jest. Mrs. Bryce looked blank. Margaret walked coldly away. She did not believe in familiarity with servants.

"Well, here's a Scotch collie puppy," went on Bryce, "with a short body and a long pedigree.

He has been given to Miss Bryce. She has no time to take care of him. Just lead him down to the barn and fix some kind of coop or corner for him and tell the cook to let you have food for him — table scraps or — or cauliflower, as you suggested. Or whatever collies are supposed to eat. See he's well fed and looked after. He's a valuable dog and all that."

McLaren was gazing at the puppy with grave interest. Not so much was he noting the appealing little face and the unwieldy shape, as the broad shoulders and the deep chest and the rounded big bones and the glint in the wistful eyes. He was forecasting from these the dog that one day was to grow out of this pudgy huddle of flesh and fur.

The gardener snapped his fingers at Kenneth. The puppy was glad of any recognition at all after this brief visit among dogless aliens. He scampered across the slippery floor to his new friend, wagging his rudimentary tail and barking in falsetto friendliness. McLaren tucked the pup under his arm and started back toward the barn.

Thus Kenneth came into the hands of some one who detested him, and thence into the care of a man who knew and loved collies as only a Scot can hope to.

The disused carriage shed became Kenneth's home, with a straw-heaped corner of it for his bed; and daily he fared forth with McLaren on the latter's rounds of the garden. Patiently he would play about amid the flower borders or between furrows while McLaren worked; and from the man's gruff voice he learned his first lessons in life and conduct.

Old McLaren was no sentimentalist. He was the sternest of disciplinarians. Even as he had disciplined and educated his own two sons until one of them had run away and the other had become a rugged pillar of the community, so he proceeded to educate and discipline Kenneth.

At Kenneth's age one's chief joys are to play hysterically and to eat inordinately and to sleep more than half the time and to get into any and every form of mischief. The eating and the sleeping were Kenneth's in ample measure, with much exercise thrown in; for McLaren knew the mighty value of these things in shaping a growing collie's body and upbuilding his health. But play was another matter, and mischief was barred. At an age when most pups know nothing more serious than a chase after their own tails Kenneth was learning the meaning of work. Also he was mastering many details as to behavior.

For example, to snatch up a dishcloth from the kitchen doorway or to roll merrily on the flower beds or to dig a tunnel under a rosebush or to yelp plaintively when put back into the shed or to chew holes in McLaren's spare overalls — all these and many other things were deadly sins and punishable by stingingly sharp spankings across the loins with a bit of switch.

Then, too, when the puppy was in the midst of a romp, the detested word "Heel!" meant he must slink slowly along behind McLaren's big shoes. And "Lie down!" and "Back!" and "Quiet, there!" and a host of other confusing mandates all had different and imperative meanings. So much must be learned — all of it distasteful.

For a space Kenneth was the most miserably unhappy collie pup in the state of New Jersey. Then, bit by bit, because he was a true collie, the brain of him awoke, and with it a glad zeal to serve this dour old man whom he had begun to love even more than he feared him. And the pup found himself trying eagerly to anticipate McLaren's commands and in win from him a grunt of approval or a careless pat on the head.

Of all his lessons, he loved best the congenial art of retrieving. To rush after a thrown stick is inherent in the nature of nearly all normal pups. But to bring it back to the thrower and lay it meekly at his feet — this must be taught. It is so much more fun to gallop away with the stick and to pretend it is a deadly foe to be chewed and shaken. Yet, in a very few days, Kenneth acquired the art of retrieving and of retrieving well. Then, before the next step in his education could be taken, several untoward events happened.

First of all, old McLaren was laid by the heels with an attack of inflammatory rheumatism. The cook kept on feeding Kenneth at the disabled gardener's orders and letting the pup out for an hour or two of exercise every day. But the lessons had stopped for a while, and Kenneth missed them. After two months of discipline he found his new freedom a bore, and he was lonely for the harsh old man who had done so much to make a self-respecting canine citizen of him.

A few days after McLaren fell ill the four Polack day laborers at Mossmere struck for extra pay and for six hours less work per week. They had chosen a bad time for the strike; for unemployment had begun to take the place of labor's post-war golden days. And Bryce's reply to their demand was to discharge all four of them.

This counter-move had not entered at all into their computations. Kilinski, the spokesman for the quartet, was jarred into a sudden loss of temper. In a bellowed avalanche of broken English, as he stood on the veranda edge, he cursed Bryce and all the latter's family. Among his fellow Polacks, Kilinski had a high repute for invective. This fame he justified for the benefit of the three other laborers, who stood grouped at the foot of the porch steps.

Bryce, at the howled repetition of one especially virulent epithet, lost control of his own temper and drove his fist to the Polack's jaw. Back over the edge of the top step reeled Kilinski, landing in the gritty gravel at the bottom of the veranda in a blaspheming heap. Instantly he was on his feet; nursing a bruised jaw with one hand, while with the other he waved on his three co-strikers to charge on the capitalist who had just assaulted him.

Mallon's car, rounding the drive and coming

to a halt in front of the steps, checked the rush. And Mallon himself, vaulting out of the runabout and reënforcing Bryce at the head of the steps, further discouraged the counterattack. One by one, Kilinski last of all, the four slouched away.

"If I were you, sir," counselled Mallon, "I'd have the village constable round up those fellows and get them run out of town. That last chap looked back at you in a way I'd hate to have my best enemy look at me. By the way, is Margaret at home, do you know?"

"I — I think so; I'm — I'm not sure," stammered Bryce, dreading the ordeal of making his daughter consent to come downstairs and see the unwelcome caller.

"How's the puppy coming on?" asked Mallon.

"I — I don't know. First rate," faltered Bryce with a guilty memory that he had not set eyes on Kenneth in weeks and that the girl most assuredly had not. "I'll — I'll send one of the maids to find Margaret. Will you come in, or would you rather —"

Margaret, ignorant of Mallon's call, came sauntering out on the veranda. "What was all the noise about?" she inquired. "It sounded like a dozen people talking over crossed telephone wires. Did —"

Catching sight of Mallon, she paused. Then she forced herself to advance toward him with frigid semblance of hospitality.

"I didn't know you were here," said she. "Was

it you and Dad who were doing all that frightful quarreling?"

"No, no," hastily interposed Bryce with a guilty look at his barked knuckles. "The Polacks wanted a raise of pay. And when I wouldn't give it to them Kilinski got noisy. So I had to send them packing. They —"

From somewhere in the rear of the house came a rapidly approaching clamor which could best be described by the old-fashioned stage directions: "Confused hubbub without." The trio on the veranda turned instinctively in the direction of the racket.

A week earlier the Polacks and a gang of stonemasons from the village had finished erecting a building which was the joy of Bryce's heart. It was a combination cowbarn and dairy and garage. It stood on a knoll, perhaps a hundred yards to the rear of the main house, hidden from it by an evergreen hedge through which wound a rear driveway. The top of the concrete building was surmounted by an enormous tank, still empty, which was planned to serve as reservoir for house and barns.

Kilinski and his crew had been cleaning up the débris around the new structure that morning when, on Bryce's return from a drive to the village, they had stopped work to make their carefully planned request for more pay and shorter hours. In gaily anticipatory mood they had trooped to the veranda of the main house. In dire disorder and led by a cursing and bleeding spokesman they had drifted back thither now, to gather up their belongings and depart.

Striding once more ahead of the rest, Kilinski woke the echoes with his tale of grievance. He called down upon Bryce every anathema he could set his ready tongue to. He vowed by all the saints and demons of Poland to have revenge. And the more he talked, the more blindly furious he became. It is not easy to talk at the top of one's lungs through a swollen jaw. But it tends to the increase of wrath.

Kenneth had just been let out for his morning run. He came capering up to the four fast-walking Polacks, galloping invitingly around them; patting his white forepaws upon the ground in playful fashion; mutely urging the men to romp with him. Life was lonely, with McLaren away.

But the four paid no heed to the friendly puppy. Once, it is true, when Kenneth's gambols brought him within reach, Kilinski aimed a murderous kick at the pup. But the kick missed its mark, by reason of Kenneth's elusive gait in circling the man. As the puppy had never been kicked, nor seen anyone kicked, he failed entirely to understand the meaning of the savage gesture.

On strode the four, Kenneth scampering gaily about them in quest of a playmate. As they reached the open door of the tool shed, where were deposited their dinner-pails and coats, a nailed-up box caught Kilinski's wrathful eye. Instantly he ceased his lurid monologue and stood stock-still, blinking at it. Through the rage mists of his slow-working brain an idea was seeping, an idea so fascinating as to focus his every faculty. Gradually the idea took perfect form.

The tool-shed adjoined the new concrete building. The nailed-up box held what was left of a case of dynamite used by professional blasters in clearing away the hardpan rock for the structure's foundations. The blasting gang were working in another part of the township that week, and had stored this dynamite, along with certain of their implements, in the woodshed; until they should return.

It was the sight of this box which gave Kilinski his masterly idea. Again and again he had watched the blasters drill rock holes and affix the old-fashioned caps to the dynamite sticks. In railroad construction jobs, too, he had handled dynamite for like purpose.

In another minute he was ripping off the nailed top of the box and gingerly drawing thence two sticks of dynamite in their paper cylinders. Then he bound together the two sticks and, delving in the box again, fished out a couple of caps and a coil of fuse. The blasters had used primitive methods, having no electric appliance for the discharge of their explosive and relying on time fuses.

Two of these sticks, with a three-minute fuse attached, tossed high in air and falling into the open and empty tank at the top of the new building, might be relied upon to change Bryce's costly garage-barn into a heap of crumbled concrete. Dynamite explodes downward. And two sticks of the size manipulated by Kilinski were ample for such a work of destruction. The fact that six valuable cows and a team of work-horses were stabled in the building added zest to the vengeance scheme, as Kilinski proceeded to outline it to his fellow strikers.

The three entered enthusiastically into the plan. It seemed to them nothing short of inspired. Moreover, they decided its execution could not be proved against any of them. They would gather up all their own belongings first.

Then, as soon as the dynamite sticks should be tossed up into the tank, they would all four take to their heels, leaving the grounds by the back way, and could be a quarter mile off before the three-minute fuse would have time to crawl to the explosive caps. It was a pretty idea, and safe withal. Nobody was within sight to spy or to tell tales.

Kenneth, with his head on one side and his furry ears cocked, stood watching interestedly the preparations. A collie, above all other dogs, is susceptible to even the best-concealed human excitement. The stark emotion of these four non-playful foreigners communicated itself at once to Kenneth. Eagerly he turned his dancing eyes from one to the other.

To save his life, he could not guess what it was that was thrilling the men so. One of them was pottering over a couple of long paper sticks, and jabbering to the others. Decidedly, there was nothing in such a scene to stir them so. Now if it had been a cat or a rabbit or even a stable rat which they were working over, that would have been quite another thing. Anyone could have understood the excitement then. But all that fuss over a couple of tied-together sticks!

In certain cases, of course, the presence of a stick was quite enough to rouse Kenneth to an ecstasy of thrills. But that was when McLaren was about to throw the stick for him to retrieve. And these glum men showed no sign of throwing the double stick. Instead, they were now tying to the end of it a thick string of some sort.

No; as far as Kenneth could gather there was no visible reason for them to take such tense interest in their queer form of play. If only they would stop pottering and throw the stick, there might be some sense to it.

Kenneth would have asked nothing better than to show off his new-learned talents at retrieving. He loved to retrieve. He loved it better than anything else McLaren had taught him.

But in the absence of any possible chance to show off or to romp he was keenly inquisitive as to the nature of the four men's quivering interest in their task, and he pattered closer. All four of them trooped out of the toolshed. Kilinski walked ahead of the others. He came to a pause just under the eaves of the new building.

There he looked all about him on every side. Then he stepped back a pace or two and brought the edge of the gaping tank within his range of vision. He gauged the distance with his eye and hefted the weight of the sticks. After which, taking out a card of matches, he struck one of them, shielding its first weak flame in the cup of his hand.

Lighting the end of the fuse, he waited only for the initial sputter of its powder. Then, shaking as if in a hard chill, he drew back his arm and hurled the twin sticks. This was the moment when the four had planned to run away. But not one of them could stir as they watched the white missile with its fizzing fuse. High in air it sped.

Kenneth had beheld the Polack's actions with fast-growing elation. Kilinski had carried the sticks well out from his body, as McLaren was wont to do when showing Kenneth an object to be retrieved. Could it be, after all, that the man was going to throw the sticks for him? And then had come the familiar gesture of drawing back the arm and of flinging. Kenneth, on his hind legs with rapture, made a glad plunge forward. Then came sickening disappointment.

The man seemed to have made a mistake. Instead of throwing the stick out onto the grass, he had thrown it up in the air toward the top of the barn. That was not fair. For a moment Kenneth was bitterly chagrined. Then, in a flash, his hopes revived. Here was an angle of the retrieving game which McLaren had barely succeeded in teaching him when illness had stopped the lessons.

Having taught Kenneth to retrieve a stick

thrown in the open, McLaren had taken the next step by throwing the stick over some obstacle and making the dog hunt for it on the other side by sense of smell. It had been hard at first for Kenneth to understand precisely what was expected of him when a stick vanished over a wall or hedge. But McLaren had been wise and patient, as all dog-teachers must be, and Kenneth had gained a tolerable knowledge of his duties in following the stick and nosing about in the grass until his scenting powers enabled him to locate it.

He had been doing this fairly well on the day McLaren fell sick. It seemed these foreigners were trying to make him do the same thing now. Hopefully, Kenneth's nearsighted gaze followed the soaring of the dynamite. Up whizzed the tied sticks with their spitting wake of powder.

As he threw, Kilinski was aware of the nervous twitches in his arm. To offset them he put extra effort into the toss. Wherefore the dynamite did not drop gracefully into the opening. Instead, it cleared the top of the building by a matter of inches, and thumped to the ground on the far side.

Around the barn flashed Kenneth, in glad pursuit. True, this bundle had not been given him to smell before it was tossed, as when McLaren threw things for him to retrieve. But there was no need to smell it in order to identify the missile. The pup had caught the pungent reek of its powder tail. That was enough. He could find it.

The smell was infinitely easier to locate than the faint human scent on the sticks and on the ball McLaren used in training him to fetch. There would be no difficulty at all in tracing it to the far side of the building or even to the far side of the county.

Away galloped Kenneth on his quest, unnoticed by the four men, who were staring owlishly at the tank edge, over which had disappeared the dynamite package. Kilinski, as usual, was first to recover his presence of mind. He had thrown too far. The only thing to do was to hurry around to the far side of the building, find the dynamite and make a second and more accurate cast. There would still be time enough, even if not quite so much time as he had hoped for. The same thought occurred to his companions. In single file the four started at a run around the barn, Kilinski in front.

But as he rounded the first corner of the building Kilinski came to so abrupt a halt as to make the three close-following men pile up against him with an unpremeditated bump that jarred him to the backbone and set his half-parted teeth clicking together so hard as to chip more than one of them. Kilinski had halted on his way to the dynamite, for the reason that the dynamite was also on its way to him.

Kenneth, dashing to the open space at the barn's other side, had had not the slightest difficulty in locating the dynamite. He located it by sight as well as by scent, little more than a brace

43

of seconds after it struck ground. He caught it up gleefully between his sharp little teeth and, whirling about, darted back at top speed toward the man who had been so obliging as to throw it for him.

The puppy was vastly proud of this new accomplishment of his. All he asked now was a chance to lay the recovered sticks at the feet of the thrower; and be petted and praised for his exploit. He had not in the least forgotten McLaren's strict teachings to the effect that a retrieved stick must always be deposited thus at the thrower's feet.

Halfway around the barn he met Kilinski face to face. He prepared to complete his retrieval work. Indeed, he checked his gallop almost as suddenly as Kilinski had checked his.

The sight of the advancing puppy, carrying enough dynamite to blow a hundred Polacks to Kingdom Come had smitten Kilinski as nothing short of a miracle. It was an impossible thing to have happened. He glared, goggle-eyed, at the frisking Kenneth. The fuse was sputtering merrily. To the men's panic glance it seemed to have burned down to a hideously short stump.

Courteously, even smugly, Kenneth bent his head to lay the burden at Kilinski's feet. But the Polack was in no mood to receive it. With a yell of sheer terror he turned and bolted, the three other men at his heels. At the heels of the four scampered Kenneth.

One cannot put down a stick at the feet of a

44

man whose feet are carrying him in the opposite direction at the rate of nearly twenty miles an hour. Therefore Kenneth gave chase. It seemed there were points to this retrieving game which he had not yet mastered. But as those points seemed to comprise a gay footrace, Kenneth was not downhearted at the new development.

McLaren had instilled in the pup's memory the rule of bringing back a thrown object, far too rigorously for Kenneth to forget or to fail in obeying the rule. He was going to place that sharp-smelling bundle at Kilinski's feet; if he should have to chase the man into the next state in order to do it.

Meanwhile the race was jolly and invigorating, despite the somewhat inconvenient heaviness of his burden. And Kenneth entered with a will into the gladsome romp. Kilinski and his fellows ran, and they kept on running. Every time one of them would glance fearsomely back over his shoulder he would see the galloping puppy close behind and would note that the wind-fanned fuse was appallingly short. The rearmost Polack began to shriek. Two of the others followed his example. They rent the air with their panic screeches.

Kenneth was gloriously elated by the noise. Much he yearned to augment it by clamorous barking. But a canine burden bearer cannot bark if the burden chances to be between his teeth, and if it must not be laid down except at the feet of a man he cannot catch up with.

To Kilinski this stark pursuit had in it no element of play or of retrieving. The Polack could see nothing in it but the Incredible and the hand of Fate. He had sought to dynamite another's property. And now, borne by a demon dog, the lighted dynamite was chasing him.

He redoubled his speed. But he gained pitiably little ground on the frisking pup. In an unconscious instant of self-protection the four men kept close together in their crazy run. They did not seek to scatter. In a scrambling bunch they fled. The same impulse, perhaps, guided mechanically their steps toward the main house; where were other humans and where perhaps might be aid.

Once, in a moment of fright courage, Kilinski stooped for a big stone and half turned to dash it at the pursuing dog. But as he looked over his shoulder to take aim he saw his brief pause had not only left him tailmost of the procession, but had brought Kenneth alongside. The fuse seemed all but touching the stick tips. Dropping the stone, Kilinski threw himself deliriously into the race again, adding his screeches to those of his comrades.

Kenneth was disappointed at this new burst of speed on the part of his quarry. When Kilinski had slowed down momentarily the puppy had supposed this to be the chance for depositing at his feet the ever-heavier bundle. But it seemed he had been mistaken. And though his baby strength was more and more taxed to carry such

46

a weight, he kept gallantly on. The fumes of the powder, too, were beginning to get into his eyes and to choke him. The game no longer was pleasant.

Around the end of the main house tore the fugitives, howling at every jump. And close at their heels followed the weary little dog. This was the strange procession which greeted the gaze of Bryce and Margaret and Mallon from the veranda edge. Open-mouthed the spectators gaped at the weird sight.

Blindly Kilinski banged against the mudguard of Mallon's runabout, on his flight toward the steps. Caroming from it, he lost his balance and sprawled full length, face downward, on the gravel of the drive. For perhaps a second the Polack lay there, half-stunned by the impact of his thick foreskull on the pebbles. Then he scrambled, crabwise, to his feet and bolted again; with fresh screeches of terror.

But that second's delay was just long enough for the accomplishing of tired little Kenneth's mission. Wearily yet daintily the dog laid down his sizzling burden at Kilinski's feet.

Kenneth's task was achieved. Well and snappily achieved, at that. He had followed McLaren's teachings to the letter, as is the way of a rightly trained collie pup of the best sort. He had overcome all difficulties. He had found the thrown object. With much skill and effort he had brought it to the thrower's feet.

Kenneth's share in the tedious sport was at an

end, unless the howling and sprinting Polack should choose to come back and toss the bundle for him again. But Kilinski seemed to have no such intent. He was making much progress in his merry race against death. His gibberings still assailed high heaven. He gave no sign of planning to continue his game with the puppy.

Kenneth was not sorry. The sticks had been increasingly heavy and unwieldy, and the powder reek had been detestable. Leaving the burden behind him, he trotted up the steps toward the three people at the summit.

Kilinski bestowed one more terrified backward glance upon his late pursuer. He saw the dynamite lying on the ground, its sizzling fuse well-nigh burned out. He saw the puppy had abandoned the game. With a yell of command to his fellows he made for the front gate, scarce slackening his pace. Not until all four were well down the highroad did they come to a shambling and jabbering standstill.

"What in the world — ?" gasped Margaret, finding her voice as the last of the runners lumbered out of sight.

But a gurgle of horror from her father interrupted her and brought her wandering gaze to something at which his wavering finger was pointing: namely, a couple of sticks of dynamite tied together and bearing a nearly spent fuse.

The sticks were lying in the driveway not ten feet from the trio.

"Take her out into the open, somewhere,"

shouted Mallon, catching sight of the explosives at the same time and gripping imperatively at Bryce's shoulder. "Carry her! *Run!*"

As he spoke Mallon cleared the porch steps at a leap that brought him into the drive alongside the spitting fuse. In practically the same gesture he snatched up the dynamite sticks and wrenched the infinitesimal bit of fuse free from the tips. Then, to make assurance doubly sure, he flung the tied sticks with all his force as far as possible from the house.

Kenneth, pattering excitedly down the veranda steps, gave instant chase. But Mallon caught the flying pup expertly by the nape of the neck as he passed, and turned back to the porch.

Bryce had been too muddle-witted to follow Mallon's instructions to hurry Margaret from under the veranda roof before the possible explosion should bring down that portion of the house on her. He and the girl stood, wide eyed, panting, their gaze fixed marvelingly on Mallon.

"It — it might have gone off while you held it," breathed Margaret, catching her breath in something like a sob. "It —"

"A second later," babbled her father, "and it would have exploded. It was touch and go. We owe you our —"

"Nonsense!" laughed Mallon, direfully embarrassed. "I'm only sorry I bawled at you so melodramatically. I was a bit rattled, I suppose. It was —"

"It was — it was *magnificent!*" declared Margaret, looking at him with an odd new expression he dared not believe he read aright. "It was — Oh, you'll stay to lunch, won't you — please? And — bring Kenneth in with you."

"Say," confided Bryce, an hour later, drawing Mallon out of earshot of the others. "I just phoned those two blasters who left the dynamite here last week. I gave them a bit of my mind, for storing explosives in my tool-house. And what do you suppose they told me? They'd left that box there because it had nothing in it but 'duds,' as they called them; dynamite sticks that were defective and wouldn't go off. They put all the defective sticks from our blast work into the box, meaning to ship it back to the dealer when they got through the out-of-town job they're on."

Mallon whistled long and low. "All my scare for nothing," he exclaimed. "Heavens! what a fool I made of myself!"

"I — I suggest," ventured Bryce, "that we say nothing to Margaret. There's no need, you know."

"No need at all," assented Mallon in a flash of sanity. "Besides — she's asked me to stay on to dinner tonight. I think I'll hunt up those two duds and have them framed."

III

JOCK

There was blurred memory, ever fainter, of a broad and shaded kennel-yard, with lawns and hills and blue water beyond its wire fence's loops, and of a soft-eyed golden mother against whose warm underbody he nestled on cold nights.

But every day these recollections waned and dimmed and merged and became more like half-recalled dreams than realities. A two-months collie puppy's mental background is sketchy, at best. And there were a million newer and unlovelier impressions, to drive out the sweet little past.

For example, the world, nowadays, was six feet long, by four feet wide, by ever so high. On three sides it was bounded by wooden partitions. On the fourth side it was hemmed in by something vast and invisible and bruisingly hard.

Beyond this plate-glass show window of the dog-and-bird shop was another world; a world unreachable and unsmellable, but starkly visible; a world of gray streets and gray buildings and of sidewalks along which streamed hordes of humans. Now and again these humans, singly or in knots, would pause at the window and peer grinningly in; or they would tap on the glass and waggle their fingers invitingly; or chirp and whistle with no sound.

But hurtful experience with the glass's unyielding hardness had taught the pups not to bounce forward against the barrier, be the onlookers' fingers twiddled ever so provocatively in their faces.

For the most part, they drowsed or else stared out through the pane. But sometimes their birthright of playfulness would lead them into mild romps and mock-fights; even in this cheerless prison of theirs. At times, too, ancestral urge would cause them to battle for a moment in clownishly gusty rage over the uninviting food they none of them yearned for.

Dan Veltin had been living in a noisy little city flat for seven years; ever since his marriage to Amy. Before that, he had lived in a noisier little boarding-house for another seven years; indeed, ever since he left his father's farm and came to New York to make a living. But his soul and his yearnings and his dreams were drenched with the mountain country where he had been born and bred and which his ancestors had snatched from the Indian-infested wilderness. Always, in the bottom of his heart, was a sick little subconscious ache for the hills and for the distances.

Perhaps that was why he took to pausing, on his walk between the subway station and his office, to peer in at the unlovely show window of the unlovelier dog-and-bird store. He had given only a casual glance to it and its prisoners, one morning. Then his gaze had focused on a mournful-eyed and fluffy and pudgy brown collie pup that was looking wistfully through the smeared glass out into the dreary street.

There was something of the country and of the open about the little dog's aspect. There was something of the same achy homesickness that pestered Dan Veltin himself. Dan stood watching the puppy so long that he was almost late at the office. Every day thereafter he stopped to watch.

One afternoon Amy came to the office to meet him. They stopped, together, to look in at the collie of which Dan had told his wife. Then they went into the smelly shop.

Five minutes later they emerged; Dan carrying a wiggly wooden box wherein pattered and danced and whined a wigglier brown collie pup.

"Yes, I know it was a fool thing to do," Dan was saying in self-excuse as he and Amy boarded the Bronx subway train for their home-flat. "I know, in the first place, we can't afford it — though if the invention ever goes through, we can afford a thousand puppies and a real place in the country to keep them in. And I know a collie has no more right in a city flat than a hawk has in a canary-cage. But — well — he'll be better off with us than in that measly window or if he was sold to some other New York chap who wouldn't know how to exercise him or take care of him. So —"

"So you were perfectly right to get him!" supplemented Amy. "I told you that, a week ago. As for not being able to afford him — I think it's always lots best to get things we want and don't need, when we can't afford them. You see, people always can scrape together enough money, somehow, for the grim necessaries of life. But the luxuries ought to be bought when they'll give the most pleasure. We oughtn't to wait till we are so rich that the luxuries won't seem luxuries at all. Besides," she rebuked, "you're not to say '*if* the invention ever goes through.' You know perfectly well it will go through. Why, the Coenen-Byng people are —"

"Lots of other people were, too, from time to time," sighed Dan. "There's no more reason to think I can put it across with the Coenen-Byng outfit than with any of them. Don't let's worry over that, though. I'll bet Ken will go wild when he sees this pup. Every boy ought to be brought up with a dog. I've always said that. And Ken is old enough to —"

"Indeed he is!" agreed Amy. "And he's a born animal-lover, too. I've told you that, ever since he was old enough to walk in the Park with me. The animals in the zoo mean more to him than anything else in the world. That's the best of living in the Bronx. We're so close to the Park, it's almost like our own back yard that we haven't got."

"He's six," mused Dan. "I was younger than that when I had a dog. I cut my teeth on the ears of Jock, our old pointer."

"The very name!" broke in Amy.

"The what?" asked Dan, puzzled.

"Jock. For the puppy. It's Scotch and it's short and —"

"And it's easy to call, at a distance," added Dan, eagerly. "That's what people ought to think of when they name a dog. Not that he'll have a chance to stray far enough in this cramped city to need any loud calling. I'm glad to have the good old pointer's name handed on. He was worth it."

Thus did the mournful-eyed brown collie puppy find a home. Thus, daily, did he become a more and more loved and honored house-mate in the Bronx flat; and make more and more of a place for himself in the hearts of Dan and Amy Veltin and of their stocky six-year-old son, Kenneth.

It was a jolly little household; though its future was bound up in Dan's tediously perfected and unsold invention and in that sad-glad word, "If." The flat held five rooms and it was on the fifth floor of a five-story walk-up apartment house.

"The only reason we live on the fifth," airily explained Dan to a puffing guest, "is because there's no sixth. The higher the cheaper. Besides, there's sunlight in every room."

Of late, six-year-old Kenneth had become a problem. The child was gifted or cursed with a queer energy. Splendidly strong and healthy, he did not know the meaning of fatigue. The walks with his mother in the Park left him eagerly unwearied. He needed the country and its all-day outdoorness as vent for his spirits and strength.

But the coming of Jock helped to ease the strain. In wild romps with the fast-growing puppy, Kenneth wore off some of his own excess energy. Boy and dog were adoring chums from the first. Their Park scampers were grand exercise for both of them, and called forth infinitely more effort and excitement on Kenneth's part than had the sedate rambles with Amy. The chums throve apace.

In the two years that followed, Kenneth took on legginess. Jock developed into a mighty and magnificent bronze-hued collie; faultless of manner, and with his intelligence deepened and humanized to the full by constant association with his three owners. Such training will do uncannily strange things to a collie's sensitive brain.

Kenneth's own brain was doing much developing, nowadays; but along one line which made his parents worry gloomily. He was as energetic of imagination as of body. In earlier years, this imagination had taken the form of sagas whereof he was the hero and wherein bears and Indians figured as his easily-conquered victims.

But when Kenneth grew older and when the romances took a less fantastic slant, both parents ceased smiling and frowned.

For instance, there was the time when he came running home and told them joyously that he had been chosen to go down to the City Hall, next morning, as delegate from Grammar School Number Fifty-nine, to present a huge bouquet to the governor of the state. There was to be a picture in the papers of it, too, the principal had said.

Thrilled at the honor to her son, Amy took a nonsparable slice of the housekeeping money and went out and bought the boy a complete new outfit of clothes for the ceremony — and never suspected the hoax until she and Dan arrived at City Hall, next day, to witness the mythical presentation.

Then there was the time when Kenneth came to the flat nursing a bloody nose and a left eye which was the epitome of all the banked thunderclouds in all the skies. A strange boy, he said, of twice his size, had been beating a little crippled girl. Mindful of Dan's lectures on chivalry, Kenneth had rushed to the rescue. He had had no great trouble in thrashing the larger boy to a pulp. But in the course of the fray a chance blow had marred the young crusader's victory by bruising his nose and eye and spoiling his looks.

Vastly proud of his son's heroism was Dan Veltin; and loudly did he boast. Then the janitor had cast murk on the shining war-episode by saying that Kenneth had merely assailed a somewhat smaller if much tougher boy because the boy refused to credit Ken's declaration that Jock had killed four wolves which had escaped from the dens in the zoo and which had pitched on to the collie during a stroll through the park.

Attacked by Kenneth, the tough boy had retaliated. Two blows only, said the janitor, had been struck in that actual fight. One was when the tough boy landed on Kenneth's nose and the other was when Kenneth's head hit the pavement. The tough youth had been bent on following up his own swift victory. But Jock had flown to his young master's relief. The collie had rolled the tough boy in the gutter and had amputated the seat of his ragged trousers; and thereafter had chased him two blocks down the street, chivvying the fugitive's legs as he ran. Had a grown man assailed Kenneth, the collie's vengeance would have been tenfold more drastic. As it was, he had treated the tough youngster with only sample-sized severity; inflicting it to an accompaniment of wagging tail and mischievous eye-glint.

Then there were other recitals of Kenneth's, which Amy characterized sighingly as "unbridled imagination" and which Dan branded bluntly as "lies."

He was their only child. Their own childhood memories were blurred. Thus there was no way whereby they could know, and find comfort in the knowledge that thousands of normally truthful children of keen imagination and mental energy go through a stormily brief phase of untruthfulness somewhere between the ages of six and eight. To Dan and Amy, the case seemed as unique as it was hopeless and hideous. They mourned the seemingly permanent demise of truth in their son.

Amy took it out in mourning. Dan, to his wife's horror, rewarded with a thrashing Kenneth's garish account of seeing a policeman fire three shots at a bald-headed car thief, a few blocks from home. Next morning, at the breakfast table, Dan read a newspaper account of the shooting — similar in every detail to Kenneth's version of it. Head in hands, the father groaned:

"What the blue blazes are we going to do, sweetheart? I can stand anything except a lie. Ken is a chronic liar. When I try to lick him into truthfulness for telling one of his luridest lies — why, the lie turns out to be true! Now I've got to apologize to him for whaling him unjustly. And that'll make him lie all the harder. Lord! Why couldn't he turn out to be anything but a little liar?"

That evening, Kenneth, newly proven truthful in the matter of the shot car thief, celebrated his rehabilitation with a really artistic account of a king cobra which had gotten out of its glass cage in the zoo reptile house and had found its way into his bedroom. By merest chance he had seen the coiled creature as he entered the room; and had crushed the life out of it by jumping on its murderous head.

Amy all but wept.

Dan said, quietly: "That was brave of you, son. Mighty brave. What did you do with the body?"

"Body?" quavered Kenneth.

"Yes. You killed the snake, just now, in your

bedroom. So its body must still be there. Go and bring it to me."

"I — I don't think mother would like to see it — not while she's eating," demurred the slayer. "It's awful messy. I stamped on it pretty hard, you see; and —"

"She will be so proud of your courage that she won't mind seeing your victim. Go and get it."

Kenneth slithered from the room. Presently — indeed, before Dan and Amy could more than exchange miserable glances — he was back again.

"It's too late, Dad!" he exclaimed, dramatically. "Jock's eaten it. I got there, just in time to see him swallow the last bit of its tail. He —"

"Dear," said Dan, solemnly, to his wife. "I'm terribly sorry about this. You see, a king cobra is about the most venomous snake on earth. Anything that eats a king cobra is certain to die in terrible agony, within a few hours, from the effects of the poison he has swallowed. Poor old Jock!"

Kenneth tried to look somber. The effort was a failure; though he loved the collie above all things, save only his parents.

"I'm going to save Jock all that torture," continued Dan. "I'm going to shoot him. That will be swift and painless. I'll take him out into the Park, at once, before the poison has a chance to act; and put a merciful bullet through his head. I hate to do it. But it's the only —"

A screech of mortal terror smashed in on the

homily. Bellowing and blubbering, Kenneth cast both arms about his worshiped chum's furry throat.

"You — you *shan't!*" he sobbed, hysterically. "You shan't shoot Jock! He — oh, Dad, it — it wasn't true. *Honest,* it wasn't, Dad! He didn't really eat the cobra. It — it must have been something else he was eating. He — You're not going to kill Jock! You're *not!*"

"You can't be certain he didn't eat the snake," answered Dan. "I won't take any chances. Amy, please get me my pistol. It's in the —"

Then burst the flood-gates; and through them gushed and spattered the truth.

"I — I didn't really kill the cobra, at all!" wailed Kenneth. "There wasn't any cobra. And it was all just a — just a lie. You can lick me again, Dad, if you want to. You can lick me all night. But you're *not* going to shoot Jock! I —"

"Good!" said Dan to himself, with a long inward breath of relief. "I've got the cure, at last."

Aloud, he said, slowly and impressively: "Very well. I won't shoot him. Now stop bawling and listen to me."

Kenneth fought back his sobs right manfully. His arms still around his squirmingly sympathizing dog, he looked tearfully up at his father.

"Ken," began the impressive voice, "your mother and I have worried ourselves sick, over this filthy habit of yours of telling lies every time you open your mouth. I've tried to explain to you what an unutterably rotten thing a liar is, and how all the world despises him. It hasn't done any good for me to tell you how unhappy we are about it. You go right on lying. But here is where you stop it."

Kenneth blinked inquisitively at the set-faced man. Dan paused, to let the boy's curiosity sharpen; then he went on:

"Mr. Coit is a friend of mine, downtown. He has bought a little home in the country. He wants a really good dog. He'd rather have a collie than any other kind. A collie belongs in the country; not in a city flat. So I'd be doing Jock a real kindness by giving him to Mr. Coit. We'd never see the dog again, of course. But we'd know he was happy out there in the fields and the woods. We'd all miss him terribly. But —"

Upon his slow-uttered harangue burst afresh the noise of heart-rent grief. Kenneth forgot once more that he was a sturdy boy of eight. He remembered only that he loved Jock with all his might; and that the collie was his chum and guard and adoring servant. Life without Jock was not to be considered, on any terms at all.

"Quiet!" ordered Dan; proceeding with voice raised above the gulping sobs. "Now this is what I want you to listen to and to remember: The next time your mother or myself catches you in any kind of a lie at all, or if we hear of your lying to anyone else, we aren't going to whip you. We aren't going to scold you. We aren't going to say a word to you about it. But you will come home from school some day and find Jock gone."

"No! *No*, Daddy! I —"

"Jock can stay here as long as he lives," continued Dan, "or he can go to Mr. Coit's place in the country. It all depends on you. Understand? It depends on *you*. If he is sent away, it will be because your lies send him. If you tell the truth, he will stay on with us. You have the say, whether we are to lose him or not. Think it over."

Kenneth thought it over. Indeed, he thought it over, for hours after he went miserably to bed that night. His processes of thought did not include any hesitancy as to the ceasing of lies.

On that he was wholly resolved. He was done with lying, once and for all. Sooner than lose Jock, he would have gone without eating or playing. There could be no question in his mind about anything like that.

Then one afternoon, on the way home from school —

"What's the names of the twin kids Miss Gusepple was telling us about?" asked Spike Burney. "The kids what lived in a wolf's den? Some queer Irish names. What —"

"Romulus and Remus," glibly answered the erudite Kenneth. "They —"

"That's the ones," assented Spike. "Some nerve those twins had, I'll say! Think of going into a wolf's den and staying there, with the wolves li'ble to chew you up as quick as look at you! Some nerve!"

"Huh!" scoffed Kenneth, loudly, stung by the wistful admiration in Spike's voice. "That's nothing. Why, one night, when I couldn't sleep, it was so hot, I got up and dressed me and I whistled to Jock to come along; and I went out to sit around in Bronx Park, where it was nice and cool. And pretty soon I got to feeling kind of sleepy and I didn't want to go to sleep out there on the benches for fear a cop would nab me. So I went over to the wolf-dens; and I just opened the first den's door, the way you've seen the keepers do when they clean the dens. The wolf came hopping out, as mad as wrath. But Jock pretty soon finished *him*. So I crawled inside the den, as easy as anything; and I lay down and —"

Something invisible clutched at his bragging throat; crushing the boastful words to a gurgling silence. Not even Spike Burney's derisive yells of incredulity could move Kenneth to further speech.

He had lied! He had told another lie! He had told it so loudly that any passer-by could easily have heard it and could run to Dad with the news. *Jock!*

Choking back his sobs, Kenneth broke into a run, deserting Spike and racing home. Jock was waiting for him at the door, as always. Kenneth could have shouted aloud in sheer reaction. Then the exaltation died. Of course, Dad hadn't had time to hear about his lie so soon; all-wise as Dad was. It might be a day or two. But Jock's fate was sealed. Dear splendid old Jock! Kenneth had lied him away.

That evening Kenneth had further respite. Dan

telephoned to Amy that he had been sent for, to a downtown hotel, for a conference with the Coenen-Byng people; who, after dropping the whole subject of Dan's invention, had been nibbling recently at it in tentative and nerve-teasing fashion. Nothing would come of the conference, Dan warned Amy over the telephone; but it was not safe to leave a single chance untaken.

As ever when there was the ghost of a hope for the invention's possible success, Amy lost herself in golden daydreams.

Thus she did not notice that Kenneth ate nothing; and that every now and then he would hug Jock spasmodically; and that he was a horribly woebegone little boy. He even went to bed without being told to. In his brain rang his mother's absent-minded words: "Daddy's not coming home till late. It is something terribly important. You'll know all about it, tomorrow — if there is anything to know."

"Something terribly important!" Dad was on the trail of Kenneth's lie. How he was tracing it to earth the overwrought boy could not guess. But he knew Dad could be relied on to discover it. Dad always got what he went after. Mother had said so, again and again.

After a million wide-awake hours of numb despair, Kenneth's desperate brain began to work. He had told Spike Burney that he had gone out into Bronx Park by night, and that he had opened a wolf-den door and had gone inside and lain down there. That was his lie. Oh yes, and

65

that Jock had taken care of the wolf! That was it. (Not that Jock couldn't thrash a whole pack of wolves, as easily as he could tree a cat. The boy had not the remotest doubt as to his collie chum's ability to overcome any foe on earth.)

Well, now, suppose! Suppose he was to turn the lie into the truth? Hey? How about doing that? Then, he could say to Dad: "It was a lie when I told it. But it's true, now!" That would square it. Just as the policeman and the car thief story was all right, as soon as it was proved to be true. Dad had apologized to him for doubting that yarn. The thing to do when one was trapped into telling a lie was to make the lie come true. That squared it.

Cautiously, swiftly, he slid out of bed and began to wriggle into his clothes. Dad might come home any time now. There mightn't be a second to lose. Jock had sprung up, eagerly, as he saw Kenneth begin to dress. The boy whispered sharply to him. Presently, holding the dog by the collar, Kenneth tiptoed down the short hallway of the flat. He peeped into the living-room as he passed. Amy was dozing in her chair, a magazine lying on her lap. The mantel clock was at five minutes before ten.

Kenneth let himself and his dog out of the house, and sped toward the Park's nearest practical entrance. The park itself had been his playground, the zoo his favorite haunt, since he could toddle. Hence, the way was as well known to him as was his own bedroom furniture. He did not even stick to the Zoological Gardens' twisting asphalt paths; but cut across, under the trees.

Past the bear-dens, past the reptile-house, he made his way, and on to the line of wolf-lairs, set against the solid rock. What was it he had told Spike? Oh, yes: "I just opened the first den's door." To the first den he went.

Like many another boy of that region, he had had long experience in dodging the casual guards during law-forbidden evening rambles in the park. To Kenneth it was pitiably easy. Easy was it, too, from frequent observing, to master the none-too-complicated door-catch of the wolf-den he had chosen for a resting-place.

As he neared the line of dens, Jock, as ever, hesitated. The dog hated wolves; and their very scent made him angry and suspicious. Thus it is with three collies out of four. More than once, Kenneth had had to scold Jock for threatening the secrecy of their evening walks by barking furiously at his enemies. Hence the collie's hesitance, now.

But Jock's night-seeing eyes showed him not only every wolf in the line springing snarlingly to the front of the dens, but also his loved young master tackling fearlessly the catch of one of these dens. Jock leaped forward to throw himself between Kenneth and the courted danger.

He was a fraction of a second too late.

The iron door swung wide. Something evil-scented and gray hurtled forth with such impetus that it hit the opening door out of

Kenneth's grasp and knocked the boy himself to the ground.

Outward the wolf launched himself; perhaps for the earth, perhaps for the boy who sprawled beneath the door. And forward flashed a tawny shape, out of the night; with a wild-beast snarl in its deep throat; forward to meet in mid-air the down-leaping wolf.

Together came the two huge furry bodies, with a breath-expelling impact. To the asphalt they crashed, in a murderous embrace. Then they were on their feet again, rearing and roaring and tearing for each other's throat.

From every den arose a chorus of lupine battle howls. The cry was taken up from spot to spot in the darkness. Far down in the lion-house, the giant carnivore smashed the night's silences with roar and scream.

Heedless, and in maniac fury, the wolf and the collie battled on, there on the dark path, bursting through shrubbery, rolling, recovering, charging, rending. Collie and wolf — thousand-year mortal hereditary enemies — they were fighting to the death, amid the ever-swelling racket of the zoo's multiple inmates.

Sublimely calm in his belief that Jock could thrash every wolf alive, Kenneth made good his lie by scrambling up into the den and laying himself at full length there; whence he proceeded to view the conflict.

The wolf emerged from a close-quarters scrimmage, and dived for the collie's nearest forepaw. This leg-breaking trick is the oldest and the favorite fight-ruse of wolves. Collie puppies copy it unconsciously in their play.

Instinctively, Jock yanked back his imperiled forefoot, out of reach of the terrible jaws. His hindleg slipped on a scrap of orange peel dropped there during the day by a park visitor. For the briefest part of an instant, the collie lurched sidewise, clawing to recover his balance. In that moment, the wolf flashed in, to gain the fatal throat-hold.

Jock shrank back to avert the grip. But he was not quite fast enough; for his balance was still uncertain. In tore the wolf, driving his teeth to the throat as Jock pulled back. He missed the jugular by a half-inch; his mouth filling with collie hair and with little else.

But his in-curving lower eyeteeth hooked upward, about the thin round collar the dog wore. Jock's backward jerk pulled the collar taut. His teeth still clenched on hair and his lower tusks hooked fast in the collar, the wolf struggled and threw himself from side to side to break free. He was tied as securely to the dog's collar as if by a rope; for the thin round loop of leather behind the curve of his eyeteeth held firm as wire.

Around and around, the battlers flung themselves; neither able, because of the absurd predicament, to bite the other. Then it was that Kenneth became aware of dancing flashlights and the rush of men's heavy feet toward the wolf-dens.

The darkness was abruptly turned into day by arc lights in front of the dens. Then a rope was passed around the wolf's neck and was held tight from two opposite directions. Out of the cage rolled Kenneth, indignant, voluble.

"What did y' want to stop 'em for?" he shrilled. "Jock was licking him, with one hand behind him. He —"

"It's the Veltin kid!" announced one of the guards. "And — yep, it's his collie, too. Tackling a timber wolf, he was! 'S a wonder that both him and the boy weren't chewed up. For the love of Mike, kid, what were you doing in that wolf-den?"

"I was telling the truth," was Kenneth's astounding reply. "And now that I've told it, I'm going home. C'mon, Jock!"

Up the long flights of the apartment house, to his own top-floor flat, Dan Veltin mounted at a run. Open he threw the flat's door and swirled in like a cyclone. Amy started from her doze in the big living-room chair and came dazedly forward to meet the man.

"Girl of mine!" he shouted, half delirious. "Girl of mine, they've taken it. They've *taken* it! The good old invention. The papers are all signed; and — look at this advance check they gave me, against my royalties! *Look* at it, I tell you! Do you know what it means? It isn't the million-dollar fortune we used to dream about, of course. Nothing like it. But it means comfort for the rest of our lives, if we live sanely. And we're going to live sanely, sweetheart. We're going to live out in the country in North Jersey, at that — you and I and Ken and Jock. All four of us! Get that, dear? Now, let's wake Ken and tell him. The janitor and the neighbors will be lucky if I don't wake *them,* too, and tell them. I've got to tell everybody in reach!"

His rapturous pæan came to a halt. He had burst into Kenneth's little bedroom; still half leading and half carrying the excitedly bewildered Amy along with him. The bed was empty. So was the bedside mat where Jock was wont to sleep.

"What — where — ?" stammered Dan.

On the heels of his first words came a fumbling at the flat's lock. Dan opened the front door, revealing on the threshold a huge dog bleeding from a half-dozen superficial hurts and a small boy much disheveled and very dirty.

"Of all the — !" began Amy.

"Where on earth have you been, Ken?" demanded Dan in the same breath.

"I've — I've been telling the truth!" reiterated Kenneth, shakily. "I've been lying down in one of the wolf-dens while Jock licked the wolf. If you don't believe me, ask the guard that has the red hair and the wart. And — and now Spike Burney can tell you anything he wants to. Whatever it is, it's *true.* I used to tell lies. I don't, any more. I don't have to. Things happen when I tell the TRUTH. Don't they, Jock?"

IV

THE "CRITTER"

"No," refused Brand, "I'm not going to sell him and I'm not going to give him away, nor yet shoot him. I was planning to do one of the three, till I went to that Chautauqua lecture, down to Paterson. But —"

"The only Chautauqua lecture, down there, that I was ever able to drag you to," interrupted his wife, "was the one on 'Small Beginnings of Great Men.' And —"

"That's the one I'm talking about," said Brand.

"But what in the wide earth has that fine lecture got to do with this long-legged fool of a collie pup?" she demanded.

Amos Brand laughed sheepishly. Yet he stuck to his guns.

"Here's the idea," said he. "You remember how the lecturer chap said that Bismarck and Mr. Thackeray and Abraham Lincoln and two or three other great men were so lazy when they was young that nobody ever had any notion they'd be worth raising? He said young Abe Lincoln used to lie around and fish and read and swap funny stories and that he'd only hustle when he had to. He said Mr. Thackeray hadn't even got the energy to graduate from his college and that he spent his time there in gambling with cards. He said Bismarck was fonder of swigging lager beer in college than of learning his lessons and they packed him home as a dunce. He said —"

"Oh, I remember all that!" put in his wife, impatiently. "But what has it got to do with — ?"

"He said," stolidly continued Amos — "he said all those fellers was some inches above six feet tall, and was built big in proportion, and they got their growth while they was youngsters; and the fast growing kept them from wanting to be of any use. Then when they had finished growing they cut loose and made big marks in the world."

"But —"

"When we came home from the lecture, there was Leggy, standing at the gate, on the lookout for us. I stopped to take a good size-up of him. He's only six months old and he's a hand higher at the shoulder than old Shep, and he's got the legs of a yearling colt, and his strength is all laying around loose on him. As I set my eyes on him, here's the thought that came to me: — 'I'll bet that's how Mr. Thackeray (whoever he was) and Bismarck and grand old Abe Lincoln would have looked at his age, if they'd been collies. The poor cuss has grown so fast, he hasn't got the pep, left over, to amount to a hill of mildewed beans. If we keep him and treat him patient and kind, likely enough he'll shape into something that'll pay us back for the nine dollars we gave that professional breeder for him when he was five weeks old.' "

"Of all the crazy —"

"Yes, Ruth, that's the very thought that come a-bizzing into my brain as I looked at him wagging his fool tail at me and looking like some ancestor of his had been a stepladder or a clothespole. And it was a hunch. I'm going to play that hunch. Leggy is going to stay on here awhile, on the chance he'll turn out to be worth the powder and shot to blow his silly head off. That's settled. He eats more than a hired man. I know that. And he tears up everything he can get his teeth into. And he 'runs' the sheep somethin' scand'lous when old Shep and me try to learn him herding. And he hasn't hardly the brains to remember his own name. But — well, a hunch is a hunch. I'm a-going to play mine. Leggy stays."

"Amos Brand!" said his pretty wife, in mock despair. "Nature used up so much wisdom in making Thackeray and Bismarck and Lincoln that she had to strike an average by making two beings that didn't have any wisdom at all. One of them is Leggy. I was dumb enough to marry the other one."

In spite of Ruth's open scorn for his hunch, Amos continued to play it. Not only did he allow the shambling giant collie puppy to continue living at the farm, but he used up an unbelievable store of patience in endless efforts to train Leggy into a semblance of a useful farm dog.

For a month or so longer his attempts were laughably — or cursably — futile. Leggy seemed unable to learn the simplest rudiments of work or of anything else. The pup was good-natured and willing and effusively friendly. But he was a fool.

He ate ravenously; he grew like a weed; he was adoringly fond of everyone he met. But he had not even brains enough to retrieve a thrown stick. Nor to keep from dashing gaily among the driven sheep or cattle, barking and harrying. In vain did Amos Brand labor and belabor. In vain did Shep, the wise little old farm collie, try to teach him by example and by thrashings. Leggy was hopelessly worthless. His master's hunch seemed to have been inspired by a bad-luck demon.

Then came winter. No longer were the cattle and the sheep sent out to the various pastures of the woody hillside farm. They were kept close, during the bitter northland weather. There was scant work for any dog to do. It was the rest season for man and beast, on a thousand farms. Beyond wood-cutting and stock-tending, Amos himself had little to occupy him.

Leggy spent his time eating and dozing or in romping deliriously in the deep snow; or in following the disgusted old Shep from place to place. He looked up to the aged collie with true hero-worship, taking Shep's snubs and thrashings with loving meekness. At last came spring. Long before the cattle were turned out to grass, half of the farm's three hundred sheep were to be sent to pasture on a rocky slope far from the house.

Shep, with no guidance at all from Brand, was wont to take them in charge on such trips; driving them to the rock-pasture with patient precision; and pushing shut the swing-gate behind him. For ten years Shep had done this sort of thing. To him it seemed ridiculously simple. He despised the harum-scarum Leggy for not having the wit to learn such tasks after a hundred teachings.

On this morning Leggy had been shut in the barn when the sheep were driven forth from their fold. Shep was getting a bit rheumatic with age. Brand did not want the old collie's toil to be impeded or redoubled by the pup's scattering of the flock.

Amos's hunch long since had begun to fade. He had decided to get rid of Leggy in the first merciful way that should present itself.

This morning, the flock was unusually hard to drive. For months they had been cooped in the fold. Their memories of being driven — if indeed sheep have sense enough to remember anything at all — were very vague. At every possible chance they would break or wheel back or try to stampede. Shep was kept busy from the moment he set out.

On this first morning Brand went along. Not

that he did not trust to Shep's brain and loyalty; but in order to watch the sheep on their entrance to the pasture. Sometimes, very early in the season, the younger ones needed a bit of over-seeing, on their initial trip.

Amos frowned in annoyance at the trouble the flock was giving to Shep, today; and he pitied the plucky efforts of the rheumatic old collie to keep them in formation and moving in the right direction. He frowned more intensely at thought of the worthlessness of Leggy, the pup he had bought to make farm work easier for tired old Shep.

As the procession reached the pasture, the gate was hanging wide. Shep drove his woolly charges straight for it; easing up on his speed, so that they might not jam or break at the gateway.

In spite of his precautions, a six-month wether wheeled in terror at a garter-snake that was sunning itself in the opening. The wether spun around and galloped off at a tangent. Some forty sheep followed.

Shep was about to give chase, when another forty or fifty sheep broke and scattered in a score of directions. Choosing to check this individual scattering, before turning back the first bunch of strays, Shep got into as active motion as his aged bones and sinews could achieve.

It was a heart-breaking task. Brand was heartily sorry for his honest helper. The man was about to join in the rounding-up process when he was aware of a new dog on the scene. At a glance he recognized Leggy. The pup had pried aside a loose board in the ramshackle barn wall and had wiggled through, at a loss of some of his luxuriant coat. Catching the trail, he had followed.

Brand groaned aloud. The situation was bad enough for Shep and himself, without having their work trebled by the aimless barking and charging of this excited pup. He drew in a long breath, to bellow an order to Leggy to come back to him. But the bellow died unborn in his throat.

To Brand's astonishment, Leggy circled the farthest bunch of galloping strays with the skill of a veteran and the speed of an express train. Deftly, brilliantly, he headed and checked them, sweeping them into alignment and driving them unerringly for the pasture gate.

It was a piece of work that would not have disgraced Shep, in the old collie's best days. True, there was a hint of raggedness and of overvehemence to it; as to the herding maneuvers of most high-spirited young collies. But it was admirably done, in the main. And it served its purpose to perfection.

Through the gateway cantered the driven bunch and out into the field; spreading and, one by one, stopping to nibble the tiny grassblades. Leggy waited only to see they were not going to double back. Then he dashed after the scattered runaways that Shep was struggling to round up.

It was a pretty sight, this swiftly efficient supplementing of the old dog's work. Incredibly soon, the strays were bunched and turned; and were trotting into the field. There, Shep nosed shut the gate, whose bar fell automatically into place.

Then the ancient sheep-dog walked across to where Leggy stood panting and grinning. Never before had Shep approached the puppy, save in castigation. Now, his moth-eaten tail awag, he touched noses with his young disciple.

In that brief contact, chumship was established and recognition was given to an able fellow craftsman. Leggy wagged his own plumed tail ecstatically at the compliment.

Amos Brand had stood staring, open-mouthed. Yet his common sense told him it was no miracle at all. Leggy had been trained and drilled into this sort of work, month after month. A hundred times he had seen Shep go through the same evolutions. The average pup would have learned long ago. Leggy's newly-awakened brain was just beginning to function.

Brand looked the pup over with new eyes. For months, he scarce had glanced at him. Now he saw a real miracle. The long winter had done more than awaken Leggy's brain. It had filled out his scrawny body to shapely leanness and to breadth of shoulder and depth of chest. It had given him a mighty coat and had chiseled his amorphous head into strongly classic lines. The silly puppy eyes had grown stern and deeper-set. A soul had been born into them.

No longer was Leggy a formlessly gangling

atrocity. He was a well-built young giant with brawn and brain. Such transformations have occurred in a million seemingly hopeless pups. But Brand was witnessing the phenomenon for the first time. Small wonder that he stared agape.

Thus began a new era in Leggy's life. From a despised nuisance, he took now an honored place in the daily routine of the farm. He was busy. But he was splendidly happy. Not only did Amos Brand and Ruth treat him with real affection and grant him the privilege of kitchen and porch; but his idol, Shep, accepted him as a loved equal. The two dogs were more and more close chums; to Leggy's manifest pride and delight. Except when work separated them, they were always together.

Not only with the wethers and older sheep, but presently with the lambs, did Brand trust the young dog. Almost at once the raggedness and the too-vehement tendencies disappeared from his herding technique. With the lambs, Leggy was as gentle as a mother with a sick child. The lamb flock was his joy. He tended it indefatigably. Once, when a mongrel stray dog ventured into the lamb-pasture, Leggy thrashed the intruder wellnigh to death.

And so the springtime and early summer wore on. With each passing day, Leggy waxed more efficient. The seemingly thrown-away lessons of earlier months were bearing rich fruit. Amos Brand rejoiced noisily in his hunch's triumph.

Then came the order for thirty of Amos's lambs to be shipped on a certain date to a dealer in Paterson. Brand selected those that were to be sent. He herded them by themselves in a high-fenced little pasture at the corner of his South Mowing. To Leggy was assigned the task of guarding them, during the few nights before shipment. Vastly proud of himself was Leggy at this welcome duty.

But as Amos, with Shep at his heels, was making his early round of the farm, the first morning after he had put the lambs into the little pasture, the man came upon a sight that sickened and amazed him.

Of the thirty lambs, two had disappeared. The others were close huddled in a corner. One of them had a hideously deep gash on its shoulder.

Leggy half-lay, half-sat, guarding the huddled flock of babies. His right foreleg trailed helpless. One of his furry tulip ears was slashed through. He was bleeding freely from a face-cut, just below the mangled ear.

As Brand approached, the young collie reared up and sought to hobble toward him, wagging his plumed tail. The attempt was too much. Pain and loss of blood made him stagger and then collapse on his side.

Amos called his hired man, bidding the astounded worker to pick up the stricken dog and carry him to the house; then to telephone to the nearest veterinary to come and set the broken leg and tend the other hurts.

Old Shep nosed his injured chum; whimpering softly in sympathy and then trotting along to the house in the wake of the man who was carrying the invalid. But for once Leggy did not respond in any way to his collie comrade's advances. Indeed, he seemed not to notice the solicitous Shep.

Left alone in the pasture, Brand began to study the trampled grass. There had been a light shower, just before dawn. Thus, the ground still held the marks of the wildly pattering lamb hoofs; and many dog footprints. Apparently, the lambs had been scared into galloping panic by their assailant, and Leggy had done much footwork in the course of their defense.

But, apart from these prints, there was nothing on the wet grass to betoken what manner of beast of prey had carried off two of the lambs and torn a third and had disabled Leggy. The thing was an absolute mystery.

Homeward went Brand, carrying the hurt lamb. He found Leggy installed on a soft folded blanket in the kitchen, with Ruth bathing his cuts and trying to ease the pain in the broken foreleg.

Grimly, Amos set to examining the slashed ear and the deep cut on the face. The wounds might well have been made with a dull knife.

"I can't figure it out," he told his wife. "Some critter has come there in the night and gotten away with two lambs, and bit another one. Leggy must have put up a good fight. But what critter could have made such a wound as either of these on him; and what critter could have broke his leg? That's what I can't work out."

"I don't know about the leg," answered his wife. "But the first minute I set eyes on the slit ear and the cut on his face, I got to remembering the fight old Shep had, that time, six years back, with Connors' big mastiff. Remember how Connors wouldn't believe a lot of dog bites could cut his mastiff so that the wounds looked like knife-slits? You told him no dog but a collie knows how to 'slash' like that when he fights. Even then, he wouldn't believe Shep's eye-teeth had made those cuts in his Tige's body. He swore you had attacked the mastiff with a knife, I remember. Well, these wounds on Leggy are just like those on Tige."

"H'm!" commented Brand. "I don't see that you've cleared it up very much. Come to think of it, there can't have been a fight at all. If any collie had been in a fight with Leggy, there'd be hair and blood on Leggy's jaws. There isn't a mark on them. I just looked. Of course, if he had had a chance to get a good big drink of water, the hair and most likely the blood would have been washed away. But there's no place in that pasture where he could have drunk. The drinking-trough is a hundred feet from where he was lying. He couldn't have got to it. Besides, how about the broken leg?"

"I — I don't know," she answered. "Unless he may have been thrown, in the fight; and the leg may have doubled under him and broken. That would have been possible."

"I tell you there wasn't any fight," insisted Brand. "You saw how he chewed up that big run-away mongrel last month — the one that got into the uphill pasture. Well, do you suppose he'd have let any dog get away without marking him? Not Leggy. His mouth and chest would have blood on them; and there'd be hairs on his jaws. No, there wasn't any fight!"

"What was there, then?"

"There was some critter that either jumped over the fence or shinned in through the bars and yanked away two of the fattest lambs and barked a third one; and had the size and strength to smash Leggy before the poor chap could even get into action. The only trouble with that idea is that there weren't any tracks such as the critter must have made. Nothing but dog footprints and lamb footprints. And I've just showed you that if it was a dog Leggy would have licked him or else he'd have done enough fighting to leave the marks on his own mouth."

"Yes," said Ruth, wearily, "you've showed me that — or you've tried to. But what does it all add up to?"

"I'd give the year's crops to know," replied Amos, despondently. "But there's one thing —"

He was cut short in his disconsolate speech by the arrival of the veterinary. Soon Leggy's fractured foreleg was in a cast, and his head-wounds were stitched and swathed. The leg-break had not occurred near a joint. Wherefore the vet assured Brand that with any sort of luck the collie would recover wholly from the fracture and would not be lamed for life.

The vet was as mystified as were the Brands, as to the cause of the injuries. He agreed with Ruth that the bone might perhaps have been broken, had the leg been doubled under the dog in a heavy fall. But he said the head-cuts had the aspect of knife slashes, rather than marks of rending by teeth.

That night, Amos Brand deputed Shep to guard the lamb pasture. He himself augmented the vigil by going thither with a twelve-gauge gun whose two barrels contained buckshot cartridges.

Brand seated himself on a rock at one end of the small upland field; wrapping his coat around him and holding the gun in readiness across his knees.

Shep lay down at his feet, his alert old eyes on the drowsing lambs; his ears pricked for the faintest sound. The collie seemed to realize that much was at stake, for he was tense all over; nor did he lower his head to his outstretched paws.

For hours the two watchers remained thus, while the solemn summer night rolled along. The air was tinged with the first chill of distant autumn. The earliest katydids were essaying doubtfully and rustily their frost-warning song. Treetoads and crickets swelled the scratchy chorus. But in and around the pasture there was no other sound.

As the night waxed later and colder, the insect songs ceased. An owl in the nearby patch of woodland began to hoot eerily. A rooster, on the farm across the river, sent out a premature challenge to the dawn. The crowing was answered from Brand's chicken-yard.

Then all went silent again. Brand's head began to nod. Shep's did not. Twice or thrice, Amos started guiltily from a half-doze. Presently he slept. The collie alone kept vigil.

Gray daybreak was crawling out of the east and over the far-off mountain wall, when Amos was waked by the discomfort of his own cramped posture. Roosters were crowing. One or two late summer birds were singing in the woods. The whole pasture was visible, in the unearthly gray light. The dawn wind was blowing.

Brand jumped to his feet. Instantly he sat down again, heavily; his numbed legs buckling. As he stamped the circulation back into his feet he peered worriedly around the little field. He had slept when he should have guarded. He was ashamed of his own negligence.

Shep was broad awake, and thumped his ragged tail on the ground in morning greeting to his master. Brand got up and, followed by the dog, made the round of the field. He counted the lambs.

All were there — alive and unhurt. Through no virtue of their owner, they had gone safely through the night. The mysterious prowler had not paid another visit to the pasture.

Relieved, if still ashamed of himself, Brand sat down again. Dawn deepened into daylight. There was a flush of shimmering gold along the line of eastern mountains. The night was over.

"Sun'll be up in another three minutes, Sheppy," said Amos, snapping his fingers to his dog. "No use of sticking around here any longer. Nothing will ever raid, after daylight comes. Let's go back to the house."

He set forth for home. Ten minutes later, as he finished changing his dew-soaked outer clothes, he remembered he had left his gun lying alongside the rock.

Annoyed at his own gross carelessness, he returned to the pasture for the weapon. As he neared the gate, he saw the lambs were huddled, bleating and milling, in the farthest corner of the enclosure.

Amos broke into a run. In another moment he was among the scared animals; hurriedly counting them.

Two were gone.

Brand had not been absent fifteen minutes in all. When he had left, the flock was intact. Now it was two short, in numbers; and the survivors were jostling one another in mortal fear.

None of them, this time, bore wounds. Nor was there any track on the trampled grass, save theirs and his own and Shep's. Yet, in that brief space of time, some intruder had entered the pasture and had carried off two of the best lambs.

Climbing a pasture tree, Amos surveyed the surrounding country. For some distance in every direction the land lay open. Not a sign of any predatory animal was to be seen. He ran to the patch of woodland, and traversed it eagerly. Nothing was there, to guide him to a clue.

"A lamb don't weigh as much as an elephant," he muttered, half-aloud, scratching his head and trying to fight back a feeling of awe. "But it weighs enough to make it a mighty heavy load for any dog or wolf to lug off. No critter could travel fast, toting one of them. But this critter has got away with *two*. Got away so fast that he's out of sight with them, in just these few minutes. Why, a grown man couldn't lug away two live lambs fast enough to have got clean out of sight in that time! It — it isn't possible. But it's happened, just the same. . . . I'll ship that bunch to Paterson tomorrow. I'm not taking any more chances."

Before he went home, he strode to the main sheep pasture on the rocky hillside beyond. There he made careful count of his flock. None was missing. None seemed frightened.

"I didn't suppose the critter would hurt them," mused Brand, "so long as he could get tender lambs. Lambs are better to eat, and they don't weigh so much to carry off."

Whereat, he turned homeward, to break the newest bad tidings to his wife.

Ruth was not content to let the matter rest so philosophically as was her husband. Nor was she willing to ascribe it vaguely to "some critter."

Her frugal soul was stirred to wrath by the wanton destruction of four valuable lambs in two short days.

She had been sitting on the kitchen floor, renewing Leggy's head bandages, when her husband entered. She had grown to love the young dog. She rejoiced that he was doing so well, after his mishap. Indeed, she found it difficult to make Leggy lie still. The cast protected his fractured foreleg. And his youth and energy made him want to be up and about.

He had proved, already, this morning, what many another healthy dog in like plight has proved; — that a strong collie can manipulate his body on three legs, almost as rapidly as on four, for short distances. A dog with a foreleg in a cast *walks* slowly and clumsily. But often he can *run* with great speed; by the great motorforce of his hindquarters.

Leggy had scrambled to his feet and had run forward to greet Ruth on her arrival in the kitchen, much to her horror. She had made him lie down again at once, and she had feared lest the exertion might have injured his leg.

Now, at her husband's news, she forgot all else save their misfortune in losing the four lambs. She plied Amos with questions, none of which he could answer. All he could tell her was that the flock had been safe when he left the field, at daybreak; and that, within a quarter-hour, two of its members had been spirited away, with no trace of their direction left to guide him.

"You say you looked all around?" she queried. "Why, from the top of that tree you could see for pretty near a mile, in every way except the woods. And you looked through those. That proves no animal or man could have taken them. There's just one way they could have gone. You looked too far. They were close by. I know it. It's the only idea that makes sense."

"It don't make sense to *me*," declared Amos. "I don't see what you're driving at."

"No man or beast could have carried two lambs a mile inside of fifteen minutes," she expounded. "You'll grant that. Well, no man or beast tried to. Any strong critter could have carried them the hundred yards or less, to the outbuildings here, in that time. He could have dragged them under the barn or under any other building or into any of a dozen hiding-places."

"But —"

"And that's what he did," she went on, unheeding. "It's as clear as the hand in front of your wrist. And it's the only answer. I thought it over, yesterday, about the other two that were stolen. This thing, today, makes me sure."

"Sure of *what?*" inquired the puzzled man.

"I had been downstairs here, working over Leggy, two or three minutes this morning, when you came in from the pasture to change your clothes," said Ruth, with seeming irrelevance. "I've been here ever since. So has he. That proves Leggy couldn't have done it, I —"

"Who in blue blazes ever supposed Leggy did

90

it?" he asked in vexed bewilderment. "What are you driving at?"

"The hired man didn't do it," she resumed, unchecked. "Because he didn't come downstairs, till a minute ago. You and I didn't do it. That leaves just *one* that could have done it. And he's the one that did. I'm talking about Shep."

"Shep?" the man echoed, in blank incredulity. "You're crazy! He —"

"No, I'm not," she denied. "But Shep is. I've read about cases like that in Dad's veterinary books. Cases where sheep dogs 'go bad,' in their old age."

"Nonsense! Why, Shep is —"

"Shep is the critter that drug those lambs away and killed them. I know it. The books said such dogs' minds go queer, and they get a sort of craftiness that makes them as clever as a fox in keeping folks from finding them out. There was a sheep dog of Dad's when he was a young man —"

"I'm telling you it's *you* who's gone queer — you, not Shep!" cried the astonished Brand. "You know as well as I do that Shep couldn't do such a thing as that, to save his life. Besides," he ended, in sorry triumph, "Shep was with me all night long. He was with me till I left the pasture this morning. So he couldn't —"

"Did he come back to the house with you?" she insisted, answering her own question by adding, "No, he didn't. I saw you come up the walk. You were alone. Here's what Shep did —

He stayed behind. The minute your back was turned he grabbed up one of the lambs and he carried it to some hiding-place under the barn or under one of the sheds. He sneaked back and got another one. Then he heard you coming out of the house and he hid. That's what happened."

Unbelieving, puzzled by her logic, Amos stood glowering at his wife. Scarce stopping for breath, she hastened on:

"Dad always said that the wiser a dog was, the craftier killer he became. That's what Shep has done. You figured no wild animal would raid the pasture, so near to the house, by broad daylight. But you didn't count on Shep. The minute he had a chance, he did it. He couldn't kill them in the night, because you were there. Even if he had been left alone on guard with them, he wouldn't have done it. He would have known we'd understand right off that it was he who did it. But he knew you wouldn't expect him to go back to the pasture, after you and he had been watching there together all night and —"

"I tell you," rasped Amos, "Strep would no sooner —"

"The thing that gave me the idea, first," pursued Ruth, "was the looks of these two cuts on Leggy's head. They are just like the slashes on the mastiff that Shep licked six years ago. No dog but a collie slashes like that. The others are only just bite and tear. A collie does those things. But he slashes, too. Just as Leggy is slashed. Leggy was guarding the lamb pasture, night before last.

92

Shep went there to steal those two lambs. Leggy tried to defend them. Shep attacked him and —"

"And Leggy could swallow Shep in two bites," interposed Brand. "He's twice Shep's size, and he's ten years younger. You saw how he can fight, the day he whipped the mongrel, out yonder, last month. Why, he'd have murdered Shep in a fight!"

"I didn't say they fought," argued Ruth. "They didn't. From the first, Leggy has never fought back when Shep has tackled him. He thinks the world of Shep. He stood guard over the lambs; and most likely he wouldn't let Shep get past him. Just stood between Shep and the lambs, like a sort of barrier. That would be Leggy's way, with a dog he loves as he loves Shep. Then Shep sailed into him. In the scrimmage Leggy slipped and fell and his foreleg broke. He was crippled, then, and Shep could steal all the lambs he wanted to. Can't you see? It's as plain as day."

The man listened glumly, striving to make himself believe her claims were absurd. Then he said, turning to the door:

"I'll find out mighty soon. If he's gorging on lambs —"

"You couldn't find where he's hidden them," she intervened, "without ripping up the flooring of every building that has an air-space under it."

"Maybe not," he agreed. "But if he's been gorging lambs, he'll be bloody; and there'll be wool all over his jaws and —"

"Unless he's had the craftiness to wash it off.

93

Likely he'd know enough for that. Shep has all the sense there is."

Without reply, Amos made for the porch. There he shouted at the top of his lungs for Shep. Several times he repeated the shout before Shep appeared from around the corner of the barn. The dog was dripping wet. Very evidently he had just returned from a wallow in the orchard brook. In any event, no trace of blood or of wool remained on him.

Long and miserably, Amos Brand surveyed the old dog that had served him so wisely and so loyally for more than ten years. Shep returned his lowering gaze, looking worriedly up into his master's face, his blearing old eyes noting the man's distress.

Then Brand went back into the house. Leggy raised his head from the blanket, wagging his tail in welcome and essaying to jump up. At a sharp word from Amos, the young collie lay back on his couch, but his tail continued to thud the floor, rhythmically.

"I'm going to prove this thing, before I shoot Shep," Amos told his wife. "And I've figured out how I'll do it. Tonight I'm going to herd those lambs into the barnyard. I'm going to sit up all night watching them. I'm going to have Shep there with me. At daybreak, I'm coming into the house. I want you to be waiting in the back attic window. From there, you can see every inch of the barnyard. You can sit a little way back in the room, so Shep won't know you're there. I'll give you the gun, to have up there with you. You're a better shot, anyhow, than I am. When I come in, watch Shep. If you see him go for a lamb — well —"

Ruth hesitated. For years, Shep had been a loved and honored member of the Brand household; tenfold earning his keep, and endearing himself much to his master and to his mistress. Yet, in a sheep-raising community there is but one doom for a sheep-killer. Ruth doubted her husband's ability to bring himself to kill the dog that had been his pal for more than a decade.

"Very well," she said, presently. "I'll do it. I'd rather lose one of my fingers or all my teeth. But it has to be done. I — I feel as if somebody in my own family had gone back on us."

At dusk, the remaining lambs were herded by Shep into the barnyard. The bars were put up. Amos Brand seated himself on the fence's top rail and began his night's vigil. Shep lay at his feet. This time, thanks to an afternoon snooze, the man was able to stay awake; though with increasing effort.

Drowsy as he was, Amos dreaded the approach of day; the time when Shep's innocence or guilt must be put to the fearful test. More than once in the darkness, he stooped down and stroked the old collie's bumpy head. At such times Shep would press caressingly against his master's foot and would thump the earth with his scrap of a tail.

Too soon the east began to gray. Amos waited as long as he dared. He knew his wife was watching, gun in hand, behind the open attic window overlooking the barnyard. He felt a foolish impulse to hide Shep somewhere. But he knew the needfully stern code of the sheep-raiser. As the golden light deepened behind the mountains, he got to his feet. He laid his hands remorsefully on his old dog's sagged shoulders. Then he left the yard and went indoors.

As he opened the kitchen door, something flashed out past him — something that ran jerkily, like a kangaroo, yet with much speed. It was Leggy. Wretchedly unhappy at the impending fate of old Shep, Amos let the crippled dog go, unchecked. If Leggy wanted to risk life-lameness by galloping on three legs while the fourth was in a cast, Brand was too concerned over Shep to waste breath in recalling the excited young collie.

The man kicked off his boots, his ears strained and his pulses athrob with miserable anticipation. As he was removing the second boot he heard the sound he had been waiting for.

The sunrise silences were split by the roar of a shotgun.

In his stockinged feet, Amos raced out to the barnyard.

Leggy had gotten up from his blanket that morning at sound of his master's step on the back porch. But as the door opened, it let in a gush of outdoor air which carried on it a faintly elusive odor which made the collie forget Brand's very existence and indeed everything except that he had a death-feud with the creature whose scent he had just caught.

Out toward the barnyard sped Leggy in his awkward three-legged gallop. His hackles were abristle. His teeth were bared.

Ruth Brand, from the attic window, had watched her husband leave the barnyard. She had gripped the gun and held it ready to aim. But, to her secret relief, Shep merely stretched himself, fore and aft, and ambled houseward in Brand's wake. The old dog did not accord so much as a backward glance at the defenseless lambs.

Still holding the gun ready, Ruth waited; on the fool chance the dog would return to the lambs as soon as he should be certain that Amos was not going to come back.

The rising sun sent its first level ray across the farm. On the instant, a huge shadow bulked black against the sun-touched grass. A second shadow swept close behind the first. Ruth looked up to learn the cause of this dual happening.

A bald eagle, fully seven feet from tip to tip, avalanched downward from the upper air. Like a flung stone it swooped.

With the speed of light it dropped among the new-wakened lambs. With the same speed it drove hooked talons into the shoulder fleece of the largest lamb and, with a mighty flapping, began to beat its laden way upward.

Its mate was close behind it, with a like swoop among the bleating lambkins.

Failing to find their prey in the little pasture, and emboldened by the earliness of the hour and by long immunity, the pair of eagles had sighted the flock here, and had come to take their toll. For a week they had dwelt among the crags of the nearer mountains, sallying forth thus at daybreak for their food.

The first eagle had not cleared the ground with its bleating burden when Leggy wriggled his painful way through the bars and was leaping at it. Well did he recall the rank scent of the birds he had sought so valorously and so vainly to fight off from his flock two days before. One of them had lanced his head with its sabre beak. A wing-blow from its mate had ended his battling by breaking his foreleg. The young dog had a score to pay.

If one foreleg was disabled, his hindquarters still had the dynamic power of a racehorse's. Upward he sprang as the bird sought to heave itself and the lamb high enough for soaring flight. Five feet in air Leggy's terrible jaws drove into the eagle's breast-plumage. They drove deep, and they hung on.

It is one thing to bear off a fat little lamb. And it is quite another to sustain the raging weight of a seventy-pound collie. The eagle dropped its ba-a-ing prey. It smote with beak and claw at the dog that had seized it. The collie's weight brought the huge bird to earth, with a crash and a winnowing of pinions.

There, for a moment, dog and eagle battled ferociously.

Leggy had found a grip where he could not well be shaken off. Deep through plumage and skin and flesh his curved white eyeteeth shore their way — and down through the eagle's breastbone.

The bird, meanwhile, was rending with beak and claw; striving to peck out the deep-set eyes; striving to rip the fur-armored young body to shreds with its powerful talons, striving to beat the dog to death with its flapping wings.

The second eagle had wheeled upward from the lamb it was grasping. Now, rushing to its mate's aid, it whizzed down at Leggy in a thunderbolt swoop.

Then it was that Ruth Brand pulled trigger.

It was a ticklish shot; and one that permitted no time for conscious aim. Yet it found its mark. The second eagle crashed into the barnyard, spinning about and flapping convulsively; with two buckshot through its silvery head.

Down it crashed, full atop the two combatants, hammering them to the ground by its weight and its spasmodic jerkings.

As Amos Brand ran into the yard, a bloody figure reared itself out of that ruck of slaughter; — a cut and bleeding collie with his foreleg in a blood-spattered cast. At his feet lay his enemy; fluttering and twisting convulsively, like its mate. The dog's eyetooth had pierced to the eagle's heart; and had ended the wild battle.

"Leggy," crooned Ruth, two hours later, as she sat on the kitchen floor beside the bandage-swathed dog — "Leggy, the doctor says you'll have a few scars, always. But he says you didn't really harm your leg in that awful fight this morning. He says it'll knit nicely. Isn't that wonderful? But" — stretching out her hand, to pat a bumpy old head just within her reach, "you didn't do anything more than Sheppy here would have done if he'd had the chance. Oh, Shep, I'm so ashamed of myself, whenever I look at you!"

The two collies, old and young, lay side by side in the morning sunshine, listening with pleased interest to their wontedly self-contained mistress's praise and crooning. Two tails — one moth-eaten and stumpy, one plumed and luxuriant — thumped the kitchen floor in joyous unison.

V

YAS-SUH, 'AT'S ER DOG!

Young Colbridge looked at Old Lee in polite disapproval. Old Lee gazed back on Young Colbridge in a disapproval that was not even polite. Each was a novelty to the other — an unwelcome novelty at that. Nature had prevented Old Lee from expressing his disapprobation in words. Courtesy now did the same for Young Colbridge. But courtesy served better than did Nature, for it kept Young Colbridge's face a mask and his bearing noncommittal. Nature on the other hand gave Old Lee full scope for an expression of opinion no less eloquent for its wordlessness.

The dog strolled once round the newcomer, sniffing superciliously at his putties, his twenty-dollar hunting-shoes, his excessively custom-made leathern breeches. The stolidly weary gaze embraced the many-pocketed suède hunting-coat and the English deerstalker cap and the three-hundred-dollar shotgun. Then Old Lee deliberately turned his back on Young Colbridge, sat down on the store's puncheon flooring, flattened his ears close to his skull, and lifted his heavy head until the barrel muzzle pointed at the rows of tin pails on the newly whitewashed ceiling. After which he gave vent to a sound that might have been a snort or a gulp, but that could not possibly have been construed into anything complimentary.

Gregory Johnson frowned at one or two customers and idlers whose faces split into ear-wide grins at Old Lee's verdict of the Johnson guest. Gregory's glower kept the grins from exploding into guffaws. But Meshek Stone — most popular "white man's nigger" in Shelbyvale — got up with unwonted suddenness from a nail-keg and scuttled to the door in reply to a mythical summons from outside.

Young Colbridge did not see any of these stifled demonstrations. He was too busy staring at Old Lee. The Northerner had heard this quail dog's praises chanted in a score of keys. He had heard them ever since his own arrival at Shelbyvale the preceding day for a shooting visit to his schooldays chum, Greg Johnson; whose father was owner not only of Shelbyvale's one hardware store but of Shelbyvale's most renowned canine. The visitor had been keenly anxious to see this paragon of bird dogs. After early breakfast he and Greg had set off for the morning's quail-shooting and had stopped at the store to pick up Old Lee. And the Northerner forthwith had suffered his first disillusion.

Young Colbridge's experience with bird dogs had been confined to the thin-skinned and attenuated pointers and the undersized and delicate setters wherewith local fashion has supplanted the honest all-rounder of other years — ultra-modern dogs that will flinch at briar or will wear down to bone and nerves after a bare three days of grueling field work. He had looked forward to seeing some such elegant and temperamental specimen in Old Lee. Instead he found himself staring dully at a dog which to casual view was a pointer, yet no such pointer as Young Colbridge had ever set eyes on at bench show or in the kennels of his friends.

He was inspecting an animal whose weight was perilously close to seventy pounds without an ounce of soft fat; a dog that stood full twenty-four inches or more at the shoulder; whose chest was as deep as a bulldog's and whose barrel and stern would not have disgraced a mastiff. The head was heavy — well nigh as heavy as a Great Dane's. The tail had strong if repressed tendencies toward bushiness. Only in the deep grave eyes did Old Lee show why he required so much brain space between his nondescript ears.

"He's — he's a pointer, isn't he?" ventured Young Colbridge, tearing away his fascinated gaze from the contemptuous dog and glancing inquiringly at his host. "Or is he —"

"Old Lee's a dropper," answered Greg Johnson. "He —"

"A — a which?"

"A dropper. At least that's what the pointer-setter cross is always called hereabouts. His dam was a prize Gordon with a pedigree as long as between drinks. She belonged to Judge Reedy, and she cleaned up twice at big field trials. But his sire was a pointer — a pointer that was brought down here for a week or so once for the shooting. Dad bought Old Lee at two months from —"

"But where does the dropper part of it come in?"

"Oh, that's just the name given to these cross-breds, because they're apt to have a way of dropping flat on their stomachs when they strike a scent, and then crawling, stomach to ground, up to the spot where they make the point. They don't strike picture-book attitudes in pointing, like the dogs you're most likely used to. You'll see the way he does; first scent he gets. Come on, if you're ready. We ought to have been out an hour ago for the best of the early shooting."

"A dropper's a novelty to me," said Young Colbridge as he began to transfer a double handful of shells from a counter box to a pocket of his elaborate hunting-coat. "Is Old Lee a one-man dog? Will he go with us, or do we take along —"

"He's a no-man dog," replied Greg. "He belongs to Dad. But Dad hardly ever hunts, so Old Lee hangs out here at the store or over yonder in the square. Mostly he sleeps here. Meshek looks after him, except when the dog happens to wander off and forget the way back or gets tied by some farmer whose house he passes. Then 'Shek always sets out on a Sherlock Holmes quest for him, and always he manages to find him, sooner or later. And —"

"But why doesn't he stay at home?"

"Because — just like I told you — he's a no-man dog. There's more excitement and more folks here and in the square than up home. Besides, everyone knows where to look for Old Lee when they're going hunting. Dad lets him go along with anyone who stops here for him."

"You mean he'll hunt with anybody?" asked the scandalized guest. "With anybody at all who — ?"

"No, suh," spoke up Meshek with undue wakefulness — for him. "No, suh, dat he won't. Ol' Lee ain't huntin' wid nobody he doan lak. An' it's him, an' not de folks, what picks out wheh dey's gwine to hunt. Ol' Lee knows better'n folks does. An' more'n dat, Ol' Lee ain't a-huntin' jes' fo' ex'cise. No, sir-ree! Let a man miss three times, hand-runnin', and 'at ol' dog is homeward bound. Ol' Lee jes' gives a bad shooter one look, an' blooey — he's settin' on dese store steps in less'n er hour. He's huntin', Ol' Lee is, not list'nin' to no s'loots bein' fired. Yas-suh, 'at's er dog!"

"I suppose Old Lee's brunette friend was stringing me just now, wasn't he?" queried Young Colbridge as he and Greg set forth for the end of town and the open country beyond. "I mean about the dog's getting disgusted when a man misses too often."

"No," laughed Greg. "That's the sad truth — and I know. He's deserted me twice for that very reason. At that," he added, "don't go believing everything 'Shek tells you about the dog. 'Shek is daft over Old Lee. He has a million yarns to tell about him, and all of them are second-hand — things hunters have told him. 'Shek's too lazy to go hunting himself. It calls for too much walking. And the only times 'Shek can ever coax himself into taking a long walk is when Old Lee gets stolen or lost. Then he strikes the trail and he never drops it till he comes home in triumph, leading the dog. Sometimes he finds him tied up behind a nigger cabin. Sometimes he finds him in a farmer's barn. 'Shek thinks more of that dog than he thinks of anything else on earth, except dollar-a-gallon gin. Dad pays him to feed Old Lee. And he always stakes him to an extra dollar or so for bringing him home when he's lost. That's 'Shek's chief livelihood. He's a cotton-handler by trade. But the warehouse is too far from Searight's gin foundry, so he doesn't work at his trade very often. Then —"

"Which way are we going?" demanded the visitor, as Old Lee turned into a right unpromising bit of pasture land and Greg prepared to follow. "Looks better over there — over along that ridge where those hazels —"

"We're going into this field," decreed Greg. "We're going into it because Lee says so. He's making for that bottom yonder. It was planted in cornfield peas and pop corn last summer and it — the fact is, the old dog has us sized up for greenhorns. That's why he's leading us to the easiest shooting; along toward the railroad. I hoped he'd head us for the rough country over by Pearson's. Lots of birds out there, but tough shooting; most of it in the heavy brush. That's where he'd have led one of the old-timers.''

Young Colbridge's eyebrows went up, but he held his peace and focused his attention on the dog.

Old Lee, going at fair speed, was working out carefully the heavy growth of gray-brown grass and weeds that upholstered the terraces of the hill's sloping side. Once and again he would turn his head to locate the two men. In gradually lessening circles he worked back to where they were moving slowly toward him. He had covered the field with lazy skill, and he had drawn blank. As soon as the dog was convinced of this, he made for the ramshackle and badly slanted rail fence which separated the field from a patch of swamp beyond. The hunters followed.

Working forward with careful deliberation, Old Lee came to the fence. Gathering himself, he leaped to its slanting top rail. There, his forefeet on the swaying rail, he halted abruptly in his jump, swayed for an instant and dropped to the ground on the same side; instead of completing the leap. Lying flat amid the weeds at the fence edge, he looked round for the men. Evidently not seeing them, he began to crawl back, snakelike, his stomach close to earth, to find them. When he had made certain that Greg and his guest saw him the old dog turned and, still crawling, led them back to the fence, where he came to a dead point.

"What's the idea?" whispered the puzzled visitor.

"He's down on a covey," announced Johnson. "The birds must be just on the other side of the fence. It's going to be a sweet job to climb it without flushing them."

Young Colbridge swung over the rotting top rail. The rail collapsed noisily under him. From almost beneath his scrambling feet, eight quail whirred up. Through the maze of swamp trees they spun. Both men fired. Both men missed.

"Will he quit us for a break like that?" asked Young Colbridge, staring doubtfully at the dog.

"Maybe not," said Greg. "He knows what a tough shot it was. No, he's moving on. Come along. Go get the singles, Lee!"

The dog led them to a clump of high meadow grass at the far edge of the swamp, before he came to a dead stand. Johnson kicked at the grass. Three birds whizzed out from the clump. The men fired. Two of the birds went down.

"I got mine!" exulted Young Colbridge, starting at a run toward one of the fallen quail.

"Don't!" cried the horrified Johnson. "Don't do that, man! D'ya want to ruin the dog? Stand still and watch him."

He signaled the pronely crouched dropper. Old Lee flashed forward, and retrieved one of the birds. He started toward them with it, carrying the fluff of rumpled feathers as tenderly as though he loved it. Young Colbridge went to meet him. The dog stiffened and veered sideways at sight of the eagerly outstretched hand.

"Give it to him, Lee!" ordered Johnson.

Reluctantly the dog obeyed, then trotted off in search of the other victim.

"Now watch," counseled Greg as Lee neared him with the bird and laid it at the hunter's feet. "In the pocket, old friend!" he commanded.

Lee picked up the bird and dropped it gingerly into the wide pocket Greg extended to him.

"Did you see how he came to a point on top of that fence back there," asked Greg, "and then backed off and moved over after us and came down on the birds a second time without flushing them? That was brain, if you like."

During the next hour Old Lee pointed five more quail — singles all — of which the hunters were lucky enough to get three. Then coming out of the field they reached the railroad right of way. And here in midspeed Old Lee dropped to a cast-iron point, his nose not five feet from the track. As he crouched there — before the men could come up — the through express roared around the curve a furlong beyond.

Straight down upon the statue-like dog thundered the train. It passed him with a rush of cinders and dust and suction that well-nigh swept him off his feet. Then it tore on, leaving him there. Not for an instant had Old Lee faltered in his point. Not for an instant now did he falter in it, though the hot cinders were blistering his tender skin. He held it until the men came up and sent him ahead to where a ten-quail covey cowered under a bramble mat a few yards on the far side of the track.

"If I owned that dog," announced Young Colbridge as they started for town, "I wouldn't waste him on the hunting-field. I'd hire him to figure out my income tax. He's all you said — and a lot more. He's an education to any hunter."

When Greg Johnson repeated this praise to Meshek Stone, who was waiting for them in the store entrance, the negro's smile of approval at the Northerner was all but a benediction. And the smile merged into a simper of utter worship when Young Colbridge said to him:

"Mr. Johnson tells me you feed Old Lee, Meshek. Well, when you buy his dinner today just tuck a sirloin steak into it with my compliments. I'm counting a lot on the next fortnight's shooting over that dog."

He handed Meshek a two-dollar bill, for the steak. The negro was stroking the bill lovingly as the young men departed.

"Lee, ol' dog," crooned Meshek, "dat young gemmen is qual'ty. Qual'ty, dat's what he sho' is. Even if he's dam Yankee. Did yo' heah dem noble wuhds 'bout a suhline steak? An' does yo' see this heah two dollahs? Dat's qual'ty talk he talked, Lee. An' he gwine hunt mos' ev'y day he's heah. Dat means mo' two dollahses, Lee. Now les' yo' an' me be movin' fo' de meat mahket."

If Searight's gin emporium had not reared its one-story bulk midway between the hardware store of Edwin Johnson & Son and the town's one meat market there is a more than negligible chance that Old Lee that day might have dined on sirloin steak. Also if common gratitude had not stirred Meshek to the desire to drink the health of the opulent young Northerner and if pride in Old Lee had not incited him to tell the story of the express-train point to other habitués of the nigger bar at the rear of Searight's.

The result of this joint combination was that Meshek and the two dollars had parted company before ever the meat market burst into view.

Wherefore, Meshek perforce fed Old Lee that night on such scraps as the proprietor of the market saw fit to let him have on credit. Not on his own credit, at that, but on Mr. Johnson's. Meshek lacked the nerve, under the circumstances, to demand a sirloin steak for the dog; knowing full well that Cottrell, the butcher, would not supply such luxuries for Old Lee without first asking Johnson if the transaction were approved.

Thus, very drunk indeed, and maudlinly ashamed of his failure to provide Old Lee with the promised feast, Meshek made his way back to the store; and served the dog with the meal of uninspired scraps. He avoided Old Lee's eye, as he dished out the dinner. He feared what he might perhaps read there, of accusation. But the memory rankled in Meshek's soul. Long he sat on the store's dark steps, Old Lee stretched out contentedly at his feet. And as Meshek brooded, his brain left one stage of two-dollar intoxication and entered upon another.

He had robbed Old Lee of a promised feast. He had used up every cent of his own available capital. Yes, this was true — and more than true. Yet all was not lost. There was hope. Meshek's booze-urged mind left vain repining behind it and soared to heights of ingenuity. In other words, he was thinking. And his thinking was all constructive. Indeed, most of Meshek Stone's best thinking was prone to be constructive.

For example, six months earlier Old Lee had gone for a ramble down the Four-Mile Pike. An officious negro had seen and captured the dog, bringing him back to the store in the hope of a two-bit reward from Gregory's father. Meshek had been the bearer of the negro's message to his employer. Quite unconsciously he had enlarged upon the dog's perils on the pike and on the rescuer's forethought and courtesy in returning him so promptly.

Mr. Johnson, moved by the tale, gave Meshek seventy-five cents to be turned over to the finder, as reward. The country darky had departed quite happy with twenty-five cents of this largesse, leaving Meshek the possessor of four bits and an idea.

Two months later, Old Lee had been missing again. This time Meshek went in search of him, returning with the dog and recounting a dolorous tale of finding him caught fast in a noose trap someone had set in a field. This netted the finder a whole dollar. So did each of three subsequent searchings.

Meshek had discovered at last a dividend-paying investment. Old Lee was worth something like a dollar a month to him in rescue fees. Meshek's only outlay was the labor of walking with Old Lee to an empty and dilapidated cabin far out in the brake, tying the dog in the one-room ruin with plenty of food and water and straw, and then of thinking up the best mode of finding him when the dog should be missed at the store.

It was very simple. And it was satisfactory to all concerned. Meshek was well rewarded for his trouble. Mr. Johnson, ever easy-going, suspected nothing except that his pet had taken to wandering in his advanced age. And he was always willing enough to pay for the dog's return. To Old Lee himself the ordeal was easy, even pleasant. It merely involved lying at ease in an old cabin for a day or so, during which time he was well fed.

But tonight Meshek's constructive thinking soared beyond these safe-and-easy means of livelihood. The memories of that two-dollar bill, and the reality of what it had gone for, were still with him. They filled him with delusions of grandeur — nay, with the virus of Napoleonism. He laid a heavy and speculative hand on Old Lee's head and he let his thought-engines race. The

113

dog in response to the touch wagged his half-feathered tail drowsily and returned to dream-land. But Meshek's own dreaming was done with wide open and speculative eyes. The negro's visions centered themselves on Young Colbridge's two-dollar bill; and radiated therefrom in aureate beams.

The Northerner had been so intrigued with a single half-day's sport with Old Lee as to lavish a small fortune on the dog's dinner. He had declared loudly his intent of shooting over Old Lee as often as possible during the next fortnight. Wherefore, should the dog become lost just now, the Yankee gold mine might readily be expected to exude wealth in huge quantities. For the return of this highly desirable comrade of the chase he would doubtless give a reward which would make Mr. Johnson's single-dollar payments looked like plugged nickels.

To the genius who should go forth and find Old Lee at a moment when the Northerner was mourning for the vanished super-dog, Young Colbridge's purse would open automatically; deluging Meshek with riches. The idea was nothing short of sublime. Drunk as he was, Meshek Stone realized that. And realization spurred him into action. Climbing unsteadily to his feet, he chirped to the sleepy dog; and Old Lee got up, stretched himself fore and aft, and followed the wavering course of the negro down the street and out into the open country.

Not until Old Lee was safely moored to a rope

in a corner of the far-away cabin, with soft straw under him and a dented pail of water at his side, did Meshek recall that he had failed to bring out the dog's wonted rations. True, Old Lee had just eaten. But to spur Young Colbridge to the needed acme of tip-giving, at least a day — perhaps more — must elapse before Meshek could return the dog to the store. Meantime Old Lee must have food — and plenty of it.

Townward, Meshek bent his still-wavering steps. Walking with a decided accent, yet with more or less speed, he made his way toward Cottrell's meat market. As he went he revolved in his mind excuses for demanding a new and large consignment of scraps for Old Lee; so very soon after the last requisition. Meshek for the moment was without money and without collateral. Searight had seen to that — in exchange for much gin. Yet Old Lee, naturally, must be fed.

As Meshek came to this conclusion for the seventh time, he brought up in front of the meat market. The windows were dark. For, unnoted by Meshek, the evening had been advancing. The hour was not far from midnight. Long since, Watkins Cottrell had shut his shop for the night. The whole crooked little street of shops was in blackness.

The vacant blindness of the vicinity cheered rather than depressed the food-seeker. For his Napoleonic mind already had surmounted the difficulty of Cottrell's absence and had even turned that absence to account. Meshek had be-

115

come a man of action.

Shuffling round to the rear of the rambling store, he gave an experimental joggle to one locked window after another. The fifth of these rattled with promising looseness. Drawing his Barlow knife, Meshek inserted its one blade deftly between the upper and lower sashes; and groped with it for the catch. The lightest of shoves sent the old-fashioned catch clicking back. And Meshek, with another furtive look round the black alley, opened the window and clambered in.

To the icebox, from the opened sash, was but three steps. Meshek, thanks to his familiarity with the store, took those steps with no shadow of hesitation. He swung wide the solid door of the refrigerator and wormed his way into the chilled interior.

Guided solely — and satisfactorily — by his sense of touch, he located a monster loin of beef hanging slablike among other slabs. Still going by touch, he brought his willing fingers to bear upon the section of loin he desired for Old Lee. Drawing his Barlow knife again, he began to hack.

"Dat gran' ol' dog's sho' gwine know now dat Meshek Stone is a niggeh of his word!" soliloquized Meshek as he wrought over the clammy mass of beef. "He's sho' gwine know dat Meshek don't take no two dollahs — not eben f'om a Yankee — not widout givin' Ol' Lee full value received. Dat dropper's gwine live on de fat of de

116

lan' all de time he's tied out — dat he is!"

Encouraging himself thus with cheery promises, Meshek cut hard and deep into the sirloin. Hunk after hunk of the gelid meat he shore off the parent loin and stuffed into his shirt bosom for safe-keeping. At last he was satisfied that Old Lee was supplied with choice viands for at least a three-day sojourn in the cabin. Whereat he groped his way out of the icebox.

"It mos' sutt'nly is coolish-like in dat li'l boodwah!" he informed himself as he swung shut the refrigerator door. "But I'd shivveh a heap mo'n dat fo' Ol' Lee. An',", he informed his faintly grumbling conscience, "him an' me ain't robbin' no one, either. De meat trus', it rob de people. De paper say so. An' no one cain't rob a robber, kin he? No, sir-ree — dat he cain't! He —"

Meshek's smug reflections came to a gobbling halt. A spear of light was ripping through the darkness of the shop and was playing with merciless gleam on the shambling body that crouched in front of the icebox door.

Wandering perfunctorily through the alley during his somnolent nightly patrol of the town, the single Shelbyvale policeman had noted the open window and had brought his electric torch to bear. Much gin and more delusions of grandeur and a hazy uncertainty as to the hour had made Meshek forget the danger from these nocturnal rounds.

At nine o'clock next morning Mr. Edwin Johnson, in his capacity of town magistrate, was constrained to sentence his pampered handy man, Meshek Stone, to ninety days on the rock pile; for the crime of breaking and entering, and for having in his possession and on his person not less than eleven pounds of choice meat pilfered from the market of Watkins Cottrell.

It was a most clear case. Meshek blinking and dizzy from the tertiary stage of his potations did not so much as attempt to deny his guilt. Nor could he advance any excuse for what he had done — especially to Mr. Johnson. His past record of purely negative worthlessness and his popularity as a factotum for all local huntsmen softened the verdict. Instead of holding the poor shaking creature for a higher court, Mr. Johnson took it on himself, with the connivance of everyone concerned, to impose sentence.

This at nine o'clock. Precisely at ten Meshek Stone was installed in due and ancient form as a member of the Shelbyvale jail's chain gang.

Neither the sovereign state nor the incorporated borough profited overmuch that day from the enforced services of the new prisoner. The gin was still mighty within him; clogging his brain, thickening his gait, making him barely five per cent efficient. But a night's resonant sleep on a plank bed restored the negro to normal; and brought back memory as well as coördination.

In the gray of dawn he woke in his cell, cold sober and sickly bewildered. He lay there peering at the window bars and trying to remember. It was his first official visit to the calaboose. But he had no trouble at all in recognizing his whereabouts. And a few minutes of concentrated effort brought memory into action, telling him why he was there.

At first Meshek was sore tempted to cry. He had all the horror of law that is the portion of a negro who has been lucky enough hitherto to escape its clutch. Here he was, in jail — his days, ninety of them, to be spent with the miserable chain gang on the road, the sport of every shrill-voiced boy in Shelbyvale; the horrible example for the more fortunate of his own race. He was disgraced — forever disgraced — here in the community where everyone had liked and — so he chose to tell himself — trusted him! Good-by to his sinecure job down at Johnson's store! The man who had sentenced him was not likely to keep him on afterward as an employee — not even in the humble office of feeder to Old Lee!

Old Lee!

Meshek sat up with much suddenness on his hard bed, his mouth ajar, his eyes bulging in despair. Old Lee!

Far out in the brake — a place not visited thrice a year except by Meshek himself — Old Lee was tied and helpless in that tumble-down cabin. There for thirty-six hours the grand old dog had lain, without food and with a fast-dwindling supply of water.

There for eighty-nine days longer must he stay. Weeks before the end of that period he must die in anguish from starvation and thirst. Old Lee!

119

The dear, trusting, lovable dog that Meshek had tolled on to his death — for the hope of a measly tip from a dam' Yankee whose clothes looked like the fool pictures on the outside of cartridge-boxes!

The negro began to weep. Not noisily, as befits a candidate for the anxious bench, or with any attempt at artistic effect. He wept as little children weep — openly and heartbrokenly and with queer strangling noises far down in his throat. Old Lee! *Poor, poor* Old Lee! Old Lee who had loved and believed in him and whom he had led to starvation!

Eighty-nine days more! In the first of those days, when the water should be gone, Old Lee would stretch himself out in high-bred patience on his rumpled bed of straw, calmly certain that the friend who had brought him thither would not let him suffer. Then would come growing and gnawing hunger and the increasing hell of thirst. The old dog would perhaps strain at his rope. He might even chew it in two. But that would be all the good it would do him. The cabin door was fast shut, to bar out inquisitive wanderers. Old Lee would not make known his plight by howling. Why, you couldn't get a yip out of that dog with an ax handle! He belonged to the iron breed that does its suffering in grim silence.

Blubbering noises, such as might be made by a man half drowned, began to shatter the early-morning quiet of the cell corridor. Meshek's dolor was reaching a crescendo; as he pictured the series of scenes in the cabin when hunger and thirst should reign. He checked his lamentations for an instant as he pondered on the plan of sending word to Mr. Johnson that Old Lee was prisoned in the brake cabin. But almost at once his woe resumed full sway.

For the stealing of meat valued at $4.84 Meshek was in for ninety days' hard labor. Over and over again he had heard Edwin Johnson, and Gregory, too, declare that Old Lee was worth a thousand dollars of any man's money. If a nigger must do ninety days for the theft of $4.84 worth of white folks' beef, then in the name of all the kings of Israel how many eternities must he stay there for the theft and the hiding of a dog worth one thousand dollars?

Morbidly Meshek tried to work out the miserable sum in his head. He got two answers. One of them gave the total at an approximate century; the other at something between two and five thousand years. Neither solution brought balm to Meshek Stone's tormented soul. In either case it would mean life imprisonment — that much, anyhow.

Moreover, it was doubtful if either of the Johnsons could find the cabin by means of his description. It wasn't in a white folks' region at best. And perhaps no Shelbyvale nigger but himself could find it. No, there was no hope. Old Lee was starving to death in that lost cabin down in the brake. And the only man who could free him was doing ninety days on the rock pile. Wherefore the lamentations of Meshek the captive assailed high heaven.

Down the corridor clumped a sleepy and none-too-genial warden. Guided by howls of dire heartbreak, he came to the gate of Meshek's cell and scowled in through the bars. At sight of him the despairing negro fairly writhed in eagerness.

"Mo'nin', Misteh Caine!" he hailed the warden, meeting the unloving glare with a tearful smile of ingratiation. "Mo'nin', suh! I sutt'nly is glad to see yo'! I got a mighty big favor to beg of yo', dis mo'nin'. Ise bleeged to git outen heah, Misteh Caine! Ise *bleeged* to! Not fo' keeps, o' co'se, but fo' jes' one li'l houh. Dat's all! One houh! I'll be back by de end of one houh, Misteh Caine, suh. I promise true, I will! But I gotta be turned loose dat long, so I'll thank yo' if yo'll jes' let me out. I promise, 'fo' God, I'll be back in jes' one houh. You-all c'n tack a extry day onto my sentence if yo' has to, to make up fo' —"

"Shut up, 'Shek!" exhorted the warden. "What the devil do you mean by waking the whole place, at this time of night? One more peep out of you and you'll take a walk to the dark cell. Now —"

"Yas-suh, Misteh Caine," cringingly assented Meshek. "Jes' like yo' says. Dat's right. Dat's c'rect. Yo's de boss heah. Yo' knows best. I'll keep still, like I was daid an' fune'led. Only jes' tuhn me loose fo' *one* houh, suh! I'm mighty sorry to bust up any of yo' rules an' by-laws, suh, but I'm jes' nachully bleeged to git outen heah fo' one houh. It's life an' death, Misteh Caine. So if —"

"Lissen here, nigger!" broke in the irate Caine. "And lissen plenty hard, too, for your own sake! You ain't going to be turned loose from this jail for another eighty-nine days; at the very best. So shut up and —"

"Den Ise bleeged to bust out de bes' I kin!" sobbed Meshek — "wheddeh you-all says aye, yes or no to it. I'll come traipsin' back soon's ever I kin git to dat cabin an' —"

"That talk of jail-breaking don't go with me," sternly interrupted Caine. "So switch it off at the start. Lots of niggers have bragged that they'd break jail here. Some few of them have done it. D'you know what happened to them? Never a one that we didn't get back! Never a one that didn't get double time for running away! Never a one of them that didn't get a ten-minute round with the good old blacksnake whip in my office when we caught him. Pris'ners ain't s'posed to be cowhided any more. But ask some of your jail-bird chums how it feels and what redress they got for it. Just ask them! Well, that's what's waiting for you, if you try to skip. Keep on remembering it! Now shut up and go to sleep!"

The warden stamped back to his own quarters, leaving Meshek quaking and gabbling. Caine had wasted an undue amount of time and admonition on this black prisoner of his. He had done it as a result of a telephone talk the previous night with Edwin Johnson.

Johnson, in mystified sorrow over his henchman's fall from grace, had asked the warden to make Meshek's lot in jail as easy as could conveniently be done; allowing the captive, for instance, to work without the chains that adorned the arms and ankles of some of the road gang's members; and employing him on odd jobs about the building. He vouched for Meshek's good behavior.

After the early-morning outburst Caine saw no cause to doubt the wisdom of Johnson's indorsement. At breakfast Meshek was apathetically meek. He plodded with sodden docility to his day's work with the road gang. He seemed too dazed and cowed to make trouble for anyone.

All day long Meshek labored with the gang. It was the hardest day's work of his long life. It did queer things to his soft muscles and stiff bones. It made him so tired he was physically sick. Yet to the best of his poor power he kept at it.

All day long before his mental eye rose the vision of Old Lee — waterless by now, as well as foodless — waiting in the cabin for the trusted friend who had brought him thither and in whom his faith would refuse to waver.

When the vision waxed too sharp Meshek would pause in his roadway labor long enough to peer out of the corner of his eye at the near-by guard. This guard with rifle eternally aslant over his arm seemed to have the uncanny gift of catching every eye that chanced to be turned his way. And as his truculent glance once and again met Meshek's the negro could have sworn that the rifle's slant suddenly became less noncommittal and more personal.

No, there was no use in courting the death of a flushed quail by making a dash for any of the tempting cover that beckoned him from every side. He went on with his loathed toil, and at the day's end he tramped back through the purpling twilight to the jail.

On the prisonward hike, Meshek whispered to the mulatto directly in front of him:

"Say, niggeh, what happens when a pris'neh gits away?"

"Hell happens!" was the succinct reply. "Jes' hell! Good ol' Baptis' hell! Not de easy 'Piscolopian kind. I'd sho hate to be him."

"H'm!" sighed Meshek dolorously, adding as a forlorn hope: "But sho'ly some of 'em mus' try it sometimes?"

"Dey does," returned the long-timer. "But not eveh twice — not de same niggeh. Dey ain't 'nough of him left arter ol' Caine gits done wid him."

Meshek lapsed into silence, dragging his aching body along step by step. Into the outer yard of the jail the gang was herded. The guard grounded his rifle as the last prisoner filed through the gate, and he reached for his pipe.

A turnkey pushed shut the gate with a languid

125

gesture. Then with a gesture that was anything but languid he sat down hard upon the dirty pavement of the yard, urged thereto by a wool-coated head that had smitten him amidships with vast force.

The closing gate was still aswing, when the same woolly head butted it into swift counter motion. Meshek Stone catapulted out through the narrow opening and into the darkness beyond.

The guard instinctively whipped his rifle to his shoulder and took a snap shot at the refugee as the gate was thrust shut behind him. The bullet slapped the running negro's shoulder in a rough good fellowship that left a bleeding wale behind it. The graze spurred the flying bare feet; as the lash of a whip might lend a speed spurt to a spent race horse.

Forgetting the ache in his every joint, the pain of the bullet slap, the fatigue and the peril that were his, Meshek sped up the dim road at a most creditable pace. At the first turning he flung himself into a wayside thicket, and thence made his journey across country, trying not to lose heart and sense of direction at sound of the hue and cry behind him.

The jail bell was ringing like mad. The jail cannon boomed twice. Thus might all hearers know that a prisoner had escaped and that a reward of fifty dollars awaited the man who should procure his return — two cannon shots for a negro prisoner, three for a white man.

126

Meshek, hearing, had no trouble in picturing a hundred folk laying down knife and fork and rising from the supper table to catch up their guns and fare forth on the quest of the fifty-dollar guerdon. Truly Caine had grounds for his chronic boast that no prisoner of his had ever been able to elude recapture! Money was too scarce and searchers were too many in and round Shelbyvale to let fifty dollars' worth of fugitive go uncaught.

But it is one thing to start the country side on a man hunt and quite another to round up the prey in the darkness. The clangor of the bell still beat in Meshek's ears as he ran. It seemed to follow him and him alone. He could hear shouts and the sound of padding feet. Once, indeed, he fell on all fours in a patch of weeds barely in time to elude two gun-carrying men who were racing across lots to join in the chase.

When the men had passed on Meshek broke cover and struck again into that clumsy run of his. At the third step the ball of his bare foot thudded flat on a small round stone. His hundred and forty pounds of weight and his momentum aided the impact. There was a snapping that sounded to the negro as loud as a pistol shot. Then an agonizing pain shot up his ankle and leg.

He had met with the mishap which has been the bane of so many cross-country runners. In stepping on the stone with full force he had broken one of the small bones of the left foot.

Meshek rocked to and fro, nauseated by the keen agony of the break. Then straightening as the banging of the bell came afresh to his ears, he began to hobble on; favoring as much as he could the foot, already beginning to swell and burn.

Handicapped as he was, it took him a full hour to limp groaningly to the cabin in the brake. As he pushed open the crazy door a welcoming whine came to him through the darkness of the musty room. In another second — sobbing, chuckling, pain sick, jubilant — Meshek had untied the rope from Old Lee's collar. The dog danced round his friend in a rapture of welcome that overcame for once his monumental dignity.

It had been lonely there in the cabin for this endless forty-eight hours. The last of the water was just gone, and Old Lee was rabidly hungry too. Small wonder he greeted with such enthusiasm the friend with whom the idea of food was always associated in his canine mind.

"Oh, Lee, ol' beautiful!" babbled Meshek, hugging the wriggling animal to his breast. "Of all de gran' dogs whatever happened, yo's dat dog! To think of yo' bein' so pow'ful glad an' friendly at me; arter de way I done locked yo' up heah an' ev'thing! Lee, I gotta pay some high fo' yo' bein' glad. I gotta do double time — back yondeh to de calaboose. An' I gotta git a black-snake whalin', too. So mebbe we're even, arter all — you an' me. An' now come help me fin' a stick I kin use fo' a crutchlike. An' den me an' you is

128

gwine have a feed what IS a feed, to make up to yo' fo' stahvin' like dis. I knows wheh dey's a windeh what kin be opened wid a knife or a splinter of wood, Lee. An' behin' dat windeh's all de high-class meat a dog kin eat in a week. C'm on!"

It was Patrolman Zollicoffer, Shelbyvale's one policeman, who recaptured Meshek Stone. Zollicoffer took his police duties very seriously indeed. By way of grounding himself in his profession he was wont to read diligently such detective literature as came his way, and to make practical use of what he gleaned therefrom. Thus it was that he had learned the fictional trait of all desperate criminals to "haunt the scene of their crimes."

Watkins Cottrell's meat market was the scene of Meshek's crime. What more natural than that the fugitive should indulge in a brief haunt of that romantic spot? Thither went Patrolman Zollicoffer, while the man hunt waged through the open country and the negro quarter. And there he found his man.

He found more. He found Edwin Johnson's dropper dog that had been missing for two days. Man and dog were seated side by side on the butcher-shop floor, just within the opened window.

Both seemed very happy indeed, until they were interrupted. Meshek was busily hewing great hunks of tenderloin from a slab of beef he had lifted from the icebox; and was feeding them to the ravenous dog, as fast as Old Lee's busy jaws could be made to assimilate them.

To Patrolman Zollicoffer it was the most natural thing in the world that Meshek Stone should thus be haunting the scene of his crime. To Warden Caine, when the prisoner was returned to him, it appeared nothing short of violent insanity. And having conscientious scruples as to ill-treating a hopeless lunatic, the warden forbore to cut patterns in Meshek's flesh with his blacksnake whip. Instead, he merely locked the returned prisoner in his cell.

There, next morning, Gregory Johnson and Young Colbridge found him. They, like Caine, were starkly puzzled to account for his antics. Nor could their most adroit questionings lure the victim from nursing his injured foot and sore shoulder in mournful silence — until Greg, as by an afterthought, asked:

"But what on earth was Old Lee doing with you? He'd been away for two days. We couldn't find him anywhere. How did you happen to run across him?"

"I — I jes' happened to — to kind of meet up wid him," shyly answered Meshek.

"But —" began Young Colbridge.

Meshek wheeled on the Northerner in a gust of fury.

"Misteh Yankee!" he sputtered; "Misteh Northerner, nex' time yo' gives a niggeh two soft dollahs to buy suhline steak wid, fo' a dog — nex'

time yo' does a high falutin' thing like dat —
well, suh, give it to some niggeh what's totin' a
rabbit's foot an' — an' all de odder voodoo
charms he kin staggeh along undeh. 'Cause dat
niggeh's gwine to have plenty o' need fo' 'em all
— an' den some!

"Still," he mumbled mournfully to himself as
the visitors left, " 'at ol' dog's wuth ninety days o'
any man's time, I reck'n.

" 'At's er dog!"

VI

FOREST LOVERS

Up the entire length of the white picket fence and then down again raged the two dogs; ravening, snarling, roaring, snapping. One detail alone kept the conflict from being epochally murderous. This was the fact that the collie was on one side of the palings and the giant mongrel on the other.

In the wide front grounds of the Crede estate dwelt the young collie; sleeping in a straw-strewn box-stall, in a stable whose dimensions and architecture were those of a dissolute cathedral. Slender, graceful, lithe he was; and the sloppily pampered pet of the whole Crede family.

He had lived there, for the full ten-month span of his youthful life, except for the first six weeks of it before he had been brought thither from the kennel of his birth by Aloysius Crede as an ornament to his grounds.

Aloysius Crede had read somewhere that a collie and a peacock are the most ornamental adjuncts to a country gentleman's lawn. Aloysius Crede was a country gentleman. He conceded that. Nay, he insisted on his right to the title. Also, he had a lawn. So he had bought a collie, and had paid a gilt-edge price for him. The dog's name was Loch. He had a pedigree that would have graced a page of Burke's Peerage. From birth he had been cosseted out of all semblance to normality.

Yes, Aloysius Crede was a country gentleman. At least he had bought this huge place in the hinterland country in the shadow of the mountains, as first step toward retiring from the soap-manufacturing business wherein he had won his fortune. Of all the many garish details which made up his uncomfortably grand surroundings, he liked best (or disliked least) this young bronze-and-snow collie.

Crede knew little of dogs; but Loch appealed to him because of a certain elfin mischief and a fieriness of spirit. Most of all did Crede admire the collie when the butcher's hulking black mongrel, Grit, chanced to loaf past on the highway that bounded the lawn.

Then, even if Loch were asleep on the porch or nibbling daintily at his carefully balanced rations, the collie would drop everything else and fly across the lawn like a furry Fury toward the big mongrel. At sound of Loch's challenging bark Grit invariably would wheel about in his leisurely road-jog and hurl himself at the white-picketed fence.

Then would begin the charging gallop, one dog on either side of the high palings. Back and forth, from side wall to closed front gate they would tear, shrieking insults at each other; snapping ferociously, clawing the pickets to push them aside and to plunge at each other's throats.

A fighter at heart himself, Crede used to thrill with admiration at the fiery gameness of the slender young collie.

"That's the thoroughbred of it," he was saying proudly today as his wife and a man guest came out on the lawn to join him in watching the frayless fray. "Loch isn't half that mongrel's size or weight. He isn't a year old yet. But he'd kill Grit if the two of them could get together. He's game, clear down to the ground."

"Pooh!" scoffed the guest, a former business associate. "That big black dog would eat your purp alive. At that, the collie would likely turn tail, if he didn't know he was safe behind the fence here."

"That shows all you know about dogs," rebuked Crede, hotly. "Why, I'll bet fifty dollars to ten that Loch would thrash the black mutt within an inch of his life."

"Fifty dollars to ten?" queried the guest. "You're on. You'll win or lose inside the next five minutes, at that."

Before Crede could guess his intent, the speaker stepped forward and flung wide the double gates that guarded the driveway and lawn from the road.

In almost the same instant the galloping dogs, one racing on either side of the fence, came out, face to face, in the open gateway; with nothing to separate them.

For the merest second the two slid to a scram-

134

bling halt and stood blinking at each other.

Then, in a business-like veteran fashion the big black mongrel lowered his heavy head and charged at his lighter adversary.

Loch met his attack gaily and halfway. Down he went under the mongrel's assault. Grit rolled him over and over in the roadway dust, nipping and bruising him.

Out of the cloud of dust and the swirl of dogs arose Grit's worrying growl. Out of the same welter soared to heaven the howls and shrieks of terrified pain wherewith young Loch made known his fright.

Loch had been a pet, from babyhood. No discipline, no proper exercise, no true comradeship had been his. To him, as to many another non-belligerent dog, it had seemed a grand game to rush up and down one side of the safe fence, to hold mock combat with a dog on its other side. He had supposed Grit regarded their daily snap-punctuated gallops in the same light.

Then, all at once, his four-footed friend was not a friend at all; but a cruelly punishing monster, hurting him dreadfully and scaring him into a panic of fright.

The puppy tried frantically to get his legs under him and to run for dear life to the nearest human protector. But ever Grit's flat paws pinned him to the dust, and Grit's teasing jaws were at work on his helpless underbody. It did not occur to the friendly youngster to try to fight back.

Then by a lucky twist of the lithe young body Loch found his feet. Tail between legs, he rushed to the portly and purple Aloysius Crede for refuge, yelping at every jump.

"It's the easiest fifty dollars I ever won," the guest was saying as Loch dashed up to his obese master.

The guying words capped the climax of Crede's astounded chagrin. Black wrath — blind, merciless, illogical — strangled him. The miserable pup had made a fool of him, had made him ridiculous in the eyes of a business colleague.

And Loch was responsible for this bitter humiliation — Loch who was rushing up to him, at that very moment, ki-yi-ing like a coward! Crede went into spasmodic action.

As Loch crouched at his feet, pressing close to him for protection and looking backward in safe defiance at the irresolutely hesitant Grit, Aloysius Crede stooped and grabbed the shivering collie by the nape of the neck, lifting him aloft. Holding him thus, he rained fistblow after fistblow on the bruised and impotently writhing and screaming youngster. Then, releasing him, he drove a hammer-hard toe into the collie's tender ribs, sending Loch hurtling through the air toward the gateway.

"Get out of here, you worthless cur!" bellowed Crede.

Loch was quite insane from terror and agony and nerveshock. Mechanically he ran at express-

136

train speed, aimlessly fleeing, bound nowhere, seeking only to escape from the hell of hurt and of fear and of successive nerve-jars that had flung him all at once out of his smugly placid young life routine and had turned his whole friendly world into a place of mortal enemies.

There lives no dog, except only the greyhound, that can outstrip or keep pace with a running collie. The mongrel Grit was left far behind. So was the smooth motor-road. So was the scattered settlement. Loch was galloping across country, his brain still crazed and his body in anguish.

Perhaps by merest chance — more likely by the atavistic instinct that lurks ever at the back of a collie's brain — he was heading toward the foothills, behind which arose the line of mountain. At its hither base lay a scattering of wilderness farms. But few human feet, except those of a casual hunter, had traversed the mountain itself.

Loch's breath was almost gone. Unused to steady exercise, it failed him while still the wiry young muscles were in perfect play. The foothills were scaled and left behind. The young dog was breasting the precipitous slope of the nearest and highest mountain of the hinterland range.

At last his fatigue and breathlessness were too strong a combination for his fear to outweigh. He dropped heavily to the rocky ground and lay there panting raucously. Long he lay, while afternoon crept on to sunset. Then a new torment urged itself upon his numbing brain. The day had been hot. His exertions had been tremendous. He was suffering keenly from thirst.

Never, except out of his sanitary drinking-dish or from an occasional driveway puddle, had the young dog lapped water. He did not so much as know it could be found in any other way or place.

But not for all the water in the world would he have gone back to that abode of torment where Grit and Aloysius Crede had mishandled him so agonizingly and where Fear had been born in his untaught heart. Yet ever his thirst grew more angrily imperative, until it all but wiped out his bruise-pains and the shuddering of his yanked nerves. The thirst itself was an increasing pain that shut out all other impulses.

Presently, under the stress of Loch's fever-craving for water, old Stepdame Nature whispered the first of her secrets into the brain of the exotically reared young descendant of the Wild.

Through no volition of his own the collie lifted his classic muzzle and began to sniff the hot afternoon air. He did not know why he was sniffing, or what he had expected to smell. Yet in a moment he was on his tired legs and padding experimentally up the side of the mountain.

Up and up he toiled, past the last few signs of human traversal; up to where the rocks lay tumbled beneath sprawling upland evergreens. There, in the thick of the bouldered slope, he found what unconsciously he had sought. Between two rocks bubbled and tinkled a deep little mountain spring. Long and greedily the collie drank from its ice-cold waters.

Then, at midnight, another primitive impulse began to plague him. Of late he had had but one meal a day; a huge dishful of scientifically balanced rations, fed to him at sunset. Thus, some thirty hours had passed now since he had eaten. He was ravenous.

Up he got; stretching his stiff body, fore and aft, in true collie fashion. Once more he found his nose was pointed heavenward and that he was sniffing the night air. Once more the farthest back recesses of his brain recorded something he was not able to formulate.

Downhill he padded.

Nature was telling him things, even as she had told them to a myriad "gone-wild" collies. Loch did not know what she was telling him, nor that he was obeying her whispered teachings. Instinct was stirring within him; the weird instinct which is a collie's birthright.

As he neared the mountain-side clearing, he stopped and sniffed again. An odd tremor swept over him as his senses recorded some rare delight that he never had known. His stealthy tread waxed catlike. Also, without knowing why, he began a wide detour which should bring him to the clearing in a direction opposite that of the almost imperceptible night breeze.

From this far side he approached the open space again, crawling with his underbody brushing the dew-drenched earth. A waning moon was just coming up. Its light was pale and haggard.

But it enabled him to see something which froze him into statue-movelessness.

In mid-clearing six or seven young rabbits were at play; chasing one another; dodging and rolling amid the bushstems and over the curly hill-grass. Into the group, from somewhere in the sky, dropped like a leaden weight a thing of fluff and beak and talons. The rabbits — all but one — scattered into immediate invisibility. The one exception was struggling in the saber-tipped grasp of the big owl that had swooped down on it.

The rabbit was plump and heavy. The owl's wings beat the air in an effort to rise to the nearest tree-limb with its prey.

But before it was half a yard aboveground something big and bronze and aflame with wild-beast excitement dashed out into the clearing; and at one bound had caught the flapping bird and borne it to earth.

Loch was making his first kill.

Even as he sank his strong white teeth into the mound of soft feathers and to the gristly flesh they guarded, the owl released the slain rabbit and fought with claw and curved beak to break free from its assailant. The heavy wings smote Loch hammeringly above the head. The beak ripped and gouged at him. The talon claws dug into his coat.

The mighty young jaws drove deeper and more grindingly. They pierced the breastbone. The owl ceased to fight. It quivered all over and hung limp between the collie's jaws.

Loch dropped the lifeless bird; smelled it all over; then sniffed at the dead rabbit. He yearned to devour them where they lay. But once more that weird instinct of the Wild was at work within him. He picked up owl and rabbit, one after the other jamming them close together between his red-flecked jaws.

Still running with a noiseless wolf-trot, he hurried uphill to the spring. There, at his leisure, he made a right glorious meal.

When everything was gone except a strew of feathers and of fur bits, Loch got up from his banquet and strolled over to the spring. There he drank heavily and long. As he ceased, still another teaching of the Wild entered his newly aroused brain.

He did not go to sleep, as before, alongside the wallow. Instead, he cast anxiously about, up and down the rocky slope, until he found what he sought. About a hundred feet above the spring, in the midst of an almost impenetrable tangle of rocks and bushes, he came upon a cliff whose lower portion had been split by some age-ago earthquake. The split formed a natural cave, masked by vines and by a cedar bush that grew directly at the opening. It was an ideal lair.

Loch curled snugly down among the dry leaves on the floor and slept.

He had come into his heritage. Nature had taught him how to find water and food and how to hide. There was little more for him or for any other to learn from her. He was coming into his wolf-ancestors' legacy — the legacy that seems to belong to the collie alone.

So began a wonderful life for young Loch. With entire ease he husked off his habits of civilization and entered with joyous eagerness into his new circumstances.

May loafed on into June. Day by day, or oftener night by night, the collie ranged the mountain from bald crest to woody foothills. He learned by experience as well as by instinct the clearings where the rabbits danced on moonlit nights and the grassy niches and root-patches where they fed.

He learned to stalk partridges as they drummed on dead logs or as they crouched for flight among the seedberries in the forest depths. He learned to pounce with unerring precision and speed upon a huddle of quail he had stalked upwind. He learned to bark harrowingly under a tree where fat gray squirrels sported, and then to lie down in seeming slumber at the very foot of the tree until that silly prey should be goaded by curiosity into venturing down within reach of a leap and a snap.

Summer was at prime. The mountain creatures, usually unmolested at this season, were more or less easy prey to the young dog. The rock spring and other springs and brook-trickles afforded him all the water he needed. His lair was dearer to him than ever had been his hygienically bedded kennel at Crede's garish estate.

Came autumn, and with it a hunter or two to the fastnesses of the mountain. But hunters were even fewer this year than usual. For word went forth that game was mysteriously scarce there.

Loch could have verified this statement with no trouble at all. Indeed he knew the supply of birds and of rabbits was running low, weeks before the hunters learned it. He was more or less put to it, after the end of the lush summer, to find enough food. He grew lean, though he was still as powerful as any timber wolf. His ribs were sparsely padded beneath their increasingly heavy coat of bronze fur. But his wit and his courage waxed, under the new urge for forage.

On an October night he heard a stamping and a snorting far up the mountain-side. He trotted soundlessly to investigate; circling, as ever, to advance against the wind. Two fallow bucks were battling, hoof to hoof, horn to horn; while nearby a handful of sleek does watched with uninterestedly mild eyes the death-conflict for their rulership.

The largest and fattest doe, of a sudden, screeched aloud and wheeled about to flee. But she could not run. At her first leap she floundered and crashed down among the dry twigs. Loch had hamstrung her. As she fell, he flashed in at her unprotected throat before she could bring her wicked fore hoofs into action. Then he leaped out again, safe and victorious.

The rest of the herd, including the two battling bucks, went thundering down the mountain-side, crashing through thickets with the noise of charging elephants. Loch was left in peace to his meal.

But when, a week or so later, he tracked this same herd to a pocket in the cliffside rocks, the leader stag turned at bay and charged him ferociously. Loch met the charge by a spring for the breast and a deeply gouging slash at the bottom of the throat. But he was knocked heels over head by the impact. And the hurt-maddened stag was upon him before fairly he could regain his feet.

Loch dived beneath the plunging antlers by a miracle of skill, eluding the pronged fore feet and slashing the hairy underbody as his enemy rushed above him. A sidelong graze of a hind hoof laid open his shoulder and knocked him breathless. But it also woke in him a vulpine fury of battle.

He dodged easily a second plunging charge; then at risk of another kick he sprang for the haunch. Down came the stag, half crushing Loch by his fall. But the collie wriggled from under and, shrinking nimbly aside from the flailing fore feet, slipped in and at the throat.

Thenceforth, and for another three months — until the small herd of deer had followed their leader in sections down Loch's shaggy throat — the wild collie had rich plentitude of provisions. True, he did not escape scatheless. In spite of his wolf-cunning and his marvelous swiftness of motion. A striking hoof more than once laid bare a rib or tore deep into his chest. But always the general result of the onslaughts was the same.

Then came a day when not a deer was to be found in twenty miles of his ranging, and when the recently padded ribs stood forth again gaunt and prominent. For the first time in his months of mountain freedom he turned his thoughts toward the abode of humans.

That night the paper window of a farmstead hencoop at the base of the foothills was broken through. In the morning two hens and a rooster had vanished. No sound had been heard in the near-by farmhouse; though, when a dog slays a chicken, the din usually can be heard for a half-mile.

Three nights later Loch descended again to this abode of highly palatable hens. As he neared the hencoop, a rank man-scent smote his nostrils. Dead short he stopped. To his preternaturally keen forest-trained hearing came distinctly the soft sound of a man's breathing, just inside the hencoop's hospitably open doorway; then the shuffle of fidgety feet. Silently Loch turned and melted into the darkness. Next morning two fowls were missing from a farm several miles distant from the scene of Loch's first robbery.

On a night when he was circling a farm whose occupants had sat up in vain, gun in hand, to wait for the supposed wolf, a soft whine checked his prowl.

From the direction of the barn it came, a full hundred feet away from house or hencoop. Cautiously Loch drew near the open barn door. No fresh man-scent assailed him here. But there was a dog in the barn. Not such a blundering farm dog as once or twice he had encountered and had eluded so easily on his winter nights of hencoop-visiting; but a female dog, young, small, unhappy.

Boldly Loch stepped in through the doorway and crossed to a stall. There in the hay crouched a gold-and-white collie; tiny, dainty, altogether captivating. By a thin rope she was tied to a manger-ring. At Loch's silent approach she jumped up and came forward to the full length of her tether. He and she touched noses. Their tails were awag; their deep-set dark eyes were shining with gay friendliness. Two minutes later Loch was leading the way out of the barn, and the golden collie was following gladly. In the stall was a dangling tie-rope, riven neatly in two by Loch's scissor-like front teeth. Padding on soundless feet, Loch made for the foothills. After him frisked and played the mate he had set free from human bondage.

Next morning Aloysius Crede drove in person to the farmhouse whence Loch had lured the little gold-white collie. A week earlier Crede had sought to enter once more the dog-fancier class by adding a new collie to his lawn. He had bought at high price a young female of perfect lineage and perfect show-points. Her name was Katrine.

Wandering desolately around the lawn the

146

preceding afternoon, Katrine had found the path gate ajar and had ventured out into the world. Aimlessly, yet interestedly, she had strayed down the road toward the foothills. (Crede's palatial estate somehow held scant appeal to any dog.)

After a mile or more of journey, Katrine met a farmer and made friends with him. Realizing she was valuable and a stray, the man took her home and tied her in his barn; there to stay until some one should advertise for her.

That same evening at the village store his son read a bulletin-board notice of Crede's loss. He telephoned the great man and told him where Katrine was. Crede promised to drive over and get her, the first thing in the morning. He kept his promise. That was all the good it did him.

The rest of the winter passed gloriously for the once lonely Loch. He and his dainty little mate were devoted to each other. Like puppies they played together among the lair-side rocks. They hunted game together. Loch brought home, from longer and solitary rambles, delicious chickens and turkeys and ducks and young sheep. It was a glad and safe and plenteous winter.

As the bitter-black nights grew warmer and as the snow and ice dripped all day long from the cliff-edges, Katrine ceased to hunt and to gambol with her mate. She preferred to snuggle down among the leaves at the farther end of the lair and to lie there for hours.

Then, one morning in late April, Loch trotted into the lair in search of her; to show her a wild mallard he had stalked and caught at the marsh edge, three miles deeper in the wilderness.

Katrine did not rise to greet him as usual. The lair was redolent of the scent of other life than hers. Nestled close against her furry side squirmed five ratlike creatures of indeterminate hue; making up for the brevity of their experience on earth by feeding most voraciously.

Katrine wagged a feebly friendly tail; and Loch came dubiously forward. He dropped the mallard beside her and then bent to sniff at his five new-born children. His mate eyed him with apprehension. But she had no cause to be alarmed. He was as proud of the babies as he was of Katrine. Silently, gravely, Loch sniffed them, one after another. Gravely he licked them. Then he lay down and shared the duck with his tired little mate.

Thenceforth he foraged alone, and with renewed zest. He seemed to realize that six mouths depended solely on him for filling. Luckily a new wave of game had invaded the mountain at this season. Rabbits and partridges abounded, for easy catching. There were occasional fawns, too; and swarms of squirrels and quail. The family waxed fat. Nor was there danger from mankind. For Loch no longer had need to invade farms.

One day he was trailing patiently a savage mother deer which would not let him separate her fat fawn from her. In seasons of stress Loch would have attacked the mother. But now there was no need to risk a cut or a gouge. There was food elsewhere, in pleasing quantities, if he should fail to capture this fawn by mere craft.

Back at the lair Katrine began to worry. Presently she set forth on a hunt, by herself, for the next meal. It was her first experience as a solitary searcher for food. She had acquired none of Loch's uncanny genius at such pursuits. Thus, instinctively, she turned toward the haunts of men.

Rabbits scurried from her path, easily dodging her efforts to run them down. Partridges rocketed noisily up in front of the inexpert huntress. She kept on.

In a field she saw a man harrowing. As she paused irresolutely at the edge of the woods, he caught sight of her. He whistled.

The man drew from his pocket a lunch sandwich and held it toward her. The scent and sight of cooked food were too strong for her caution. She trotted shyly up to him.

Ten minutes later, hanging back against the rope that encircled her furry neck, Katrine was on her way to the magnificent country estate of Mr. Aloysius Crede.

The farmer considered that the reward for her capture would far more than repay him for his loss of time at the harrow. Nor was he minded to risk losing this reward by tying her up again and giving her another chance to escape.

Back to the lair jogged Loch. Over his shoulder

swung a fat fawn. His game of waiting and of cunning had been rewarded.

No Katrine.

The pups set up a multiple yapping squawk at sight of their sire. But he paid no heed to them. Never before had their dam left her babies alone. Loch was troubled.

Instantly he found her trail. More and more unhappy at every step, and more and more apprehensive, he loped along until he came to the spot where her scent was joined by man-scent. Then, seeming to read the dire omen aright, he broke into a run.

True, the trail was bearing him to the loathed dwelling-places of humans. And by glaring sunlight, at that. But "perfect love casteth out fear." Madly worried as to his adored mate's plight, he had no thought but for her rescue.

On the lawn of his estate stood Aloysius Crede, beaming down on the newly recovered Katrine as she cowered before him at the end of the farmer's rope. Taking the impromptu leash from her captor with one hand, with the other Crede delved into his cash pocket for the reward.

"Thanks, Muller," he was saying. "And you've done a good day's work for yourself. I paid four hundred dollars for this collie. I wouldn't have lost her for —"

Katrine broke into a sharp barking. She ceased to cringe. Ears up, she was fairly dancing with glad eagerness. Gone was her forlorn hopelessness of demeanor. She tugged at the rope and pawed the air with fast-moving white forepaws, as she strained to verify a new scent and the pad of flying feet.

Annoyed at the interruption, Crede gave a vicious yank at the rope, upsetting the little dog's balance and sending her sprawling. He was about to bring her to her feet again with a second yank, when suddenly he dropped the leash as if it were white hot.

A tawny thunderbolt had cleared the picket fence — although the path gate stood open only a few yards farther on — and launched itself at the human who had just thrown down Katrine so brutally.

Rending jaws ripped Crede's fat hand to the bone. In almost the same move Loch was hurling himself at the reeling man's throat. Roaring and foaming, Loch sprang. His jaws missed the jugular by a bare inch. But they laid open Crede's priceless raiment from neck to waist. The impact on his chest destroyed Crede's balance. Bellowing with pain and terror, he sat down abruptly.

Loch did not follow up his own advantage. Crooning, whimpering in stark eagerness, he turned to Katrine. As if she understood, the little collie wheeled and darted out through the path gateway. At her heels rushed Loch. The two collies gained the highroad outside the gateway. A huge black mongrel happened to trot around the corner. It was Grit, the butcher's formidable cur, on his way home from a morning ramble. At sight of Loch the black dog apparently remembered the jolly time he had had, a year agone, in bullying the helpless young collie.

Merrily he flew at Loch, to roll him over once more. In mid-charge he was met by an incarnate bronze devil that smote the mongrel obliquely on one shoulder and knocked him off balance; then ravened at the falling Grit's throat and underbody. Valorous and doughty as was the mongrel, he had no chance against this wild beast, either in speed or in skill or in rabid savagery.

Men came running up. As they approached, Loch jumped back from the slaughter. Whimpering to the admiring Katrine, he dashed down the road; shoulder to shoulder with his regained mate. Nor did they pause in that wild scamper, until the foothills were reached. Then Loch halted long enough to scissor the rope noose from around Katrine's panting throat.

The two breasted the steep mountain-side right merrily in the glad climb toward their sumptuous breakfast of tender fawn and to their impatiently yapping babies and to the life-long jubilant freedom that henceforth was to be theirs together.

VII

HEROISM, LIMITED

Until Rance met The Girl, this vacation at the seaside had been an unflawed spree to Andeen. Never before had the collie been within a hundred miles of the ocean.

This meant she had never before been tossed and rolled by the combers as she charged hysterically among them. Never before had she dived clean from the end of a dock, like a flung spear, and come up sputtering and barking, to let the breakers catch her and sling her shoreward. Never before had she chased squeaking sandpipers along miles of wet brown beach or galloped stomach-deep into the surf after clamhunting white gulls.

Oh, there were a million things a questing collie could find to amuse her, in this new water-edged world whither Rance had brought her! Pleasantest of them was to romp along the beach ahead of her master on the ten-mile hikes he reveled in; and to snore blissfully at his feet in front of a blue-shot driftwood blaze, all evening; while the waves hammered a drowsy accompaniment to her snores.

153

Then The Girl had smashed into the countless joys of seaside life.

From the first, Andeen could see that Rance liked The Girl. And presently the collie's queer sixth sense told her The Girl was beginning to like Rance more and more. But that same sixth sense told Andeen that The Girl did not care in the very least for dogs, that she was even a bit afraid of them and had no experience whatever with them.

Between Andeen and her adored master The Girl was forever pushing her way, spoiling the completeness of their romps and taking Rance's mind off his collie pal. Andeen grieved. Into her white canine heart resentment never had entered. But she was as keenly unhappy as only a high-strung female collie knows how to be. Neglect was cutting into her like a knife.

Then of a morning The Girl and Rance went out to the end of the pier to watch the net haul. So did a hundred other summer boarders. So did Andeen, trotting glumly along at the heels of her unnoticing master and hoping vainly for his old-time jolly word of cheer to her or the rumpling gesture of his dear hand on her ears.

There was a goodly scattering of children in the pier-end throng. One of these — a fluffy five-year-old girl in a pink linen dress — leaned far over the stringpiece to see if she could discover Jonah's whale in the greenish depths just beneath her.

There was a panic squeal as the child lost her

balance and toppled off the pier-edge. Twenty men began to rip off their coats. They were too late. Andeen had flashed forward at the baby's scared cry. The collie's tawny body smote the lazy water a bare second after the child's.

The youngster's billowing pink dress brought its wearer bobbing momentarily to the surface. In that moment, Andeen had lunged forward and clutched at the dress's stout shoulder. Swimming with all her wiry strength and holding her head high to keep the kicking and yelling baby from immersing her screwed up face in the water, Andeen struck gallantly out for land.

In shallows a dozen human volunteers caught the crying child from her rescuer and bore her ashore; Andeen padding along behind, her coat close plastered to her sinewy body.

All day long Andeen was the heroine of the beach. People vied with one another for the privilege of patting and feeding her. Cameramen snapped her picture. Rance was his old friendly self, vastly proud of his heroine dog. Even The Girl deigned to pet Andeen's silken head and to gaze upon her with a wholly new expression.

Anyone who knows collies will understand how this wholesale adulation went to the dog's head. Andeen reveled in the limelight. Her vanity swelled at every new bit of approbation.

Then, in course of time, the chorus of praise ebbed. (Lindbergh himself is not cheered, now, every time he sits down to breakfast.)

Being only a dog, Andeen could not understand how or why she had ceased to be the most prominent figure on the beach. But, being a member of the most uncannily wise of all dog breeds, she recalled clearly how and why she had won her brief hour of fame. If such fame could be achieved once, it could be achieved again.

On another net-haul morning, the usual crowd was at the pier-end, children and all. Glancing around to see she was not observed, Andeen sidled unobtrusively up to a curly-headed baby boy in rompers who stood on the stringpiece. A butt of her head in the small of his back sent him tumbling out into space.

By the time he struck water, Andeen was at his side. Once more the splendidly heroic rescue scene was enacted. Once more the collie was surrounded by applauding and petting and feeding crowds; as she shook herself dry on the beach. Once more the adulation of her human admirers thrilled her to the very heart. Once more Rance made much of her. But, alas! these plaudits died down as the days went by, even as they had done before!

Rance stooped to pick up his dropped tobacco-pouch, a few days later, as he and a clump of other vacationists stood near the end of the pier to wait for the net haul. There, with his eyes only a foot or so above the level of the pier, he saw something that made him gasp in unbelieving horror.

Between the legs of the men in front of him he saw Andeen glide, swift and noiseless. He saw her lower her classically chiseled head and deliberately butt a romper-clad youngster in the small of the back.

The child had been dancing up and down on the stringpiece. At that impact she shot forward over the edge. In practically the same instant, Andeen launched herself in pursuit.

. . . Rance was not among the noisy group this time, which pressed in around the rescuer and the rescued; as Andeen deposited her bawling and soaked charge, unhurt, in shallow water, and stood proudly to receive the homage of the crowd.

Rance was thinking. He was thinking hard. He was enlisting, in his thoughts, all his considerable knowledge of collie nature. That day he was vague and undemonstrative in his replies to the horde of congratulations which poured in upon him on his ownership of the magnificent life-saving collie.

Almost ungraciously he vetoed an eager suggestion that a fund be raised to buy a gold medal for the heroic dog that had rescued no fewer than three children from a hideous death in less than a single fortnight.

That night, when he went with The Girl for a moonlight stroll on the beach, he shut Andeen into his room before he set forth. He wanted to make certain the collie should not stage any more rescues in his absence.

Andeen crouched unhappily on a mat beside her master's bed. Not only did she resent being imprisoned like this, but she was puzzled at Rance's newly disapproving manner toward her. Then a maid came in to turn down the bed and to bring fresh towels. Furtively, Andeen slipped out of the room and out of the house. With no difficulty at all she caught the trail of Rance and The Girl, and she started along it at a hand-gallop.

Strolling very slowly and very close together, the two humans made their way to the pier-end; deserted, but for them, at this hour. The moon sent a track of shaky silver across the ocean toward them. The Girl sighed happily; stepping up on the stringpiece and stretching forth her slender arms to the glory of the night. Then her sigh of happiness merged into a cry.

Over the edge she lurched into the black water below. Rance, with a louder cry, dived after her. But, before he could throw aside his coat and kick off his low shoes, a tawny shape had whizzed past him and leaped down into the depths.

"Oh, the wonderful, *magnificent* dog!" The Girl was sobbing, as she and Rance and Andeen toiled up the beach through the shallows. "To think of her following us here — she must have had an intuition of the danger that was waiting for me — and saving my life! Darling, you must let her stay with us as long as she lives! Forget what I said about not wanting her. It was wicked and foolish of me. I didn't understand. I can never be happy unless she is with us — the gorgeous little heroine! I — I must have had a dizzy spell. It seemed almost as if something struck against me and made me fall over the edge. . . . Promise me Andeen shall always live with us. *Promise!*"

"I promise!" agreed Rance, solemnly; adding under his breath:

"And thank heaven we live a hundred miles inland! If I can fix a guardrail around the bathtub, there isn't going to be any more self-starting heroism."

VIII

THE COWARD

It began when Laund was a rangily gawky six-month puppy and when Danny Crae was only seven years old. Danny had claimed the spraddling little fluffball of a collie as his own, on the day the boy's father lifted the two-month-old puppy out of the yard where Laund lived and played and slept and had a wonderful time with his several brothers and sisters.

On that morning Ronald Crae ordained that the brown-and-white baby collie was to become a herder of sheep and a guard of the house and farm. On that morning, seven-year-old Danny announced that Laund was to be his very own dog and help him herd his adored bantams.

Now, Ronald Crae was not given to knuckling under to anyone. But he had a strangely gentle way with him as concerned this crippled son of his. Therefore, instead of the sharp rebuke Danny had a right to expect for putting his own wishes against his sire's, Ronald petted the wan little face and told Danny jokingly that they would share Laund in partnership. Part of the time the puppy should herd the Crae sheep and do other farmwork. Part of the time he should be Danny's playfellow. And so it was arranged.

A year earlier, a fearsome pestilence had scourged America, sending black horror to the heart of ten million mothers throughout the land and claiming thousands of little children as its victims. Danny Crae had but been brushed lightly by the hem of the pestilence's robe. He did not die, as did so many children in his own township. But he rose from a three-month illness with useless legs that would not move or bear a fraction of his frail weight.

Quickly he learned to make his way around, after a fashion, by means of double crutches. But every doctor declared he must be a hopeless and half-helpless cripple for life.

Small wonder his usually dominant father did not veto any plan of his stricken child's! Small wonder he skimped the hours of herd-training for Laund, in order to leave the puppy free to be the playmate of the sick boy!

In spite of this handicap, young Laund picked up the rudiments and then the finer points of his herding work with an almost bewildering swiftness and accuracy. Ronald Crae was an excellent trainer, to be sure; firm and self-controlled and commonsensible, if a trifle stern with his dogs; and a born dogman. But the bulk of the credit went to the puppy himself. He was one of those not wholly rare collies that pick up their work as though they had known it all before and were remembering rather than learning.

Crae was proud of the little dog. Presently he began to plan entering him sometime in the yearly field trials of the National Collie Association, confident that Laund would be nearer the front than the rear of that stiff competition.

Then, when the puppy was six months old, Crae changed his opinion of the promising youngster — changed it sharply and disgustedly. It happened in this wise:

Of old, Danny had rejoiced to go afield with his father and to watch the rounding up and driving and folding and penning of the farm's sheep. Now that he was able to move only a little way and on slow crutches, the child transferred his attention to a flock of pedigreed bantams his father had bought him and which were the boy's chief delight.

Like Ronald, he had a way with dumb things. The tame bantams let him handle them at will. They ate from his wizened fingers and lighted on his meagerly narrow and uneven shoulders for food. Then it occurred to him to teach Laund to herd and drive them. Luckily for his plan and for the safety and continued tameness of the little flock of chickens, Laund was as gentle with them as with the youngest of his master's lambs. Gravely and tenderly he would herd them, at Danny's shrill order, avoiding stepping on any of them or frightening them.

It was a pretty sight. Watching it, and Danny's delight in the simple maneuvers, Ronald forgot his own annoyance in having to share a valuable puppy's valuable training-time with his son.

One day Danny and Laund sat side by side on a rock, back of the barnyard, watching the bantams scramble for handfuls of thrown feed. Among the flock was a tiny mother hen with a half dozen downily diminutive chicks. Anxiously she clucked to them as she grabbed morsel after morsel of the feast, and tried to shove the other bantams aside to give place to her babies where the feed was thickest.

As the last of the flung grain was gobbled, the flock dispersed. Most of them drifted to the barnyard. The mother hen and her chicks strayed out toward the truck garden, some fifty feet in front of where the boy and the dog were sitting.

Of a sudden the tiny mother crouched, with a raucously crooning cry to her children, spreading her wings for them to hide under. As they ran to her, a dark shadow swept the sunlit earth. Down from nowhere a huge hen-hawk shot, like a brown feathery cannon ball; diving at the baby bantams and at their frightened dam.

"Laund!" squealed Danny, pointing to the chicks.

The six-month puppy leaped to them. He had no idea why he was sent thither or what he was supposed to do. He did not see the swooping hawk. Never had he even seen a hawk before, though hawks were plentiful enough in that mountain region. But he noted the flustered excitement of the hen and the scurrying of the

163

golden mites toward her and the alarm in Danny's loved voice. Wherefore he bounded alertly into the arena — to do he knew not what.

As a matter of fact, there was nothing for him to do. As he reached the hen, something dark and terrible clove its way downward, so close to him that the air of it fanned his ruff.

A chick was seized and the hawk beat its way upward.

Instinctively, Laund sprang at the bird, before its mighty pinions could lift it clear of the earth. He leaped upon it right valorously and dug his half-developed teeth into its shoulder.

Then, all the skies seemed to be falling, and smiting Laund as they fell.

A handful of feathers came away in his mouth; as the hawk dropped the mangled chick and wheeled about on the half-grown puppy that had pinched its shoulder.

The drivingly powerful wings lambasted him with fearful force and precision, knocking him off his feet, beating the breath out of him, half-blinding him. The hooked beak rove a knife-gash along his side. The talons sank momentarily, but deep, into the tender flesh of his underbody.

It was not a fight. It was a massacre. Laund had not time to collect his faculties nor even to note clearly what manner of monster this was. All he knew was that a creature had swept down from the sky, preceded by a blotty black shadow, and was wellnigh murdering him.

In a second it was over. Even as Danny yelled

to the bird and as he gathered his crutches under him to struggle to his feet, the giant hawk had lurched away from the screeching and rolling puppy; had snatched up the dead chick, and was beating its way skyward.

That was all. On the recently placid sunlit sward, below, a frantically squawking hen ran to and fro amid five piping and scurrying chicks; and a brown collie wallowed about, waking the echoes with his terror yelps.

In all his six months of life Laund had known no cruelty, no pain, no ill-treatment. He had learned to herd sheep, as a pastime to himself. He had not dreamed there could be agony and danger in the fulfilling of any of his farm duties.

Now, while still he was scarcely more than a baby — while his milk teeth were still shedding — before his collie character could knit to courage and tense fortitude — he had been frightened out of his young wits and had been cruelly hurt and battered about; all by this mysterious and shadow-casting monster from the sky.

Through his howling he was peering upward in shuddering dread at the slowly receding giant hawk. Its blackness against the sun, its sinister sweep of pinion, its soaring motion, all stamped themselves indelibly on the puppy's shocked brain. More — the taste of its feathers was in his mouth. Its rank scent was strong in his nostrils. Dogs record impressions by odor even more than by sight. That hawk-reek was never to leave Laund's memory.

The pup's wails, and Danny's, brought the household thither on the run. Laund was soothed and his hurts and bruises were tended, while Danny's own excitement was gently calmed. The doctors had said the little cripple must not be allowed to excite himself, and that any strong emotion was bad for his twisted nerves.

In a few days Laund was well again, his flesh wounds healing with the incredible quickness that goes with the perfect physical condition of a young outdoor collie. Apparently he was none the worse for his experience. Ronald Crae understood dogs well, and he had watched keenly to see if the pup's gay spirit was cowed by his mishandling from the hawk. As he could see no sign of this, he was genuinely relieved. A cowed dog makes a poor sheepherder and a worse herder of cattle.

Crae did not tell Danny what he had feared. If he had, the child would have given him a less optimistic slant on the case. For more than once Danny saw Laund wince and cower when a low-flying pigeon chanced to winnow just above him on its flight from cote to barnyard.

It was a week later that Laund was driving a bunch of skittish and silly wethers across the road from the home fold to the first sheep-pasture. Outwardly it was a simple job. All that need be done was to get them safely through the fold gate and out into the yard; thence through the yard gate out into the road; thence across the road and in through the home-pasture gate which Ronald Crae was holding open.

It was one of the easiest of Laund's duties. True, there was always an off-chance of the wethers trying to scatter or of one of them bolting down the road instead of into the pasture.

But the young dog had an instinct for this sort of thing. Like the best of his ancestors, he seemed to read the sheep's minds — if indeed sheep are blest or cursed with minds — and to know beforehand in just what direction one or more of them were likely to break formation. Always he was on the spot; ready to turn back the galloping stray and to keep the rest from following the seceder.

Today, he marshaled the milling bunch as snappily and cleanly as ever, herding them across the yard and to the road. On these wethers he wasted none of the gentleness he lavished on heavy ewes or on lambs. This, too, was an ancestral throwback, shared by a thousand other sheep-driving collies.

Into the road debouched the baaing and jostling flock. As ever, they were agog for any chance to get into mischief. Indeed, they were more than usually ready for it. For their ears were assailed by an unwonted sound — a far-off whirring that made them nervous.

Laund heard the sound, too, and was mildly interested in it; though it conveyed no meaning to him. Steadily he sent his wethers out into the road in a gray-white pattering cloud. Through the yard gate he dashed after them, on the heels of the hindmost; keyed up to the snappy task of making them cross the road without the compact bunch disintegrating; and on through the pasture gateway where Crae stood.

As his forefeet touched the edge of the road, a giant black shadow swept the yellow dust in front of him. The whirring waxed louder. Frightened, gripped by an unnameable terror, Laund glanced upward.

Above his head, sharply outlined against the pale blue of the sky, was a hawk a hundred times larger than the one that had assaulted him. Very near it seemed — very near and indescribably terrible.

A state forest ranger, scouting for signs of mountain fires, glanced down from his airplane at the pastoral scene below him — the pretty farmstead, the flock of sheep crossing the road, the alert brown collie dog marshaling them. Then the aeronaut was treated to another and more interesting sight.

Even as he looked, the faithful dog ceased from his task of sheep-driving. Ki-yi-ing in piercing loudness, and with furry tail clamped between his hindlegs and with stomach to earth, the dog deserted his post of duty and fled madly toward the refuge of the open kitchen door.

Infected by his screaming terror, the sheep scattered up and down the road, scampering at top speed in both directions and dashing anywhere except in through the gateway where Ronald Crae danced up and down in profane fury.

The plane whirred on into the distance, its amused pilot ignorant that he was the cause of the spectacular panic or that a fool puppy had mistaken his machine for a punitive henhawk.

After a long and angry search, Laund was found far under Danny's bed, huddled with his nose in a dusty corner and trembling all over.

"That settles it!" stormed Crae. "He's worthless. He's a cur — a mutt. He's yellow to the core. If it wasn't that Danny loves him so I'd waste an ounce of buckshot on him, here and now. It's the only way to treat a collie that is such an arrant coward. He —"

"But, dear," protested his wife, while Danny sobbed in mingled grief over his collie chum's disgrace and in shame that Laund should have proved so pusillanimous, "you said yourself that he is the best sheep dog for his age you've ever trained. Just because he ran away the first time he saw an airship it's no sign he won't be valuable to you in farm work. He —"

" 'No sign,' hey?" he growled. "Suppose he is working a bunch of sheep near a precipice or over a bridge that hasn't a solid side rail — suppose an airship happens to sail over him, or a hawk? There's plenty of both hereabouts, these days. What is due to happen? Or if he is on herd duty in the upper pasture and a hawk or an airship sends him scuttling to cover, a mile away,

169

what's to prevent anyone from stealing a sheep or two? Or what's to prevent stray dogs from raiding them? Besides, a dog that is a coward is no dog to have around us. He's yellow. He's worthless. If it wasn't for Danny —"

He saw his son trying to fight back the tears and slipping a wasted little arm around the cowering Laund. With a grunt, Ronald broke off in his tirade and stamped away.

More than a month passed before he would so much as look at the wistfully friendly puppy again or let him handle the sheep.

With all a collie's high sensitiveness, Laund realized he was in disgrace. He knew it had something to do with his panic flight from the airship. To the depths of him he was ashamed. But to save his life he could not conquer that awful terror for soaring birds. It had become a part of him.

Wherefore, he turned unhappily to Danny for comfort, even though his instinct told him the boy no longer felt for him the admiring chumship of old days. Laund, Danny, Ronald — all, according to their natures — were wretched, in their own ways, because of the collie's shameful behavior.

Yet, even black disgrace wears its own sharpest edge dull, in time. Laund was the only dog left on the farm. He was imperatively needful for the herding. He was Danny's only chum, and a chum was imperatively needful to Danny. Thus, bit by bit, Laund slipped back into his former dual position of herder and pal, even though Ronald had lost all faith in his courage in emergency.

A bit of this faith was revived when Laund was about fourteen months old. He was driving a score of ewes and spindly-legged baby lambs home to the fold from the lush South Mowing. There was a world of difference in his method of handling them from his whirlwind tactics with a bunch of wethers.

Slowly and with infinite pains he eased them along the short stretch of road between the pasture and the farmstead; keeping the frisky lambs from galloping from their fellows by interposing his shaggy body between them and their way to escape, and softly edging them back to their mothers. The ewes he kept in formation by pushing his head gently against their flanks as they sought to stray or to lag.

Even Ronald Crae gave grudging approval to strong young Laund coaxing his willful charges to their destination. Try as he would, the man could find nothing to criticize in the collie's work.

"There's not a dog that can hold a candle to him, in any line of shepherding," muttered Crae to himself as he plodded far behind the woolly band. "If he hadn't the heart of a rabbit there'd be every chance for him to clean up the Grand Prize at the National Collie Association field trials, next month. But I was a fool to enter him for them, I suppose. A dog that'll turn tail and run to hide under a bed when he sees an airship or a hawk will never have the nerve to go through those stiff tests. He —"

Crae stopped short in his maundering thoughts. Laund had just slipped to the rear of the flock to cajole a tired ewe into rejoining the others. At the same moment a scatter-wit lambkin in the front rank gamboled far forward from the bunch.

A huge and hairy stray mongrel lurched out of a clump of wayside undergrowth and seized the stray lamb. Crae saw, and with a shout he ran forward.

But he was far to the rear. The narrow by-road was choked full of ewes and lambs, through which he must work his slow way before he could get to the impending slaughter.

Laund seemed to have heard or scented the mongrel before the latter was fairly free from the bushes. For he shot through the huddle of sheep like a flung spear, seeming to swerve not an inch to right or to left, yet forbearing to jostle one of the dams or their babies.

By the time the mongrel's teeth sought their hold on the panicky lamb, something flashed out of the ruck of the flock and whizzed at him with express-train speed.

Before the mongrel's ravening jaws could close on the woolly throat, young Laund's body had smitten the marauder full in the shoulder, rolling him over in the dust.

For a moment the two battling dogs rolled and

revolved and spun on the ground, in a mad tangle that set the yellow dust to flying and scared the sheep into a baaing clump in mid-road.

Then the two warriors were on their feet again, rearing, tearing, rending at each other's throats, their snarling voices filling the still afternoon air with horrific din.

The mongrel was almost a third larger than the slender young collie. By sheer weight he bore Laund to earth, snatching avidly at the collie's throat.

But a collie down is not a collie beaten. Cat-like, Laund tucked all four feet under him as he fell. Dodging the throat lunge he leaped up with the resilience of a rubber ball. As he arose, his curved eyetooth scored a razor-gash in the mongrel's underbody and side.

Roaring with rage and pain, the mongrel reared to fling himself on his smaller opponent and to bear him down again by sheer weight. But seldom is a fighting collie caught twice in the same trap.

Downward the mongrel hurled himself. But his adversary was no longer there. Diving under and beyond the larger dog, Laund slashed a second time; cutting to the very bone. Again he and his foe were face to face, foot to foot, tearing and slashing; the collie's speed enabling him to flash in and out and administer thrice as much punishment as he received.

The mongrel gained a grip on the side of

Laund's throat. Laund wrenched free, leaving skin and hair in the other's jaws, and dived under again. This time he caught a grip dear to his wolf-ancestors. His gleaming teeth seized the side of the mongrel's lower left hindleg.

With a screech the giant dog crashed to the road; hamstrung, helpless. There he lay until Crae's hired man came running up, rifle in hand, and put the brute out of his pain with a bullet through the skull.

For a mere second, Laund stood panting above his fallen enemy. Then seeing the mongrel had no more potentialities for harming the flock, the collie darted among the fast-scattering ewes and lambs, rounding them up and soothing them.

In his brief battle he had fought like a maddened wild beast. Yet now he was once more the lovingly gentle and wise sheep-herder, easing and quieting the scared flock as a mother might calm her frightened child.

"Laund!" cried Ronald Crae, delightedly, catching the collie's bleeding head between his calloused hands in a gesture of rough affection. "I was dead wrong. You're as game a dog as ever breathed. It's up to me to apologize for calling you a coward. That cur was as big and husky as a yearling. But you never flinched for a second. You sailed in and licked him. You're *true* game, Laund!"

The panting and bleeding collie wagged his plumed tail ecstatically at the praise and the rare caress. He wiggled and whimpered with joy. Then, of a sudden, he cowered to earth, peering skyward.

Far above flew the forest-ranger's airplane, on the way back from a day's fire-scouting among the hills. With the shrill ki-yi of a kicked puppy, Laund clapped his tail between his legs and bolted for the house. Nor could Crae's fiercest shouts check his flight. He did not halt until he had plunged far under Danny's bed and tucked his nose into the dim corner of the little bedroom.

"Half of that dog ought to have a hero medal!" raged Crae, to his wife, as he stamped into the kitchen after he and the hired man had collected the scattered sheep and folded them. "Half of him ought to have a hero medal. And the other half of him ought to be shot, for the rottenest coward I ever set eyes on. His pluck saved me a lamb, this afternoon. But his cowardice knocks out any chance of his winning the field trials, next month."

"But why? If —"

"The trials are held at the fair grounds — the second day of the Fair. There's dead sure to be a dozen airships buzzing around the field, all day. There always are. The first one of them Laund sees, he'll drop his work and he'll streak for home, yowling at every jump. I'm due to be laughed out of my boots by the crowd, if I take him there. Yet there isn't another dog in the state that can touch him as a sheep-worker. Rank bad luck, isn't it?"

So it was that Laund's return to favor and to respect was pitifully brief. True, his victory prevented the Craes from continuing to regard him as an out-and-out coward. But the repetition of his flight from the airship all but blotted out the prestige of his fighting prowess.

The sensitive young dog felt the atmosphere of qualified disapproval which surrounded him, and he moped sadly. He knew he had done valiantly in tackling the formidable sheep-killer that had menaced his woolly charges. But he knew, too, that he was in disgrace again for yielding to that unconquerable fear which possessed him at sight of anything soaring in the air above his head.

He lay moping on the shady back porch of the farmhouse one hot morning, some days later. He was unhappy, and the heat made him drowsy. But with one half-shut eye he watched Danny limping painfully to the bantam-yard and opening its gate to let his feathered pets out for a run in the grass.

Laund loved Danny as he loved nothing and nobody else. He was the crippled child's worshiping slave, giving to the boy the strangely protective adoration which the best type of collie reserves for the helpless. As a rule he was Danny's devoted shadow at every step the fragile little fellow took. But at breakfast this morning Crae had delivered another tirade on Laund's cowardice, having seen the collie flinch and tremble when a pigeon flew above him in the barnyard. Danny had seen the same thing himself, more than once. But now that his father had seen and condemned it, the child felt a momentary disgust for the cringing dog. Wherefore, when the little fellow had come limping out on the porch between his awkward crutches and Laund had sprung up to follow him, Danny had bidden him crossly to stay where he was. With a sigh the dog had stretched himself out on the porch again, watching the child's slow progress across the yard to the bantam-pen.

Danny swung wide the pen door. Out trooped the bantams, willingly following him as he led them to the grassplot. Supporting his weight on one of the two crutches — without which he could neither walk nor stand — he took a handful of crumbs from his pocket and tossed them into the grass for his pets to scramble for.

Laund was not the scene's only watcher. High in the hot blue sky hung two circling specks. From the earth they were almost invisible. But to their keen sight Danny and his scuttling chickens were as visible as they were to Laund himself.

The huge henhawk and his mate were gaunt from long-continued foraging for their nestlings. Now that the brood was fledged and able to fend for itself, they had time to remember their own unappeased hunger.

For weeks they had eaten barely enough to keep themselves alive. All the rest of their plunder had been carried to a mammoth nest of brown sticks and twigs, high in the top of a mountain-side pine tree; there to be fought over and gobbled by two half-naked, wholly rapacious baby hawks.

Today the two mates were free at last to forage for themselves. But food was scarce. The wild things of woods and meadows had grown wary, through the weeks of predatory hunt for them. Most farmers were keeping their chickens in wire-topped yards. The half-famished pair of hawks had scoured the heavens since dawn in quest of a meal, at every hour growing more ragingly famished.

Now, far below them, they saw the bevy of fat bantams at play in the grass, a full hundred yards from the nearest house. True, a crippled and twisted child stood near them, supported by crutches. But by some odd instinct the half-starved birds seemed to know he was not formidable or in any way to be feared.

No other human was in sight. Here, unprotected, was a feast of fat fowls. Thrice the hawks circled. Then, by tacit consent, they "stooped." Down through the windless air they clove their way at a speed of something like ninety miles an hour.

One of the bantams lifted its head and gave forth a warning "chir-r-r!" to its fellows. Instantly the brood scattered, with flapping wings and fast-twinkling yellow legs.

Danny stared in amazement. Then something blackish and huge swept down upon the nearest hen and gripped it. In the same fraction of time the second hawk smote the swaggering little rooster of the flock.

The rooster had turned and bolted to Danny for protection. Almost between the child's helpless feet he crouched. Here it was that the hawk struck him.

Immediately, Danny understood. His beloved flock was raided by hawks. In fury, he swung aloft one of his crutches; and he brought it down with all his puny strength in the direction of the big hawk as it started aloft with the squawking rooster in its talons.

Now, even in a weak grasp, a clubbed and swung crutch is a dangerous weapon. More than one strong man — as police records will show — has been killed by a well-struck blow on the head from such a bludgeon.

Danny smote not only with all his fragile force, but with the added strength of anger. He gripped the crutch by its rubber point and swung it with all his weight as well as with his weak muscular power. The blow was aimed in the general direction of the hawk, as the bird left ground. The hawk's upward spring added to the crutch's momentum. The sharp corner of the armpit crosspiece happened to come in swashing contact with the bird's skull.

The impact of the stroke knocked the crutch out of Danny's hand and upset the child's own equilibrium. To the grass he sprawled, the other crutch falling far out of his reach. There he lay, struggling vainly to rise. One clutching little hand closed on the pinions of the hawk.

The bird had been smitten senseless by the whack of the crutch-point against the skull. Though the force had not been great enough to smash the skull or break the neck, yet it had knocked the hawk unconscious for a moment or so. The giant brown bird lay supine, with outstretched wings. Right valorously did the prostrate child seize upon the nearest of these wings.

As he had seen the first hawk strike, Danny had cried aloud in startled defiance at the preying bird. The cry had not reached his mother, working indoors, or the men who were unloading a wagon of hay into the loft on the far side of the barn. But it had assailed the ears of Laund, even as the collie was shrinking back into the kitchen at far sound of those dreaded rushing wings.

For the barest fraction of an instant Laund crouched, hesitant. Then again came Danny's involuntary cry and the soft thud of his falling body on the grass. Laund hesitated no longer.

The second hawk was mounting in air, carrying its prey toward the safety of the mountain forests; there to be devoured at leisure. But, looking down, it saw its mate stretched senseless on the ground, the crippled child grasping its wing.

Through the courage of devotion or through contempt for so puny an adversary, the hawk dropped its luscious burden and flew at the struggling Danny.

Again Laund hesitated, though this time only in spirit; for his lithely mighty body was in hurricane motion as he sped to Danny's aid. His heart flinched at sight and sound of those swishing great wings, at the rank scent, and at the ferocious menace of beak and claw. Almost ungovernable was his terror at the stark nearness of these only things in all the world that he feared — these flying scourges he feared to the point of insane panic.

Tremendous was the urge of that mortal terror. But tenfold more urgent upon him was the peril to Danny whom he worshiped.

The child lay, still grasping the wing of the hawk he had so luckily stunned. With his other hand he was preparing to strike the hawk's onrushing mate. The infuriated bird was hurling itself full at Danny's defenseless face; heedless of the ridiculously useless barrier of his outthrust fist. The stunned hawk began to quiver and twist, as consciousness seeped back into its jarred brain.

This was what Laund saw. This was what Laund understood. And the understanding of his little master's hideous danger slew the fear that hitherto had been his most unconquerable impulse.

Straight at the cripple's face flew the hawk. The curved beak and the rending talons were not six inches from Danny's eyes when something big and furry tore past, vaulting the prostrate child and the stunned bird beside him.

With all the speed and skill of his wolf ancestors Laund drove his curved white tusks into the breast of the charging hawk.

Deep clove his eyeteeth, through the armor of feathers, and through the tough breast bone. They ground their way with silent intensity toward a meeting, in the very vitals of the hawk.

The bird bombarded him with its powerful wings, banging him deafeningly and agonizingly about the head and shoulders; hammering his sensitive ears. The curved talons tore at his white chest, ripping deep and viciously. The crooked beak struck for his eyes, again and again, in lightning strokes. Failing to reach them, it slashed the silken top of his head, wellnigh severing one of his furry little tulip ears.

Laund was oblivious to the fivefold punishment; the very hint of which had hitherto been enough to send him ki-yi-ing under Danny's bed. He was not fighting now for himself, but for the child who was at once his ward and his deity.

On himself he was taking the torture that otherwise must have been inflicted on Danny. For perhaps the millionth time in the history of mankind and of dog, the Scriptural adage was fulfilled; and perfect love was casting out fear.

Then, of a sudden, the punishment ceased. The hawk quivered all over and collapsed inert between Laund's jaws. One of the mightily grinding eyeteeth had pierced its heart.

Laund dropped the carrion carcass; backing away and blinking, as his head buzzed with the bastinade of wingblows it had sustained and with the pain of the beak stabs.

But there was no time to get his breath and his bearings. The second hawk had come back to consciousness with a startling and raging suddenness. Finding its wing grasped by a human hand, it was turning fiercely upon the child.

Laund flung himself on the hawk from behind. He attacked just soon enough to deflect the beak from its aim at the boy's eyes and the talons from the boy's puny throat.

His snapping jaws aimed for the hawk's neck, to break it. They missed their mark by less than an inch; tearing out a thick tuft of feathers instead. His white forefeet were planted on the hawk's tail as he struck for the neck.

The bird's charge at Danny was balked, but the hawk itself was not injured. It whirled about on the dog, pecking for the eyes and lambasting his hurt head with its fistlike pinions.

Heedless of the menace, Laund drove in at the furious creature, striking again for the breast. For a few seconds, the pair were one scrambling, flapping, snarling, and tumbling mass.

Away from Danny they rolled and staggered in their mad scrimmage. Then Laund ceased to thrash about. He braced himself and stood still. He had found the breasthold he sought.

For another few moments the climax of the earlier battle was reënacted. To Danny it seemed as if the bird were beating and ripping his dear pal to death.

Beside himself with wild desire to rescue Laund, and ashamed of his own contempt for the dog's supposed cowardice, Danny writhed to his feet and staggered toward the battling pair, his fists aloft in gallant effort to tear the hawk in two.

Then, as before, came that sudden cessation of wing-beating. The bird quivered spasmodically. Laund let the dead hawk drop from his jaws as he had let drop its mate. Staggering drunkenly up to Danny, he tried to lick the child's tear-spattered face.

From the house and from the barn came the multiple thud of running feet. Mrs. Crae and the men were bearing down upon the scene. They saw a bleeding and reeling dog walking toward them beside a weeping and reeling little boy. From the onlookers went up a wordless and gabbling shout of astonishment.

Danny was walking! Without his crutches he was walking; he who had not taken a step by himself since the day he was stricken with the illness that crippled him; he whose parents had been told by the doctors that he could never hope to walk or even to stand up without his crutches!

Yes, he was one of the several hundred children — victims of the same disease and of other nerve-paralysis disorders — who regained the long-lost power over their limbs and muscles; through great shock and supreme effort. But that made the miracle seem none the less a miracle to the Craes and to the former cripple himself.

In the midst of the annual field trials of the National Collie Association, the next month, a gigantic and noisy airplane whirred low over the field where the dogs were at work.

If Laund heard or saw it, he gave it no heed. He went unerringly and calmly and snappily ahead with his tests — until he won the Grand Prize.

He saw no reason to feel scared or even interested when the airship cast its winged shadow across him. A few weeks earlier he had fought and conquered two of those same flappy things. He had proved to himself, forever, that there was nothing about them to be afraid of.

IX

A CRIME OR SO

The ancient teller's hands remained obediently over his head. But, with one groping toe he found and pressed the floor button under his desk.

Instantly the drowsy silences of the bank and of the street outside were split by a deafening clangor of the newly installed alarm bells.

The thief spun about, making for the door at something better than record speed. His motorcycle was parked in the alley. He had timed his visit when the sole day policeman of Gusepple was due to be at the far end of the mile-long Main Street.

His pistol swung menacingly from left to right as he dashed for the door. The few people in his path flinched from it. This was due to be a safe getaway.

His ignorance that an alarm system had just been installed here in the antique Aaron Burr National Bank had made his foray a failure. For even as he had reached with his free hand for the stack of pay-roll money the teller was sorting, that miserable multiple ringing had crashed forth. Still, his road to safety was clear; if he used haste. And he was using all the haste he had.

He was in the open doorway, whence a single bound would carry him down the low flight of steps into the village street. In another ten seconds he could reach his motorcycle.

Townsfolk were running from both directions, drawn by the unearthly banging of the gong. But none of them was likely to risk a bullet by trying to stop his flight. He gathered momentum for the leap through the doorway and down the steps.

The leap was made. But not at all as the thief had planned it.

From somewhere among the tangle of cubbyhole rooms at the rear of the bank, a furry gold-red catapult whizzed past the panic-held group of clerks and depositors. Like a flung spear it flashed through the air, its seventy-pound body smiting the fugitive squarely between the shoulders from behind. A double set of powerful jaws raked the nape of the thief's neck. Four curved white eyeteeth shore their way through flesh and muscle, almost to the bone.

Under that flying impact the thief's balance was destroyed. Spread-eagling, he floundered through the air and down the low steps. On all fours he landed on the sidewalk; the pistol tumbling from his loosened hand into the gutter, the gold-red collie still raging for his jugular.

The victim got to his feet with the quickness of a monkey. In what seemed a single gesture he rose from his breath-taking fall and grabbed the ravening collie tightly around the throat. The dog snarled and snapped impotently in that strangling grip.

But in almost the same moment a hatless man dashed out of the bank and into the fray.

The thief saw him coming, too late to do more than toss the dog aside and try to meet the onrush. A hard-driven left fist caught him flush on the point of his chin. The blow's force was doubled by the hatless man's momentum. Over the belatedly upflung guard it smashed, and to its mark.

The thief's knees turned to tallow. With a curiously bewildered look on his lean face, he crumpled peacefully to the sidewalk; and lay there.

The hatless man caught the collie by the ruff, holding him back from further onslaught. Five valiant townsfolk fell belligerently on the stricken thief, pinioning him and bawling for the police.

The episode was over — the most exciting thirty seconds in all the sleepy history of the sleepy little 3,000-population North Jersey town of Gusepple. It had been true melodrama. It had furnished substance for a month's recital by everyone in Preakness County. It was due to pass into local history as a deathless legend.

Still holding the dancing collie by the ruff, the hatless man turned back into the bank. Through the clump of goggling onlookers in the doorway, two incredibly old and wizened men advanced upon him. One of them was orating shrilly to the other.

"See that, Lamech? Did you see it? Remember how you grouched, awhile back, when I let Hilda Greer bring this collie of hers to the bank with her, every day? You said a dog didn't belong in a bank and it was a pest and it took away from the institootion's dignity. That's what you said, Lamech. Your own very words. Well, maybe you've changed your mind. If it wasn't for Heather, that crook would be at large right now, laying plans to rob more banks. Maybe this one. Monty Trent never would have got to him in time. It was Heather that pulled him down. I was back in the file room when it all started. Heather was lying there, dozing. I yelled to her: '*Sic* 'im, Heather! *Get* 'im!' Just like that. And likewise she did. . . . Turn off that alarm, somebody! I can't hear myself think."

Seldom did Ephraim Crayne lose an atom of his saturnine self-control; even when he was quarreling with his lifelong crony, Lamech Judd. But the oldster had been jarred out of all semblance of calm by the past half-minute's turmoil. Forgetting his senile aloofness as president and chief stockholder of the Aaron Burr National, he fairly spouted. Before Judd could speak, Crayne was patting the collie fervently and was saying to the man at her side:

"Not that I don't give some of the credit to you, too, Monty. That was a good swat you landed on the feller's chin. And maybe it kept him from doing Heather a mischief. You thought quick and you acted quick. You helped catch him, even if Heather was ahead of you with it. I won't forget it. I'll — well, how'd you like a whole holiday Tuesday? It's no more'n your due. And Tuesday's a light day here. I like to reward zeal in a subordinate. . . . Your knuckles are barked. Go wash them and put something on them."

Thus Ephraim Crayne dismissed the case and went forward to meet the policeman who came running up. Monty Trent was looking at the president no longer. From the little group of employees he had singled out a face and was gazing eagerly at it. It was a pretty face, strong, sensitive, highbred — the face of Hilda Greer, to whom he was engaged. In her big eyes now, as she returned his look, a hero-worship shone.

At sight of it Monty Trent's own eyes brightened. For an instant the lately habitual sullenness was gone from his visage. Hilda had seen him strike that mighty blow. She had seen him overcome another man — a desperate man, at that — in hand-to-hand combat. There was enough of the vainglorious primal male in Trent's makeup to thrill him at the thought. Few are the chances for a modern man to show himself to such spectacular advantage, to the woman he loves.

"You were splendid, Monty!" the girl whispered as he went past her on the way back to his desk. "Oh, it was *magnificent!* But — he might have hurt you, dear!"

Smiling at the mother-tone and words, Trent

touched her hand surreptitiously. Then he continued his journey through the tight-packed group and toward his little office. It was several minutes before the droop came back to his mouth and the sullenness to his eyes. But back they came eventually, as ever they did nowadays.

He and Hilda had been schoolmates at Gusepple and next-door neighbors. Together they had gone to business college in Paterson. Hilda had found a job in New York after they were graduated, and Trent had come back to Gusepple to take a clerkship in the Aaron Burr National.

The Aaron Burr was an old-fashioned small-town institution. And it was run in an old-fashioned way by its ultra-old-fashioned president, Ephraim Crayne. But it prospered. It was the bank not only of the town itself, but of the rich farming region around it and of one or two small factories and mills. Crayne was laughed at for his back-number methods. But he was trusted and his bank was rock-solid.

By drearily slow degrees Monty Trent had worked his way up from under-clerkship to the job of trust officer. Then it was that Hilda Greer's father died. The girl had had to leave her work in New York and come home to look after her lonely mother. Her father had left a little money. Her earnings were not needed to keep the home going.

Old Ephraim had been fond of Hilda since she was a child. She was one of the rare soft spots in

191

his hidebound nature. He made a job for her at his bank, though her work could easily have been distributed between two other employees. Now she was chief clerk and assistant trust officer; the immediate subordinate of her sweetheart, Monty Trent.

Ephraim still further had gone against his grim record by allowing Heather to come to the bank daily with her adored young mistress. More in defiance of Lamech Judd and the bank's other elderly directors than out of any fondness for animals, he had even gone out of his way to make friends with the collie.

At noon each day, Hilda and Monty were wont to lunch together in the file-room at the back of the bank. There, with Heather to play propriety, they ate the contents of their lunchboxes and chatted for the half-hour allotted them. It was the pleasantest part of the whole long workday for them both. At least it had been so at first, and for many months thereafter. But lately —

Today, Hilda was the first to reach the file-room. Arranging the handkerchief-sized table for the meal, she said to Heather:

"Go tell Monty I'm waiting."

At the command the dog wagged her plumed tail in glad excitement. This was her daily chance to perform a trick which she had taught herself; and in which she reveled with all a true collie's love for showing off. To Trent's office she cantered gaily. There, barking once, sharply, she lifted from the corner of the desk a battered lunch-box; and started back with it for the file-room. Monty looked up from his work, grinned at the dog's prideful eagerness, and followed her dancing footsteps to where Hilda waited.

By chance, one day, Heather had gone through this simple performance probably more with the idea of hastening the moment when she should share the two lunchers' tidbits than with any idea of summoning Trent. But both man and girl had praised her extravagantly for the exploit. And, collie-like, that confirmed her in it.

Hilda looked up with a shade of anxiety as Trent came in. She found what she was looking for and what she had learned to dread — that seldom-absent discontent and sullenness at the back of the man's eyes and in his mouth corners. She gave no sign of what she saw. Instead, she went on arranging daintily the contents of the two boxes, and she led the talk to the morning's adventure. Yet, the ill-spirit would not be banished from Trent's eyes. Presently, as she talked, it burst forth into angry words.

"The old mummified cheese-parer!" growled Monty. "You heard the grand reward he offered me for knocking out that crook! For making all the banks in the state safer from hold-ups — the Aaron Burr along with the rest — for risking a shot or a knife-poke in the ribs! I get a whole day off from this mangy treadmill! Any other bank would have given me a bonus or maybe a raise. But Ephraim picks out the lightest banking day in the week and says I can have it to stay home in. If the thief had stolen 100,000 and I had gotten it back from him, the old tightwad would have broken his heart by letting me stay home a day longer. He —"

"Oh, don't feel like that about it, boy of mine!" she pleaded. "I know Mr. Crayne ever so much better than you do, and he's pure gold. Honestly he is. And —"

"Pure gold! That's right. He's been amassing it all his life, and he never let a penny of it be pried loose from him. He ought to be one hundred per cent gold by now. To think of paying for a stunt like mine by giving me a measly holiday! He ought —"

"That's only his way, dear. You will gain *much* more by it, soon or late. I know him. He'll never forget what you did. It has boosted you ever so much in his esteem. "Some day —"

"Some day, when I am ninety," he railed, "Granther Parsons will fall apart from old age. Then Hendry will get moved up to cashier (if he hasn't dried up and blown away before then) and I'll get Hendry's job. Then I'll have enough pay for us to marry on. It's a cinch I'll never have, till then."

"But we're both young, dear. We can wait. Aren't we worth waiting for?"

"Not if we could get married without waiting. Gee! When I think of all the cash lying around loose in the world, while I'm working on starvation pay! There's Vroom, down at the Hapton

Trust: He had the same job and the same pay I have. He got a hot tip about the C.G. & X. merger, from his cousin in Wall Street. Vroom drew out every cent of his savings and put a mortgage on his bungalow; and plunged, on margin. He cleaned up more money in that one deal than I'll ever have if I live to be as old as Ephraim Crayne. If I could strike a bonanza like that, we could get married tomorrow! I've been studying the market, too, and Vroom says —"

"Don't, sweetheart! *Don't*," she begged, in genuine terror. "That's the way fifty speculators go broke, to one who wins. And even those who win are sure to keep on till they're ruined. Don't talk so! Don't *think* so! Why, we were so gloriously happy, just to be engaged, till you began getting these ideas about making a fortune overnight, and being discontented with your job! Can't you — ?"

"No, I can't. I love you. I want to be able to marry you. I want us to have a home of our own. That's the right of every man. And, at the pay I'm getting and likely to keep on getting, I'll be gray-haired before I can earn a marrying salary. Hendry's job would carry enough pay. Hendry is nearly seventy. But people are kept on here till they crumble into dust. Not a chance of my —"

"Perhaps when we're old we'll be glad the Aaron Burr keeps its white-haired workers on, instead of turning them out to starve. I don't wonder you feel resentful at getting ahead so slowly. Mother says Dad felt that way when he and she were engaged. She says he told her every low-salaried man, in love, feels that same glum illogical resentment because he can't afford to marry. But Dad said it ought to be used as a motor to drive them to harder and better work, not to make them sour or to try to get rich quick. He —"

"Yes, and if your father had been working for Crayne, you'd never have been born. For he wouldn't yet have gotten a marrying salary. . . . When I think of all the money that's lying around loose! Right here in this bank, a lot of it. Why, there's enough in Lamech Judd's strongbox, alone, to set us up for life! If I had a double-handful of it, to play the market with on a tip Vroom gave me — !"

"Monty!" cried the girl, her eyes full of unshed tears, her soft mouth trembling. "You hurt me so, when you say things like that! Oh, I know you don't mean them! I couldn't stand it if you did. But you've brooded over all this; till you aren't normal any more. It's —"

Heather created a diversion by reaching daintily upward from where she lay on the floor and taking from Hilda's fingers a sandwich which had remained neglected there so long that the collie supposed it was now public property.

"The dog has more sense than I have!" exclaimed Trent, glumly. "When there's something of value to her, within reach, she helps herself to it. . . . Time's up," he added, glancing at his watch. "Back to the treadmill for both of us! To pile up a few more dollars for Ephraim, and nothing for ourselves! Dear girl, I'm sorry I've been so cranky. I've spoiled my lunch hour, and yours, too. I didn't start out to. But that magnificent reward from Ephraim got under my skin. Besides, maybe I'm a bit keyed up from slugging that fellow. I'm sorry."

On his way back to his desk, Monty Trent found new fuel for the anarchistic grievance which was obsessing him. Old Lamech Judd had come bustling into the bank and to the private offices at the rear. Catching sight of Trent, he accosted the sullen youth much as he might have hailed an office boy; bidding Monty get his strongbox from the vault and carry it for him to one of the cooplike compartments which were for the use of the bank's box-holders.

Without replying, Monty went with Judd to the vault and to the boxes which lined three sides of the walls. Lamech fumbled in his wallet for a dirty strip of paper whereon was typed the combination of his box. Shrewd as he was in other ways — a shrewdness which had made him the richest man in the township — Judd never could remember the cabalistic list of figures which made up his deposit-box's combination. Thus, always he carried the figures in his wallet; to pore over as he worked the box's knob, and then to restore with crafty caution to the wallet's inner recesses.

Inspired small-town business man though he was, Lamech had an abiding distrust in the safety of banks. This, ever since, fifty years earlier, all his boyhood savings had been swept away by the collapse of a privately owned bank in the adjoining county. Wherefore, he would not keep a checking account.

All his transactions — and some of them were large — he conducted on a cash basis. He would take to the bank such money as he received; get the Aaron Burr's cashier to change it into big bills, and then would put the bills in his strong-box. There they would lie — sometimes a goodly amount, sometimes less — until he found the right investment for them.

The occasional sight of these stacked bills, as the box was opened or closed, had begun to rouse Monty Trent to an absurd fury. Hilda had been right. Trent had allowed himself to brood over his supposed ill-treatment at the hands of fate and of Crayne, until no longer he was normal. Today, as Lamech transferred a fat sheaf of bills from the box to the wallet, he eyed the old man with a blank face which masked feelings of which he had the grace to be ashamed.

"Got a chance to snap up first mortgage on the Stellings place," said Lamech, airily, as he watched Trent put back the box into its numbered niche. "I want to land it before Eph Crayne gets ahead of me. If I didn't, I'd wait till tomorrow. That's the day I've got six interest payments and a couple of dividends coming to me. A lot more'n I need for this Stellings mortgage. But I've done most of my best business by never waiting. That's a wise rule, young feller. Take it to heart. If you'd waited a few seconds this morning that robber would have got away from you. Eph acted handsome about that, too, giving you a whole lazy holiday just for hitting one crack. Goo'day, son."

At a little before noon next morning Lamech Judd was back at the bank; stopping at the cashier's window to change a mountain of many-denomination bank notes and two checks into large bills. Evidently, the expected interest payments and dividends had arrived. The money in hand, he made his way toward the vault. Monty Trent had been staring at Judd, glassy-eyed, during the changing of the bills. Now he came forward to escort him into the vault.

His hands still stuffed with money and with some mail that had arrived for him in care of the bank, Lamech fumbled for his wallet and drew awkwardly from it the greasy combination strip. He put his burden of bills and envelopes down on a stool while he twirled the box's knob. Grabbing them up again, he followed the box-bearing Trent to the nearest coop.

For some minutes he was closeted there. When he emerged, Trent was waiting for him. Lamech made his leisurely way toward the vault, while Monty went into the coop to retrieve the deposit-box. There, he noted, two or three of the envelopes had fallen to the floor while Judd had been stacking away his precious money. Idly, Trent stooped to pick them up.

Then his heart stood still.

Close beside one of them lay a greasy strip of paper.

Acting on no conscious volition, Trent swooped upon it. On a deposit blank he scribbled with lightning speed its contents: *"Right 2 to 27. Left 3 to 18 twice. Right 12 to 15."*

As he slipped hurriedly out of the coop with the heavy box under one arm, Lamech Judd came charging back, nearly knocking Monty off his feet as they collided. Trent dropped the box noisily; clinging to Judd as if to keep from falling. In that brief instant, he thrust the combination strip into a gaping upper waistcoat pocket of the plunging and excited old man. It was an absurdly simple thing to do. It called for no more legerdemain than to slip a coin into an unsuspecting child's pocket. Lamech was far too self-absorbed in the loss of his precious combination slip to have noticed a far more violent jostle.

Followed minutes of stark uproar and confusion at the Aaron Burr. Everyone from office boy to president milled around, searching, questioning, explaining, seeking to lure the bellowing Lamech Judd back to sanity and evading his shrieked demands that the police be sent for. At long last, the frantic old man yielded snarlingly to Crayne's oft-repeated suggestion that he search his pockets to see if by any chance he might have stuck the combination strip therein. Protesting ferociously that he had done nothing of the sort, Lamech ran his fingers in perfunctory fashion through his clothes.

His jaw drooped and he looked the complete fool he felt himself when he fished the precious strip from the same waistcoat pocket which held his wallet. Shamefaced, he slunk out of the bank; deaf to Ephraim Crayne's shrill derision.

The following day, Monty Trent found legitimate business for himself in the vault, when nobody else chanced to be there. Working swiftly, yet with curiously self-detached calm, he opened the door of Lamech Judd's deposit-box, drew forth the box itself, and took from it the topmost bundle of bills. Riffling them with trained speed, he counted $27,000. This packet he thrust inside his shirt. Then he shut the box and set the combination.

The thing was done. With this money he could take advantage of the hot Wall Street tip which Vroom had given him. Playing on margin, he was certain to clean up enough profits to restore the "borrowed" $27,000; and still to have a tidy little fortune.

Enough to marry on!

Over and over he said that to himself. Still, there must be nothing left to chance. If the loss should be discovered and the police sent for and everyone searched — !

He went to his desk. There, he opened his flat lunch-box and dumped its contents out of the window. Choosing a big manila envelope, he put the $27,000 into it, and deposited the envelope, unsealed, in the empty lunch-container. Leaving the box's lid a fraction of an inch ajar to allay suspicion, he went on with his work. Nobody would think of looking for stolen money in a lunch-box which lay, not even tight closed, on the corner of a desk. Tonight, he would take home his plunder and find fit hiding-place for it, until he could turn it over to the bucket-shop patronized by Vroom. Everything was safe. It had all been ridiculously easy.

Mechanically, Trent went through the morning's routine. It was as if he had used up his every emotion in the acquiring of the $27,000; and was drained dry of any power to think or to feel. His office brain functioned in a daze. So bemused was he that he lost count of time. Only when he chanced to pass the file-room and saw Hilda setting out her sandwiches on the table, with Heather sniffing ingratiatingly at the feast, did Monty realize that the noon hour had come.

"I'm — I seem to have a headache — or indigestion — or something," he heard himself babbling to the girl as he paused in the doorway. "I won't eat any lunch today. But if you'll wait a minute till I give Pete these letters to mail, I'll sit there with you while you eat."

But if Trent was not hungry, Heather was. Long experience had taught her that this delectable noonday meal, with its guerdon of crusts and meat scraps for herself, could not begin until both her human deities were seated at the file-box. Self-importantly and hungrily, Heather frisked to his office on her own account.

She found the lunch-box in its wonted place on the desk corner. But, for once, no divine odor of food gushed forth from it to greet her. The food-scent was faint and stale. Heather was annoyed at this unpardonable lack. Hence, instead of lifting the box from its place with her usual daintiness, she caught the protruding corner of it in her jaws and gave an impatient yank. The box slipped from her careless mouth-hold. It fell to the floor and the unfastened cover flew open.

Out tumbled a long and thick envelope, its only contents. Now, this assuredly was not food. But the envelope bore the scent of Monty's touch. And it was Heather's self-imposed duty to trot back to the file-room with the lunch or with the nearest approach to it. No use lugging the empty box. She picked up the envelope, with no great zest; that she might not incur rebuke by going back empty-mouthed. Carrying it thus un-interestedly, she started for the file-room. As she went she heard an outbreak of loud and wrathful voices from somewhere in front of her. Stirred, as ever a collie is by prospect of human excitement, she broke into a gallop.

Lamech Judd had received that morning a $2,000 timberland payment which was not due until the next week. Instantly he had driven into town with the money, to deposit it in his strong-box. As Trent was in another part of the one-story building, Lamech commandeered a clerk to take him to the vault and to carry his strongbox hence to the coop. The moment he opened the receptacle he saw the topmost stack of bills was gone. His yell brought Ephraim Crayne and several others running to the coop.

Monty had gone in search of the office boy, to give him the morning's letters to mail. He had overhauled the lad on the outer steps, on the way to lunch. Thus, he had missed the babel which followed Lamech's discovery. Coming back to the file-room, he found Crayne and Lamech standing on its threshold, where Judd had paused to thunder his loss to Hilda. Trent stopped short, his stomach sinking, his brain afire.

It was then that Heather came cantering toward her mistress, bearing the envelope and agog to learn the cause of all the noise. As the dog brushed past Crayne, who blocked part of the doorway, the envelope was knocked from its loose hold between her teeth. It fell at Lamech Judd's feet. The jar of the fall pushed back the unsealed flap. The sheaf of big bills slithered out and lay fanwise in front of their gasping loser's toes.

The two old men had gone; Judd still blithering dizzily as he clutched his money; Crayne as wildly ecstatic over what he termed Heather's "miraculous sixth sense" as he was bewildered over the treasure's mysterious loss and far more mysterious return. The bank had settled down to its usual busy quiet.

For the first time, Trent forced himself to raise his eyes to Hilda's. The girl's face was bone-white and drawn. In every line of it was stamped incredulous horror. There was no need of words. She had seen Heather patter away to Trent's office. She had seen the collie return with her strange burden. Furthermore, love let her read Trent's stricken countenance as though its import were in large print. Hilda understood.

Long and wordlessly, Trent stared into the big eyes from which all youth and hope and sunshine suddenly had been driven. Into the man's very soul, like white-hot iron, that expression seared. Heedless of what his own aspect might reveal, he stood dumbly, in mortal agony; as though he had just slain all he loved. Presently, with a mighty effort, Hilda spoke. The words were banal enough, though they came gratingly through a throat sanded by heartbreak.

"Was it worth it?" she asked. "Was it worth the sick terror I saw in your face when the money fell out? Is there anything valuable enough to steal? Is anything worth such craven fear? *Is* there, Monty?"

She fell silent. The man did not speak. Presently he drew a long breath. Then he turned on his heel and walked fast out of the room. In vague new disquiet Hilda sprang up and followed him. As she saw him push open the door of Ephraim Crayne's private office her own steps quickened. With the impulse which makes a mother strive to shield an imperiled child, she ran to the door of Crayne's office and forced herself into that sacred retreat almost on Monty's heels.

Old Ephraim glanced up from his work, frowning at this unheralded dual intrusion. Then at sight of the invaders he grinned. He was certain he understood.

"Come to announce the date of the wedding, hey?" he asked, scanning the two perturbed visages. "It's in the very nick of time, too. Because we're pensioning Hendry next month. That rheumatism of his won't let him stand another winter in this climate. And we've slated you, young man, for his job. You see, I've been watching you and your work for quite a spell. If you'll live always economical, you two, you ought to get along real nice on your new pay. I wasn't fixing to tell you, for another week or so. But when you screw up your courage to come in here together to tell the old man you're —"

"I didn't," Trent interrupted the flow of paternal prattle. "We are not going to be married."

"Hey? But —"

"I shan't be here. I shall be in jail. I stole the combination of Mr. Judd's strongbox. Then I opened the box and stole $27,000 from it. I hid it in my lunch-box. Heather found it there somehow and brought it to him. I am a thief. A worse thief than the one I knocked out last week. That's all. Now phone the police."

Hilda drew her breath in a great sob. She caught Trent's limply cold hand in both her own.

Ephraim Crayne's leathern face was set and expressionless.

"Tell me about it," he demanded.

Curtly, extenuating nothing, Monty Trent told his story; from the very outset of the obsessing urge for a marrying wage. Silent, expressionless, Crayne listened. Once or twice Hilda Greer sought impulsively to interrupt. But Trent stilled her sobbing protests. Then the sordid tale was finished, and silence fell again — a silence broken only by Hilda's sobs.

"That's all," said Trent, after a moment. "I'll dictate it and sign it if you like. Send for the cops, please. I hate to have Hilda kept here suffering like this. Let's get it over with. She —"

"No!" cried Hilda. "*No!* Mr. Crayne, you won't do that? You won't? Let him go! No man with the nature of a thief could ever have confessed to you when there wasn't a shred of suspicion against him. Can't you see that, sir? If you'll let him go, I'll work here for the bank, for nothing, for all the rest of my whole life. I promise I will. He's so splendid! And it was on *my* account he confessed. Just because I was silly and thought for a minute that he — that he wasn't as wonderful as I've always known he was! He —"

"Please, Hilda!" murmured Trent. "*Please* don't! You're only making yourself all the unhappier. Will you call up police headquarters, Mr. Crayne, or shall I? Let's get this ended."

Ephraim Crayne looked at the wall clock.

"You folks' lunch hour is over," he said, his dry

voice as expressionless as his face. "You're wasting the bank's time. Get back to your work, the both of you."

Trent's jaw fell ajar. Hilda cried out as if in sharp physical torment:

"Mr. Crayne!"

"He has a right to play cat-and-mouse with me, if that's his pleasure," said Monty, recovering from his daze. "Won't you go now, please, little sweetheart? I don't want you to see them take me away. I —"

"I told the two of you to get back to your work!" rasped Ephraim Crayne. "If that isn't plain enough English, then here's a mouthful more: If I wanted a feller to represent the bank down in a country where there's danger of smallpox, I'd pick out someone who's had smallpox. He couldn't have it a second time. I want a feller to take the responsible job Hendry is leaving. So I pick out somebody who's had a nice virulent attack of temptation and who has seen what hell it can bring him to."

"Mr. Crayne! Then Monty — ?"

"I figure he's immune for life. He has learnt that crookedness and self-torture mean the same thing. Lots of folks take a lifetime to learn that. . . . I don't make many blunders in the men I pick for jobs here. My best enemies grant me that much credit. I —"

He broke off, cleared his wizened throat, and peered again at the wall clock.

"Get back to your desks, you two," he commanded, "or I'll dock the pair of you! . . . Hilda, here's fifty cents. Buy Heather a hunk of good tender steak for her supper, on your way home. Tell her it's from me. She's sure earned it."

X

"HUMAN-INTEREST STUFF"

Nobody knew how many world-famed champions' blood coursed through the veins of Tatters. One thing alone was certain as to those champion ancestors of his: no two of them could possibly have belonged to the same breed.

Yet he was beautiful. By some freak of nature his generous mixture of breeds had proved a blend, not a cross. Deep-chested, mighty of coat, powerfully graceful, he had the "look of eagles" which is supposed to go only with flawless canine or equine lineage.

Whence he came, what had been his upbringing, who his first owner or owners — these were mysteries never cleared up. As far as our story is concerned, life began for him in the Midwestburg dog-pound. It was there that Benny Craig found him.

This on the morning of Benny's tenth birthday. Five crumply dollar bills were throbbing and burning in the lad's hip pocket; gift of his big brother, Mel Craig.

Five dollars was wealth to the ten-year-old youngster who seldom had had one-fifth of such a fortune at any one time. Whereat, as soon as his brain cleared from the shock he made his own supreme life dream come true.

Always he had craved a dog. Long ago he had decided on just the kind of dog he yearned for. It was to be a Boston terrier, like Dode Townsley's. But of course a billion times nicer. And it was to be named "Tatters," in honor of the canine hero of a Sunday-school book he had read. Not that Bostons are in the least tattery, but because there was a lure to the name.

Dode Townsley had bought his Boston at the Midwestburg dog-pound for three dollars. Thus, to the pound fared Benny Craig, his incalculable five-dollar hoard pulsing hotly in his pocket.

Before he had time to make the entire rounds of the pitiful place, he saw Tatters. The big dog did not yelp or growl or brawl as did the rest of the common pen's occupants. He stood apart from the milling throng of luckless captives; heartsick, proud, silent. He looked up as Benny peered over the top of the rough enclosure.

His eyes met the boy's. Not in cringing appeal nor in hostility nor in blankness; but as one lonely soul speaking with another. Benny didn't want a big dog. He wanted a Boston. Yet with no volition of his own he found himself pointing a grubby forefinger at Tatters and bidding the bored attendant fetch the cross-breed out to him. Deep had called to deep. Lonely dog to lonely child. And, hurried on by something outside himself, Benny Craig responded.

Two dollars was the price demanded and paid for the purchase of Tatters. Another dollar went for a collar and a chain. With his new dog, and with two whole dollars still left in his pocket clamoring to be spent, the lad made his way through the more crowded streets to his riverside home in the suburbs. On the journey he stopped to buy two pounds of raw meat. Tatters was well-nigh starved. Yet he ate the luscious fare daintily, instead of wolfing it down.

By the way, this is not a juvenile yarn. Benny's share in it is practically at an end. Tatters' is just beginning.

Mel Craig slouched in to dinner that night from a long day's trucking, to be met by a tearful kid brother and by an irate mother. Benny did the sniveling; their mother did the first and most vehement part of the talking.

"Look at that big brute, Mel!" exhorted Mrs. Craig, waving a reddened fist at Tatters, who lay dozing beside the stove. "See what Benny spent most of your five-dollar present on! SEE him. Big as a house and due to eat more'n a human. Takes up more room than a cow. That's what Benny's wished on us. Bought him at the pound, he says. Bought him by the ton, *I* say. Him wanting a nice genteel tiny Boston that wouldn't have been in anybody's way, and then getting this elephant. I won't have it! He's got to take the beast back, first thing in the morning."

"Aw, Mel, he's — he's grand!" whimpered

Benny. "I'm calling him 'Tatters,' and he's learned his name already. Can't I — PLEASE, Mel, — can't I keep him? Aw, Mel —"

"If that big hyena stays, *I* don't!" announced Mrs. Craig, fiercely. "Mel, if you've got the spirit of a man, instead of a mouse, you'll —"

"Cut it out!" ordained Mel Craig, in a tone his mother was not used to. "Cut it out, the two of you. And, Ma, you don't have to show me a hunk of cheese, to find out am I a man or am I a mouse. I gave the kid the cash to go buy himself a present. If he's picked out this one, and if he likes it, the mutt stays. Get that? He *stays*."

"Mel!" rebuked Mrs. Craig.

"Aw, gee, Mel, *thanks!*" blithered Benny in the same breath. "You're — you're swell!"

Tatters waved his plumed tail, got to his feet, stretched himself fore and aft; and came across the room courteously, to make closer acquaintance with the beetle-browed giant who had countersigned his right to remain. Mrs. Craig's mouth flew ajar. A covert wink from Mel made it fall slowly shut.

"Take the purp out for a run before we eat, Benny," commanded Mel. "These big dogs needs lots of exercise. Bring him back in five minutes or maybe more."

Thrilled at his victory, Benny fastened the chain to Tatters' new collar. Boy and dog stormed forth into the twilight. Mel turned on his mother, forestalling a sizzle of words that bubbled to her ample lips.

213

"Listen, Ma," he said, sinking his voice lest Benny still be within earshot. "I don't aim to have that oversize critter blocking up our whole house, any more than you do. But it's the kid's birthday and —"

"I tell you I won't have —"

"And I'm telling you we aren't going to have!" interrupted Mel. "I had it all figgered out the minute I set eyes on him. But there's no use making the kid cry on his birthday, is there, when there's nicer ways to settle it? Make out you like the mutt. Say he c'n sleep here in the kitchen, to-night, by the stove. Then —"

"I tell you, I won't have —"

"Then," pursued Mel, unheeding, "when the kid is sound asleep, I'm going for a walk. See? A walk. And this Tatters dog is going with me. All quiet-like, so as not to wake Benny. The purp will go along with me, because there'll be a rope around his neck. And when I get to the landing stage, I'll get a nice big rock from that ballast pile down there, at the edge of it, and I'll tie the rock to the far end of the rope. Then the mutt and the rope and the stone will all three drop off the dock together. And that'll be that."

"But when Benny wakes up —"

"When Benny wakes up in the morning, he'll find his tramp cur has sneaked off and left him. The kid will traipse around the neighborhood, asking folks have they seen his grand new dog. And he'll keep on hoping Tatters will maybe come back soon. That way he'll be hoping till he

214

forgets about him. While he's doing that, I'll buy him a Boston. If we'd made him get rid of the big cuss, he'd maybe have cried himself sick. And he'd of been sore on the two of us. There's plenty of better ways of not paying a board bill than by kicking the landlady in the face. So, when the kid is asleep —"

"Mel!" exclaimed Mrs. Craig in doting admiration. I've always said you had all the brains your dear dad had. And then some. I —"

"Dad's brains landed him in the hoosegow," corrected Mel. "Mine is due to land me in the big money before I'm done, if I get any kind of breaks. So —"

"Ma!" shrilled Benny, storming back into the kitchen, Tatters tripping him up exultantly with the chain at every hopping step. "Ma, he knows how to shake hands and he knows how to speak! I tried him. Gee, Tatters, of all the dogs that ever happened, you're — you're that dog!"

Late in the evening, Tatters lifted his head from the mat by the stove. Some one was leaning above him and fumbling at his neck. The dog saw his visitor was Mel. Drowsily Tatters blinked. His tail smote the floor welcomingly.

Even when Mel slipped off the new collar and replaced it with a rope noose, the dog continued to wag his tail. In this warm house of kind treatment and good fare he feared none of the ills that had befallen him during his weeks of bewildered wanderings from his earlier home to the pound.

215

Obediently he got to his feet as Mel twisted the rope and chirped to him. It was monstrous pleasant to snooze cosily there by the stove. But an accredited member of his new household was giving orders. Out through the street door tip-toed Mel, the dog following in friendly docility at his heels. Tatters did not so much as pull back on the six feet of rope which dangled between his throat and Mel Craig's hand.

It was only a furlong or so to the landing-stage that stuck out into the black river. On both sides of the stage the banks shelved steeply into the water, deep enough to drown any dog. But Mel made doubly certain by leading Tatters out to the far end of the stage.

He paused in his progress to fumble in the dim light, among the rocks of the ballast pile along-side the float. Thence he picked out a stone whose weight made him grunt; a stone which seemed to have enough angles and bumps to keep a tied rope from slipping loose.

When the tying was done, Mel lifted the stone in one hand, and slipped his other arm under the stomach of the astonished Tatters. With a heave that called on all his great strength, he flung the rock and the dog far out into the fast-running water.

At least, that was the maneuver as Mel Craig planned it. It did not work out that way.

On a cloudy night and at the outer verge of a slime-coated float, smooth-soled shoes do not get the surest of footings; when the body is only half balanced by reason of a violent effort. Like ancient tires on a grease-splotched concrete road's curve, Mel's feet skidded.

He wrenched sideways to recover his balance. The awkward move jerked the stone behind him, in the convulsive waving of his arm. Then gravitation took charge.

A sixty-pound dog shot forward at one end of the rope. A thirty-pound stone made a like evolution on the other end of it. This by reason of Mel's tremendous outward heave. But now the short length of rope between dog and stone chanced to be directly behind Mel's neck instead of in front of him. Also his soles still were slipping aimlessly about in the green slime of the float's edge.

The force of the throw sent Tatters and the stone well out into the depths. But between these two weights the taut rope jerked a third object into the water. This object was Mel Craig.

And never in his twenty-seven years had Mel taken the trouble to learn to swim.

Over the verge he was yanked. His big body was carried outward for several feet before it hit the water. Then, like the dog on one side of him and the stone on the other, he went deep beneath the surface.

Down and down he sank rapidly, toward the ooze of the river-bottom. Vaguely he was aware that Tatters no longer was sinking, but was struggling to make his way upward. The new unevenness of the pressure on either side told him that.

But the stone was pulling Craig and the dog downward, sidewise, despite Tatters' game efforts. Mel's aimlessly frantic squirmings added to the dog's difficulty in fighting his way to the air above.

As any night fisherman knows, there is an art in tying a rope securely around an anchor stone. This art Mel Craig had lacked. To such ineptness he owed his life. For presently his subaqueous plungings and twisting caused the noose to slither free from the rock.

To the surface bobbed the man, after centuries of strangling in the black depths. He had swallowed much water. His lungs were afire. His head came up into the air. His first breath was blazing anguish. It choked back his half-uttered yell for help.

He felt he was beginning to sink anew. The horror of dread made him thrash around crazily in an effort to keep his nostrils free. And these insane gyrations drove his nostrils below the surface once more.

Then it was that he felt a bruising grip on his shoulder. Something had seized him there and was trying to lift his writhing, sinking body to the top. By some minor miracle Mel had the sense to cease his suicidal gyrations and to lie still.

At once his inert body began to move toward the steep bank at the left of the float. The marvel of this cleared his brain enough for him to realize that Tatters was fighting with every wiry sinew, to drag him shoreward.

Slow, agonizingly slow, was the dog's progress; even though now the man was helping him by lying moveless and limp.

After several eternities Mel's dragging toes scraped and bumped against the bottom. The touch galvanized him to life. With his last strength he scrambled up part of the bank and sprawled, panting and hiccoughing, along its precipitous side.

Tatters was exhausted. The dog's breath came in long uneven gasps. He lay down beside Mel and licked the man's streaming face.

For the first time since he was a child Mel Craig broke into hysterical weeping.

"Tatters!" he choked, drunkenly. "*Tatters!* If — if it wasn't for you, I'd — I'd be down there yet — there in the black water — for keeps! And — and I was trying to drown, you, Tatters — God forgive me! And you got me out! There ain't a — a bloody thing to say to you, Tatters. Only — only —"

Raucous sobs shook him afresh. The dog moaned in quick sympathy and fell again to licking the wet face.

But it was a stoically self-contained Mel Craig who strode into the kitchen half an hour later. Close at his side marched Tatters, monstrous proud of himself and of the rescued man's petting and praise.

Mrs. Craig was waiting up for her son, to learn definitely that the dog was disposed of. At sight of Tatters — his shaggy coat still as dank and dripping as were Mel's own clothes — the woman broke into a stream of angry queries. Mel cut her short. Speaking in the dully authoritative tone she heard so seldom from him and which even her ready temper dared not oppose, Mel said:

"Tatters stays. Never mind why. He stays. And he is going to have every break we can give him. If it wasn't for him, you and the kid would be hunting for a new meal ticket tomorrow. Never mind why. And there'd be one fewer truck, hauling for Chaggers & Comp'ny. He *stays*."

"But, Mel," quavered Mrs. Craig, "Benny woke up awhile ago. Woke up cross. Said he was sorry now he hadn't got a Boston, like he aimed to do. Said he don't like big dogs, nohow. Said he only got Tatters on a fool hunch —"

"A fool hunch that'll keep him and you from going on the Relief, next winter," interposed Mel. "But I'm glad he wants a Boston, instead. I'll get him one. From the pound, at that. I'll hunt up Spike Shevlin tomorrow and slip a piece of coin to him. In less'n a week there'll be a dozen nice Bostons in the pound for the kid to choose from. Spike'll see to that."

"Then we can send Tatters back to — ?"

"I told you once already Tatters stays. He's *my* dog, from now on. Not Benny's. Mine. Till the one or the other of us dies. . . . While I'm getting these soaked shoes off, will you trot to the icebox and give him that slab of steak you was saving for my breakfast, Ma? He sure rates it. . . . No, never mind why. I paid for the steak, didn't I? Well, I bought it for Tatters. I didn't know it then, or I'd of bought him a whole steer."

That was how Mel Craig acquired his first and last dog, he who had not cared for animals. From then on Tatters slept at the foot of his bed every night and lay at his side during meals and rode with him on his truck during work hours.

The acquaintance had begun queerly enough. But there was nothing queer in the way the acquaintance grew into friendship and then into mutual devotion. Tatters was that kind of dog. And, though never had he suspected it, Mel Craig was that kind of man.

He was a good worker, was Craig, and according to his own lights he was more than indifferent honest. But always he had been lonely; despite his throng of acquaintances — some of them with little in common with Cæsar's wife — and always subconsciously he had longed for a real pal. Now he had found the chum he had craved.

Tatters' cleverness and loyalty and all-around companionableness delighted Mel as much as they astounded him. He had not guessed dogs were like that. And ever at the back of the man's brain lurked a little sting of self-abasement at memory of his attempt to kill the dog, and of Tatters' strange form of reprisal.

From the bottom of his heart Mel hoped the dog did not know of the effort to drown him. Whether the animal's ever-increasing devotion to himself was in spite of that knowledge or from an ignorance of the attempt, Mel did not know. He did not want to know. But he had found a friend — a friend every day dearer to him.

Besides the truck which he kept in a closed shed on the edge of Midwestburg, Craig owned a rattletrap sedan of ancient vintage. Whether on his work rounds in the truck or on his country drives on Sunday afternoons, Tatters rode always beside him on the seat.

When Mrs. Craig and Benny or a neighbor or two were sharing the Sunday drives, Mel let them do the talking. He was not an inspired conversationalist. But when he and Tatters drove alone together, Craig fell into the habit of so many lonely men, of chatting fluently and long to the dog — the dog that could not understand one word in twenty but that loved the man's rumbling monotone, and was vastly proud that it should be addressed to him.

One Sunday afternoon Mel had deposited his mother and his small brother at their home, after a ride. Then with Tatters he set forth to the shed where the antique sedan was stored alongside the scarcely less ancient truck.

Patrolman Guttman chanced to reach the patch of road alongside the shed; on his wonted beat, that day, as Mel and Tatters drove up. Guttman had been exiled to this suburban beat a week earlier, from a far more profitable and congenial post near the center of Midwestburg. He was avid to roll up a record which should cause his return to civilization. Still more eager was he to form lucrative financial contacts here in the sticks, to tide him over until such return.

Speculatively he approached Mel as Craig finished backing the tumbledown sedan into the tumbledown shed.

"Let's take a look at your licenses, feller," he suggested.

"Both of them is in the car pocket," answered Mel, puzzled. "What's the trouble?"

"Maybe no trouble," said Guttman, enigmatically. "Maybe quite a plenty of it. I'll take a looksee."

He pushed past Craig and tugged at the car's nearest door. In a flash he was staggering back, with Tatters raging at his throat. The first — almost the only — lesson Mel had taught his beloved dog, was to guard the car and the truck from the touch of all strangers. Tatters was obeying orders, now, to the letter, in assailing this outlander who was laying vandal hands on his sacred charge.

Knowing and fearing the police from childhood, Mel Craig caught up his dog and pushed him into the sedan; slamming the door shut behind him. This barely in time to bring his own hulking body between Tatters and the patrolman.

For Guttman had whipped his pistol from its holster. Incidentally, he was gobbling with ire and with the knowledge that he must pay out of his own pocket for the damage the teeth rents had wrought on his uniform coat.

"That mutt of yours tried to kill me!" yelled Guttman. "He —"

"I've learned him not to let strangers tamper with the car," soothed Craig. "He didn't mean any harm. When he saw you grab the door and open it, he thought —"

"Stand clear!" stormed Guttman. "The cur won't do any more thinking about anything. I'm going to fit a slug of lead into the thing he does his thinking with. He's 'incurably vicious' and he attacked an orfcer in the pursoot of his dooty. It'll go on the blotter as such. Stand clear, I'm telling you, if you don't want —"

His left hand shoved Craig far to one side. Tatters roared with anger at sight of the rough treatment dealt out to the man. The dog hurled himself snarlingly against the thick glass. The ancient car shook and groaned under his vain attempt to break out and attack the stranger who had assaulted his master.

Mel Craig reeled under the vehement shove. He caught his balance as Guttman took aim at the raging dog through the glass of the car door. The patrolman was too wise to open the door and take a chance at his bullet reaching Tatters before Tatters might reach him.

The hurting impact of the push and the peril to his chum ripped Mel's last remnants of self-control. He went Berserk.

With one fist he knocked the pistol out of Guttman's hand, just as the policeman pulled trigger. The ball flew wild. The heavy-caliber cartridge's report echoed far, as it rent the Sabbath silences.

Then, with both hands, Mel had Guttman by the throat; strangling him, shaking him insanely. Down went the bluecoat, battling in futile fashion with the screaming maniac who crashed to the ground atop him and who seemed trying to tear out his victim's jugular. The muffled roars of the dog imprisoned in the car added to the godless din.

Folk ran out of their houses. Two policemen, returning to the station, heard the shot and the clangor a block away, and came up on a run.

With all the strength and science acquired in riot work, they pried Mel loose from the half-swooning Guttman, and dragged him to the station.

There a lieutenant jotted down the facts on the desk blotter.

A sleepy-eyed youngster was lounging against the desk. He listened with mild interest to the tale of strife. In a less mild pity he scanned the prisoner. As a precinct reporter, he knew well the treatment Mel was likely to receive, in his cell that night, for the unforgivable crime of beating up the sacrosanct body of a policeman. As soon as the captain should return from supper, to give sanction to the carnage, the work would begin. In court next morning, the prisoner's hideous condition would be accounted for by the injuries he had sustained in

225

his self-started fight with Guttman.

Then the sleepy reporter came wide awake. For Mel Craig gave a sudden start, shaking off the apathy which had gripped him ever since he woke from his Berserk fit. Memory was pouring in on the captive; memory and coherent thought.

"What'll I get for this, sir?" he asked the lieutenant, his voice still uncertain and wavery from the groundswell of his rage.

"Six months, or maybe a year," replied the officer, adding merrily for the reporter's benefit, "But the first half of it'll be spent nice and cozy in the hospital. So don't —"

Craig heard no more. Even the sinister threat of eligibility to a hospital's accident ward did not touch him. His bemused mind centered on one dread, alone.

Tatters!

The dog was locked in the sedan in the shed. Days might pass — perhaps weeks — before anyone might think of looking for him there. Days, weeks, of starvation, of torture from thirst; in that cramped space. Growing weaker and weaker, and ever in more and more suffering, and wondering pitifully why his loved master had deserted him to such a black fate!

The thought was crazy anguish to Craig. Not yet was he calm enough to realize that he could perhaps get word to his mother and to Benny, next day, to let the dog loose and to care for him until Mel's jail term should be ended. However, there was a strong chance that he himself would be in no mental or physical shape, after the punitive night in the cell, to communicate with anyone.

"Tatters!" he mumbled, dazed.

Then life rushed back to his numbed muscles. Hitting out on both sides, he won his way clear from the men who guarded him on either hand. In a single bound he was at the station door.

If only he might keep ahead of the chase until he could reach the shed where he had stowed his car! If he might get there and unlock the door and let Tatters out and order the dog to run home — well, then they were welcome to catch him and yank him back to the station and stick him into a cell and lam him with the rubber hoses until he should be dead. Tatters would be safe.

Wide he flung the station door. He launched himself outward with all his strength and speed, on his rescue race — just as the tip of Patrolman Guttman's flung night stick knocked him senseless.

"Coming to, is he?" asked the reporter, ten minutes later. "*I* figured it was a fracture case. But that's the only thing I've been able to figure out. Why'd he ever sail into a cop? And then why did he try to make a getaway when he must have known he didn't have a Chinaman's chance to? He isn't drunk, either. It doesn'a make any sense at all to me. But the less sense the better story.

Mind if I drop down there and try to make him talk?"

"Chase ahead," assented the lieutenant, "but you won't get anything. Just a case of blowing up from the heat or something. No story to it."

"For Monday papers," expounded the reporter, "there's a story in things that wouldn't rate three agate lines any other day. I'll tackle him, anyhow. Thanks."

The lieutenant bent over his blotter again, to straighten the day's returns before the captain should come in to relieve him. He knew it was not wholly regular to let a police reporter ask questions of a beaten-up prisoner under such conditions. But this particular reporter, young O'Leary of the *Clarion*, had given him more than one bit of useful publicity and was likely to give him more. It is well to handle such pests with gloves. They can sting when they are sore on an officer.

Presently O'Leary came up from the cells, less sleepy of aspect and more lively of gait than was his wont.

"Get any story from him?" boredly asked the lieutenant.

"Only a dog story," responded O'Leary, adding, "S'pose the captain will be at his flat, now?"

"Likely. Finishing his supper. But he'll be here in a little while. Why don't you wait? Whatcher want him for, anyhow? *I* can —"

"I want to tell him a dog yarn," said O'Leary.

"These big silent brave police guys love dogs and dog stories. If you don't believe that, read some of the dear 'human interest' blitherings in the papers. Maybe in tomorrow's *Clarion*."

"Remember it was me at the desk, not the cap'n, when you write your piece," adjured the lieutenant, "and don't forget how I —"

"I won't forget," promised O'Leary. "So long. If the story's printed, your name will go into it. But I'm hoping it won't be printed."

This was cryptic enough to leave the lieutenant blinking stupidly after his caller. But then the newspaper boys were always saying things a sane guy couldn't understand. Part of their patter, most likely.

Police Captain Bourke had finished supper. He was squirming into his uniform coat as O'Leary strolled in on him. Bourke was genuinely glad to see the reporter. Here in the suburbs the captain received little enough newspaper mention. If this were to be an interview —

"Evening, Captain," O'Leary hailed him. "I'll walk back to the station with you, if you don't mind. There's something I want to get off my chest."

"Sure. Come along. Have a drink, first?"

"No," said O'Leary, with real regret. "You see, I never drink when I'm working. But then," he continued more cheerily, "I never work very long at a time. Let's go."

As they set forth on their walk, the reporter told tersely the tale of Mel Craig's arrest and its cause and of the attempt at bolting. Captain Bourke's hard face set harder as he listened. He quickened his stride. The punishment could not begin until he should arrive at the station to sanction it. But O'Leary continued to move along as slowly as before. The fuming captain was forced to slacken his own eager pace.

"I had a talk with the prisoner," O'Leary was saying. "He wasn't very coherent. He was just convalescing from night-stickitis. But I got the main idea. It's the best human-interest yarn that has broken, out here, in six months. And — and I'm hoping I can't use it!"

"Huh?"

"Craig was putting up his car," resumed O'Leary, "when Guttman breezed along and wanted to see his licenses. There hadn't been any accident. So Guttman had no right to ask for them. It was the first move in a petty shakedown, of course. So —"

"Guttman must have —"

"He had. He tried to open the car, to grab the licenses. Craig's dog had been trained to guard the car. So he went for Guttman. Craig pushed the door shut on the dog, and Guttman pulled his gat. He gave Craig a swat. Then he opened fire on the purp. He missed. And Craig beat him up. They got Craig to the station. Then Craig happened to remember that his dog would probably starve to death in there — which he wouldn't — and he makes a break to get back and let the mutt out. He —"

"Yep," mused Bourke, absently, his mind still centering on the penalty to be meted out in the cell block that evening; to the thug who had dared assault a policeman. "Pretty good story, just like you said."

"*If* it's printed," amended the reporter. "And I told you I'm hoping it won't be. That's why I chased around for a chat with you."

"I don't get you."

"No," said O'Leary, with a queer tightening of his slack manner, "you wouldn't. But you will, now. At least, I hope you will. For your own sake."

"Oh, speak United States!" rumbled Bourke. "Put it in language. Whatcher getting at?"

"Maybe I'm getting at you and your stuffed-shirt lieutenant and especially at your wife's cousin, Herr Guttman. But I hope not. It's up to *you*. Ready to stop thinking about rubber-hosing Craig for a minute, and do some listening?"

"Whatcher getting at?" repeated Bourke, falling back on his nearest conception of scoffing repartee.

"At this," answered O'Leary, still tighter of lip and of diction. "I'm asking you to go back to the station and to do one of the pretty stunts with the blotter that you do when you get orders from the City Hall. I'm asking you to find so many flaws in Craig's arrest that you'll turn him loose. Then that you'll pass word along to Guttman and the rest that he's to be let alone in future. How about it?"

"You're batty!" grumbled Bourke, in amaze. "Or are you being funny? Here's a bum who beats up an officer who's in pursoot of his dooty, and then resists arrest, and then slugs two other men of mine in trying to break loose. It's a clear open-and-shut case. And you ask me to turn him loose! It's a laugh!"

"It isn't yet," demurred O'Leary, "and when it is, the laugh's due to be on *you,* Cap. Use your head, man. I'm giving you your chance. Best take it. S'pose I chase back to the office and write this yarn, the way it ought to be written. The yarn of a poor workingman who loves his dog. The cop who tries to shake him down and then gives him a smash and tries to kill the dog that's protecting the man. And then Craig risking his own freedom, to save his dog from getting killed; and then risking worse to get back to the car to keep his dog from dying or starving. If I know a human-interest-Monday-morning story, that's a pippin."

"But —"

"The case will come up before Magistrate Vanderslice, in the Cooper Market Court, in the morning. Is there a police magistrate on earth who doesn't read all the crime news of his district, in the morning paper, before he goes into court? Vanderslice will be all primed with that yarn. He'll have sense enough to know it's the kind of story every afternoon paper will pick up and that the A.P. and the U.P. will wire all over the country. What kind of verdict do you figure he'll give? The very worst Craig can get from him is a suspended sentence. You know that, as well as I do. Then —"

"But I'm telling you, O'Leary —"

"No. I'm telling *you*, Cap. I'll be on hand there. I saw Craig, and I know just how much signs he gives, right now, of what's been handed him from Guttman. I'll be watching him when he comes into court. If he looks any worse then, I'll know why. And I'm warning you I'll spill it to the evening papers crowd. It'll make a grand mouthful for the *Banner*, in that crusade of theirs against police brutality. Likewise, where will you and Guttman and Company be; when Headquarters and the Big Feller find what a sweet mess of newspaper publicity you've hauled the administration into? Tell me that?"

"If a roustabout and a mangy cur can —"

"They can. And they will. That's the kind of stuff the dear public understand. They understand it fifty times better than they'd understand an exposure of tax-juggling or street bond scandals. They'll do some writing, and some yelping, and next month some voting. And papers from Georgia to Oregon will write editorials on it. Nice publicity for our fair burg, hey? And who'll pay? Think it over, Cap. Then think it over some more. And think fast, both times."

O'Leary fell silent. For a space the big man and the little man cropped meditatively along, shoulder to shoulder. It was Bourke, not the reporter, who was doing the bulk of the thinking.

233

The longer the thought the drier grew his throat. Bourke was far from being a moron. His mental processes, once started into motion, traveled straight and true.

Better and stronger political climbers than himself had had their careers smashed to a pulp by lesser causes. He was visualizing the slimy sob-sister stories of the hero who risked mayhem and prison to save from peril the dog that was his best friend.

Dearly he would have loved to clasp both huge hands around this wretched police reporter's skinny little neck and throttle him into eternal silence. But Bourke knew well that a policeman who damages a reporter is in dire danger of bringing the whole newspaper fraternity down upon him for the rest of his days.

They had reached the steps of the police station. There they came instinctively to a halt in their walk and in their ruminations. Bourke's wide face broke into an affectionate grin as he slapped his palm agonizingly down between O'Leary's meager shoulder-blades.

"Come on in!" he invited, with much effusion. "I hear there's been a blunder made here while I was out. My fool lieutenant pulled a boner. So did my wife's ivory-head cousin, Guttman. I've got to set it straight. It won't take but a minute. Then I'll turn your friend, *Mister* Craig, over to you; to take back to his rotten mutt of a hound. Come on in."

"Thanks, Cap," said O'Leary, with real gratitude. "I owe you something for that. And I mean to pay it, some day. You see, I promised Craig I'd either get him out of the coop or get his dog out of the car, inside of an hour. And if you'd said 'No,' then it would have been up to me to chase over and let out the dog. And he might have bitten me. I hate dogs. . . . Thanks."

XI

SNOW WHITE

When Boskirk Robin Adair was four months and one day old his cash value was well above $300. Many a fancier, who foresaw in him a flawless show collie, would have invested several hundred dollars gladly in the wonderful pup, on the chance of his not coarsening or "going back" or dying from distemper. This at four months and one day, remember.

When Boskirk Robin Adair was four months and two days old his cash value as a show dog was something less than thirty cents.

This because on the morning of that fateful day he ran playfully out to meet a delivery truck that was bringing some provender to the Boskirk Kennels. The truck happened to arrive during the puppies' exercise hour. Out in front of the swift-moving vehicle scampered Robin. The driver applied all brakes. The kennel man at the same moment yelled to Robin to get out of the road. The puppy and the truck both sought to obey orders. Neither was quite fast enough.

As Robin leaped back, the left front wheel nipped his luxuriant tail. An hour later the local veterinary saved the rest of Robin from blood poisoning by slicing the tail off, midway between its roots and its plumed tip.

The veterinary made a good job of it. But incidentally he amputated nearly a hundred per cent of the pup's worth. A tailless or half-tailed collie is of no use in the show ring. And the show ring was the objective toward which Robin and ten generations of his ancestors had been guided.

Kin Hodgers was carting a load of cedar shavings from his mill to the Boskirk Kennels — for anti-flea bedding, at a dollar ninety cents per hundredweight — when the tragedy's second act ended. The veterinary had finished his work. Orrin Boskirk was empurpling the air with gusts of language, at loss of his best show-prospect pup. Kin listened with awed interest to the kennel owner's harangue.

"Too bad!" he commented as Boskirk paused for breath. "What are you going to do with the pup now, sir?"

"Do with him?" sputtered Boskirk. "There's nothing left to do. The vet did it all. I sent for him because I figured he might be able to save the tail — put it in splints or something. What does he do? Cuts it off, and then has the acid nerve to stick me for five dollars for the operation. I'd have seen him in blazes before I paid it, if it wasn't that I'm li'ble to need him again. It's like that, with vets. When you need 'em you need 'em bad. Can't afford to fall out with 'em. Now I've paid out five good dollars and I've got the job of

237

shooting the pup, besides. He's no good to me or anyone, as he is. He'll eat as much as any of 'em, and never bring in a cent."

Kin Hodgers looked down at the puppy, stretched on the barn floor, gallantly choking back any sign of pain and meeting the new human's eyes so honestly and appealingly.

Kin's big cross-breed Newfoundland — his chum and guard and sole daily companion for the past ten years, since the day when old Deacon Hodgers had left the sawmill and nothing else to his lonely eighteen-year-old son — had died of old age, a month earlier. The little mill and the smaller house behind it had been doubly lonesome since then. On sudden impulse Kin spoke.

"I'll give you the five dollars the vet charged you," said he, "and you can give me the pup. It'll be cheaper for you than to shoot him. Take it or leave it."

That night the dead cross-breed's enormous kennel coop had an occupant that did not half fill it — a sorrowful-eyed collie pup whose bisected tail still was done up in the vet's best bandages.

But before the week was out Robin Adair was sleeping at the foot of his new master's bed in the three-room house. And the kennel coop once more was empty.

There is something wondrously appealing and lovable about any collie pup. And Robin was of the best sort. Almost from the first he and Kin became pals. By the time the hair had grown cascadingly over the tail stump the collie's education was well under way. Kin had a natural gift with dogs — a gift vouchsafed often to the lonely. Under his instruction Robin learned as fast as his master could teach him. Constant comradeship with the man tended to develop his brain rapidly and to humanize him. Kin took to talking to him as if the collie were a fellow man. Which is also the way of the lonely and which is a marvelous education for any dog.

At the close of day they were wont to sit side by side on the handkerchief-sized back porch, overlooking the thicket-bordered millpond. Pipe in mouth, Kin watched the play of sunset light over the patch of water, and dreamed the dreams of the lonely and heartsore. Close by his knee the collie loafed drowsily, starting up in eager interest whenever the man chanced to speak his name.

One such evening, when Robin was about a year old, they sat lazily there, at the end of a hard day's toil at the mill. Kin put into half-coherent words one of these idle dreams of his.

"Robby," he mused, "wouldn't it be grand if we was to be setting here like this, sometime, just you and me, Robby, like it was now, and there should come a rustling in that bunch of alders over yonder, and a beautiful young lady with blue eyes and yellow hair and a white muslin dress should come out onto the edge of the pond, Robby?"

At the repetitions of his name Robin Adair's

half-length tail smote the porch boards resound-ingly and his deep-set sorrowful eyes scanned with keen curiosity his master's brooding face. Kin went on, reflectively:

"She'd have been out for a walk somewheres, Robby, and she'd have lost her way. She wouldn't see the pond till it was too late for her to stop. And she'd fall, slapbang, right into it. She wouldn't know how to swim. You'd hop in after her, Robby. So would I. The two of us would haul her ashore here, safe and sound. Then maybe she'd be so grateful to us that she'd fall in love with me, Robby. We'd get married, her and I. And the whole three of us would live here happy f'rever after. How's that, Robby?"

He glanced down shamefacedly at the dog. Robin's dark eyes were on his master's. In their depths was no ridicule. In them was nothing but dumb adoration, tinged with the wistful mischief that ever underlies a collie's look. Encouraged, Kin resumed:

"She'd be just every bit as nice as she was pretty, Robby. She'd never make small of me for being bashfullike and awkward, like one girl did — a girl with those colored hair and eyes and clothes, Robby. Never mind that. It's all past and gone. She'd think I was grand. And she'd *know* you was grand, Robby. I guess anybody'd know that, anyhow.

"It'd be kind of nice to have somebody to work for and make much of. Some human, I mean, Robby. Somebody with yellow hair and blue eyes

240

and a white dress — to make me forget that other one. It'd be nice to come in, evenings, from the mill, and find her setting out here on the stoop, with a white apron and a blue dress and with her sewing in her lap, and maybe singing to herself, all soft and sweet, just waiting for me to come home to supper. Supper with saleratus biscuits and honey, most likely. Gee, but I wish she'd come through that alder copse right now, Robby! It's kind of long waiting."

Again he glanced down at the dog. Robin Adair was paying still more flattering interest to the tale, for he was staring across the narrow belt of pond toward the mass of alders, as though expecting momentarily to see the wonder maiden emerge. His tulip ears were pricked. There was a light of quick expectancy in his eye. Vastly flattered at this show of attention, Kin enlarged on the theme.

"There'd be a sort of rustly sound in the alders, Robby, and a glimmer of white muslin. Then they'd kind of part, and —"

A low-breathed growl from the collie interrupted him. Robin was staring more intently at the alders. He had half-risen to his feet. His chiseled nostrils were sniffing the still air.

"Hold on!" adjured Kin. "*That* wouldn't be any way to welcome her, Robby. Not by growling when the bushes commenced to rustle and —"

He broke off, slack-jawed, eyes abulge. The alder bushes *were* rustling. More, they were moving. Kin sat agape at this phenomenon.

241

Gradually, and at almost the very spot which Kin had indicated to Robin by a shift of his pipe stem, the alder stems parted. Something as white and shimmery as a muslin skirt glinted through the green of the copse. Kin held his breath.

A face, then a head, then a chest and a pair of shoulders emerged silently through the parted alder stalks. A fox stood there on the brink of the pond.

Yet it was no such fox as Kin Hodgers had ever beheld or heard of in all his twenty-eight years of rustic life. For the beast was as white as swirled snow.

For a long quarter-minute the strange creature stood facing the moveless man and dog across the pool. Its reflection in the still water was as snowy and as distinct as in a mirror. Infinitely dainty and beautiful it was. Nor had it any of the slinking timidity of its kind.

It was Robin Adair who broke the spell. With a bark and a plunge, the collie leaped forward. Before Kin could speak, Robin was tearing through the waterside thickets in delirious pursuit of the fox.

The latter, with a swift backward movement, seemed to melt into the green of the copse as it vanished. For a space the evening silences were broken only by the sound of Robin Adair crashing through the coverts in mad chase of his elusive prey.

Now the wolf is blood-brother to the dog, especially to the collie. But the fox, at best, is a distant cousin. At that it is a cousin with far too much of the cat about it to permit of any amalgamation with the dog. Wherefore, dog and fox are wellnigh as inimical to each other as are dog and cat.

Instinct told Robin Adair that this white visitant was his hereditary foe. Never before had he seen a fox. But he needed no second command from his subconscious mind, to send him off in furious pursuit of the stranger.

Kin Hodgers sat blinking incredulously, as the sound of the chase died away. In the slack months of late autumn and early winter Kin was wont to eke out his slender sawmill income by roving the mountains with a gun and a set of traps over his shoulder and a borrowed mongrel foxhound at his heels; in quest of foxes. Red foxes these. He had heard of no other variety.

A Paterson furrier gave him $10.50 for every good fox pelt. The furrier then cured and dressed the skin, equipped it with snappers; and sold it for $75 as a neckpiece. Kin was skilled in this difficult art of fox-tracking — a knowledge he had gleaned from his father. In good seasons he annexed sometimes as many as twenty skins. He was well content with the price paid him for them. The Paterson furrier was more than seven times as content.

Now, as his daze cleared, Kin moved instinctively toward the house, for his gun. If a red fox was worth $10.50, a snow-white fox assuredly must be worth fully twice as much.

Then he paused. The season was late summer. Not yet was any fox's pelt "in prime." Nor would it be for another two months or more. Off-prime peltry found no good market anywhere. And yet —

Out yonder, some laps ahead of the pursuing Robin Adair, many dollars' worth of rich fur was running. By late autumn — by the time the mountain frosts should have thickened and enriched that fur — the fox might well be fifty miles away. Or a luckier hunter might bag the rare prize. Kin was loath to lose the chance. The sight of the glorious animal had thrilled him with the urge of possession. He saw a possible solution to the problem.

Putting his calloused fingers to his lips, he whistled shrill and long. At the summons Robin Adair, far away, ceased reluctantly from his fruitless chase and came panting back to his master. The collie's coat was snarled with burrs and his nose was scratched by brambles. But he had had a wonderful time.

Trained to instant obedience, it had not occurred to him to turn a deaf ear to his master's call. But he grudged the need of minding. Humans were always calling dogs back, just when fun was at its height.

"You'd never catch him in a year, through all that mile of undergrowth, Robby," Kin informed him. "It's the kind of growth that stops a dog, and where a fox can skin through like he was greased. Besides, you've never learned to track foxes. They've got more tricks in a second than the sharpest dog has in a year. Not but what you've got more real worth-while wiseness than any fox, Robby. But you gotta learn their ways before you can catch 'em."

Robin lay down, with a thump, on the edge of the porch, his tongue out, his furry sides heaving with the speed and obstacles of his run. In mild curiosity he eyed his master as Kin exhumed from a cupboard a mass of steel and wood and springs and levers.

"This is the best fox-trap there is, Robby," explained Kin. "Dad invented it, and he knew what was what. Besides, it catches 'em alive and it don't torture nor pinch 'em. I've known foxes to be caught in this that never could be took in by any other kind of trap there is."

As he spoke he was assembling deftly the trap's parts, anointing each from a vial of rank-smelling oil. He had drawn on thick gloves before starting to work.

"Get the idea, Robby?" he asked. "Foxes don't do anything by accident. Every move is all worked out. The white fox we saw — well, that fox didn't just happen to stray here. Either he came to drink, because there's no other pond nor brook in a mile, or else he came for one of my ducks. Anyhow, here he came. And the worst that happened to him was to get chased by a dog he had no trouble in shaking off. That means he's due to come back when he thinks it's safe. You and me are going to do our living and our sleeping in the mill for the next few days, Robby. Likewise, we're going to round the ducks into their pen. After 'em, Robby."

At his gesture, the collie sprang into the pond and struck out for the spot where a little flock of tame ducks were feeding on watergrass. With practiced skill the swimming dog rounded them up and set them in motion toward their water-side pen. With little difficulty he drove them to it and herded them, quacking and flapping, in through its gate.

Kin shut the door upon them, saw that the coop was safe from possible marauders; and then returned to the porch for his trap. Skirting the pond, he came to the place where the fox had appeared. There, deep among the alders, he set and baited the snare.

That night he and Robin slept on the floor of the mill; leaving the waterside house deserted. It was so the next night. Through the day, they did not go near the pond; except when Kin brought food and water to his prisoned ducks.

On the third morning, when, from the mill's roof, Kin looked down, as usual, at his trap among the alders, he saw his forecast had been correct. In the trap box something white and ghostly moved from side to side, with the repeated furtive iteration of the Wild. The fox was caught.

Leaving it to grow tired with endless assaults on the bars, Hodgers set briskly to work making a coop and yard for it. Digging a hole a foot deep

246

and ten feet long by eight feet broad, he carpeted the bottom of this with a double layer of chicken wire. Then he flung back the twelve inches of displaced dirt over it, and surrounded the enclosure with a fence, three feet high. The fence was also of doubled chicken wire. A layer of the same wire roofed it over.

In one corner of the eight-by-ten yard he set up a small packing-box whose bottom was strewn with hay and whose only opening was a circular hole about twelve inches in diameter. When food-and-water vessels had been affixed to the inner side of the wire walls and filled, and a door cut in the end of the yard, the fox's temporary home was ready.

"You see, Robby," Kin explained to the collie who was watching these proceedings with grave curiosity. "Foxy's skin isn't worth much of anything, this time of year. But if we can keep him alive till late November, it's due to be worth a whole lot. Likewise we're going to keep him alive till then, if we have luck. First of all, when I get him in his yard, I'm going to point him out to you and tell you to leave him alone. I know you'll do it, once you understand what I mean."

Drawing on his thick gloves, and shutting Robin indoors, Kin skirted the pool to where his prisoner wove to and fro in the trap. As the man approached, the fox forbore to press against the bars in search of a weak place in them. He crouched low and he showed all his teeth in a hideous smile.

Undaunted by the menace, Kin opened the door just wide enough to let his hand in; and reached for the prisoner. The fox reached for him at the same time and with far greater speed and accuracy. The pin-sharp teeth drove deep into the leather of the glove and into the fingers beneath. But in another instant Kin had him by the scruff of the neck and was drawing him forth from the trap.

Suddenly the fox went limp, lying, a dead weight, in his captor's grasp. Too experienced to be taken in by this possum-playing ruse, Kin bore his captive to the yard prepared for him. He dumped the fox in through the doorway and closed the wire door behind him, fastening its lock.

The fox lay where Kin had dropped him, a drift of dazzling white against the brown earth. Hodgers looked down on the seemingly dead creature. Yes, at close view, he was every bit as beautiful and as unbelievable in coloring as at that first brief glimpse. Save for a very few blackish hairs at the tail tip, he was as white as a season's first snowfall. No mere Alaskan white fox this, but a greater rarity — an albino. Never had Kin Hodgers dreamed of such an animal.

Leaving him lying there, and making sure the food-and-water dishes were full, he went noisily away. Climbing to the low roof of his mill, he looked down at the prisoner. For several minutes, the fox did not stir. Then cautiously he opened an eye and peered around.

Finding himself alone, he got to his feet. With uncanny speed he raced around his roomy inclosure, seeking means of egress. After sniffing cautiously at the aperture of the packing-box house, he whisked inside, only to emerge again almost at once. Next, making sure that he was still unobserved, he began frantically to dig, choosing a spot close to the wire wall.

In a few minutes he had burrowed through the twelve inches of earth and had come to the double layer of chicken wire.

Slowly, disconsolately, he backed out of the hole, his showy coat smeared with dirt. Then, shaking himself clean, he walked calmly over to the food dish and began to eat.

Kin frowned perplexedly. He had forseen all the other moves. But that a new-caught and panic-scared fox should eat — this was far outside his experience. Then, the explanation dawned on him.

"I — I might 'a' known!" he exclaimed, aloud to the excited collie. "That's no wild fox. That's an escaped pet. No wonder it wasn't more scared of Robby and me, the other evening! That's a pet. But any fool knows a fox can't ever be made a pet. First chance they get, they'll run. Pet or no pet, its skin ought to be worth a lapful of money. That's good enough for me."

Descending, he let Robin Adair loose and took him over to the yard. The fox paid scant heed to their coming. Seeming to recognize that he was once more in loathed captivity, he gave over his

249

former wiles. He contented himself with snarling horribly at the approaching visitors. His slitted eye pupils grew round and greenish.

"Robby!" said Kin, speaking slowly and with much emphasis. *"Leave — it — alone!* Understand? *Leave — it — alone!"*

Robin had been advancing with gay ferocity upon the cornered fox. Now, at his master's words, he halted; then turned and walked away, head and bobbed tail adroop. He understood. So far as he was concerned, that hated fox was as safe as if they were miles apart. But it irked the collie sharply to lose such a chance for attacking a hereditary foe.

"Good old Robby!" approved Kin. "That's the dog! Maybe sometime you can get a chance against a wild fox, to make up for it."

He plodded off to his day's work, the dog at his heels. Purposely he had built the fox-yard in a hidden corner where no possible visitor would be likely to see it. He was not minded to have dozens of curiosity-seekers crowding his place, to stare at the phenomenon. Still less was he minded to have some light-fingered neighbor steal his treasure trove, under cover of night or during one of his own rare absences.

As he was about to stop work, for lunch, he looked up from his lathe to see a woman standing in the doorway of the one-room mill. It was the first time a woman had stood there since the death of his mother, twelve years earlier.

Owlishly, Kin regarded the caller. Then his

glance contracted in a recognition that held a tinge of pain. The intruder was Olive Madden, teacher of the two-mile-distant district school.

Robin Adair had started up truculently at sound of the light step rendered all but soundless on the sawdust of the dooryard. He stared at the woman. Then, gravely and courteously, he stepped forward to greet her. Kin wondered at this strange show of hospitality. The collie was decidedly a one-man dog; and Hodgers was the one man. Robin was not given to such show of cordiality to outsiders.

Bobbed tail awag, he thrust his muzzle into her cupped hand and stood looking up at her with quiet friendliness. She stooped to caress the classic head.

"Good morning," said Kin, stiffly, aware all at once of his own unshaven shabbiness.

To offset his sense of shame, resentment came to his aid.

"What do you want?" he asked, gruffly.

The woman winced slightly at the tone. Kin noted it and it roused him to surly self-defense.

"You can't much wonder at me for not being tickled to see you again," said he, "if you'll stop to remember the last time I met you. That'll be three years ago. But likely you'll remember."

"Yes," said the woman, "I remember. And I don't blame you, Kin. But it wasn't all my fault, either. How could I know you were — were asking me to marry you? I had never even dreamed you cared anything about me. You had

251

been so — so shy and — and almost sullen. Then when you blurted it out, all upside down and stammering, why, I — I thought you were trying to be funny or trying to give an — an imitation or something. And I laughed. It wasn't really funny, Kin. I only laughed because I thought you were doing something you thought was funny. So I laughed, and — and I said I wished you'd do it for our school entertainment. It wasn't till you gave me that awful blank look and went straight off home that I — that I dreamed you'd been in earnest. I'm so sorry! I —"

"S'pose we let it go at that," he grumbled, in a torture of embarrassment. "There's nothing gained by digging up things that's dead. I got over it, all right. All it did was to leave me hating the thought of women that have yellow hair and blue eyes and wear blue dresses and white aprons. I never can bear to think of them kind of women, even yet. Just because they're like you. I never do think of 'em, either. That's all the harm it did, so far as I'm concerned. Forget it. Like I have forgot it. Now what do you want here?"

Strangely enough, the churlish words and tone no longer made her wince. She even glanced sidewise at his frowningly averted face. In her blue eyes was a flicker of wistfulness that was all but maternal. She steadied herself to meet him on his chosen new ground.

"I came here because I thought you could help me," she said simply. "Will you?"

"Can't you find enough folks to 'help' you,

among the fellers that are always hanging around you?" he snapped, cut and angry. "Why do you have to come to — ?"

"First, because there aren't any fellows 'hanging around' me," she made answer. "Perhaps they saw it wasn't any use. Perhaps I'm not as attractive as I used to think I was, when you knew me. And anyhow, there's nobody but you around here who could help me in this special worry of mine. Can I tell you about it?"

Taking his dull silence for assent, she went on:

"Last year my brother ran down from Canada to see me. He is still trapping up there. He brought me some lovely furs and he brought me a baby white fox for a pet. An albino. It was a darling little thing. I got ever so fond of it. He warned me it was certain to run way if ever it got a chance to. So I kept it in a pen that he made for me. I kept it hidden behind the cellar, for fear the boys or the dogs might find it and tease it. Or it might get stolen."

His rancor and heartache jarred away by this revelation, Kin stood pop-eyed, listening to her.

"Two weeks ago," she continued, "it gnawed its way out and escaped. I gave up any hope of finding it again and I was ever so unhappy. Then, last night I went to the meeting of the Grange. And after that I was worse than unhappy. Four different men got up and told how their hen-roosts had been robbed during the past fortnight. Fifty-one chickens in all were killed or taken, they said. One man said he got out of bed just in time to see his best rooster being carried off, in the dark, by something that looked snow white. He said it might possibly have been a dog with white patches of fur. The only part of him that was visible in the darkness. But one of the other men said that a dog couldn't carry off a chicken without its waking the whole neighborhood, and this animal didn't make a sound or let the chickens make a sound. They said they'd be sure it was a fox, 'only foxes are red and not white.'"

She paused. Still Kin did not speak.

"I knew then that it must be my fox that was doing all the killing," she said. "You can imagine how I felt — how I still feel. Just think! Fifty-one chickens! And nobody knows how many hundred more there will be before it's ended. And it's all my fault! If people knew, I'd probably lose my school. And whether they know or not, I'm every bit as much to blame. At least, I will be if I let it go on. That's why I came to you."

"Huh?"

"You have the name for being the best fox-hunter anywhere around here," she replied. "You told me yourself you have the best fox-trap that was ever made. Oh, can't you set it, somewhere that my fox is likely to be? Can't you? Can't you catch him, *somehow?* Kill him if you have to. Only I wish you could catch him alive. I'm so fond of him! But whether he is caught alive or shot, he's got to be stopped from destroying people's chickens. I can't let that go on.

If it does, I'll have to risk losing my school by coming forward and telling all about it and pay for the chickens that are already killed. I am going to pay for them, anyhow; only I dare not do it yet, for fear of being found out. You — you can imagine what a terrible lot it means to me, when I can come and beg help from *you* — after — after —"

" 'Scuse me for butting in, as the feller said," boomed a voice from the doorway, "but I'm here on business."

Dick Roehl, local police chief, swaggered into the mill; his vast bulk dwarfing the small place. Nodding with covered head to the schoolmistress, he favored Kin with a less courteous nod, then turned a truly baleful glare on the collie.

Robin viewed the newcomer with even less favor. Seeming to sense a hostile presence in his master's sacred precincts, the young dog bristled. And he moved unobtrusively between Kin and Roehl, a growl starting far down in his furry throat.

"Quiet, Robby!" adjured Kin, adding: "Well, Chief, what 'business' are you on, here?"

"Eleven of my chickens was killed, three nights ago," returned the chief. "At least, I came home by broad daylight, along supper time, and found 'em killed. On my way home, not three minutes earlier, I heard you whistle. And this big bobtailed cur of yours came bounding past me from the direction of my house; when he heard you. I got back home and I found the chickens dead. They weren't even cold yet. Couldn't have been dead longer'n half an hour. Maybe not five minutes."

"H'm!" mused Kin to himself. "No wonder the fox was making for the nearest place where it could get a drink!"

"I had my suspicions," continued Roehl, "but I hadn't any proof that was downright legal. Then last night at the Grange — you was there, Miss Madden — Sim Zabriskie told how something white and kind of small had run off with one of his fowls, right under his eyes, in the dark. That set me to thinking. In the dark, the only part of a critter that would show is the white that's on him. Sim said he saw a patch of white about twice the size of a cat."

"Well?" said Kin, instinctively shifting his body so it hid from Roehl the face of the trembling girl. "What then?"

"Just this," summed up the chief, "and taken together with what I saw on my own way home, three days back; the white ruff and frill of that big collie cur of yours is just about double the size of a cat. And in my opinion that's what Sim Zabriskie saw sneaking off with his rooster. The cur had —"

"Listen, friend," interposed Kin, with dangerous softness, "that's the third or fourth time you've spoke of Robby as a 'cur.' If you were half as thoroughbred as Robby is, you wouldn't have had to threaten suit against that county-historian feller for proving your great-grandmother was a

256

Lenape squaw. So go easy on calling names to those that's better bred than what you are. Now, as to the rest of your charge against this collie of mine —"

"No!" cried Olive Madden, hysterically. "*No!* Let me —"

"Please don't interfere, Miss Madden," commanded Kin, sternly. "And if you don't mind, I'll ask you to go; and come back some other time. I'll see can I find the kind of hardwood you want for your class in manual training, and I'll let you know. Now, then, Chief, this collie of mine —"

"This cur of yours," flared the chief, black with anger at the unlucky mention of his Indian great-grandmother, "is under grave s'spicion of being the killer we are looking for. I believe we can prove it on him. If we do, I'll get a court order to kill him, and I'll execute the order myself on your own premises. I don't care how much store you set by him. He —"

"Yes," said Kin, ruminatively, "I set plenty of store by Robby, all right, all right. He's all the c'mpanionship I got. He's all that cares whether I'm alive or dead. I'm — I'm wondering whether it's worth making myself lonesome once more, just for the sake of someone that don't give a hoot for me. If I was a story-book hero I'd most likely own up that Robby did those killings and let him get shot, by law; so that — somebody might be saved a little trouble. But a dog that loves me is maybe worth more than a — a human that don't."

"What's all that?" broke in Roehl, striving to catch the mumbled words.

"Nothing at all," growled Kin.

"You're right — partly right, Kin," spoke up Olive, whose keener ears had caught the drift of his revery. "It isn't worth it. That's why I'm going to clear Robby and you, here and now, by tell—"

"Telling what, Miss?" prompted the chief as a vehement interruption from Kin checked her.

"Oh, she has an idea about the killing," said Hodgers, wearily. "You know how women are, Chief. She heard talk at the Grange, same as you did. And she's got a theory."

"Theory!" snorted Roehl, with true ancestral contempt for woman's brain power. "We aren't bothering with theories, Miss. Teach those to your school kids. We're after facts now. And I'm after that bobtailed collie. I want Judge Frayne to see him and —"

"All right," was Kin's indifferent answer. "Take him along with you — if he'll go. — *Robby!*"

The last word was almost a whisper. A queer intonation went with it, that electrified the collie to lightning alertness. The chief strode forward to grip him by the ruff. Then he yanked back his hand with ludicrous speed. The suddenly slashing jaws had missed the flesh, but had gouged a rent in the thick sleeve of the coat. The chief reached back toward his hip.

"Hold on," suggested Kin, as if tiring of the

258

game. "You can cut out the Western two-gun stuff and save yourself a lawsuit. If you've had enough of this silliness you can stand still and listen to me while I clean up the mystery for you. Suppose I know who did that chicken slaughtering? Well, I know the law of this State, too. Though, from your bluff about a court order to shoot, you don't seem to think I do. Dad read it to me once. The law says if any critter can be proved to have killed livestock, that critter's owner shall be responsible for the cash value of such livestock, 'and shall, if nec'ssary, furnish bond for the future good behavior' of said critter. Nary a word about killing the critter, unless the bond is forfeit or unless he busts loose again or unless he c'n be proved to be an old offender. Is that the law or isn't it?"

"It's —"

"Is that the law or isn't it?" insisted Kin.

"If I can prove —"

"Never mind all that. It's the law and you know it. Now, a critter of mine did this killing. I can't swear to it, but I'm willing to admit it. So I'm willing to pay for the dead fowls, at the law's price of one dollar per head. But as the critter isn't an 'old offender,' I won't have him shot. Nor yet the law can't make me have him shot; so long as I'm willing to put up a reasonable bond for his good conduct. Which same I am. Is that sat'sfactory, Chief?"

"I — I s'pose so," assented Roehl, disgusted to find his opponent had such uncomfortable familiarity with the state's livestock laws.

"Good!" said Kin. "Come out here to the door. Come along, Robby."

In the road, a flock of Hodgers' chickens were sunning themselves. One long-legged old hen was at some distance from the others. Kin pointed her out to Robin Adair.

"Get her, Robby!" he ordered. "*Get* her!"

Like a flash the dog was after the flustered hen. The chase was brief, but it was accompanied by a godless amount of dust-raising and barking and frenzied squawking. The din could have been heard for a quarter-mile. As the dog was about to grab his cornered prey Kin whistled. Robin trotted back to him, vastly elated over his minute of mischief.

"Chief," said Kin, "you've just seen what happens when this dog goes for hens. I leave it to you or to any justice of the peace, whether Robby can be the critter that was able to kill fifty-one chickens and carry most of 'em away, and not have any sound made that could be heard six feet off."

"But you just said —" began the puzzled Roehl.

"I said a critter of mine did the killing. I didn't say Robby was that critter. He isn't. Come along with me, once more."

This time he led the way behind the mill and across the small field back of it. Rounding a big clump of tangled briar rose, he pointed to a wire yard hidden by the shrubbery. Chief Roehl stared, speechless, at the snow-white fox basking fearlessly in the dirt of the yard's flooring.

Olive Madden had followed, as perplexed as Roehl himself. Now, at sight of the fox, she cried out in amaze. But before she could speak, Kin was pattering forth his story.

"This fox came from up around Hudson Bay," he explained, profoundly, to Roehl. "He got loose a fortnight ago. But I caught him, this morning. And I'm ready to gamble he can't ever get loose from the pen I've fixed for him, now. Likely enough, while he was loose, he did all that chicken-killing. I'll admit he did, sooner'n stand suit. I'll pay for the chickens, and I'll drop down to Judge Frayne's, this afternoon, and sign a bond for his good behavior and safe-keeping in future. I'll meet you there, at two o'clock. Now if you've gawped at the critter long enough, just let me remind you you're on my property without a warrant, and ask you to chase off'n it. That's all. Good-by."

Almost by force he hustled the dumfounded Roehl out of the yard, keeping up a volley of loud talk which drowned out Olive's repeated efforts to speak. Shutting the gate behind the officer, Kin turned back into the yard and faced his other guest.

"Well," he said, sullenly, "it was the only way out. I caught him in that trap of mine, this morning. In a week or so I'll make you a present of my white fox. So you'll have your precious pet back, all right, all right, and no harm done. After that it'll be up to *you* to keep him safe. I might 'a' been a measly hero and let Robby take the blame. Or I might 'a' done a passel of other fine things. But it seems to me I did the only *sensible* thing that was to be done. I've saved the fox, you set such store by. And I've saved Robby. And I —"

"And you've lost fifty-one dollars," she reminded him. "Or at least you would lose it if I didn't send you a check for it the minute I get home; as I'm going to. But, oh, thank you a billion times for —"

"Oh, that's all right," he muttered, ungraciously, adding, as he turned toward the house: "Not wanting to hurry you, but I'm due to eat. And it's time for your own lunch. So don't let me detain you any longer. Next week I'll send the fox down to you with a letter giving him to you, and —"

"You're right," she said, abruptly. "It *is* lunch time. What are you going to eat?"

"A slice of bread," he answered, wondering at the question, "and a hunk of cold pork, and a pickle."

"You are not," she contradicted, with much decision. "You are going to have scrambled eggs and broiled ham and buttered toast and a cup of coffee and some berries. That is what *I* am going to have, too. Show me where the things are kept, and then sit down on the porch there while I get lunch ready. If you really want to do something worth while, you might even shave while you're waiting. I won't be long."

Stupidly he stared at her, unbelieving, his mind a blank. Then his bulging eyes seemed to read some impossible message in the far blue depths of hers. For he came to life with a galvanic start and a gasp.

"Likewise," he dictated, breathlessly, "we'll have saleratus biscuits and honey! And — and after today I'll have to ask you to wear a — a blue dress and a white apron while you're getting my — *our* — food ready. . . . Robby, I wonder does a marriage license cost as much as a dog license. This afternoon I aim to find out."

XII

"MASCOT!"

Midwestburg was mildly proud of its G.A.R. post. The Memorial Day parade was headed by no fewer than twenty-eight Civil War veterans; each and all of them spry enough to tramp stiffly for the entire half mile from post headquarters above the firehouse, to the cemetery.

True, there were one or two maudlin oldsters in the sidewalk crowds along the line of march who could recall that three hundred and forty-three recruits had gone to training-camp from Midwestburg in the 1860's. But a residue of twenty-eight, after all those decades, was no poor showing.

The *Clarion*'s Memorial Day stories lauded the post's numbers and vigor. And rotogravure sections of several big-city newspapers had brought fine publicity to Midwestburg by using photographs of the marching twenty-eight.

These photos were taken, head on, as the handful of blue-clad and white-headed ancients approached the cemetery. So the pictures were focused on two agèd men, as alike as the hackneyed brace of peas, heading the procession. Be-

264

tween the two strutted vaingloriously a big gold-red collie, brushed and fluffed to perfection of coat and with a tricolor ribbon and the post's official badge dangling from his collar.

Seven years earlier, a seeker for press mention had given the post a mascot — a three-months-old registered collie pup — and had conferred on his gift the memory stirring name of "Antietam." The *Clarion* ran a human interest yarn, along with a half-tone of the puppy. The paper called attention also to the appropriateness of the mascot's name. On the red hill slope above Antietam Creek, in 1862, Midwestburg had lost more men than had any other town in the state.

Now, the G.A.R. post had no keen desire to own a mascot which must be fed and cared for. But, after that splendid newspaper send-off, it could not well reject the offering. The problem became one of face-saving; apart from the cost of the collie's upkeep. And Post Commander H. Abiff Mason called for volunteers.

In a wheezily eloquent speech he pointed out to his twenty-seven myrmidons that the post treasury had no funds for the feeding of a dog, and that its headquarters (shared alternately with three other organizations) had no place for him to live in. He asked that some comrade step forward and pledge himself to assume the care and expense of Antietam's upkeep.

A moment's pause, to an accompaniment of embarrassedly scuffing shoe soles. The twins, Caleb and Ehud Horne, muttered back and forth

265

to each other, in hurried undertone. Then —

"I and Caleb will take on the job of guardeens for little Antietam, here," announced Ehud Horne. "Our own grand old dog died, couple of months back. And it's kind of lonesome, to home, without a purp underfoot all day. We'd like fine to have him. And we'll prodooce him whenever the post has any big doings that calls for a mascot's presence."

A rheumatic multiple flutter of relief, followed by a vote of thanks to Comrades Caleb and Ehud Horne; and the thing was settled. The brothers led the wildly frisking puppy home to the half-portion cottage wherein they had been born and where — except during their war term — both of them had passed the ensuing sixty-seven years.

The Horne twins were as salient features of Midwestburg's life and local color as was the lightning-stabbed steeple of the Second Baptist Church or the ante-Mexican War tavern which had been Abraham Lincoln's abiding-place for the best part of a month.

Between the twins was a strange oneness, bred of some mystic birth-bond quite as much as by propinquity. Neither of them had married. They had spent the best part of their first half-century in tending lovingly their bedridden mother and in scraping together enough money to meet an endless succession of bills for doctors and for nurses and for the other super-costly expenses of invalidism.

After old Mrs. Horne died there was more

cash to spend and less hustling and scrimping. The brothers hit on a fiscal plan which promised to work out well. In turn, a month at a time, each would assume the running of the home; including all expenses, catering and cooking, and every other detail. They were happy, in their own gruffly smug way, and they were incredibly congenial.

If anything could have capped their routine contentment with life it was the advent of their canine ward. They shortened Antietam's name to "Anti," and they made fools of themselves over him.

In spite of the spoiling and the silly adulation that were his, the young collie waxed as stanch and wise as he waxed majestic of aspect. He was one of the rare dogs which develop shiningly in the face of the most indiscreet upbringing. The results of his collie heritage were unflawed by the twins' unwitting efforts at discipline-killing.

He seemed to look on the two old men as might a well-bred child upon doting and loved grandparents, humoring them tenderly, shutting his brain to their absurdities.

The major thrill of Anti's life came yearly, on Memorial Day. Then, groomed to lustrous wonder of coat and adorned with ribbon and badge, he took his place between Ehud and Caleb in the vanguard of the bumpily moving squad of twenty-eight Civil War veterans on the half-mile march from headquarters to cemetery and back.

The pompous throb of fife and drum, the presence and the plaudits of the curb throngs, the snapping of cameras, the indefinable thrill of emotion behind the cheers as the veterans stumped along — these things went to Anti's head. They were the breath of life to him. He reveled in every minute of the march; from the starting signal outside headquarters, on through the clamorously rhythmic journey and the call of Taps above the flag-marked graves; to the puffing and weary dispersal of the twenty-eight on their return to the hall above the firehouse. It was all an unforgettable rapture to Anti.

Strutting, swaggering, on these marches, he paced between the twins, vibrant with drunken pride.

For seven successive Memorial Days Anti led the G.A.R. contingent, with one of his ancient guardians on each side of him. Collie-like, he remembered each parade, throughout the whole year. The annual march was his Moment.

Then came the smash-up.

And like most of the worst smash-ups, it had its rise in a crass triviality. But it twisted the lives of the twins and of their dog.

May of this year was Caleb's month to run the cottage's affairs. One wet morning Ehud awoke with a searing bite of sciatica. All five of his remaining indigenous teeth registered a raging ache. To an accompaniment of groans he limped into the kitchen-dining-room, in a state of mind and body which bred in him all the lovable friendliness of a sick wildcat. There he found Caleb pottering over the range, getting breakfast, and droning cheerily off key the "Battle Hymn of the Republic." Caleb was offensively happy.

Anti trotted forward gaily to greet his co-guardian. Ehud shoved the dog aside with surly gentleness. Vaguely he resented Anti's merry spirit at a time when all existence was an ache-shot horror. He loved the collie too slavishly to resent the frolicking welcome. Yet something or some one must pay for the old man's rheumatic pains. He glowered balefully upon Caleb. Unnoting, Caleb hailed him with:

"Morning, Ehud! Sleep good? There's chipped beef for breakfast."

Then Caleb went on with his off-key droning, while Ehud snarled in virulent ill-will. If there was one dish Ehud abhorred it was chipped beef. His sciatic soul screeched for a vent. Caleb, still bent over the range, chanted:

"He has stomped upon the vineyard where the grapes of wrath is stored.

"He has —"

" 'Taint, neither!" shrilled Ehud, grabbing at the nearest handle to his grievance against the world at large. "And if you got to sing it so out of tune, get the words right, anyhow. Any punkin-head ought to be able to do that much. It's: 'He's *tromped* upon the vineyard.' Tromped. Not stomped. If you couldn't fight no better'n you can sing, you'd never have got that medal from

Congress. Not that you earned it, square. Besides . . . chipped beef ain't fit to feed to a hawg. You know I hate it like pizen. That's why you keep a-having it so often when it's your turn to keep house. I don't eat it none. And you save cash for yourself that way. Moreover, and besides all that —"

He paused, interrupted by a howl from his brother. Turning his head to listen to Ehud's rapid-fire tirade, Caleb had forgotten to turn his hand. Two fingers were burned deep by the range's gas-jets. In mingled physical hurt and mental outrage, Caleb flared into a sputter of speech.

Ehud did not let him finish his first blasting sentence before contributing a further share to the mutual fireworks. For nearly ten minutes the twins brawled in senile fury, while Anti stared from one to the other of them in an impotent frenzy of unhappiness.

Awful things were shrieked quaveringly back and forth. The deeps were churned up, bringing to the befouled surface a dozen forgotten or overlooked grievances; grievances dating from the ante-bellum day when Ehud borrowed Caleb's skates and lost one of them in an air-hole on Gusepple Lake; from the day a few years later when Caleb shot one of Ehud's trained homing pigeons by alleged mistake.

It is the petty beginnings, not the mighty grievances, which rip life-long friendships to shreds. As this hour of idiotic recrimination murdered the sixty-seven-year-old brotherly love between

Ehud and Caleb Horne; and left them snarlingly sharing the same house, but a house that no longer was a home to anyone except the worriedly confused Anti.

For nine days not one word was exchanged between the once-loving brethren. In the heart of each of them the new hatred festered and maturated and spewed internal venom. Then it became needful to break the gangrened silence. Needful, because Memorial Day dawned.

"I'm not marching with you, Caleb," curtly announced Ehud as he came in to the morning meal, wearing his oft-turned old blue uniform and his medals.

"Nor yet me with you, Ehud," retorted Caleb, glancing up with loathing from his work at the kitchen range.

(He was cooking chipped beef for the ninth time since the quarrel, though plethora of the fare had taught him to hate chipped beef as acutely as did Ehud. But he ate it, ever, with vengeful satisfaction, because he was spiting his brother by serving it.)

"How'll we settle it?" grunted Ehud. "Which'll march with Anti, and which'll stay home? I brushed Anti last night and I put the red-white-and-blue ribbon on his collar, and the badge, too. If it wasn't for that, we c'd both stay home. But Anti counts on that Memorial Day parade like human kids count on a circus. I ain't aiming to dis'point him. Neither are you. So which takes him along and which stays here? How'll —"

"S'pose we throw dice for it?" suggested Caleb. "That's fair. One throw. Loser stays to home. Winner goes. And Anti."

"Forgot how we stuck our b'ckgammon board into the garbage-can when we stopped speaking?" Ehud reminded him. "Dice was in it, along with the pieces. How'll we toss dice when we got none to toss? Hey? Just you tell me that, you're so smart!"

"Easy enough. I'll step 'cross the street to McNomee's and borrow the loan of his parchesi dice. Wait, and I'll be back in a minute."

Out onto the handkerchief-sized porch hurried Caleb. Anti frisked along with him. The early sounds of the fife-and-drum rehearsal, in front of the G.A.R. headquarters, a block away, had told the collie what day it was. That and his own ribbon-and-badge adornment. He was trembling with anticipation of the year's event. Perhaps that was why he galloped so heedlessly, barking in plangent excitement, across the street, ahead of the slow-moving Caleb.

Around the corner whizzed a touring car, driven by a young speed maniac. Caleb yelled a shaky warning. But he was an instant too late. At the end of that instant the driver had vanished in a dust-cloud. Behind him in mid-street, two old men jumped up and down like rheumatic patent toys, howling falsetto curses. Behind him, too, in mid-street, lay inert a tumbled mass of fluffy red-gold fur which so lately had been a gloriously living collie.

Slowly, sniveling, and weeping the difficult tears of age, Ehud and his brother bore the limp body indoors and laid it on the kitchen table. Caleb took down the big American flag he had draped over the porch that morning. Reverently he covered with it the pitiful huddle of fur and flesh and bone.

Ehud helped him in the process. During the brief task, the brothers' hands met. So did their wet eyes. Then, across Anti's inert body, their hands met again, and clasped.

"If — if it wasn't for us spatting like two nasty little kids," blubbered Ehud, "he'd be alive. He —"

"Come!" broke in Caleb, briskly, gouging his eyes with his knuckles. "There's the ten-minute signal from the firehouse bell. We c'n bury him — bury him with mil't'ry honors — when — when we get back from the parade. He'd want us to lead the line of march — like we've always done since we had him. We —"

"C'mon!" wept Ehud, his hand stretched out like a blind man's. "C'mon — Cale."

Hand in hand the twins left the desolate cottage and made their way to the firehouse. Fast as they stumbled along, they reached the G.A.R. headquarters barely in time to take their places in the van; before the starting bugle was sounded.

Fife and drum burst into "The Girl I Left Behind Me." Instinctively Caleb and Ehud straightened and set off smartly in step, left foot

273

first. Behind them all but two of the other twenty-six survivors, in fours formation, followed, in rickety correct formation. Post Commander H. Abiff Mason took his wonted position, three paces to the left of the column; while Hiram Tyre, the antique drummer of the company, took up his station, three paces to the right. The march was on.

Caleb and Ehud Horne stepped out dizzily, trying not to cry. Then it was that something smote with soft fervor against them both; throwing them almost off balance and out of step. They glanced down.

Strutting waveringly, yet swaggeringly, between them marched a dust-streaked collie, from whose head a scalp wound still exuded a few drops of blood. From his collar swung the badge of the post and the three-colored bow of ribbon. The twins stared down at Anti in slack-jawed unbelief. Their minds were awhirl, even while olden discipline and habit kept their bodies straight and their tottery feet marching in time to the music.

Anti had no way of telling them the car's fender had smitten his skull a glancing blow, stunning him — that he had come to his senses on the kitchen table, no worse off than is a trained pugilist after a knockout — that he had caught the scent of their footsteps and that he had been guided by the direction of the music — that he had cantered dizzily after them, feeling more like himself at every stride, and had

274

dropped proudly into his wonted place between them almost at the very outset of the parade. To the twins, in their crazy gush of happiness, it was all a heaven-sent miracle.

On the handkerchief-sized porch of the Horne cottage, that noon, sat two old men. Their feet ached. They were tired all through from the double march — a whole mile in all — and from the ceremonies above the graves. But through their hearts surged a happiness that all but choked them. Sprawled drowsing at their feet, in the noonday sunlight, a huge red-gold collie snoozed. Anti had had a deliriously happy morning; a morning of continuous thrills. He was sleeping it off. Ehud said, at last, breaking the happy silence:

"I heard that soprano lady singing the — the Battle Hymn, on the platform. I listened real close."

"So did I," agreed Caleb.

"She must 'a' got the words right," pursued Ehud. " 'Cause she was reading 'em off'n a sheet of print. And in that line we — you — sang — couple weeks back —"

"The word was 'trampled,' " added Caleb, as his twin hesitated. " 'Trampled out.' Not 'Stomped upon.' Nor yet 'Tromped upon.' We — we was both of us —"

"Both of us was wrong," finished Ehud. "Dead wrong. Like we was, from first to last, all through that measly squabble of our'n. Oh, Cale — !"

"Anti likes chipped beef, fine," exclaimed his twin, seized by an inspiration. "Let's go inside and round up all the filthy stuff that's left. And feed it to him. He sure rates it. C'mon! C'mon, Anti. I and Brother is giving you a party."

XIII

MY FRIEND, THE GENTLE MAN-HUNTER

A fourteen-year-old lad, Grover A. Whalen, Jr., was leaving his father's Dobbs Ferry, N.Y., estate, for prep school. This was on September 27, 1935. Early on the day he was to go he made a round of the neighborhood to say good-by to some friends.

And he didn't come back.

The telephones were set to work. No trace of the boy, who had planned to come home an hour earlier. Then the hue-and-cry was raised. The New York City police were notified. So was Troop K of the New York State Police, at Hawthorne Barracks.

Official motorcycles whizzed questingly in every direction. Folk were questioned. Cars were examined. Telephone lines were tapped. Neighbors turned out to dragnet the woods and hills. All the law's mighty machinery was in action. The hunt was vehement. And the hunt was futile.

There was no reason to think Grover had run away. There was every reason to think he might have been kidnapped. His father was wealthy, prominent, famed as a greeter of celebrities landing in New York; a man who might well have roused vengeful vows in crooks he had assailed during the years when he was Police Commissioner.

The web of the police was spread far and wide. And the web of the police caught nothing in its costly meshes. The Whalen boy had vanished as wholly as if he had dematerialized.

Then it occurred to the authorities, as a last and possibly hopeless resort, to listen to the urgent plea of an athletic young giant in uniform. This athlete — Captain Christopher Kemmler, of Troop K, New York State Police — said over and again that the kennels in the troop's Hawthorne, N.Y., barracks contained three bloodhounds which never yet had failed to track down their quarry. He begged that they be allowed a part in the chase.

Permission was given. This, after many hours had passed and after countless clumping human feet had been allowed to stamp out or confuse any possible trail. Kemmler telephoned a curt command to the barracks. As fast as a state car could carry them, Troopers William Horton and George Gaydica were at the Whalen house. In the car's tonneau lounged a brace of unspectacular dogs. One was rufous. The other was black and tan.

They were Red and Queenie (good friends of mine, by the way), smallish in stature, friendly of heart and of aspect, with ridiculously long lop ears and hanging dewlaps. Each wore a black leather harness with a greenish three-foot woven leash. A trooper was holding to the far end of each leash.

The two hounds wagged their tails pleasantly as they blinked at the crowd. They were as different from the bloodhounds of stage and of fiction as Charlie Chaplin differs from Attila the Hun. Nobody possibly could be afraid of these two peaceful brutes. And nobody was supposed to be.

A coat of young Grover's and a pair of his shoes were brought from the house and were handed to Captain Kemmler. The captain held these personal effects in front of Red and Queenie. Gravely, both hounds sniffed at coat and shoes, as a detective might study some pictured face with a view to memorizing it.

During the sniffing process they lost their air of impersonal friendliness. Both were intent on what lay before them. Then, heavy muzzles to the earth, they cast about. Presently, through all that maze of alien footsteps, they struck the boy's trail. Gaydica and Horton leaned back on the thick leashes to keep from being pulled off their feet.

The hunt was on.

Finally Red and his mate stopped short, midway on a path which ran atop a culvert at the edge of a ravine. Still with nostrils to earth, the hounds plunged over the almost clifflike side of the gulch.

At the bottom they looked pityingly down at a huddled body, hidden in underbrush.

Human hunters had passed and repassed that spot again and again. They had seen nothing, sensed nothing. But the dogs had found at once what they had been sent to seek.

Young Whalen had been walking the clifftop path when his foot had slipped. He had plunged to the bottom of the ravine. There his skull had crashed against a jut of rock. And there, but for the two hounds, he might still be lying. For he was helpless and in grave need of medical care.

Later, I paid a visit to the two sleuth-hounds who saved the Whalen boy, and to their sad-eyed old kennelmate, Hamlet. And I pumped questions into Captain Christopher Kemmler.

When the trio of man-hunters accepted me willingly as a friend, Captain Kemmler thawed out a bit and talked without restraint of his hounds, which are also his life hobby.

"I have worked with other breeds," he told me. "But I like bloodhounds best. Several kinds of trackers may be almost as good, but some of them are likely to be vicious. I don't care to set dogs on the trail of some lost child or of someone whose mind is wandering, and then to have them wind up the chase by biting chunks out of the person they have run to earth. Our bloodhounds never do that."

He laid a hand on the black-and-tan head of Queenie. She wriggled with pride at her master's singling her out.

"Now, Queenie, here," he expounded, "has different ideas from Red and Hamlet. Her methods aren't theirs. Sometimes she is invaluable in a chase. Sometimes the two others are worth ten of her. Here's the idea (and it applies to the ways different bloodhounds do their work):

"Let Queenie out on a trail and she sniffs around till she strikes the tracks of some one she decides to go after. Then she runs that person down, no matter how long or how hard the trip may be. Sometimes it's the right person. But sometimes it isn't. That's why she's splendidly useful in many cases, and why she is useless in others.

"But if we let Red and Hamlet loose they won't bother to cast about for any trail at all, till they have some piece of clothing held to their noses. Then they'll sniff at that, to register the odor, and they start out to locate it. They won't turn aside for any other track — human or animal — till they run down the scent they have been put on.

"We've had these three dogs here, in service, less than a year. They were an experiment. The experiment has been a big success. In ten months they have discovered more than a dozen lost persons — mostly children — who were still alive when they found them, and who might not have stayed alive if they hadn't been found. They have trailed almost as many people who — who weren't alive when the trail ended.

"I don't want to use names. In the Whalen case we had to. For that story had 'broken' before our dogs were called into use. But most people don't like to have the names of their crazy or suicidal friends put into print, when those friends stray from home. So I ask you not to use names, in the case or two that I am going to tell you about. If you think I am stringing you, you are at liberty to verify what I say.

"There was a sick old woman" [naming the unfortunate and the place], "last December, who wandered away from home while she was out of her mind. We were called in. We took Queenie and Hamlet ('Ham,' we call him; he belongs to the famous Leon Whitney, who trained him) to look for her. Both hounds led us through woods and into steep ravines and over hills, to the Croton Reservoir. At the brink, side by side, they came to a standstill.

"Queenie, here, sniffed at the bank. Then she lapped at the water — she had had a long run — then she lay down beside Sergeant Charles LaForge, who was on the other end of her leash. Her 'share in the evening's entertainment was at an end.' But Hamlet plunged into the reservoir, yanking the leash out of Trooper Gaydica's hand. He swam around and around in a circle, about twenty-five feet from shore, till he was worn out. Even then he didn't want to come back to the bank at my command.

"That night there was a sharp freeze. Next morning the ice on the reservoir was too thick for smashing through. But on the first day in the spring when the ice was gone, men dragged with nets and hooks, from the spot where the dogs had halted at the water's edge. They found the woman's body, caught in the mud, twenty-five feet from shore.

"Another time, a few months ago, an insane man was missing. We let 'Ham' and Red smell a shirt of his. Off they went after him. By and by they dragged us to a house. The people who lived there declared they never had seen the missing man. But the hounds tore through the house and out of the back door.

"A long distance farther on they came to his body. He had killed himself.

"We cross-questioned the people in the house and we broke down their denial. By-and-by we made them admit the poor demented man had run into their house and through it.

"This use of bloodhounds by Troop K is an experiment several communities are watching closely. Police officials from two other states" [which he named] "have been studying our methods at first hand. They are planning to buy bloodhounds. They want it kept secret for a while.

"About four times a week I send some man in a car to a distant bit of country. There I have him get out and walk for several miles in a twisty zigzag course. The next day or the next night (at night we use flashlights, so as to accustom our hounds to the glare and the uncertainty of them)

I let out the three bloodhounds at the place where he left his car or his motorcycle, and I give them some article of his clothing to smell. Off they go, with a trooper hanging to the leash of each of them.

"I arrange always that the hunted man shall be at the end of the trail, with a slice of raw liver to pay the dogs for their work. Never do they fail to find him, no matter how he may have tried to confuse his tracks. That form of training keeps the hounds fit and on edge. And it costs us nothing, except an eighth of a pound of liver."

A State Police bloodhound, a few years ago, solved a "lost child" mystery that had a gruesomely different ending from the Whalen case — a mystery that paralleled in its chief details the Lindbergh tragedy. The story is worth your reading.

At 2 A.M. on June 1, 1920, Mrs. George H. Coughlin, of Norristown, Pa., woke with the involuntary cry:

"What does God want with me?"

She thought she had been dreaming. She and her husband settled down once more to sleep. Less than half an hour later she was waked again. This time with an impression of hearing a child's muffled cry and the tinkle of glass.

Her thirteen-month-old baby son, Blakeley, slept in the next room. He was getting over a bad cold. Vaguely worried, Mrs. Coughlin sent her husband into the nursery to make certain Blakeley was all right.

The crib was empty. The top of a ladder showed above the sill of the open window.

Followed the usual ghastly weeks of police search and of false clues and of increasingly threatening ransom notes. At last the kidnapper ordered the Coughlins to drop a package containing $6,000 from a window of the Atlantic City Flyer, between Philadelphia and Egg Harbor, on a given afternoon. Coughlin was to scan the track until he should see a white sheet tied between two trees somewhere along the line. Just beyond this sheet he was to toss out the money.

Some minutes ahead of the Flyer that afternoon a shabby-looking special train was sent out. It was full of plain-clothes policemen and state troopers. At various "zones" on the journey men got out and vanished into the woods. In one corner of the special's rear car sat Corporal John Russell, of the Pennsylvania State Police's Troop A. Between his knees stood a leggy and dismal reddish bloodhound, Commissioner by name. A dog destined to make criminal history that day.

At the edge of a long stretch of marshy woodland, a mile or so from a way station, a smear of white showed against the green foliage. It was the signal sheet, hung between two trees. The special train thudded on for another mile and around a curve. Then it came to a jarring stop. The horde of plain-clothes men jumped to the ground, Commissioner yanking at his leash and whimpering. They plunged into the woods, making in a semicircle for the spot where they had seen the sheet.

Most of them reached their chosen hiding-places before the Flyer was due to arrive. But Corporal Russell and his hound were delayed a few minutes by the swamp they blundered into.

Then the Atlantic City flyer whizzed by. Just after it had gone past the sheet, a package was tossed to the trackside from an open window of one of the cars.

The trap was set.

Presently the crouching plain-clothes men in the woods saw a man stroll along the railroad right of way. The stranger glanced idly at the money package. But he did not stoop to pick it up. He sauntered on. Then he hesitated and turned back. What next he may have planned to do was not done. For he caught a glimpse of one of the hidden watchers in the undergrowth. He wheeled about as if to bolt. And another policeman grabbed him from behind. The posse closed in.

That seemed to be all the good it was going to do them. The trap had sprung. But was anything caught between its jaws? The man had not touched the package of money. He might be, as he declared, an innocent passer-by. He denied all knowledge of the sheet. He said he had not so much as seen it, still less hung it to the trees. He behaved, in fact, as any harmless pedestrian might who suddenly is surrounded by a bunch of detectives.

Then it was that Commissioner came up, dragging Corporal Russell at his heels. The mud-splashed dog was panting and crooning with eagerness. Straight to the sheet Russell guided him, without going within many yards of the prisoner. The red hound smelled long and thoughtfully at various parts of the sheet, especially where hands had been busy tying its corners to the trees.

As soon as he had established the scent to his own satisfaction, Commissioner dashed away. Straight through the clump of police he ran. He halted in front of the prisoner, rising on his hindlegs and bracing both splayed forepaws on the man's chest. Then he waked the echoes with a bugle-voiced long-drawn bay of triumph. His work was done.

Where trained human wits had failed to establish a link between the captive and the signal sheet, one sad-eyed, lop-eared old red bloodhound had forged that link past all chance of breaking.

After weeks of police grilling the prisoner, August Pascal, broke down and confessed. He had stolen little Blakeley Coughlin from the crib. Blakeley had begun to cry. Pascal had swathed the child's head and face tightly in a coat, to stifle the sound. He stifled not only the sound, but the baby as well. Blakeley smothered to death. Pascal threw his weighted body into a river.

The kidnapper got off with a sentence of life imprisonment. But for the genius of one reddish old bloodhound he might perhaps have gone free.

A little girl wandered from her home in the Kentucky foothills. She had been seen last at the edge of a deep pond. After police and neighbors had hunted everywhere for twenty-seven hours, Captain V. G. Mullikin was sent for; to bring his best bloodhound into the search, on a "cold scent." At midnight, Mullikin and his hound came to the edge of the pond wherein the lost baby's body was supposed to be lying.

With a sniff of contempt for such a theory, the hound made for a wooded hill in the distance. Mullikin and the father followed as best they could. Presently they tripped over a tree root in the darkness and fell. The hound jerked the leash from his master's grip and forged on alone.

Half an hour later Mullikin and the father came up with him standing above a new-wakened little girl, whose arms were tight about his shaggy neck. The formidable man-hunter was licking her face and trying to comfort her. Truly an anti-climax scene for those to whom "bloodhound" is a name of terror!

I think it is this name, "bloodhound," which has given its bearer his undeserved repute for savagery. Yet the name's origin was harmless enough. When a wounded deer or other game, centuries ago, escaped from the ring of the encircling killer dogs, leaving a trail of blood, this breed of hound was brought up; to trace the gory trail to its maker's final place of refuge. Hence the term "bloodhound," or "blood-tracking hound."

Harriet Beecher Stowe and her imitators added vastly to the grim ill-fame of my pal, the bloodhound, by making him chase innocent folk. If Eliza and her child had but paused in their hopping flight across the ice-cakes of the Ohio River, long enough for the bloodhounds to catch up with them, they might have found the terrible four-legged trackers the nicest playmates on all the length and breadth of the stream. From the entire pack they would have received less physical hurt than from a single hungry anopheles mosquito.

Long years ago, I forgathered with the immortal "Chaplain McCabe," the Yankee prisoner who first made popular "The Battle Hymn of the Republic" by teaching his fellow captives in Libby Prison to sing it as a rollicking chorus; in 1863. McCabe told me a secret confided to him by an ancient negro slave; when the rumor spread that bloodhounds would be used in tracking down any Union soldiers who might escape from Libby.

"Fill yo' pocket wiv red peppah, Pahson," counseled the negro, from long experience in such escapes. "Spatteh some of it along de groun' behine yo'! De blood-dog he gwine folleh, sniffity-sniff-sniff! An' when he sniff up de fus' noseful of dat red peppeh, he gwine f'get all 'bout yo'. He ain' even gwine 'member deah's

289

any Civil Wah a-goin' on, a-tall; poo' suff'rin' cuss!"

Hideous treatment for a friendly dog! A hound whose sole motive in catching up with his prey seems to be a craving to enroll such prey among his human pals.

The tabloid saga of another historic brace of bloodhounds, and I am done. They belonged to Dr. J. B. Fulton, of Pueblo, Colorado. They flourished in the first few years of the twentieth century, though their exploits are local legends to this day. They were X-Ray and his mate, Jo Jo. Never did they turn aside by a hair's breadth from a trail, once they had struck it. They followed it to victory. For example:

In 1903 a burglar was looting the neighborhood of Oneida, Kansas. Dr. Fulton and his two dogs were summoned. The burglar heard the hounds were coming. He knew their miraculous tracking prowess. He decided this was no part of the country for him to linger in. So he stole a horse and buggy, and he drove at top speed for the state line.

When the hounds and their master reached Oneida, the only clue available was a currycomb that had been used for a long time in grooming the stolen horse. X-Ray and Jo Jo sniffed it, and recorded the scent of the horse it had massaged. Then they set off. For nearly one hundred and fifty miles they followed the trail, pausing only for short rests and for food. The long run ended at Elwood, Kansas. There they caught up with their man.

Jo Jo's self-imposed rule never to swerve from the track of any fugitive had grim results. A year or so after the chase for the burglar and the stolen horse, Dr. Fulton put her on the trail of an escaping thief. This was at Pueblo. The fugitive had crossed a railroad trestle above a wide gorge.

Nose to the track, Jo Jo followed her quarry's footsteps. An express train roared out onto the trestle in front of her. She had plenty of time to shrink to one side or the other. But that was not Jo Jo's way when she was on the trail. She knew her job. Straight ahead she loped, hot on the scent; until the locomotive hit her and crushed her to death.

Perhaps many a human has died less gloriously in the shining pursuit of duty.

XIV

"ALL IN THE DAY'S WORK"

The auburn setter stood disconsolate for a moment in the cellar whither his wrathful mistress had banished him. The dank dimness of the room was echoing still to the vicious bang she had given its door when she thrust the dog into his prison.

Harking back to his earliest puppyhood, Rusty could call to memory a horde of babyish sins for which he had been punished, in order to turn him into a decent canine citizen. But he had no faintest idea what fault he had committed, this day, that he should be scolded and then locked ignominiously into the cellar.

Rusty hated the cellar. It was a loathsome place. Moreover, it was associated with punishment.

And, after all, what fault had he committed? This morning, when he had been let out before breakfast, he had gone as usual over the hedge fence into Vance Calvert's back garden; there to romp with his beloved comrade, Rags, Vance's big mongrel.

A thousand times he and Rags had played together. Between them there was one of those oddly devoted chumships which sometimes spring up between two dogs. Again and again he and Rags had snoozed side by side on the moon-drenched porch of Fay Lanning's home in the spring evenings, while Fay and Vance sat needlessly close together, talking.

Last night, for instance, Rusty and Rags had snoozed thus in drowsy content on the porch, until they had been awakened by the grating change of tone in the two human voices. With a dog's psychic sense they had realized that their deities suddenly were at odds.

Thus Vance had gotten to his feet and had departed for his own home, Rags frisking along at the glum man's side. Fay had gone indoors, calling Rusty to follow her. There, to the setter's dismay, his self-controlled mistress had sunk down on a hall chair and had wept hysterically.

He had been wild with sympathy and he had sought to thrust his cold nose between her tight-pressed hands and to lick her face. But she had pushed him away and run up to her own room.

This morning, midway in his romp with Rags, she had called angrily to him. Then she had shut him by force into this abominable cellar.

Rusty looked unhappily around him. And as he looked his unhappiness vanished. Before him was an absurdly simple means of escape.

Coal had been dumped into the cellar the day before. The window had been left open. A scrambling rush up the steep and shifting hill of black fragments and Rusty was out through the window. He was free.

Instantly he beheld Rags, dancing forward to greet him. When Fay had called Rusty to her, Rags had followed. She had slammed the front door in his face. But a far stronger hint would have been needed to show the friendly big mongrel he no longer was welcome where so long he had been an accepted guest.

Like Mary's pseudo-historic lamb, Rags had "waited patiently about," even when Fay opened the front door again and ordered him sternly away. And now his wait was rewarded. Rusty had joined him again.

The two dogs touched noses. Then both of them caught sight of a neighbor's cat which was stalking an oriole at the other end of the lawn. With a gay rush the comrades charged the cat.

The cat scrambled up an elm, her tail swollen to double its normal size. From the lowest branch crotch she spat right virulently down at her pursuers; as they circled the tree at a gallop, to an accompaniment of plangent barks and of futile leaps at the trunk.

They were having a beautiful time, even if the cat was not.

The din brought Fay Lanning to an upper window. She stared unbelievingly down at her supposedly imprisoned setter and at the disreputable mongrel.

Once more she sallied forth. Seizing Rusty by the scruff of the neck, she dragged him indoors, scolding him as they went. Rags trotted alongside, much concerned at his friend's plight and seeking to soften Fay's heart by patting playfully at her white skirt with his muddy paws.

Fay thrust the setter into the house. Rags prepared to follow. She turned on him fiercely, driving him from the porch. To reinforce her act of eviction, she picked up a small stone and threw it in his general direction.

The stone was not tossed with any force; as it was designed only to make Rags run home, and not to injure him. It missed its large and furry mark by several feet.

Ricocheting from the lawn grass, it smote the treed cat lightly on the side just as pussy had ventured to descend to earth again after her climb into the elm. The impact of the pebble would not have bruised a mouse. But it sent the cat scuttling indignantly homeward. Rags beheld her irate flight and merrily he gave chase.

Fay went indoors again. There she found that Rusty had gone to the cellar, for once, of his own accord, and had escaped again through the coal window.

The setter joined Rags in the futile chase of the stonestruck cat. As the latter dived for safety under her owner's veranda, on the far side of the wide suburban street, the two dogs trotted off to the woods together for a rabbit-hunt. It was nightfall before they came back to their respective homes, happily tired, and coated with swamp mud and with clots of burrs.

Meantime, several things had happened.

Ten minutes after the episode of the cat, Fay Lanning received a hand-delivered note from a neighbor who lived directly across the broad suburban street and whom the whole neighborhood disliked. The note ran:

DEAR MISS LANNING:

With my own eyes, just now, I saw something I would not have wanted to believe on hearsay. I had come out of the house to look for darling little Fluffy, to give her her morning milk. I was in time to see you hurl a rock at her, striking her with cruel force. Then I saw you set Mr. Calvert's detestable mongrel dog on her and then your own red setter.

Fluffy managed to escape from their murderous attack, terribly injured though she was by the wound from the rock you flung at her. She is almost delirious from pain and fright.

I have telephoned the veterinary. If he finds her injuries are as serious as I know they are, I shall not only notify the S.P.C.A., but consult my lawyer. I have never witnessed, nor even imagined, such an instance of cold-blooded brutality toward a helpless dumb creature.

Very truly,
LUELLA V. TODD
(MRS. K. JACKLYN TODD.)

Through her natural ill-temper at the letter and its crazy misinterpretation of the cat's adventures, Fay Lanning was aware of a great and growing sense of worry.

No suburbanite or country dweller needs to be told that more rural neighborhood disputes and trouble and general ill-feeling are caused by live-stock than by all other local mishaps put together. And here was a quarrelsome woman who might well be able to make the court or the S.P.C.A. believe that Fay Lanning had actually stoned a harmless cat half to death and then had set fierce dogs on the stricken creature. The story would look ugly in print. There might be heavy cash damages to pay. At the very least, the foundations were laid solidly for a perpetual neighborhood feud.

A new turn of thought shifted Fay's perturbation to anger.

It was all Vance Calvert's fault! Yes, the whole thing could be traced directly back to him. If he had not behaved so abominably, the night before, Fay would not have been urged to drive his worthless mongrel from her grounds. No stone would have been thrown. No cat would have been hit. Hence there would have been no trouble with that loathly Mrs. K. Jacklyn Todd.

The logic was irrefutable. It was as clear as crystal. Vance Calvert was to blame, and nobody but Vance Calvert. It was just the kind of thing she might have expected from such a man.

Her righteous indignation against the miscreant was too tense to permit of delay in expressing it. Besides, note-writing is infectious. Fay sat down and began to scribble. Then she sent her letter across to the Calvert house by the Lanning man-of-all-work.

That evening, Vance came home from his law-office in the city, hot and tired from a strenuous day's work. On the porch he was met ecstatically by an equally hot and tired mongrel, whose furry coat was miry and burr-crusted and whose nose was scratched by briars.

Indoors, on the hall table, Vance saw Fay Lanning's note. A tender smile touched the corners of his mouth as he tore open the envelope.

"Poor little sweetheart!" he muttered to himself. "She's sorry she behaved so rottenly to me last night, and she's writing to say so. I'll chase over there, on the jump."

He had started for the front door, on this mission of reconciliation, before his eyes fell on the first lines of the letter. Then he stopped short in his tracks, and read:

DEAR MR. CALVERT:

I am writing to ask — to demand — that you keep your mongrel cur off our premises. He is a neighborhood pest; what with tormenting defenceless cats, and so forth. Everyone knows that. Including Mrs. Todd.

But my personal complaint against him is that he comes here and lures my setter, Rusty, to run away with him, and that he tramps his muddy feet all over our veranda, and that he has just ruined a new white skirt of mine with those same muddy feet.

Besides, when strangers pass by our home I don't want them to see an ugly mongrel there and to carry away the false idea that we would harbor such a dog. It is humiliating.

When I ventured to say very courteously to you last evening that a thoroughbred dog (like Rusty, for example) always has far more beauty and intelligence and better manners than any mere cross-breed can hope to have, you flew into a fit of temper at this supposed slur on your dog, and thus you showed me once and for all the true nature of the man I had once been so foolish as to consent to marry.

In the conversation that followed you said things I shall try to forget.

Enough of that. My letter is solely for the purpose of warning you to keep your dog off our land and off our porch. I think you will not need to be told again that the same request applies to yourself.

Very truly,
FAY LANNING

Normally Vance Calvert had a level head. If he had not been a lover, he would have laughed delightedly at this bit of ludicrous babyish crankiness.

But he *was* a lover — an ardent lover. The silly letter plunged him into utter despair. His whole world lay in ashes. The future stretched out before him dreary and barren as a rainy sea.

Fay had not repented of her idiotic behavior of the preceding night. Worse, she was now insulting him and the dog that was his pal, and was ordering both of them to keep off her father's land. It was terrible; a deathblow.

(Let him who never has made a fool of himself during the drunkenly dizzy era of first love sneer at the disconsolate Vance.)

Rags sensed his master's unhappiness and pressed close to him, thrusting his great honest head into the man's inert palm.

"She doesn't want us around, old friend," said Vance, stroking the dog's lopping ears. "She's done with us, both of us. We're — we're *out!*"

The next morning Vance awoke early. He would have sworn he had not slept a wink all night. To clear his head for his long workday in town he set off at sunrise for a hike through the woods and over the hills.

As always, Rags danced joyously about him, thrilling at the prospect of a walk. The mongrel's gay barks split the early-morning stillness of the pretty suburb.

The barks did more. They reached the sleeping setter, Rusty, on his mat in the Lanning front hallway. They bore him a message that brought him instantly to his feet.

For there is as wide a difference between the various kinds of dog barks as between the inflections of human speech. To Rusty this hail of Rags' told of expectancy, of fun, of adventure, and it seemed to extend a welcome to all the world to join therein.

Through the kitchen darted Rusty, and thence to the swing door that led down to the celler. In another five seconds he was slithering up the coal pile toward the open cellar window that had served him so well yesterday.

Before Vance Calvert and Rags had traversed a quarter mile of their hike, Rusty had not only caught their trail, but was ranging alongside, his feathered tail awag, his topaz eyes alight.

Vance stopped short, perplexed as to the new angle which Rusty's arrival had put on the situation. If Fay should chance to learn that her setter had joined him and Rags on their tramp, might she not well believe that the crime-smeared Vance had coaxed her dog from home and taken him along with him, in order to spite her?

On the other hand, if he should escort Rusty back to his owner's veranda and tie him there, he would be breaking her cruel command not to trespass. She might even see him, from a window, stealing away, across the lawn, and she might draw the inference that he had been spending the night in penitence under her casement.

That would be infinitely the worst thing that could happen. Vance started on again, both dogs gamboling in front of him. Their hearts were as jubilant as his was shattered.

But it is hard to remain a Blighted Being; when one is breasting steep hills at sunrise, with two dogs for comrades, and with the dawn wind in one's face. Before he realized what he was doing, Vance Calvert had begun to whistle. He broke off in this, to shout encouragement to the two dogs as they tore away in pursuit of a rabbit which bounced out of a thicket just ahead of them.

Suddenly Vance realized, to his horror, that he was having a good time. Aghast, he fought his way back to a mood wherein he had been picturing the fickle Fay Lanning as weeping at his deathbed, and himself whispering words of divine forgiveness to the heartbroken penitent.

Still more to his dismay, he found the brisk five-mile hike had given him a most unromantic appetite for his breakfast.

Fay Lanning had awakened, wretchedly unhappy, from a night of broken sleep. As she came out on the porch to call the mysteriously absent Rusty into the house, she paused horror-struck.

From where she stood she had an excellent view of the Calvert house beyond the hedge fence which separated the two modest estates. At least it was an excellent view for anyone who might care to look in that direction. This, Fay vowed sternly she would not do. This, then, she did.

And she was just in time to see her recreant ex-*fiancé* going indoors from his walk. More, she saw him stoop to pat Rusty and Rags just before he went in. There could be no doubt both dogs had been his companions on the hike.

When Rusty ambled carelessly home to his

302

own breakfast his mistress eyed him with cold aversion.

He was her pal. She had reared him from puppyhood. She had done everything for him. And now this four-footed auburn-coated Benedict Arnold had gone over to the enemy.

He had sneaked off — or had permitted himself to be coaxed off — for a jolly tramp through the hills with the man who was her sworn enemy; the scoundrel whose vile conduct had broken her heart, the miscreant who had not even had the decency to add fuel to her resentment by writing an irate letter at once in reply to her stinging epistle of the day before.

Rusty had a vague sense of being in disgrace. He did not in the least know why. But being a dog, and with all a dog's wondrous friendliness, he sought pathetically to make friends with his icy mistress.

He brought her the morning paper — an exploit which almost always earned him a word of praise — and then he brought her his ball, in case she should crave a romp. Last of all, he pattered up to her room. Thence, one by one, he brought down to her both of her bedroom slippers.

All in vain. Not a word or a glance would she bestow on him or on his offerings. These humans were strange folk. There was no understanding them. All day the aloofness continued, and all day Rusty was puzzled and sad because of it.

But next morning Fay had thawed enough to

303

whistle him to join her in a walk. This to the setter's wild rapture. He felt himself forgiven at last for the sin, whatever it might be, that had estranged him from her for a whole day.

It was Sunday. Every bright Sabbath, for months, directly after early church, Fay and Vance had gone together for a jaunt through the primitive country which crowded almost up to the suburb's one long street. Always, both dogs had gone along. It had been a continuous gala occasion.

Today, Rusty peered expectantly toward the Calvert house, in search of Vance and of Rags. But Fay spoke abruptly to him and she set off in the direction opposite to that which she and Vance always had taken.

With a defiance she found ever harder to maintain Fay strode down the street and toward the country. She yearned to look back over her shoulder, to see if Vance and Rags by any chance were in the offing. If they were, she would toss her head haughtily and hurry on. Indeed, she practiced the gesture, and she tried to make herself believe it had not more the air of a nod of invitation to follow.

But whatever it resembled, the toss of the head was thrown away; so far as Vance Calvert was concerned. For he and Rags had started on their Sunday walk a full fifteen minutes earlier.

Lest Fay Lanning might think he was trailing her, if she too should take a Sunday stroll through their olden haunts, Vance had chosen

304

deliberately the direction opposite to their usual road. Gloomily he plodded along, his heart full of bitter memories of earlier Sabbath rambles.

Rags was enjoying it all. He was fairly bubbling with high spirits. In vain he tried to make his master join in the fun. But for once Calvert was oblivious to his mongrel chum's blandishments.

Indeed, he himself was getting so little pleasure from the walk that presently he turned back. One might as well stay at home and read, as undergo such a bristle of sore memories.

Vance had crossed the railroad track, just beyond Hairpin Curve, and had begun to mount Panther Hill when this resolve came to him. Rags had cantered on ahead, in chase of a squirrel. The squirrel refused to play fair, and resorted to the unsportsmanly tactics of climbing a tree; even as had Mrs. Todd's cat.

Wherefore the dog was less averse to obeying his owner's call and of retracing his way than he would have been if the squirrel had stayed manfully on the ground. Obediently, if with no great zest for this curtailing of his hike, the big young dog trotted in his master's wake on the homeward stretch.

Then, as they neared the railroad track again, Rags pricked up his lopping ears and bounded forward. A girl and a dog had come in view, moving toward them.

By scent, sooner than by sight, Rags recognized his dear playfellow, Rusty. So they four were going to have their happy Sunday afternoon walk together, after all! Rags galloped across the track to greet the setter. His clubbed tail was wagging furiously. He was a picture of canine joy.

It was then that Fay Lanning caught sight of the oncoming Rags and, behind him, of the slower-moving Calvert.

Her ruse to avoid meeting him had had the effect of bringing them together. She was sharply vexed at the unbidden throb of happiness at her heart on sight of Vance. The man would think she had followed purposely, that she had thrown herself deliberately in his way!

She came to a quick standstill. Rusty had started to brush past her, to meet the advancing Rags. Fay caught the setter by the ruff and held him. Rags came bounding up. She made a forbidding gesture at him with the light walking-stick she carried.

She meant the motion to be only monitory. But Rags was coming on like a clumsy hurricane. The girl misjudged the distance and the force of her movement. The stick smote the happily capering mongrel painfully and hard, full across the face.

Rags shrank back at this blow from a girl who always had been so friendly to him. Vance Calvert caught his breath ragingly. Then he called the mongrel to him; and turned toward the roadside woods as if to get himself and his dog out of the girl's path.

Rags came at the summons, head and tail

adroop. The blow hurt his face, and still worse it hurt his sensitive feelings. He was glad to go to his master for comfort and reassurance.

It was then that the electric train swung around Hairpin Curve. It made no sound that could be heard above the babble of the near-by creek and of the summer wind in the tops of the trees. It was moving fast, to make up for an earlier delay.

Poor Rags had just ambled to the very middle of the railroad track, in response to Vance's recall, when the train struck him. There was a single frightened yelp. Then the big furry body hurtled through the air like some grotesque bundle. Straight forward it was flung. And it fell directly athwart the track, just ahead of the train.

The engineer jammed his brakes on, belatedly. But there was no earthly chance of his coming to a halt before the foremost wheels should cut the dog's big body in three.

Vance flung himself forward at top speed. But he was much too far away to be of use. Fay screamed, and ran futilely toward the body huddled so lifelessly there in midtrack. The third spectator had not waited for orders. As the train had tossed Rags into the air, Rusty had wrenched himself free from the girl's detaining grasp on his ruff and had gone into action.

There was a flaming auburn streak that flashed onto the track, under the very nose of the train. Without checking that whirlwind rush, the setter stooped and caught Rag's limp body by the middle of the back, and plunged onward, half dragging, half carrying the heavy inert weight.

The engineer evidently changed his mind about stopping for a mere dog. For the train thudded past.

For a moment, Fay Lanning stood alone on the hither side of the track, as the cars slid in front of her. Dreadingly, she scanned the rails for signs of what perhaps had been a double slaying.

Then, after what seemed a century, the train was gone and she could see the road just beyond it.

On the ground, still in that unnatural huddle, lay Rags. Above him stood Rusty, sniffing at the chum for whom he had risked his own bright life.

In the road sat Vance Calvert, holding Rags' head in his lap. The man's lean face was working as he stared in dumb grief at the motionless creature that had been his adoring comrade and slave.

"Oh, Vance!" sobbed the girl, throwing herself on her knees beside man and dog. *"Vance!"*

Sobs choked the words she fought so hard to say. Vance Calvert glanced across at her, dully, impersonally, his face dead.

"Won't you please go on?" he said, his voice as dead as his aspect. "You and your dog? Please go on, won't you, and leave me here with — with this friend I've lost? You've nothing to wait for. You've got your wish. You wanted my 'ugly mongrel cur' to be kept away from your house. Well,

308

he'll be kept away, and you won't be shamed by having strangers think you are harboring such a worthless mutt."

"*Vance!*"

"You can see for yourself that he'll never bother you again," rasped Calvert. "Neither will I. Now that you're rid of us both — now that you've got what you wanted — won't you go? I don't mean to speak rudely. But it's little I'm asking of you. I just want to be alone with —"

He broke off with a gurgling yell of amaze. On his knees he could feel a tremor shoot through Rags' body. Then the mongrel lifted his shoulders and his head from his master's lap and blinked dazedly around him.

Slowly, waveringly, the big dog staggered to his feet. He stood peering drunkenly from one to the other of the dumfounded onlookers.

(When the veterinary examined him, half an hour later, he found the train had thrown the mongrel in air with no worse results than a few bad bruises; and that he had landed on his head when he hit the track again. He had been stunned. But the thick skull had not been injured.)

Vance Calvert would not let his miraculously revived dog walk; but carried his great weight tenderly in his arms to a furlong-distant garage, whence he could commandeer a car to take Rags to the nearest vet's.

Weeping, crushed, utterly humbled, Fay Lanning followed. Neither she nor Vance had spoken since Rags had come to life. There seemed nothing to say — or too much to say.

With stately tread Rusty moved along at his mistress's side. For the moment, nobody paid any attention to the setter. Recognition — and much of it — and praise and petting, would come later; when these deeply absorbed humans should have scope to recall the grand thing the setter had done.

On to rheumatic old age Rusty was destined to be an honored inmate of their home and a hero to their children.

In the meantime he was placidly content with what he had done. Perhaps he knew his all but suicidal dash onto the tracks had saved Rags from being killed and mangled under the deadly wheels. Perhaps he had been moved only by a swift canine instinct to yank his pal out of danger. Who can follow the trend of a dog's brain processes?

Just now his mistress was crying. His friend, Vance Calvert, was stalking along with misty eyes and set teeth. Ordinarily the setter would have overwhelmed them both with eager sympathy. But something in his strange mental cosmos whispered to him that they both were gloriously happy, whether they might realize it or not; and that neither of them stood in the faintest need of sympathy.

It was the same occult sense which had made him forbear from giving voice to the awful death howl, there on the tracks, when these humans were making such a fuss over the seemingly dead Rags. Rusty had known his rescued playmate was still very much alive.

As for his own glowing exploit — well, it was all in the day's work, wasn't it? — all a part and parcel of what humans know as "a dog's life."

XV

MAROONED

Down the mucky lane toward the lake straggled the procession. It was headed by a thick-shouldered man who half-led, half-dragged, a collie dog on the end of a rope leash.

Behind the two ambled a half-score idlers who had deserted the steps of the village's only store for the fun of watching a helpless animal put to death.

As Mitch Gallet had slouched past the store on his lakeward journey he had answered a loafer's careless question by saying:

"I'm heading for the water; and when I get there I'm not going to turn myself into a bathing beauty, neither. I'm going to hunt for a thirty-pound stone that's not too smooth to tie one end of this rope to. Then the purp and that stone are going for a swim together off the boat dock. If the stone forgets to float, the cur is out of luck."

That was quite enough for the loiterers. As one man they arose and followed.

There was more to this performance than the mere drowning of a friendly dog. And the crowd were avid to be in on the final scene of a little drama that had been the theme of much of their store-steps chat.

All of them knew the love Old Man Keegan had borne for this gold-red young collie, Jock, which now hung back so reluctantly on the rope. The dog and the crippled oldster had been familiar sights along the roads, on their daily walks.

All of them knew the hate that had flared between Keegan and his son-in-law, Mitch Gallet: a hate the younger man had held in careful abeyance because Keegan's money kept the Gallet home going and because the father-in-law might readily change his will and his place of abode.

Gallet's detestation had even included the young collie. Now, on the very day after Keegan's death, he was revenging himself.

The collie himself seemed to have some premonition of what was afoot. For as they neared the lake he hung back more and more; and tried to gain claw-hold in the loose mud. At every such attempt a vicious yank of the rope brought the luckless dog again into motion.

A turn in the lane brought to view the ramshackle wooden dock that jutted some twenty feet out into the water for the mooring of rowboats. On the end of the rotting pier a man sat hunched over, peering glumly down into the lake.

He was so engrossed with his own thoughts that he did not bother to glance around as the group drew near, nor even when Mitch Gallet sought and found the kind of stone he wanted and fastened it to one end of the six-foot rope.

Indeed, the sitter did not look up from his grim survey of the water until Gallet gathered the squirming, protesting collie in his arms, along with the stone; and strode out onto the dock. Even then the man did not note what was happening until Gallet lifted dog and stone high in air to fling them into the lake.

Then, as he saw what Gallet planned, the gloomy sitter came to life with a start that brought him to his feet. But before he could raise a protesting arm or even speak, the dog hurtled past him through the air and splashed loudly into the water below.

But, though the stranger had not time to interfere, he had time to see the doomed collie's eyes were fixed on him in a silent agony of appeal, as though recognizing him instinctively as the only humane person there. That lightning-brief look did something to the man's brain.

Without pausing to consider, he dived from the dock; striking water just as the weight of the stone began to drag the wildly struggling dog beneath the surface.

The group on the shore broke into a wordless gabbling. This was even more worth seeing than they had dared to expect. The gabbling swelled in volume as the heads of the man and the dog came into view just beyond the dock.

The man had caught the rope, under water, and had passed it over the back of his neck; so the stone hung from one shoulder and the dog from the other. Thus encumbered, he clawed for the nearest outjutting boatstake; caught it and drew himself to the dock itself.

Along the side of the dock he worked his way, thus, from stake to stake, until his feet touched bottom. Then, gathering the dog in one arm, he waded shoreward. As he moved he groped in a pocket, with his free hand, and tugged forth a knife. With it he hacked savagely at the rope.

The last strand severed as he reached shore. The stone plopped into the shallows. The man set the dripping dog down carefully, but kept one hand on his ruff. Cascades of water ran down from rescuer and rescued. They were a disreputable sight. Someone in the group broke into a guffaw at their wretched aspect.

The laugh roused Mitch Gallet from a momentary daze of astonishment. He stamped over to the drenched man and towered above him, glowering down into his wet face.

"That's *my* dog!" he announced. "And I was drowning him. Who told you to butt in? Hey? Tell me just that, feller!"

"There wasn't time to wait for an invitation," answered the other. "Yes, I saw you were drowning him. And I inferred he was yours. He asked me to help him, and I did. That sounds cuckoo to you. But it's true, all the same. People only drown animals they don't want. So I figure you don't want this collie. I'll take him off your hands. That's about all, I think."

Still with his fingers on the dog's wet ruff, he started up the low bank toward the lane. Again, some one in the group laughed. Mitch Gallet put a ham-size hand on the stranger's shoulder and spun him around.

"The purp's mine," he reiterated, a snarling note creeping into his heavy voice, "and he's going to be drowned. That's a big piece of satisfaction I've been promising myself for more'n a year. And now is when I make good on it. I hope old Keegan is where he can see me. Let go of him, you!"

As he spoke, he gripped the collie's soaking neck. The dog made a motion of the head, almost too swift for the eye to follow. Gallet sprang back with a yell. The fleshy part of his thumb was slashed to the bone.

In his two years of life, young Jock had known nothing but affection and kind treatment from his agèd master. Never till today had an unfriendly hand been laid on him. He had endured the rough leading to the lake; still not understanding that he was willfully ill-treated. Not until Gallet had lifted him, to throw him into the water, had he grasped the whole situation. Then this newcomer had saved him. And now Gallet was at him again. A flare of resentment, inherited from some far-back wolf ancestor, sent the dog into raging action.

The stranger's lightly firm hold on Jock's ruff kept the collie from following up his first punitive slash; the only angry bite, thus far, in all his short life. With a gentle word or two the man sought to soothe the fury-vibrant beast.

But the sting and blood of the hurt had completed the wreck of Mitch Gallet's never calm temper. Mouthing and roaring, he rushed headlong at the dog, swinging his heavy boot in a really murderous kick.

With a motion that had in it none of the roughness of Gallet's earlier rope yankings the stranger drew the dog deftly to one side. The kick lost its force on the empty air. This time the whole group laughed. Gallet recovered his balance and bore down upon the dog and the dripping man, with foam flecking his thick lips.

"Since you won't give me the dog you were trying to drown," mildly suggested the stranger, making no move to get out of Mitch's way, but still keeping the angry collie behind him, "I'm ready to pay you a fair price for him. How much?"

Checked momentarily by the unwonted prospect of cash, Gallet hesitated. Then he remembered that his father-in-law's death yesterday had left him better off financially than ever he had dared hope to be.

"I'm not selling!" he declared. "I'm killing. Leggo of Jock and stand outer my way."

"No," said the stranger, ruminatingly, as if giving some thought to the suggestion, "I think not. The collie defended me, just now. Besides, one takes a liking to people and things one has helped. I'm keeping him. If you won't give him to me or sell him to me — well, suppose I fight you for him? Would that suit you better?"

The idlers fairly buzzed with sudden excitement at this unexpected offer. Decidedly, the hot trip down the lane to the lake had been well worth the trouble involved in quitting their comfortable seats on the store porch.

And there was more to it than this: Among the winter gangs who went logging, up on the Reginskill, from November to April, there was not a local lumberjack who could hold his own, in a finish fight, against Mitch Gallet. Mitch's bearlike strength, his savagery, his unwieldy bulk, all made him a neighborhood terror; when it came to a physical clash.

This smooth-spoken stranger was fully three inches shorter and thirty pounds lighter than Gallet. It was nothing less than suicidal for him to urge a fight on the giant lumberjack. Yes, this was due to be a sight almost as sportsmanly as the grudge-drowning of a friendly young dog. And far more spectacular.

The crowd formed a ring about the two potential battlers. But Zenas Crope, the storekeeper, spoke a perfunctory word for mercy.

"Hold on, now, Mitch!" he soothed, timidly laying a dirty hand on Gallet's arm. "Hold your horses. This young feller is off his bean. You can't fight him. You'll li'ble kill him, and do time for it. He's — he's an invalid of some kind. I know, because I've asked. He comes down to the store for supplies. He's rented the Graynor camp, up yonder, for the summer, to get well of something or other. Lives there, all alone. Just mountain-climbs and fishes and moons around by himself. Graynor told me. From New York City, he is. Rented the camp from Graynor because he said he had been smashed up somehow and wanted to 'find himself,' whatever that means. Name's Eldon. Pierce Eldon. You can't go beating up a sick man. Take a feller of your size, Mitch."

"O.K.," agreed Gallet, sulkily. "Let him gimme my dog and clear out of here, and I'll let him off. I wouldn't do even that much for you, Crope, if you hadn't helped me out by letting my bills run, sometimes. Chase, Mister Pierce Eldon, Esquire. And keep on going till you get to that backwoods shack of Graynor's! I'll take the dog off your hands. He's due to get extra trimmings on his drowning, 'count of that bite and —"

"My noisy friend," gently intervened Eldon, "the water is still in my ears. Perhaps it's made me a little deaf. But I didn't hear your answer to my offer to fight you for Jock. You won't give him to me. You won't sell him to me. I heard you say that much. Will you fight me for him? Or shall I take him away with me?"

He set off in leisurely fashion toward the forest trail which skirted the lake. The collie fell into step, right willingly, close at his side.

Like the average dog, Jock's sense of gratitude was egregiously strong. This soft-spoken stranger had rescued him from a man who had tried to kill him. Thus, and by his voice and touch and magnetism, he had won the collie's devotion. Gladly Jock walked by his side, ready to accompany him anywhere, everywhere.

But Mitch Gallet would not have it so. Before man and dog had gone three paces, Gallet was barring their way, fairly stammering with fury.

"You mangy little shrimp!" he growled. "Trying to put your New York City ways over on me, are you? Well, you've had your chance. You asked for a fight. You're due to have one. Want to put up your hands? Or will I just take you across my knee and paddle you?"

As he finished speaking, Gallet swung his enormous right hand, palm open, for Eldon's cheek. It was a slow and awkward blow, intended as punitive rather than combative. But, like his recent kick at Jock, it wasted itself on the lakeside air.

This because Eldon, in one seemingly careless motion, stepped clear of the collie's impeding body, and made a slight shift of his head which eluded the fervent slap by less than an inch. At the same time he danced away a step or two.

At sight of this attack on his newfound deity, Jock sprang forward; hackles bristling, teeth bared from his upcurled lip; charging at Gallet.

"Jock!" called Elden, sharply. "Heel! Keep out of this."

Speaking, he dodged a mighty left swing from the wrath-blinded Gallet. Almost in the same gesture, he stepped lightly in, setting himself; and drove a short-arm uppercut to the lumber-jack's throat.

The blow traveled a bare ten inches. But behind it was an amazing concentration and scientific force. The impetus was doubled by the fact that Gallet was lurching forward and met it halfway.

Mitch stopped in mid-charge; and sat down very hard indeed; gurgling as the blow momentarily paralyzed his windpipe.

But on the instant the big man was up again, leaping in, yelling ferocity at the stripling whose presumably chance blow had made him the laughingstock of his store-porch cronies.

He charged like an infuriated bull. Such an attack, among his slow fellows of the lumber-camps, had ever proved irresistible. Nothing could stand against it.

And now, as before, nothing stood against it.

Without seeming to exert himself at all, Pierce Elden avoided the clumsy bull-rush. Stepping lithely aside, he planted a terrific punch in the giant's meridian and another on his slobbering mouth.

The double counter shook Gallet to the very heels.

As he wheeled to meet his elusive foe, he encountered another sickening smash to the throat and a fairly stiff blow to the heart. And again Pierce Elden was dancing easily away.

For a moment Gallet paused for breath and to

plan afresh his campaign against this mosquito-like adversary, who stung and then faded so mysteriously out of reach. In the interval, Elden called out almost gaily to the storekeeper:

"Mr. Crope, it was something besides my body that got cracked up and brought me to the Graynor camp. My body's always been all right. And my exercise this summer has kept me just as fit as when I won the amateur middle-weight championship last year. Watch!"

While he was calling he changed in a trice from the defensive to aggression. No longer did he bother to move far out of reach to avoid Gallet's clumsily deadly rushes. Easily preventing any of the giant's sledgehammer blows from landing with harmful force, he bored in to the assault.

He was in and out and all over and everywhere and nowhere, ever smiting with fearful scientific force at the nearest unprotected part of Mitch's big anatomy. As a bit of punching-bag work it was commendable. The sharp impact of punch after punch echoed and re-echoed from the unwieldy body of the giant.

Mitch Gallet was enduring terrible punishment and was imparting practically no real injury in return. His flail-like arms drove their incomparably heavy blows at the evading form in front of him, but without adequate results.

His life-long experience with lumberjacks as awkward and slow as himself, and less powerful and enduring, had not prepared him to cope with a modern scientific boxer. Nor had a steady course of boozing and of physical laziness put him into any such condition as was his wiry opponent.

Finding he was worse than helpless at long range, he rushed and sought to clinch. Four times Pierce Eldon sidestepped or ducked these abortive clinches with ridiculous ease, always sending in a volley of stingingly unrequited short-arm punches.

The fifth time he did not seek to get out of the way. Instead, he slipped in, eel-like, under the doughty arms outflung to mangle him. His body clashed with his antagonist's. His left hip squirmed behind Gallet's, and a little below it. His left arm encircled as much of Mitch's ample meridian as it could hold. In the same move, Eldon's muscles tensed. His heels drove into the earth. He twisted and heaved with the swift accuracy of a steel spring.

Forward shot Mitch Gallet, through the same air he had been punishing with fist and boot toe. His head was the first part of him to touch any solid substance. It crashed against one of the dock-stakes, splitting the wood from top to bottom and sending a spray of yellow splinters in every direction.

There he lay, half in, half out of the water, his face a bloody mask, his clothes torn, his fat body a splotch of red bruises, his breath coming in stertorous gasps.

The collie had been dancing madly around the battling pair, seeking to dig his white teeth into some part of Gallet's vast anatomy. Now that the giant lay spent and helpless and half-stunned, the dog drew back.

Pierce Eldon snapped his fingers. Instantly Jock was at his side. Turning, Eldon set out along the lakeside trail to his forest cabin-camp. With joyous steps Jock frisked along in front of him. The collie paused, at every few steps, to look back to make certain of their direction, or else to trot up to his new master and thrust his cold muzzle into the palm of the man's battered hand.

And so, at last, they came to the rustic camp which Eldon had chosen for his summer solitude.

Eldon's brief exhilaration over the fight was spent. He felt tired and sick. He sat on a stump outside his cabin, to rest. Jock came across to him and stood expectantly in front of him, head on one side, tulip ears inquiringly pricked. When Eldon did not notice him, the collie came a step closer and laid one white little forepaw on the man's knee.

With a start Pierce came out of his glum revery. As his eyes fell on the tensely adoring gold-red dog, his brows contracted into a scowl.

"Jock," he mused, half-aloud, as if speaking to a fellow human, "you complicate matters. I've made myself responsible for you. If I turn you away, that obese Gallet brute is liable to get hold of you again. I've got to look after you till I can find a decent home for you, Jock. That means I'll have to postpone what I was going to do."

Naturally, the collie could not understand the meaning of one word in ten. But the occasional repetition of his own name set his plumed tail to waving. He whimpered softly, far down in his throat, and his deep-set dark eyes grew wistful. Again he laid one forepaw encouragingly on his master's knee. Aroused once more from his black revery, Eldon spoke again.

"Jock," he said, "do you know what I was getting ready to do when you and your paltry affairs interrupted me, half an hour ago? I was going to step off the end of that dock down yonder. The water is too shallow along the shore, up here. And I was going to let myself sink. That wouldn't have been hard, Jock. Because, you see, I don't know how to swim. Funny, isn't it, that an all-round athlete never took the trouble to learn even the rudiments of swimming? Well, it just happens I never did. It was the only line of sport I hadn't tried. (So you see when I made a fool of myself by diving off the dock after you, I was as helpless as you were. I'm glad you didn't get thrown out any farther than you did.) I was going to drown myself, Jock, because nobody knew I couldn't swim and it would seem an accident. She wouldn't have known I did it on purpose. Even if she'd happened to read about it in the papers, Jock."

As before, every repetition of his own name brought an enthusiastic tail-wave from the collie. Eldon rumpled the dog's tulip ears in rough affection, and meandered on:

"I spoke of 'she,' Jock. 'She' is Hilda Deene. Pretty name, isn't it, Jock? A pretty name for a pretty girl. But she smashed me. Worse than I smashed that man-mountain who was drowning you. That's why I'm out here, Jock. She was everything to me. When she threw our engagement out of the window, and my life along with it, I had to get away somewhere for a while. To shape the world over again for myself, if I could.

"I gave it a fair trial, Jock, old boy. But it kept getting worse instead of better. That was why I was going to wind up the whole hideous business today. . . . And now you've gone and spoiled everything, you worthless collie. I've got to postpone it till I can find some way of settling *your* problem. If only Gallet had waited ten minutes longer before he brought you to the lake — !"

He broke off in his rumbling incoherent harangue, shamefacedly aware that he had been talking to a mere collie, as a child might talk to its doll — unaware that he was not the first, nor the millionth, lonely man who thus has spoken his inner thoughts aloud to his dog.

"Come on, old chap," he resumed, getting to his feet. "Let's rustle some supper for both of us. Tomorrow I'll write to a couple of men I know, and see if either of them wants a collie for a chum."

For the first time in his miserable three months of brooding in the wilderness, Pierce Eldon began to find a certain pleasure in forest

326

life. The collie was a splendid comrade; on the long mountain tramps and on fishing-jaunts and during the heretofore dreary camp-fire evenings. He had come into Eldon's endless solitude just when that solitude had eaten dangerously into the man's sick mind and nerves.

The dog adored his new master, and was even quicker to learn than was Eldon to teach him. He had had a protective fondness for the agèd man who had been his first master and whom Mitch Gallet had hated. But it had been as nothing to his gay devotion toward this younger and more companionable chum.

In spite of himself, Eldon began to find a certain real pleasure again in being alive; and in the magic of the summer forests and the hush of the solemn nights under the stars and the dozen wilderness interests to which he had been blinding himself.

Always at his side was this jolly four-footed comrade, eager to share his every exploit, his every mood.

Forest life is a collie's ancestral heritage. Jock blossomed under its spell. He learned to trail rabbits, to anticipate their "doubling," as he gave hot chase to them; to bring such game proudly back to camp and lay it at Pierce's feet. (Once he brought a skunk he had slain thus. To his disgust, Eldon scrubbed him for an hour in lake water and yellow soap; and for several days discouraged the dog from coming near him.)

Until his fight with Gallet, Eldon had been

wont to go to the two-mile-distant logging village for his supplies. Now, unwilling to meet the looks and the comments of the porch loafers who had witnessed the flashily melodramatic scene at the dock, he was accustomed to walk three miles to the nearest highroad and there take a bus for the county town of Gusepple, some fifteen miles away. There he would stock up with such provisions as he needed for the next month.

At such times he shut Jock into the cabin until his return. For, while the collie was happily obedient in all things else, Pierce could not keep him from trying to follow. And bus lines do not accept big young collies as passengers.

One morning in the autumn, after the night of the first white frost, Eldon arrayed himself in a town-going suit and prepared to go to Gusepple for another fortnight's food, as well as for a set of thicker camp blankets against the steadily colder weather. Ruefully, Jock submitted to being called into the cabin and to having its one door shut upon him. With a sigh of resignation he stretched himself on the deerskin rug in front of the hearth and prepared for the several hours of waiting.

But the wait was far longer.

When Pierce Eldon had made his last purchase, he crossed Gusepple's busy main street, his arms laden with bundles, and headed for the bus's stopping-place. He had all but reached the sidewalk when a fast-driven motor-truck spun around the corner from a side street.

The pavement was slippery. The truck skidded. It sideswiped the bundle-laden camper, knocking him several feet. Eldon's head smote the edge of the curb with sickening force and he lay very still.

All day, Jock waited with ever-increasing worry and restlessness in the lonely cabin among the lakeside firs. Never before had his adored master been away from him so long. It was dull there without Pierce. Again and again Jock went to the shack's only window and peered wistfully out, only to return to the cold hearth to wait.

He was hungry. He was thirsty. He was ill at ease with the nameless dread which sometimes assails the best type of collie when trouble overtakes his distant master. He began to pant, though he had taken no exercise and the cabin was chilly.

There was no water in the cabin to ease his growing thirst. True, there was two days' rations on the shelf. But from puppyhood Jock had been taught that snooping food from a shelf or a table is a deadly canine sin. It did not occur to him to steal the rations or even to sniff at them.

When the next morning dawned cold and gray, Jock's worry and hunger and thirst had reached a climax. Over and over he went to the tight-shut door, scratching at it and even throwing his sixty-pound weight against its planks. But the hasp held firm.

At last, in desperation, he prepared to do a

thing which was against all his teachings in regard to the sanctity of human property. Backing
to the farther wall and gauging the distance, he
made a dash across the room and flung himself
with all his strength and weight against the single
window.

There was a shivering of the pane and a buckling of the flimsy wooden sash. Amid a hailstorm
of broken glass and of splinters Jock landed on
the ground outside the cabin.

His first action was to trot to the lake and there
to drink for nearly three minutes without stopping. Then he cast about, nose to earth, until he
found Pierce Eldon's cold trail. This he followed,
at a hand-gallop, through the woods and over the
hill until he came to the state road. There
abruptly it ceased at the point where Pierce had
boarded the bus.

Once again Jock cast about for the lost trail.
Not finding it, he followed the original trail back
across hill and woodland to the cabin.

He was wretchedly unhappy and he was
scared. But, being a young and exuberantly
healthy dog, he was also ravenously hungry, and
there was no food; none at least except the stores
on the cabin shelf. These were sacred to the perfectly trained collie. Starvation itself would not
lure him into touching them. Therefore, other
food must be found.

Now it was that the lore he had picked up
during the summer came to Jock's aid. For his
own amusement he had learned the art of rabbit-

hunting and the sly stalking of game birds, and where to dig in soft mold for field mice. It was time to put his attainments to practical use, and he did so.

In this lush autumn season the forests and sering meadows were alive with game. The law was not yet off on the shy creatures of the wild. They had not been frightened back into deeper solitudes by the daily thunder of guns and the clumping of countless hunters' boots. For a dog of Jock's speed and cleverness there was plenty of food for the catching. The problem of warding off hunger was no longer a problem.

Far afield he ranged. Yet ever he came back at night to the cabin, leaping through its single sash-broken window and sleeping on the hearth. Sometimes, in mid-hunt, he would run wistfully to the cabin, often miles away, to see if Eldon had come back. Never did he cease to grieve and to pine keenly for the man.

The brilliant and risky operation on Pierce Eldon's shattered skull, at the Gusepple General Hospital, made surgical history and immortalized the surgeon who dared perform the seemingly impossible miracle. But a full three weeks passed before the patient came fully to himself from the fevered delirium which followed it.

Then, one October day, the invalid awoke, clear of mind, if babyishly weak of body. He stared blankly at the white ceiling of his hospital room. A moment earlier, it seemed, he had been aware of the motor-truck lumbering down at him. And now —

When a nurse in crackling uniform explained soothingly to him what had happened, he lay for nearly an hour; still blinking at the stretch of snowy veiling, piecing together what he remembered and what he had just learned. He was content to lie thus, drowsy and lethargic. Nothing seemed to matter.

Then through his tired dullness flashed a thought that stung his brain to activity as though a hot needle had pierced it.

Jock! *Jock!*

He had shut the dog into the cabin; with no way of getting out, with no one to care for him. The few rations on the shelf would scarce have kept the collie in food for three days at most. Then starvation must have set in — starvation and thirst. For there was not a drop of water in the cabin. The dog that had been his loved comrade had been condemned to a lingering death, mured up in that closed shack. And — what had the nurse said? — it was three weeks and more since Eldon had shut him there!

Pierce lifted himself weakly on his elbow, frantic with remorse and sorrow. There was a chance — a pitifully bare chance — that a spark of life still remained in the starved prisoner in the cabin. Someone must go there instantly and let him out and feed him and nurse him back to health.

"Nurse!" panted Eldon, noting vaguely that a woman had just come into the room and was standing by his side. "Nurse! Some one has got to go up to my camp, in a rush, and —"

His voice trailed away and his jaw dropped. Unquestionably he had slipped back into one of his myriad impossible fever dreams. For this woman smiling down on him was not the primly efficient white-clad nurse who had talked to him with such professional gentleness. This was a younger and smaller woman — a woman whose soft eyes were shining with tenderness and with something far greater and deeper.

"Hilda!" he mumbled stupidly. "Hilda Deene! *Hilda!*"

"Hush, dear!" the girl was saying, her dear hand on his forehead. "You mustn't excite yourself. The doctor says so. I've — I've been here every day — every day since I read about it in the paper. It seemed to calm you to have me in the room. That's why they let me keep on coming. I had tried so hard to find you, all these months! But all my letters kept coming back to me. At your rooms they said you had gone away last spring and hadn't left any address. I wanted to tell you how silly and wicked I had been in our idiotic quarrel, and to beg you to let things be as they used to be. That is, if you still cared. And the things you kept saying when you were delirious told me you *do* care. So —"

"Hilda!" he muttered, unbelieving, his tired head on her shoulder. Things were happening too fast for his tired senses to grasp them all. Later, it would be time enough to understand and to rejoice. To rejoice? Again the white-hot memory stung him.

Jock!

"Listen!" he bade the girl. "There's something you must do for me. You must do it *now*. Get a car or a bus, and go out to Witchfire Lake. It's less than twenty miles. You can make it in less than an hour. Take along a lot of raw meat. I'll tell you how to get to the camp after you reach the lake. And you'd better hire a car; and tell the driver to step on the gas, all the way. Don't forget the meat. Lots of it. I — . . . Oh, don't look at me that scared way, dear! I'm not out of my head. It sounds so, but I'm not. This is life or death to a pal of mine. A pal that kept me sane and kept me alive. The chances are twenty to one it's too late, even now. Listen."

Quickly, disjointedly, he told of Jock's plight.

When the girl had gone, Pierce slumped back on his pillow, as exhausted as though he had been fighting twenty-five fast rounds. Nature claimed its own and he fell into the sleep of utter fatigue.

When he woke, Hilda Deene was sitting beside his bed again. In response to his volleyed questions, she told him she had found the cabin empty, its moldering little stock of rations untouched on the shelf and the window sash knocked clean away. She had searched the nearer reaches of woodland, along the lake, calling the collie's name. But she had found no trace of the dog. Nor had he been seen by any of the several village folk and farmers from whom she had made inquiries.

"Good old Jock!" said Eldon. "He had sense enough to get out of jail, anyhow. And he knows enough about hunting to keep himself alive for a while, if Mitch Gallet doesn't run across him. It was just like Jock not to break the Law by eating the provisions he had been told to leave alone. As soon as they'll let me out of this sickbay, we'll drive up to the camp and collect my things and close the place. We'll go early in the morning and I'll make an all-day hunt for him and post a reward in the store. But — but I doubt if ever I get news of the dear old chap. I'd rather have lost anything and everything else — except you. It was Jock that kept me going when the going had stopped seeming worth while. He did what he was sent to do. And now that it's done, I've lost him!"

Jock was waked from a fitful sleep on the cabin hearth by the reiterated banging of shotguns, from near and far. The first morning of the hunting season had dawned. The clangor of guns added to an uneasiness that had obsessed the dog ever since an evening when he had come back to the cabin to find it tinged with the alien scent of a stranger. Some one had been wandering around in there during his daily absence. The knowledge was vaguely disquieting to the sensitive collie.

This morning Jock fared forth as usual, on his day's foraging. But as he started along the twisting path that led from the shack he came to an abrupt halt. A man had just come into view, around the bend in the trees — a man with a gun over his shoulder and a game-bag swinging from his hip. At sight and scent of the intruder Jock's white eye teeth glittered from under his upcurled lip.

Mitch Gallet halted with equal suddenness, and brought his gun down from his shoulder. He recognized the collie as quickly as Jock had recognized him. Red hatred flamed high in the man's heart — a hatred which had smoldered there for months.

This dog was the cause of his lost prestige in the village where once he had strutted as an unconquerable fighter. Snickers from the store-porch groups, whenever he slouched past, reminded him eternally that his ignominious thrashing at the hands of a man smaller than himself was still a theme for neighborhood mirth. Even yet there were scars on his fat visage from that battle.

And now, here was the dog, at last, at his mercy. Yes, and the dog's new master was not here now to help him. Mitch, like everyone else in the village, had read of Eldon's accident and that the recluse was lying at the point of death in a Gusepple hospital.

Mitch Gallet smiled in perfect happiness. With the slow appreciation of an epicure he brought his gun into position. True, it was loaded only with birdshot. But a charge of birdshot at this close range would do the work.

At Mitch's threatening gesture, Jock's momentary daze of astonishment vanished. This man, his mortal enemy, was invading his lost master's premises, the premises Jock had been taught to guard. The dog gave a wild-beast yell and sprang at Gallet's throat. At the same moment Mitch pulled trigger.

But the collie's unexpected onslaught and lightning shift of position unsettled the aim. A single pellet of shot raked Jock's side stingingly. The rest of the charge went wild. Before Mitch could club his single-barreled gun, the dog was upon him.

Gallet clawed wildly at the furry whirlwind of whale-bone and muscle which ravened at his throat. Back he staggered and all but fell. Then through the din of conflict the sound of his own name penetrated the rage-mists that clouded the collie's brain.

Pierce Eldon and Hilda had rounded the turn in the path on their way to the cabin. Hilda cried out in alarm at what she saw. Impulsively Pierce shouted to his dog.

Gallet was aware of an immediate ceasing of the dog's mad efforts to get to his throat. He recovered his balance and turned bewilderedly around. Apparently Jock had found a new antagonist. The dog had hurled himself upon Eldon in a paroxysm of rapture, screaming with joy, sobbing, panting, seeking ludicrously to lick his master's face and feet at the same time.

Mitch Gallet picked up his empty gun and crept on tiptoe and at top speed into the shelter of the forest. Nor did he slacken speed till more than a mile lay between him and the man and dog he dreaded.

XVI

SEVENTH SON

Behind the kitchen stove was a widish space where, ordinarily, firewood was stacked. Tonight the space was given over to a shallow packing-box, roomy and blanket-floored. Within the box a shaggy little collie sprawled in tired comfort. Close against her furry underbody squirmed and nestled and muttered several rat-sized newborn puppies.

Rhodes crossed the kitchen, from the living-room beyond. Chirping to the wearily triumphant mother, he stooped over the impromptu brood nest.

"Steady, Lorna!" he quieted the worried collie as she sought to nose aside his exploring hand. "I'm not going to hurt them. You ought to know mighty well I'm not. I'm just playing census-taker."

Petting her silky head, he called to his wife in the living-room beyond.

"There are still six of them. There haven't been any born since noon. So that's the whole litter. Six. Lorna's fourth family, and the first time there haven't been seven . . . Lord, but it's a

339

brute of a night!" he broke off as a swirl of gale-scourged snow scratched the windows with a million claws and as the house jarred afresh to the storm's buffetings.

He was turning back toward the living-room when a hammering at the kitchen door made itself heard above the wind.

Rhodes hurried to answer the summons. In that semi-primitive corner of Preakness County, neighborliness was still an instinct rather than a virtue. Nobody was likely to be dropping in on such a night for the mere pleasure of a stroll and a fireside chat. The knock meant need.

Lorna had heard the hammering at the door far more distinctly than had her master. Her abnormally keen ears had even caught the muffled tread of clumping feet on the kitchen porch, through all the racket.

Her watch-dog training swept aside her fatigue and lassitude. Before Rhodes could turn at sound of the knock, the collie had sprung out of her packing-box brood nest and was flashing past him toward the porch. Hackles bristling and eye teeth aglint, she danced impatiently as Rhodes unbolted and swung ajar the door.

Her master had scant time to catch her by the scruff of the neck as she sprang.

"Down, old girl!" he commanded, bracing himself against the inrush of wind and snow, and continuing more loudly: "Come in, whoever you are. If I leave this door open half a minute there'll be a ton of snow on the floor. Lively!"

Over the threshold was propelled a coonskin-wrapped figure, panting and choking as from a race.

"Thanks," said the man as the door shut behind him. "Sorry to bring all this snow into your house. I was on the way to Paterson. It was heavy going, but I thought I could make it. Then I hit a drift about a mile high, just outside your gate. The poor old car went spang out of business. Not another inch of go left in her. I saw your light. I thought maybe you'd tell me how to get to the nearest inn or roadhouse where I can put up for the —"

"There's the Minnehaha Inn, about half a mile from here," answered Rhodes. "But it's closed for the winter. At least, they padlocked it, last October, for six months. Then there's the New Paradise Inn. The best food in Preakness County. But that's a good mile farther on and you'd have to make a couple of turns to get to it. You'd never find it, a night like this; even if you could keep on your feet that long. You'll have to stay here with us. We can make you fairly comfortable. We've finished supper, but my wife can easily enough fix up some for you. Take your coat off."

"Thanks," said the stranger, beginning to breathe more naturally. "That's white of you, Mr. — Mr. —"

"Rhodes. Milo Rhodes. I —"

"You aren't *the* Milo Rhodes?" queried the other. "The Rhodesian Kennels? Why, this was

341

one of the places I was planning to stop at; on my way South. You and I have had more than a little correspondence in our time, Mr. Rhodes. Remember? I'm H. P. Callon. If it hadn't been I wanted to see your kennels I'd have been in Paterson before now. I took a round-about way and got lost."

Rhodes' heavy face brightened at sound of the guest's name. And he gripped the other's thick gloved hand with wince-evoking heartiness.

"Of course I remember!" he assured Callon. "Why wouldn't I? And it wasn't a month ago I had your letter about wanting to stop off here on your way to Florida for the winter. I —"

"Thais!" he broke off, turning to his young wife, who was coming down the three steps from the living-room. "This is Mr. Callon. I've read you some of his letters. The great Midwestburg collie man. He and I have been chewing the rag on paper for a year or more, over one collie matter and another. His car's broken down, right outside here. He's spending the night with us."

At sight of the slim young woman, Callon removed the big cap he had lugged far down over his ears and eyes and shook off his ice-stiff gauntlet. As he stepped forward to greet his hostess, he was at first glance a half-grown boy, not only in figure but in face. Then the face resolved itself into lines and angles and a handful of wrinkles which gave the lie, startingly, to the idea that he bore any semblance of youth.

"Take your things off, Mr. Callon," Thais

Rhodes was saying. "It won't be more than a few minutes before I can get supper ready for you. The fire is —"

"If you don't mind," interrupted Callon, "I'll butt my way out to the car and get my suitcase, before I shed this coat. It won't take me a minute. . . . Hello! That's a good collie you've got there!" he exclaimed, his snow-and-darkness-blurred gaze focusing for the first time on Lorna as she stood unwelcoming and vigilant at her master's side, eyeing the visitor with sullen disapproval.

Thus does the average collie mother regard strangers who intrude too near her brood nest when her pups are only a few hours old. Moreover, the sudden advent of Callon out of the tumultuous loneliness of the night and into the same room with her adored pups had done things to the mother dog's hair-trigger nerves.

Callon looked approvingly at her, noting the classically clean head, the deep-set dark eyes, the deep chest, the massive coat, sizing up her show points with the eye of an expert. He snapped his fingers invitingly at her. Lorna snarled; forbidding friendliness.

She did not like this pleasant-spoken stranger. She did not like him at all. Which proved nothing whatever, either bad or otherwise, as to Callon's inner nature. There is no more egregiously asinine lie in all the billion asinine lies of caninity than that a dog can tell instinctively whether some human is or is not trustworthy.

"There's the reason why she isn't friendlier with you," explained Rhodes, pointing to the squirmy knot of collie babies in the center of the brood nest's tumbled blanket.

Callon glanced at the pups, then nodded his full understanding.

"Six, eh?" he said, taking a step toward them. "Fine husky-looking bunch, they are, too. Here's hoping you won't have a squeaker in all the lot. They —"

Lorna had growled murderously as he moved nearer the brood nest. Now, slipping between it and the man, she crouched, to spring, should he continue his advance.

"Lorna!" cried Rhodes.

"It's all right," laughed Callon. "I ought to have known better. I'll go out for my bag, now."

As he went to the door, Lorna followed. Few dogs like to be laughed at. The guest's laugh had not lightened Lorna's distaste for him. She intended to keep an eye on this potential devourer or kidnapper of her six pups.

Rhodes had kicked off his slippers and was struggling into his knee-boots.

"I'll go with you," he volunteered. "Or if you'll tell me where to find the bag, I'll —"

"No, thanks," refused Callon. "It's in the rumble, and the rumble is locked. Don't bother to come out in all that filthy weather. I can get it all right, alone."

But Rhodes had pulled on his mackinaw and picked up a flashlight, and was standing with his hand upon the latch.

"Make it snappy," he warned, "both going out and coming back. Don't let's bring any more of the blizzard in here than we have to. Ready?"

As he spoke he opened the door halfway, and held it while Callon hastened through after him. Lorna slipped out, at Callon's heels, with all the eel-like swiftness of a collie; unnoted by either man. Thais Rhodes was busy over the stove and she did not see the dog follow the two.

In another minute Callon and Rhodes were back again; entering the house even more rapidly than they had left it. That brief battle with the storm had made them avid for the bright warmth of the kitchen. The night was savagely cold. The bitter chill tore at faces and hands, like rusted pin points.

Rhodes came in first, carrying the suitcase. Callon whipped into the room behind him with almost ludicrous haste; slamming shut the wind-buffeted door behind him — slamming it, unconsciously, against the very nose of the close-following dog; shutting her out.

Lorna scratched imperatively for admittance. The sound was lost in the yell of the tempest and in the jolly chatter of voices from inside. Failing to gain ingress, the little collie lay down miserably on the drifted door mat. She was shaken by sudden sickness and pain. The blast tugged at her heavy coat, seeking to penetrate to her heart. It caked her fur with sleet. It half-buried her in snow. Thus she lay, bodily torment half-ignored in terror for the fate of her six deserted babies.

Perhaps half an hour later, Callon pushed back his chair from the table. He was replete with hot food and with a sense of comfort. His glance fell on the brood nest. Several times during the meal he had looked at it.

"I'm afraid that good collie of yours is a bad mother," he commented. "Some of them are. I've watched; and she hasn't been near those pups of hers since we came back into the house. They're apt to get chilled, that way."

"Lorna!" called Rhodes, staring about the room. "Where are you, old girl? Come back to your babies.... *Lorna!*" he shouted as she did not patter up to him as usual at first sound of his call.

The shout penetrated the thick door and the noise of the storm. Obediently, eagerly, Lorna sought to answer it. Whimpering, she reared herself feebly to her feet and scratched once more at the door panel. This time, amid the momentary silence from inside, she was heard. Rhodes ran to the door and flung it open. On the mat crouched the wretched little mother, amid an ever-larger drift of snow.

But, at her master's penitent outburst of invitation she did not hurry into the house. Instead, she peered imploringly up at Rhodes, whimpering as if trying to make him understand something. She made no move to trot past him to where warmth and food and her babies were waiting for her. Instead, she continued to lie there, whimpering and imploring.

Rhodes stooped, picking her up gently by the nape of the neck and, depositing her on the floor inside, shut the gale-hammered door behind them.

"Poor little thing!" he said, stroking her. "She was so scared and chilled she couldn't even come into the house by herself. She —"

Lorna broke away from him and ran feverishly back to the door. There she scratched and whined, in dire anxiety to get out again. Through a moment's lull in the screech of the tempest came faintly to the wondering humans an all but inaudible squeak. The sound made Lorna frantic. She tore furiously at the panel.

Rhodes, his jaw slack from bewilderment, lifted the latch. Instantly, Lorna was nosing her way, with all her wiry strength, through the crack of the door.

Her forequarters disappeared into the lofty drift where once had been the door mat. Backing out again, she wheeled and ran into the house and to her brood nest.

Between her teeth she carried tenderly a snow-smeared newborn collie puppy.

It was half frozen and more than half dead; — this seventh and last pup of the litter — the pup which belatedly had been born while its mother cowered there in panic among the porch drifts — the pup she had been forced to leave to its doom when Rhodes had leaned out in the dense blackness and had lifted her bodily into the kitchen.

Amid the exclamations of the three humans,

Lorna snuggled the moribund infant close to her, lying down in the brood nest and nosing it against her warm underbody. But Callon was not content with her ministrations.

"Please hold her, one of you," said he. "I don't crave a bitten hand as a reward for life-saving. . . . So!" he went on as he picked up the frozen pup, while Lorna writhed ferociously in Rhodes's grasp, to get at him. "Now, Mrs. Rhodes, if you've such a thing in the house, I want three drops of brandy. Not for myself. My own dosage is somewhat bigger. Please put it in a teaspoonful of hottish water."

As he talked, he unbuttoned his coat and waistcoat and the top buttons of the two shirts beneath. Then, with infinite care he deposited the feebly stirring puppy close under his left armpit, next to his skin, leaving the garments above wide enough open to permit it to breathe.

"That's about the hottest part of the body," he said. "And it's a good many degrees hotter than the pup would be if he was against his mother's fur. Presently she'd find he wasn't going to live. Then she'd push him away from her, the way dog mothers do when something tells them there's no hope for a sick puppy. I'd suggest you wrap him in warm flannel and put him in the oven to thaw out, Mrs. Rhodes. But, thanks to my getting here so late and the gorgeous supper you cooked for me, the oven is so hot it would roast him. So this is next best. Got that spoonful of brandy and water ready? . . . Thanks."

Without taking the chilled puppy away from its warm nook under his arm, he forced open gently the set jaws, while Rhodes trickled the contents of the spoon, drop by drop, down the infant's almost paralyzed throat.

"In an hour or so," prophesied Callon, "the pup will either be dead or else he'll be well enough to put with his mother again. If I were making a bet on the outcome, I'd wager something like twelve to one against his living. But it's always worth the try."

"Lorna's had seven pups to each litter," said Rhodes as they sat down again. "And I was just wondering why she had broken her rule by having six this time. All those six in the brood nest there are males, too. That doesn't happen once in fifty times. And —"

"This one under my arm is a male, too," answered Callon. "That makes seven. He's her seventh son — the seventh son! Say, Rhodes, what a corking registration name for him, if he lives! 'Seventh Son!' 'Rhodesian Seventh Son!' Why, there's magic in a name like that! If there's anything in magic, the pup will be a winner — a wonder — a second Sunnybank Thane! And, by the way, didn't you tell me Sunnybank Thane is his sire? If I had a red carpet and a calico canopy with stars on it, I could forecast a future for this pup that would make Thane look like a piker. That is, if the pup doesn't die, presently. And most likely he will."

But Seventh Son did not die. Bit by bit, under

his arm and against his chest, Callon could feel the puny body grow warm and flaccid, then warm and firm, then warm and squirming. Warmth, outer and inner, was reinforcing the three drops of stimulant, and both were aiding in what Rhodes always insisted on calling a miracle.

At an hour's end the snow-born baby was as healthy and as vigorous as were any of his six brethren. Rhodes was for putting him back with them, under Lorna's flank. But Callon intervened. Laying the resuscitated pup in his lap, he bade Rhodes bring him any two of the other babies.

"Now," he ordered, "take them all three into your own hands for a few minutes, close to the stove. Put this one between the other two and hold them all three close together. That will get rid of the 'stranger scent' on him. If you give him to her right away, she's apt to kill him. Dogs go by scent, not by sight. If he smells like me, she'll never believe he's hers. And he's worth saving. I tell you this youngster's due to make his mark. Aren't you, Seventh Son?"

Presently, Seventh Son was laid beside his mother, again; in company with the two brothers whose brief absence had so worried Lorna. She sniffed at the newcomer, doubtfully, once or twice. Then, reassured by the scent of Rhodes's hands and of her two other babies, on the ratlike gold-brown coat of her last-born, she snuggled him against her, crooning softly to him an invitation to eat. An invitation the newborn puppy accepted with greedy haste.

"It isn't every pup that gets a drink of good pre-war brandy before even he tastes his first drop of milk," commented Callon. "That's another omen for you, Rhodes. At this rate, you'll have the super-dog we've all been looking for."

"No," denied Rhodes, "I'm afraid I won't. You see, we've sold all this whole litter in advance, to be delivered at three months. Sold them at seventy-five dollars each for males and sixty dollars each for females, to Conrad Gryce of the Longlane Kennels, down at Wyckoff. Seventh Son will have to go with the rest. That's the contract. But I hate to let him go when such a famous collie man as you has taken so much trouble with him. Still — let's see — seventy-five times seven is — is — How much is it, Thais?"

"It's just five hundred and twenty-five dollars," promptly answered his wife. "Not a bad price for a winter litter, the way collie prices run lately. If we had one of the famous collie kennels, I suppose we could get double that for them at three months. Still, for third-raters like us, it isn't bad for a blanket price on a whole litter."

"I'm a man of hunches," Callon told them, squatting low in his chair, his young-old face queerly sharp in the red light from the stove. "And I've a hunch about Seventh Son, there. Suppose I offer you seven hundred and fifty dollars flat for the whole litter as it stands this minute, and let you deliver it to me, up at

Midwestburg, when I get back from Florida. I'll pay you here and now in cash. And if any of the pups die before then — as probably one or two of them will, after all that time away from their mother, this evening — I'll stand the loss. Seventh Son won't die. I'll gamble on that. Well, how about it?"

Husband and wife glanced at each other. It was the calmly level and assured look of man and woman who love and understand each other and whose love and understanding the years have welded into steel. Between such there is no need for noisy words, to learn each other's minds.

"No," replied Milo Rhodes. "We'll play it as it lies, that being our way. Thank you just the same, Mr. Callon."

"But, man, you'd clear two hundred and twenty-five dollars, by taking my offer; even if all seven of the pups live, which isn't likely! And —"

"Perhaps you didn't quite understand, Mr. Callon," said Thais. "You see, Milo passed his word."

"But who's to know?" asked Callon, in genuine bewilderment. "*I'm* not going to tell. And the Longlane Kennels have no way of knowing that any of the pups lived. Many a litter dies, one and all. You can just send the Longlane people a postcard, saying Lorna's pups didn't live, and you can pocket the seven hundred and fifty dollars, as safe as a church. Nobody can prove anything."

"Yes," contradicted Rhodes, "there's one man

who can; a cuss named Milo Rhodes. He's the chap I've got to live with till I die, same as I've had to since I was born. If I let him turn crooked, that means I've got to live chained to a crook — and so has Thais. That seven hundred and fifty dollars sounds mighty attractive, especially in these hard times in the collie game. And maybe a lot of breeders would think it was a grand idea. But — well, what's the use of me making Sunday-school speeches? You get my meaning, I guess."

"But if —"

"I'm sorry to have to disappoint you and I'm sorrier to lose the extra cash. But there's nothing to do about it. Of course, you can go to the Longlane folks and buy in this Seventh Son puppy, if he lives. And you can get him a whole lot cheaper, at three months, than seven hundred and fifty dollars or than half of seven hundred and fifty dollars. Shan't we let it go at that?"

There was a short silence. Outside, the storm continued to scream and to pound away at the stanch old house and to scratch at every northeast window with its myriad angry snow fingers. Indoors, the light shone softly and the stove glowed and the kettle chuckled to itself. From the brood nest arose the sleepy mutterings of the pups against their sleeping little mother's side.

Then from the nest came a querulous squeak. It stirred the Rhodeses to instant anxiety. Callon smiled, observing half under his breath:

"There starts the first squeaker. There will be

others. At seventy-five dollars per. You'll notice it isn't Seventh Son."

To a layman his careless words would have meant nothing. To a dog man they and the peevish sound which evoked them were full of sinister meaning.

A "squeaker" is a very young pup which, for no known reason, refuses suddenly to nurse. A pup which makes known his inner discomfort by a series of squeaks, ever more feeble, until death puts him out of his troubles.

Veterinaries know the precise cause and the cure of "squeaks." The only catch is that almost no two of them agree as to such cause and cure. As a result newborn puppies die yearly by the thousands, from the mysterious ailment.

Two days later, several hours after the county snowplows had cleared the highroad of its worst drifts and had permitted Callon to proceed on his interrupted journey toward blizzardless Florida, the sixth of the squeakers had succumbed. Of Rhodesian Lorna's seven collie babies six were dead — from exposure, from colic, from any or no known cause; in other words, from the squeaks.

The sole survivor was Seventh Son. To him went all the nourishment and care which nature had provided for a septet of puppies. He throve apace.

It was just three months later that Callon headed his car for Midwestburg, after his Florida sojourn. He made a point of stopping for an hour at the Rhodesian Collie Kennels, on his homeward run. Idle and bantering as had been his forecast of Seventh Son's career, yet he felt an odd interest in the puppy whose life he had wrested from almost certain destruction.

Moreover, there are one or two not-infallible signs whereby an expert may guess at a just-born pup's future quality. At birth, and up to the age of two or three days, the skull formation foretells sometimes the shape the head will take at maturity. This before the head lapses into the pudgy bluntness it is to wear for the next month or more.

Seventh Son's head had been sharply coffin-shaped. His chest and shoulders had been almost grotesquely massive for such an amorphous body. More than once, such signs had enabled Callon to pick a born winner. More than once the same signs had proven worthless. The man was mildly interested in seeing whether, at three months, Seventh Son still gave promise.

It was a drippily soggy early April noon when Callon halted his mud-smeared car in front of Rhodes's gate and tramped up to the porch whereon Seventh Son had been born. Milo greeted him with eager warmth; insisting on his staying on for midday dinner and, in the meantime, making an inspection tour of the kennels.

"First of all," Callon insisted, "show me Seventh Son, unless you've already shipped him to the Longlane people. You said he was to be deliv-

355

ered to them at three months, didn't you? Has he gone yet?"

"No," returned Rhodes, glumly, "he hasn't gone. They're sending down here for him, by car, sometime this week. Gryce of the Longlane Kennels is going to stop for him on his way back from the Paterson show. He was here for a look at him, yesterday. If ever a man looked sick at having to keep a bargain, Gryce was the man. At having to shell out seventy-five good dollars for a mutt like Seventh Son. But the Longlane outfit is square and Gryce is keeping his word. The pup isn't worth five dollars. He isn't even pretty enough to sell for a pet. You were lucky I didn't take you up on that seven hundred and fifty dollar offer of yours, last January, Mr. Callon. I was sore at myself then for passing up seven hundred and fifty dollars and getting only a tenth of that for what was left of Lorna's litter. But when I see Seventh Son, I figure Longlane is the real loser."

As he talked, he had been leading Callon through the field behind the house and between rows of wire runs wherein rain-slicked muddy collies were dancing expectantly at sight of their master and leaping high against the wire walls of their inclosures. Rhodes stopped at a small kenneled yard that stood by itself to one side of the street of runs.

"There he is," said he.

The yard's occupant lurched gaily forward to welcome the two men. Rhodes swung open the wire door and the puppy shambled out to him.

"Shambled" is perhaps the least severe word to express the crablike gait which his hindleg action imparted to his whole locomotor processes.

"Rickets?" said Callon, more in assertion than in query.

Rhodes nodded. The pup had skittered up to his master; and Rhodes stooped to pet him. There was a tinge of pitying tenderness in the man's action; grotesquely like that of a mother's with her crippled child.

The puppy gamboled adoringly around Rhodes's muddy feet and patted at his ankles with clumsy forepaws. But he did not rear himself on his hindlegs, nor leap up at the man, as is the wont of frisky three-month pups. The defective hindquarters would not bear the weight of his pudgy body in a perpendicular position, nor permit it to leave the ground.

Callon was studying the youngster with much the expression of a collector who views the ruins of a smashed piece of priceless porcelain.

The pup was a rich bronze in hue, save for his snowy ruff and mane and legs and tail tip. Young as he was, his coat gave gorgeous promise. His head was beginning to shape, clean and strong and classic. The mischievous deep-set dark eyes had a far-back glint of sternness — "the look of eagles."

But there all excellence ended. The shoulders and chest were largely developed, as Callon had foreseen. But the angle of the weak hindquarters rendered them grotesque in pose and action.

The legs spraddled wide.

"Up to six weeks old," Rhodes was saying, "he was a beauty. Then — rickets. For no reason at all. You're more of a dog expert than I am, Mr. Callon. So you don't need to be told that the only one hundred per cent sure maxim for a kennel is that Anything At All Can Happen; no matter what pains a breeder takes. Well, that's the answer. At six weeks he was a comer, if ever I saw one. At three months he's a dead loss."

He picked the wrigglingly happy youngster up in his arms and led the way back toward the house.

"At that," he said, "I wish I could keep him. I told Gryce so when I offered to let him off the deal. But Gryce holds me to the bargain — out of charity, I'm afraid. You see, Seventh Son has more brain and pluck and a sweeter disposition and more of the true collie nature than any other pup of his age I ever saw. We leave him loose most of the time — or we did till yesterday, when I got the Longlane check for him. And we have him in the house a lot. He's a natural house dog. A natural chum dog, too. Never have to teach him anything a second time. Yes, I'd keep him if I could. Thais and I have gotten mighty fond of him."

"H'm!" replied Callon, with faint contempt and with no interest at all.

Rhodes fell to remembering something a disgruntled breeder had said about Callon, whose dogs had beaten his at three shows in succession.

"Callon is only interested in the outside of a collie," the breeder had declared. "He looks on it as a cash asset and as nothing more. He has about the same tender chumship and love for his dogs that a garbage man has for his garbage. And there are too may breeders like him."

Rhodes had set this speech down as one of the innumerable jealous slurs — most of them baseless — which garnish dog-show conversation. He had refused to think such a thing of this man whom he admired and to whose expert collie-lore he always had deferred. Yet now —"

"Seventh Son," remarked Callon, with sour jocoseness, as they reached the house, "I owe you a grudge. You've chipped off the corner of my vanity. I picked you as a winner and I kept you from dying. It's the first time I ever went out of my way to lend a hand to a born failure. I'm ashamed of myself. From the neck forward you look like a million dollars. From the neck back, you're a canine crime. And the longer you live the worse you'll get."

The puppy snuggled lovingly in Rhodes's strong arms and struggled to lick his master's momentarily clouded face. Rhodes tumbled the pup's ears in rough goodfellowship. Surreptitiously he fed him an animal cracker.

"Just the same, sonny," said he, "I'd buy you in if could."

Conrad Gryce, of the Longlane Collie Kennels, was an elderly Englishman whose forebears for seven centuries had been dogmen. Even as the unluckily extinct old-time vets did not know the Latin name for "distemper" and yet could cure it by ancestral recipes, so Gryce was steeped in practical dog-knowledge for some twenty generations back.

Not once, but countless times, in the old country, he had seen the most obstinate cases of rickets cured when the patient was young enough. He himself had cured case after case of it, in homely fashion which would have horrified a modern vet with a college degree.

At sight of the stricken Seventh Son he had assumed a poker mask; and had even spoken gloomily of the bargain he had made. Yet he was athrill, to the core of his thrifty soul, at buying such a prospect at such a price. He noted the marvelous head, the hunched but mighty forequarters, the wealth of coat. His educated fingers ran over every inch of Seventh Son's fat anatomy as Paderewski's fingers might test out a new piano.

A week after Callon's visit Seventh Son was carried to the thirty-mile-distant Longlane Kennels. On the same day Gryce began his homely course of strengthening and straightening the pup's wabbly hindquarters and in building up his general condition. Gently and with infinite skill he wrought over the seemingly hopeless case. Bit by bit, as so often in his experience, he saw results. On the day when the eight-month pup could clear a three-foot fence in his swinging stride, Gryce looked upon his work and saw that it was good. Before him romped a magnificent collie, sound and shapely, a rare treat for any dogman's eyes.

Twelve weeks later Conrad Gryce fell from the ridgepole of Longlane barn, whose shingle repair he was supervising. His neck was broken.

A month thereafter, Callon received this letter from Milo Rhodes:

DEAR MR. CALLON:

I'm writing this in drydock — at the St. Simeon Hospital at Paterson. An appendix-fancier got hold of me last week and I've another week or more to stay here before they'll let me go home. But I'm doing fine and I think I look rather better without my appendix than I looked with it. The only thing I'm grouching over is that I'll have to miss the night's visit you promised us for next week, when you drive through on your way home from Miami.

So I'm writing to ask a favor of you. Here's the idea:

Thais told me yesterday that she read the Longlane Kennels are going to be broken up and sold at auction in a month or so, on account of poor Gryce's death that I sent you a newspaper clipping about. I'm wondering if you'd mind driving past there, on your way (it's only a dozen miles out of your route), and try to buy Seventh Son for me. Before the auction the Longlane people may be glad to get rid of any of their stock that is dead wood, and I think you can pick up the crippled little chap for a song. Even if you have to pay a real price for him, I'll stand it.

You'll josh me, maybe, but I can't get that pup out of my memory. Neither can Thais. He had more personality and sense than a dozen ordinary dogs. I want him back. So does my wife. By now he'll likely be even clumsier and worse shaped than he was. But we don't care. We're all-fired fond of him, and we want him for a pet and a house chum for as long as he lives.

Thais would go there, herself, and buy him in, but she's a woman and they'd probably run up the price on her if they thought she cared about him. You'll know how to work the deal. I'll mail you my check the same day you write me you've bought him. I'm a bit short, thanks to the price I'm shelling out for this operation. But I'll go as high as $100 if I really have to; for I sure do want him. Will you do this for a worthy and distressed friend, please?

MILO C. RHODES

The letter reached Callon on the day he was starting homeward. It touched him, almost as much as it roused his amused contempt. He liked Rhodes and he was glad to do him this tri-fling service. He wired to the convalescent:

362

If Seventh Son can be bought or bagged or stolen or otherwise annexed, I'll land him in your kennels inside of a week. Delighted you're progressing so finely in drydock.

"Gee, but there's one white man!" sighed Rhodes as he read the telegram. "Next time I hear a dog-show Knocker's Chorus hammer him, I'm going to start something."

"I've always had a sore little spot in one corner of my heart. Ever since we let Seventh Son go," said Thais. "It's funny how missable he is. It'll be wonderful to have him back again. I'm almost beginning to like Mr. Callon. Perhaps you were right about him, after all."

" '*Perhaps?*' " repeated Rhodes, with convalescent crankiness. "That's just like a woman. You hadn't a single thing to dislike him about, and you know you didn't. You said so yourself. I'm glad you're changing your mind. These intuitions that you women brag about have no sense in them. I've told you that a billion times. But, say! Won't it be grand to have the pup back again? Callon's wire has done me more good than all the slops and dope these health-patchers have slung into me. *Good* old Callon! I wonder how soon I can hear from him. In less than a week, his wire says, doesn't it?"

It was a week to the day. But instead of hearing from Callon, the convalescent met him face to face. Rhodes was sitting up, shaky but himself again, in a lounge chair on the hospital balcony, when Callon was announced.

"Glory be, you've cheated the devil this time!" exclaimed Callon, setting down beside the chair a basket of fruit he had brought his host. "You're looking like ready money, Rhodes. But," his smile fading, "I've some bum news for you. I'll spring it straight, without beating about the bush. Seventh Son is dead. Died of distemper, three weeks ago. There was an epidemic of it at Longlane. Brought from one of the March shows, most likely. Fourteen of the collies got it. Six of them died. Seventh Son was one of the lot they couldn't pull through. The Longlane people were sore as a boil about it. Because they said Gryce had cured him of every single bad effect of rickets and he was a grand pup. The only comfort is that you'd never have gotten him for one hundred dollars or for anything near it. Lord, but I'm sorry to bring such disappointing word to a man who ought to be cheered up!"

Rhodes's face went a sicklier white. But his mouth and eyes gave no sign of the sharp wrench that was his at the downfall of his hopes of having his good little chum back again.

"That's all right, Callon," he made shift to say. "And I'm thanking you for the trouble you've taken. Sit down, won't you?"

"I must go in a few minutes," said the guest, seating himself on the balcony rail. "It took me longer than I expected, to make the detour to Longlane, this morning; and I'm due in New York at one o'clock, for lunch with some of the

American Kennel Club crowd. I —"

"Is that your car down there?" interrupted Thais, turning back from the rail where carelessly she had been glancing down into the street below. "The maroon one, I mean. The one behind my runabout. Because that delivery truck almost rammed it, just now."

"No," Callon assured her. "I didn't know what the parking rules are, up here around the hospital. So I left it in a garage parking space, somewhere down yonder."

Thais strayed along the balcony, humming idly to herself as she went. Rhodes looked reproachfully after her. Except for her first stiffly civil greeting, the query about the car was the total of her conversation with this guest who had tried to be of such kindly service to them. Apologetically, Rhodes threw himself into an effort to talk entertainingly to Callon and to make the man forget Thais's rudeness.

Presently the two were deep in the mazes of dog chat; speaking eagerly the language of the Initiate — a lingo as incomprehensible as Choctaw to the average layman, but glib and voluble on the tongues of veteran kennel folk.

Time flew, under the spell of caninity, Deep calling unto Deep. Dog after dog that had won fame in the past fifty years — from Metchley Wonder to Sunnybank Thane — came under discussion and anecdote. At last Callon blinked at his watch and got hastily to his feet.

"I'll never make New York by one o'clock!" he

complained. "I must hustle. By-by, Rhodes. Quick recovery to you! And the best in the shop, in everything! I'm sorrier than I can tell you that I fell down on that mission of getting back Seventh Son. I was planning to make you a present of him if he'd been alive. Besides —"

Thais strayed back onto the balcony from the long window of her husband's room.

"That is beautiful of you, Mr. Callon!" she exclaimed, with an effusion that more than made up for her earlier iciness to the guest. "Do you really mean it? If Seventh Son weren't dead, would you really *give* him to Milo? As a 'getting well' present? Would you, honestly? Or was that just a polite thing to say? I ask, because even the *wish* to do it means so much to Milo. His face all lighted up when you said it."

"Of course I would, Mrs. Rhodes. I made up my mind to that, the moment I got his letter, down in Miami. I was prepared to pay anything in reason for the dog —"

"Just as a present to Milo?" she reiterated, in admiring wonder.

"Just as a present to Milo," Callon assured her. "Naturally."

"You are the truest sort of a true friend!" she gushed; adding: "I've had so little chance to see you, this visit, I'm going down to the door with you. May I?"

Milo Rhodes smiled after the departing man and woman.

How sweetly Thais had made up for her earlier

incivility! And how tactful she had been, to leave the two men to hobnob together for a full half-hour over their cryptic dog talk! More than ever did Milo feel all-encompassing pride in the wife who was his chum.

Thais, meantime, led the way down the corridor to the floor elevator-gates. There she paused, without pressing the call-button, and faced Callon.

"Mr. Callon," she said, "I want to tell you again how splendid it was of you to say you would give Seventh Son to my husband as a free gift. It —"

"Would *have* given," corrected Callon. "Because the poor pup is dead, worse luck! So there's nothing but empty words in what I said; and I don't deserve any of the flattering things you're telling me. You see —"

"Think back, a minute," she urged. "You didn't say 'would have given,' Mr. Callon. I asked 'If Seventh Son weren't dead, would you really give him to Milo? Or was it just a polite thing to say?' And you told me, 'Of course I would, Mrs. Rhodes.' I heard you distinctly. So did Milo. So did Dr. Blayne. He is my cousin, you know; and he's one of the physicians here. I asked him especially to stand just inside the window and listen. At first he didn't want to. But when I explained, he said he would. That makes three witnesses, doesn't it? One of them disinterested."

"Witnesses to what?" asked Callon, puzzled.

"I don't catch the drift of any of this. What's — ?"

"I read once," returned Thais, "something about simple faith being better than Norman blood. But somehow I've never been able to make myself feel that kind of faith in you, Mr. Callon. I never knew why, till this morning. Then, when you started to tell Milo that story about Seventh Son being dead of distemper — well, I don't know why, but all at once something told me you were lying."

"Mrs. Rhodes!"

"Don't go getting all noble and indignant, till you've heard the rest of it," she soothed him. "I went to the floor phone, and I called up the Longlane Kennels. It was Mrs. Gryce who answered me. I asked her all sorts of questions, and she gave me the answers. Perhaps I made her realize what it meant to me. But she didn't tell me anything I hadn't already guessed pretty straight."

"I —"

"She told me how you came there this morning and asked to see Seventh Son. She told me you looked at him, all over, and then asked her how much she'd take for him. She doesn't know much about dogs and she needs ready money. You beat her down to two hundred and fifty dollars. And you carried him away with you. On the way out, you told her kennel man that Seventh Son is the finest collie you've seen in a year, and that he is easily worth two thousand dollars of any fancier's money. That was a brag.

But it is the truth. I know, because I've just gone all over him, myself."

"I — I don't understand. It —"

"I asked about your car. You said it was in a garage parking space. There is only one garage with a parking space, on the route you must have taken from Longlane to get here. It's only a couple of blocks away. The owner knows us well. We've been parking there, for years. He has bought a couple of dogs from us, too, and he's been at our kennels. So when I drove there and told him I had come after one of our collies that you had left in your car and that I was to call for, he didn't make any objections at all."

"You mean that you — that — ?"

"There were only about a dozen cars parked there, in all, and I found yours right away; by its state license plate. I opened the door. And beautiful Seventh Son came bounding out. I knew him in a second. Yes, and he knew me, too, after all this long time, the darling! Oh, what a beauty he is!"

Queer static noises sifted from between Callon's backdrawn lips.

"I took him along; and I stopped by at my brother's store," she resumed, sweetly, "and I told him about it, and got him to promise to take Seventh Son to his place right away, and keep him there carefully locked up till Milo goes home next week; and then to have him waiting for us at our house when we drive in. It'll be a lovely homecoming surprise for Milo. It will brace him up more than a trip to Europe. I — I wasn't sure how much time I had left, so I hustled back here and got hold of Dr. Blayne. I was going to face you with the whole story, but just as I came out on the balcony you said that generous thing about giving the dog to Milo, and you saved me all the trouble of a horrid scene. It was dear of you, Mr. Callon."

"If there's a law in this state —" exploded Callon, finding his breath and his wits in a rush.

"There is. Oh, indeed there is!" she reassured the apoplectic little man. "And Milo and I are inside of it. *Well* inside it. Or — if I happen to stick outside of it at any point, just bring suit and tell a jury how you tried to cheat a sick man who trusted you — and how you lied to him about the dog he loved. Isn't that what the newspapers call 'human-interest stuff,' Mr. Callon? I feel quite sure they'll give you an immense lot of publicity on it. Think it over."

For a full minute Callon stood glaring, purple and mouthing, at the level-eyed woman who smiled back at him in such a friendly way. Then —

"I know you went to Longlane as a favor to Milo," she continued, gently. "I know you meant to get the dog for him. Perhaps you even meant it for a gift. A poor misshapen, crippled collie would cost almost nothing. Then you saw Seventh Son. You saw him as he is today — a fortune and a pride to anyone who owns him. And friendship went out of business. You played safe.

370

Your kennels are a thousand miles from ours. We'd never have seen him or known the difference. The only thing you stumbled over was one of those aimless 'woman's intuitions' that Milo says have no sense. He —"

Callon shook himself impatiently, as one who comes out of a nightmare. Once more the habitual smile was on his lips, if not in his puckered eyes. He drew from his pocket three slips of paper, and with a fountain pen scribbled a line on the back of one of them. Then he handed the three to the perplexed Thais.

"Seventh Son's registration certificate and his certified pedigree and his bill of sale," he pointed out. "I've endorsed the bill of sale over to Rhodes. A dog is incomplete without his 'papers,' you know. And I never like to give an incomplete gift. . . . Good-by, Mrs. Rhodes. Your husband may have his money in his own name, but he's got his brains in yours. I shan't see you again. But here's hoping — here's hoping Seventh Son gets hydrophobia and bites you!" he finished, his hard-held self-control exploding.

"Good-by, dear Mr. Callon," cooed Thais. "Here's hoping if ever *you* should get hydrophobia you'll be terribly careful not to bite *yourself!*"

XVII

THANE

There were seven of them — a mystic number. By some miracle there was not a "cull" or a "second" in the lot. The whole septet proved at once their royal ancestry. Their sire was my red-gold Champion Sunnybank Explorer. Their dam was my gentle leaf-brown Sunnybank Bauble. Their grandsire was Champion Sunnybank Sigurd; the "Treve" of my book of that name.

Presently one of the seven alone was left. The six others had been sold, and at record prices, as befitted a royal litter. The seventh I had marked from brood-nest days, as a dog I wanted to keep. He was Thane — later Champion Sunnybank Thane.

I had been saving up that half-royal Scottish title, for years; waiting for a dog that should merit it. In this pale-gold youngster's deepset dark eyes, almost from birth, I read the true "look of eagles"; the look I had been watching for so long. In his ungainly and pudgily overgrown baby body I read a future of mighty bone and lion-like power and symmetry and of tremendous coat. Here was a born champion. Here was a pup preordained to wear my stored-up name of "Thane."

Perhaps you have been warned against the risks of gambling on Wall Street. You may even have been told that margins are not the solidest forms of investment, and that futures imply some slight risk which savings-banks avoid.

The most daringly risky form of speculation that I have tackled — one which makes oilless oil-well stocks seem like United States government 3's, by contrast — is the raising of pedigreed collie dogs.

To the lay mind it seems a simple enough thing to raise a litter of fluffy collie puppies and to keep those one wants to keep and to sell the rest of them at a good price.

So also it is simple to buy a speculative stock at rock-bottom price and to wax rich by selling it again for ten times what one paid for it. But the poorhouses are full of people who discovered too late that there was a catch somewhere in their plan.

A collie puppy is either the easiest animal on earth to raise — or else he is the hardest. Litter after litter will be born and will grow and flourish into splendid dogs. With no special care, they thrive egregiously. Disease and accident make as wide detours around them as around a lake. They are almost one hundred per cent net profit.

Why? *I* don't know. Nobody knows.

Again, litter after litter of collie pups will be

born, under the most ideal conditions, and will receive as careful skilled treatment as the children of an emperor. It is no use. One after another the pups die, and all the nursing and all the veterinary skill can't keep them alive. Some of them will be born dead; others of them will die during the first week; and still others may seem ruggedly healthy up to the time they are from a month to three months old, and then may die for no understood cause.

Why? *I* don't know. Nobody knows.

All I know is that a breeder's investment for a year may prove a total loss, through no fault or oversight of his own. Again, through no special care or sense of his, he may raise every pup of the year and sell the lot of them at a big profit.

When you buy a collie pup, and the breeder asks a fairly large price for him, just remember what I have been saying about his risks; before you call him a robber. You are paying not merely for the pup you buy. You are paying, your share of an "overhead" which may be crowding the breeder toward bankruptcy.

So when I say seven pups were born in this litter which included Thane, and that all seven grew to high-quality maturity, I am making a loud and warranted brag.

But there is something more to it than that:

Here is a brood nest. In it sprawls a collie mother. Against her furry underbody nestle five or six or seven or eight or nine shapeless ratlike atoms of caninity. Of the lot, some may be runts, some may be coarse or may be thick-headed "throwbacks." One or two may or may not be future champions.

After they pass the third day of their mortal lives, and until they approach their fourth month, no human can tell which are to be epoch-making dogs (if any) and which are going to sell merely as pets. During the first three days — especially on the first day — there are certain not infallible signs to go by. I studied those signs when I inspected the day-old litter which included Sunnybank Thane.

From the lot I picked out a mouse-colored, rat-sized, sightless half-pound creature whose head was shaped like a coffin. His rudimentary ears were not half the size of a squirrel's, but they were plastered high and close to his oblong rectangular little skull. I handled gingerly the baby ribs and chest. Then I dropped a blob of scarlet and fire-bright mercurochrome on the white patch behind the neck; as a means of identification.

In another few days, I knew, he would grow snub-nosed and round and would look exactly like his brothers and sisters. I must mark him while I could. On the same day I sent to the American Kennel Club — the Supreme Court of dogdom — an application blank for the registering of *"SUNNYBANK THANE. Sire, Champion Sunnybank Explorer; dam, Sunnybank Bauble. Whelped March 26, 1927. Color, sable-and-white. Breeder, Albert Payson Terhune; Sunnybank*

Collie Kennels (Registered)."

The resultant certificate was Thane's admission card to immortality. Also it was legal proof of the flawlessness of his ancestry.

I like to boast that I picked Thane out, at a glance, as a future king. I did. But with shame I confess I have made the same prophecy about many a youngster which never proved to be better than passable. True, I had made a like forecast for Champion Sunnybank Sigurd and for Champion Sunnybank Sigurdson and for Cavalier and for Jock and for Champion Sunnybank Explorer and for a few other canine winners. But — well, why use up space by citing all the not-quite-good-enough collie pups for which I have foretold an equally shining future?

Show me the breeder who can pick them out, infallibly, at an early age; and he can name his own salary to act as consultant at my Sunnybank collie kennels. I am safe in saying that. For such a man is not born yet. Or else he died the day before I was born. It is all a gorgeous gamble, this breeding of pedigreed dogs. Therein lies its lure. When our prophecies come true, it is fun to boast. When they fail — which is oftener — silence is very golden indeed.

When Thane was left alone in the wide and shaded kennel yard which once had held seven brethren and sisters, it was up to me to lighten his loneliness. Incidentally, it was up to me, if I wanted him to amount to anything, to educate him beyond the mere rudiments of obedience which already he had learned.

So every day for an hour or two I would take him out by himself, for an educational hike, or to accompany me on my round of The Place, or to lie in my study while I worked. Much I talked to him, on these outings. Not merely giving him orders or training him; but accustoming him to my voice and letting him learn its inflections. Naturally, he did not understand one word in fifty that I spoke to him. But he grew to understand my mood, whatever it might be, and to get a general idea of the simpler meanings I was trying to convey to him.

Meanwhile I was teaching him, by patient training, the few needful things I wanted him to learn. Also I was giving him sweeping uphill gallops to deepen his chest and broaden his shoulders and establish the straightness of limb and complete bodily poise I sought for him. Incidentally, I was giving him two raw eggs and a pound of fresh raw beef a day, in addition to his regular kennel rations of bread and milk and bones, and I was grooming, his blanket-like coat as one would groom a racehorse.

Does it seem silly to you that I should have wasted all this time and meticulous care on a mere dog? Well, if you can't understand a dog's jolly companionship and the joy of developing it to anything beyond its ordinary limits, then perhaps the financial side of the task may appeal to you.

Later, I refused three thousand dollars for

Sunnybank Thane. His cash income, from shows and otherwise, climbed well toward a thousand dollars; before the dawn of his second year. There are worse investments.

Perhaps you are picturing a gigantic gold-and-white collie, with a stern aspect and with the grave dignity of a prime minister. At casual glance, when he was on the show-block, that describes Thane precisely. In every other respect, that is precisely what he was *not*. He was an overgrown and lovable and super-energetic puppy. That is all he ever would become. And therein lay the bulk of his charm.

The play traits cropped out when he and I began those fast daily walks. He would enliven the hike by strenuous efforts to tear the straps from my puttees when I was striding along at top speed. That was a favorite pastime of his, all his life, and one which lost me perhaps a score of puttee straps and more than once all but broke my neck. Another feat of his was to yank my handkerchief from my pocket and lure me into knotting it and then throwing it for him to retrieve. These were but two of Thane's uncountable pranks, all performed with a certain stately grace which had nothing of the harum-scarum in it.

Then there were his toys. He played with them as might a child. They amused him for hours. Yet never did he destroy them, as would the average playful dog. They were his dear possessions, to be treated as such. For example:

When he was less than a year old he had a Teddy Bear which was an endless delight to him. He would play dramatically, yet gently, with it, by the hour. One day he left it on the lawn when he came into the house. Sandy found it there. (Perhaps you remember reading about Sandy in my "Biography of a Puppy," in my book, *The Way of A Dog*.) Sandy in those days had a morbid love for destructiveness which never before have I found in a grown collie. He fell upon the luckless Teddy Bear and tore it into small independent republics.

Thane and I came out of the house, just as the work of demolition was at a climax. Thane took in the scene at one horrified glance. There, in fifty ragged pieces, lay his adored bear playmate. With a sound more like a human yell of fury than any ordinary canine utterance, he hurled himself at Sandy; bearing him to the ground as might some golden hurricane, and ravening madly at his throat.

It was the first time I had seen the gentle young giant out of temper. Gaily he had withstood the teasing and rough romping of his fellow dogs. But the sight of his destroyed plaything roused him to what might well have been murder if I had not jumped into the fray and stopped it.

I bought him another bear, as much as possible like the first. He played with it, once in a while; but more dutifully than ardently. His heart was with its torn-up predecessor.

Ormiston Roy, foremost of Canada's collie experts and judges, called on me in October of 1927. He looked over the kennels, alternately dealing out praise and mordant criticism. Presently he reached Thane's yard. There he halted. For a full minute he said not a word. Then he walked into the yard and began to "go over" the seven-month pup; as Paderewski might test a piano. Presently he turned to me and said:

"I'll not ask you if you'll sell him. Nobody would. He's — he's a *collie*."

That was all. Roy is not given to gushing. But during the next month or two, on one pretext or another, the chief collie authorities of the Western Hemisphere chanced to drop in at Sunnybank. The news had gone forth.

Joe Burrell, Mrs. Lunt, Genevieve Torrey, H. H. Shields, Avery, Mrs. McCurdy, Arden Page, John Gamewell, Rolfe Bolster, Hugh Kennedy, Isabelle Ormiston, Dr. de Mund (president of the American Kennel Club), Carlotta Goodnough, a half-dozen others of the collie chieftains, found occasion to call and to bring the talk around to Thane, and then ask to see him.

The dog magazines began to contain squibs about the wonder-puppy which was to "clean up everything in sight" at the annual Westminster Kennel Club Dogshow at Madison Square Garden in February of 1928; and at the Collie Club of America show, in the same month.

Far and near, Thane was hailed as the world's coming collie. I began to preen myself in advance as breeder and owner of still another Madison Square Garden winner. The Westminster Dogshow is the classic canine event of all America.

By the way, do you recall that I said this dog-breeding game is "a gorgeous gamble"?

On the morning of the last day of December, 1917, I let Thane out of his yard for our daily hour or so together. Slowly, painfully, he came forth, in utter variance to his wonted dynamic rush. He reached feebly for one of my puttee straps. But he decided it was not worth playing with. I tied my handkerchief into a knot and tossed it for him to retrieve. He took an undecided step toward it. Then he slouched back to me and laid his head against my knee.

He was panting heavily and there was a wheezy noise far down in his furry throat. I knelt and listened to his breathing. Then I lifted his seventy-four pounds of languid weight and carried him down to the stables, calling to the men to clear out the biggest box stall for him; and bidding my English superintendent, Robert Friend, to telephone our veterinary to drop everything and drive over to Sunnybank at top speed.

The vet verified my snap judgment. He said my glorious young collie paragon was a victim to pneumonia.

Now let me stop an instant in this rambling talk, to make another confession: Thirty years ago I knew everything about dogs that could be known. I had spent my life among them. But, after more than another quarter-century of studying them, even more closely, day after day, I admit I don't know anything at all about them.

As fast as I learn or evolve some supposed canine fact, that fact disproves itself. The only nugget of unimpeachable wisdom I have been able to glean from my lifetime of intensive dog study is summed up on this one grim axiom:

"Anything can happen!"

It had been my theory that a collie should be allowed to stay out-of-doors day and night; except when he chooses to go into his south-facing kennel-house; and that the wintry elements toughen and strengthen him and give him a tremendous coat. This had been the mode of life meted out to Thane from babyhood, as to a hundred other Sunnybank collies. Yet, for the first time in my life, I had on my hands a case of canine pneumonia which was not preceded by distemper.

The grand young dog was sick, grievously sick. My experience has been that thrice out of four times a very sick dog is a dead dog. I had no hope of saving Thane. Yet I worked over him as seldom I had worked before. Robert Friend worked even harder.

Inside of an hour the invalid was incased in an oiled-silk-and-woolen double "pneumonia jacket," from which corset-like casing his head and his hindquarters emerged in masses of golden fur. Day and night Robert Friend and I wrought over him — Robert more faithfully than

I — rubbing him, giving him his bi-hourly medicines, making him inhale (to his disgust) the fumes of benzoin-and-hot-water, etc.

For a week or so it was nip-and-tuck with death, down there in the dim box stall. The dog lay, breathing noisily, on a bed of blankets, in one corner; languid, dull, a pathetically patient shadow of his vivid self.

Then, in a flash, he was not sick at all. At least he did not *feel* sick, although the doctor said he must remain in his box-stall hospital for at least a month longer and must still have his medicine and an occasional "steaming." His fever temperature had vanished and his wildly gay spirits had come back.

(By the way, your own normal temperature is about ninety-eight and a half. A dog's normal temperature is one hundred and one and a half. So is a cat's. So is a cow's. A horse's is one hundred. A pig's is one hundred and two and a half. A sheep's is one hundred and four. A fowl's is one hundred and seven, a temperature at which no human could sustain life.)

Thane's temperature dropped gradually from one hundred and six to normal. His strength came rushing back to him, and with it his love of fun. He began to play assiduously with his bear and with an old shoe and with other toys we put into his stall.

One of these toys was a huge round cat's head, black and made of rubber. Like the bear, it would squeak, lamentably and loudly, if it was squeezed. At first Thane would press the rubber cat between his jaws, listening with critical enjoyment to its squeaks. Then he found he could produce the same sound without biting.

He would chivvy the spheroid toy into the center of the stall. There he would press his forefoot on it, with changing degrees of intensity, for minutes at a time, reveling in the varied noises evoked by the pressures. (Yet they say dogs cannot reason anything out!) This was a never-ending source of joy to the convalescent giant. When any human visitor came to see him, invariably he would fetch forth his rubber cat and set his forefoot to work in producing these entrancing screeches.

Also, he invented a game in connection with a two-inch rat-hole in one corner of the stall. When Robert or myself came in with the medicine spoon Thane would rush over to this rat-hole and make spectacular efforts to crawl into it, fluffing his coat up to about double its normal size in the idiotic attempt. The sight of the medicine spoon always was a signal for a dive toward the hole.

By the second week in February he was pronounced well. Heart and lungs once more were in perfect condition. The vet said it would be safe to take him to the Madison Square Garden Show; more especially since he was still under a year old and therefore need stay at the show for only a single day. Fanciers clamored for me to show him there, prophesying that he would win every prize in sight.

But I kept him at home. I would rather have a live chum than a dead champion. Perhaps I am foolish. Assuredly, I miss many valuable dog-show prizes and points in that way. But I sleep the better o' nights for knowing I am not jeopardizing the life of a dog-comrade for the selfish sake of a scrap of ribbon and a few dollars or medals or cups.

I don't seek to defend this attitude of mine, for which I have received much good-natured guying from wiser and less mawkish dog-fanciers. To my biased way of thinking, all dogs die too soon, at best; even though I and so many other humans seem to live too long. Why shorten, wilfully, a collie's pitifully short span of normal life by making him take needless chances for his owner's self-glory?

So Sunnybank Thane stayed smugly at home all winter, in his box stall, with his toys; while lesser collies were rolling up points toward their championships and were annexing cash prizes.

He was a gallant invalid, giving no sign of the pain and restless discomfort that at first were his, nor moping at the narrow quarters which replaced his miles of daily gallop and romp.

It must have been deadly stupid for him, cooped up there all winter in a box stall; he who had had the run of the Place. Yet he bore it all right gaily, and he devised game after game to lighten the tedium. During that winter, too, he waxed strangely humanized, thanks to his dependence on us for companionship and amusement.

At last he was out of danger. The heart and the lungs were back to their old form. On dry days he could go out for an hour or two and wander at will. The corset-like pneumonia jacket was cut off, too, much to his relief.

According to all precedent, the weeks of high fever and the galling of the air-tight jacket ought to have stripped the hair from his sides and back, and left him well-nigh naked. Instead, he emerged from his box-stall winter with the most incredibly mighty golden coat I have seen on any collie of his age. Once more — *"Anything can happen."*

Incidentally, he is the first dangerously stricken Sunnybank collie to emerge alive from that "incurables' ward" box stall. I had grown to hate the sinister room. In it have died Jock and Bobby and Treve, and other unsparable collie chums of mine whose wistful ghosts still haunt my memory. (One more great dog, later, was to die there. As you shall see.)

Well, springtime came. With it came the great annual out-door dog show of the Morris & Essex Kennel Club at Madison, New Jersey, May 26, 1928. A notable assemblage of collies was to be there, some of them champions, others that had won renown in the big winter shows. I entered young Thane for the Novice Class and for several other and harder classes, at Madison. Never before had the huge youngster been to a show. Never before had he been in a motor-car or away from Sunnybank.

Even an ordinarily fearless collie may flinch at the ordeal of plunging for the first time into an assemblage of three thousand strange and clangorously noisy and odorous dogs, and of having thousands of strange humans staring at him and chirping at him. With some curiosity I watched for the effect of the ordeal on our home-bred and home-kept Thane.

He trotted into the show, on his leash, as unflinchingly as a clubman might thread the crowds on Fifth Avenue. True, everything and everybody interested him hugely. But it was a pleasurable interest. There was no fear in it. He was having a glorious time.

Then came the collie judging. I led Thane into the ring; where, with several other untried collies, he was to test his fortune in the Novice Class.

Enno Meyer was the collie judge that day.

Thane went through the needful ring evolutions — the parade, the trotting back and forth, the posing on the block, the expert handling of the judge and all the other tiring tests. He went through them with evident joy. In fact, he frisked through them.

He was having a beautiful spree. When the judge gave him the blue ribbon — first prize — of his class, there was a burst of handclapping from the spectators on all four sides of the ring. The applause seemed to please him almost as much as had the squeaking of his rubber cat.

He was in several classes that day. He won in every one of them. Then came the gruelingly hard Winners Class; the supreme test in which the winners of all the earlier classes — Puppy, Novice, American-bred, Limit, Open, etc. — must compete for the purple rosette which carries with it a certain number of points toward a championship. The number of points depending on the number of dogs shown.

Again Thane thrilled merrily to the skirl of hand-claps which followed upon Enno Meyer's awarding him the rosette.

My home-bred youngster had been acclaimed Winner; and at his very first show he had received four of the fifteen points needful to a championship.

I did not take him back to his bench at once, but let him stay out in the Maytime shade of the cool green grass with me for a while. Crowds came up to congratulate me on his victory. Wise-eyed veteran collie experts came close to examine him and to pass verdict on him and to praise him to the skies and to foretell a meteoric show-career for him.

And Thane? How did all this hurricane of adulation affect him? Did it turn his head? (It came rather close to turning *mine*. For this was the reward of years of breeding experiments on my part.) This is how Thane received it:

As his show work was over for the day, I had given him a fair-sized beef bone. He lay sprawling on the grass, in benign content, gnawing happily on it, while the waves of approval surged over him and while I was fingering his purple rosette and his sheaf of blue ribbons and the medals and the handful of gold pieces he had won.

Personally, I was hard put to it to bear in mind the first half of my own kennel motto:

"To win without boasting; to lose without excuses."

But his triumphant debut and his long stride up the championship climb and the praise of the collie experts and the still more flattering scowls of some of the collie exhibitors meant to Thane only that he was monstrous comfortable sprawling on the shady grass with such a meatful beef bone to pick clean.

The Paths of Glory Lead but to the — *Bone!*

Then the photographers swarmed up. And once more the young dog must pose majestically — this time for a clicking battery whose sounds amused him almost as much as had the hand-clapping of the rail-birds. When they had gone, he threw himself on the grass again and made growling, terrifying dives at the Mistress's feet, to coax her into a romp with him. Next, he rolled on his back with an imbecile expression and with all feet in air; looking like an utter fool, a canine Village Idiot.

Then he tried to pick my pocket for animal crackers; and at last he returned to his beef bone.

Such was his victory conduct. It was worthy of a silly puppy, and it was ludicrously amiss for a

389

huge and stately creature which had just been acclaimed as Thane had been acclaimed. In brief, he had posed statuesquely as long as such pose was commanded by his Master.

Then, the day's work being over, he lapsed into grotesquely unstatuesque puppyhood.

A month later, at the Rye, New York, outdoor dog show, he repeated his initial triumph; piling up three more points and defeating all collie competitors. He had earned, now, the "two shows, of three or more points each," which are the necessary and hardest part of any dog's championship struggle. The rest of his fifteen points he could pick up, if need be, one at a time, at small outdoor shows, during the next five years; should he live so long. The toughest part of the struggle was over.

Moreover, hot weather was coming on — hot weather, sticky weather, breathless weather, weather in which a wealth of coat like Thane's is as much a burden as would be a collegian's coonskin overcoat in the tropics. I was advised most urgently to send him on the circuit of summer shows, to clean up his championship in a rush.

But — a few minutes ago I told you I would rather have a live chum than a dead champion. Also, during the stifling summer heat, I would rather have a dog of mine snoozing comfortably in my cool study or splashing deeply in the chilly lake, than chained to a hot bench under a hotter tent roof; or made to stand and to parade in a sun-scourged judging-ring.

Therein, I was foolish. I admit that, without argument. But there are plenty of autumn shows, where the heat torture is absent. If he should not have shed all his immense coat by that time (which I was certain he would have done), perhaps he could pick up one or two more points at near-by outdoor dog shows to which he could be driven by motor in an hour or less. Or perhaps he might not win anything at these. It was all a gamble. Meanwhile, he was happy here at home.

More dogs are killed by dog shows than by motor-cars and by mad-dog scares combined (which is a sweeping statement)! Distemper is the deadliest foe of dogdom. And distemper claims a hideous number of victims at shows. True, there are wise American Kennel Club rules to curb its presence there. But these rules depend on the squareness of human nature. There is too often a catch in it somewhere.

In sending or taking any dog to a show, the animal's owner must sign a statement that "there has been no case of distemper within the period of six weeks prior to this date, in any kennel in which the dog or dogs here entered have been quartered during any part of that time."

Fine and good! The American Kennel Club has done all that is humanly possible to prevent abuse of its rules. But, a dog has distemper and is recovering from it — which happens barely five times in ten — or there is distemper in the owner's kennels, but the dog to be shown has not yet had it. The dog is taken to a show, and with him he brings a billion distemper germs in his coat or in his nostrils.

He touches noses with other dogs there. Or some one pats him and then pats another exhibited dog. The germs are spread. Through the whole show they scourge their way, chiefly assailing young dogs, but often infecting older dogs as well.

Similarly, veterinarians are supposed to stand at the entrance to a show and to give careful inspection to every dog that enters, washing their hands betweentimes. I can testify that I have taken dogs to dozens of shows at which no veterinary laid a finger on one of them; nor accorded the entrant more than a casual distant glance, if so much as that.

I have been to other shows where a veterinarian examined the nose and mouth of dog after dog, without disinfecting his own hands; thus cheerily inoculating a dozen dogs from any one of them which might chance to be in the earlier and less distinguishable stages of the terribly infectious disease.

Most vets are clean and conscientious in their inspection work at shows. I have seen some who were not.

As a result of these lapses on the part of owner or of vet, or both, there have been big dog shows which have been followed by (literally) hundreds of distemper deaths and by almost the wiping out of entire kennels.

There is infinitely less danger in an outdoor show than at an indoor show; infinitely less at a one-day show than at a show that lasts for two or more days.

That is the chief reason why I won't let a Sunnybank dog spend more than six or seven hours, at most, at any show. That is why I pick outdoor shows, by choice; and why the Mistress or Robert Friend or myself or one of the Sunnybank men is always stationed in front of the Sunnybank benches, at a show, to prevent anyone from patting or even touching one of our dogs.

That, also, is why we bring our own drinking-pans and see to their filling. I have seen dog-show attendants dump the contents of half-emptied drinking-pans into the pails wherewith other pans were to be filled. Another cogent and potent way of spreading disease.

For two days before Thane went to his shows, he was dosed regularly with Delcreo, a safe and harmless distemper preventive. The moment he left the shows, his nose and his lips and the pads of his feet were sponged with grain alcohol (which he hated); flaked naphthaline was rubbed deep into his coat; and he was treated to a mighty swig of castor oil — a nauseous dose which dimmed for the moment his faith in human kindness; but which is the best thing I know of to avert distemper. The same treatment has been given to all my show dogs.

I have written prosily, here, of the perils of dog

shows in general. And, at that, I have not touched on many of them. For instance, on the panic terror which such shows arouse in some dogs — a terror which too often takes the form of violent fits — fits which sometimes end in death — nor of the long and cramped journeys in crates, from show to show, where, for weeks, a dog's existence is divided between his crate and the bench and the tiny exercise inclosure.

But it may be worth your while to remember some of these things, the next time you go to a dog show. You may look at the luckless beasts with a less unconcerned eye when you realize the black risks some of their owners make them take for the sake of a scrap of blue ribbon. You may also decide I am less of a maudlin fool than you thought, for refusing to let my collies take such risks.

It is a fine thing to rush one's dog through to a championship in a mere handful of shows. It is a finer thing (I am silly enough to believe) to allow one's dogs to stay alive and well. Thane might easily have been a champion before he was a year old. Also he might still more easily have died in agony from distemper or fits.

Meantime, he was *alive*. Which pleased his maudlin master infinitely more than would all the championship certificates the American Kennel Club ever issued. I would rather have had his Paths of Glory lead to the Bone than to the destination named in Gray's Elegy.

Balzac and Sue and several other continental

writers used to delight — as do some of the moderns — in carrying their stories through successive generations of one family, and in showing how ancestral traits crop out. Few writers live long enough to make an actual study of a several-generation family in real life.

We dog-breeders are luckier. We can trace inherited characteristics — mental, physical, even moral — through an endlessly long canine family line. (When you stop to realize that a dog often is a grandsire by the time he is three years old, you will understand how many generations may make up a single decade.)

To me, it has always seemed far more interesting and worth while to try to perpetuate in my dogs certain desired traits of courage and cleverness and sense and elfin fun and stanchness and originality and the like, than to seek mere physical perfection by the successive mating of certain arbitrarily correct types.

Now and then — as in Thane's case — I try to produce a fine show specimen. Sometimes I succeed. Sometimes I do not. Sometimes — once in a great while, as with Thane — I can evolve a dog which combines both the inner and the outer traits I am looking for.

If he can inherit only one set of these traits, then I prefer to have him inherit the nature rather than the appearance of the type I am aiming at. That, also, is silly. I admit it. But it is fun to eliminate unpleasant traits and build up pleasant ones, by wise breeding.

For example, there was a magnificent merle collie of blazingly savage temper. He was Champion Grey Mist. His beauty was blurred by his savagery. I secured the best-tempered of his daughters as a mate for my great Bruce, whose temper was sunny and whose disposition was sweeter than that of any other dog I have owned. At the same time Bruce was as fearless as was savage Champion Grey Mist.

From this mating, our grand old Sunnybank Gray Dawn — hero of my book, *Gray Dawn* — was born; with all the grandfather's savagery bred out of him, except such as every good watch-dog needs; and with Bruce's and Grey Mist's courage and size and beauty. Dawn's son, my Sunnybank Sandstorm ("Sandy") has many of the best of these traits. So has Sandstorm's black son, my Sunnybank King Coal. So have Coal's children.

Again, Thane's grandsire, my Champion Sunnybank Sigurd — the "Treve" of my book of that name — had a certain eerie mischief and a fund of humor and of queer melodramatic originality — the changed remnants of one or two unpleasant ancestral peculiarities which had been bred out of him.

Treve's three best sons, Sigurdson and Cavalier and Explorer, differed as much in nature as ever did three diverse men. All three were gentle and playful with accredited humans. But with other male dogs Cavalier was savagely quarrelsome. Champion Sunnybank Sigurdson was alternately fierce and frolicsome, and in many ways like his sire. Champion Sunnybank Explorer was almost colorless in his conduct.

Explorer was one of the quietest and most diffident and sensitive dogs I have owned. Yet his son, Thane, was almost the physical and mental reincarnation of his own grandfather, Treve. I found myself — as did the Mistress — involuntarily calling him Treve and speaking of him as Treve; although golden Treve had been dead since June of 1922. Character and appearance skipped a generation and cropped out to an uncanny degree in Thane.

These "generation skips" are frequent.

Bruce sometimes went to sleep, lying with his head at such an angle as to look as if his neck were broken. Never had I seen a dog do that. Years later, Bruce's grandson, Sunnybank Sandstorm — "Sandy" — lies with his head at that same impossible angle. (He sprawls thus at my feet as I write this.) It is a petty detail, perhaps; but it may help to emphasize my point.

Yes, these experiments in heredity are to me the most interesting things in collie-breeding; these and the often successful effort to breed out such traits as I don't want and to intensify manifold the few traits I am looking for. Among humans, where eugenics never can be practiced successfully on any large scale, this feat is difficult. Among dogs it is comparatively easy.

Yet, even there, I fail disastrously, sometimes. I fall to wondering at some unexplainable phase of character and of mentality in a puppy; and I try to figure what remote ancestor it comes from or from what Mendelian blend of ancestry.

Forgive this long digression — which, after all, may perhaps be interesting in its way — and let's get back to the none-too-patiently waiting Thane.

I have seen dogs which very evidently knew and cared when they had won or lost in the show ring. They would leave the ring, strutting or slinking, according to whether or not they happened to have received a blue ribbon. Any observant dog-breeder will bear me out in this. Yes, there are many dogs to which victory or defeat means much.

But Thane was not one of them. To him, the ring and the crowds and the competing dogs seemed to be component parts of a thrillingly amusing scene, set for his benefit. I do not believe he had the faintest idea what it was all about or that he himself was on exhibition. He posed or paraded at command; and he did it all well. Not with Sigurdson's calm perfection, nor with Explorer's glum distaste for crowds, nor with Treve's absurd sense of the occasion's dramatic values.

No, Thane behaved in the ring precisely as he behaved at home, and with not an atom more of self-consciousness. In all his short life he knew nothing but friendliness and good-fellowship from humans; and he did not know there could be anything else. Therefore, he suffered the judge to handle and examine him; even as he permitted Sunnybank guests to pat him.

He felt the keenest interest in the other dogs in the ring, and he tried gleesomely to lure them into romps. When I drew him away from them he looked reproachfully up at me, as though trying to tell me that I was spoiling the beginning of a jolly friendship.

I did not have to "show" him — in other words, to attract his attention by means of some squeaking toy or bit of fried liver, so that he would stand alertly at attention. The sight of other exhibitors, showing their dogs, was an endless delight to him. Unwittingly they were "showing" my dog along with their own. For he followed all their sometimes frantic gesticulations with a joyous interest. He was vividly on the alert, from nose to tail tip.

Ever, at the back of his gay brain, I knew, was the promise of that after-sprawl on the cool ringside grass, with his beef bone to gnaw at. That was the supreme moment of the show for him.

Yes, the Paths of Glory led but to the Bone!

LATER — *Much* LATER:

You have just read the life story of my golden Champion Sunnybank Thane, as I wrote it for a national magazine in the summer of 1928. Would you like to hear the rest of it?

When September of 1928 brought cool weather, I took Thane to three more dog shows.

At all of them — Tuxedo and Cornwall and Westchester — he received the "Winners" award as well as "Best of Breed."

At the Cornwall show the collie ring was within a yard or two of the bandstand. As the collies of Thane's class paraded into the ring, the many-pieced band burst into a thunder of jazz, just above their heads. This in spite of bribe-fringed entreaties that the playing be delayed until after the classes should be judged.

Never before had Thane heard such a roaring burst of sound. Well might he have cringed or bolted. I whispered to him,

"Steady, son! STEADY! *I'm here.*"

This as the first blare of cacophony roared over him. The gallant young dog heard me and he obeyed me.

Vibrant with the ear-cracking novelty of the din, he glanced questioningly up into my face. Then he went through his ring paces as calmly as if he were in the practice ring at home. He won his class. He received "Winners" and then "Best of Breed."

In five shows, in a space of less than five months — including the torrid weeks when I had kept him at home — my golden collie had won the fifteen points which, by American Kennel Club law, made him a "Champion of Record." He became "CHAMPION Sunnybank Thane." And he was acclaimed everywhere as the greatest collie of the decade.

I do not believe in showing champions, in the

ring; and thus deterring some younger or lesser dog from working his way up to the all-important title. Thane was a champion. Therefore, for the rest of his days, Thane should remain at Sunnybank; unexhibited, and reaping the reward of his prowess.

But only a handful of time remained for him to enjoy his laurels.

He won his championship in late September, 1928. On the morning of April 26, 1929, he and I went for a walk together. The dog was wildly gay and active. When I went into my study to work I shut him in his yard. An hour later my superintendent showed a party of unbidden visitors — strangers — motor tourists — over the kennels. He told me later that they lingered long in front of Thane's yard, several of them; while the rest moved onward with their guide. What they did or did not do, I don't know. For what other kennels — if for any at all — they were emissaries, I don't know.

But half an hour before lunchtime, I went out for an inspection tour of Sunnybank. I let Thane out of his yard. Instead of dashing forth, as always, like a burst of golden flame, he lurched slowly toward me, head and tail adroop, panting and in evident agony.

As when he had had pneumonia, I gathered him up in my arms and carried him to the box stall that had been his sick-bay during his earlier siege of illness. And I shouted to my superintendent to telephone for the veterinary.

Twelve hours later Champion Sunnybank Thane was dead. Nobody knows how or why.

He was born on the 26th of the month. He was registered on the 26th of the month. He went to his first show on the 26th of the month. He went to his final and crowning show on the 26th of the month. He died on the 26th of the month, at the beginning of the 26th month of his shining young life.

Somehow, since then, dog shows haven't interested me overmuch. I haven't shown any of my few surviving collies. It isn't a question of sulks, but genuine dearth of interest.

Queer, isn't it? And peace to Thane's bright memory!

The employees of G.K. Hall hope you have enjoyed this Large Print book. All our Large Print titles are designed for easy reading, and all our books are made to last. Other G.K. Hall books are available at your library, through selected bookstores, or directly from us.

For information about titles, please call:

(800) 257-5157

To share your comments, please write:

Publisher
G.K. Hall & Co.
P.O. Box 159
Thorndike, ME 04986